OSIRIS

BOOK ONE OF THE OSIRIS PROJECT

E. J. SWIFT

DEL REY

1 3 5 7 9 10 8 6 4 2

First published in the US in 2012 by Night Shade Books
Published in the UK in 2013 by Del Rey, an imprint of Ebury Publishing
A Random House Group Company

The Random House Group Limited Reg. No. 954009

Addresses for companies within the Random House Group can be found at
www.randomhouse.co.uk

A CIP catalogue record for this book is available from the British Library

The Random House Group Limited supports The Forest Stewardship Council®
(FSC®), the leading international forest-certification organisation. Our books
carrying the FSC label are printed on FSC®-certified paper. FSC is the only
forest-certification scheme supported by the leading environmental organisations,
including Greenpeace. Our paper procurement policy can be found at:
www.randomhouse.co.uk/environment

Printed and bound by CPI Group (UK) Ltd, Croydon, CR0 4YY

ISBN 9780091953065

To buy books by your favourite authors and register for offers visit:
www.randomhouse.co.uk

For my parents, Andrew and Veronica Swift

PROLOGUE

He sits on the balcony with his legs hanging over the edge and his face pressed between two railings. Beyond the bars lies the great vault of the city and its pale roof of sky. He does not see an architectural masterpiece, although there are lines of beauty here that exist nowhere else. What he sees is a maze of luminous shapes, ignited by the sun.

He has spent hours in this space, high in the eyries of Osiris, where gulls and other birds wheel and screech their hunger. Sometimes he stands and leans over and peers into the depths of the morning mist. Other times he perches on the railings, with death at his side like a neighbour. Occasionally he sleeps. The cold is hostile, and he is not dressed to face it. He wakes in the frost, trembling, surprised still to be here.

In the brittle air he feels, acutely, the internal heat of his body battling with the outside draught. His blood pulses, torrid and bright. His heart tattoos a rhythm in his chest. Icy stone pushes against his bare feet. When the storms come, the elements sweep around him in multilingual conference. Rain lashes the windows and his skin, wind claims the moisture back. He has forgotten that he is afraid of storms. He turns his face to the heavens and closes his eyes.

Once, people came and found him here. They spoke to him, and when he was silent they begged him to talk and when he talked their eyes grew strange and harboured clouds. But it has been a long time and the findings are things of the past, things that lie almost beyond the reach of memory. He holds onto only one. He cannot remember her name, but she tumbles through the world: bold, vital and violent. He cannot let her go because she knows no fear.

People still watch, although he is unconscious of their surveillance and the whispers that shroud him. These stories skip along bridges, ride up and down the glass lifts. From unseen lips, they echo in the hollows of a dozen ears. They make good copy. There are episodes when he leaves the balcony, even leaves the penthouse it is attached to, and then the Reef field buzzes and tingles in the keys of many different voices. But days pass, and his expeditions become rarer. He keeps time for the city, watching it dissolve around him.

He knows there is something he has to do. A mystery he has to solve. It is in the water. It is in the ice.

One morning, in the lilac hours before dawn, he lifts his arms as if they are wings. They have spoken at last. It is in the water, he knows it now. He climbs the railings. For a moment he poises, absolutely still. The city is hushed.

But now he hears it. At first barely audible, then louder, as it has been growing these past few months, or even years. Hooves beating on the skin of the waves. They run like streamers in the wind. Foam flies about their salted coats; the horses.

No one is awake to see him fall. His body hurtles earthwards, faster than the diving gulls, faster than a rumour. The air rushes against him. Windows flee his reflection. He crashes into the sea and vanishes instantly beneath the surface, leaving only a faint trace that is quickly gone.

PART ONE

1 ¦ ADELAIDE

A delaide first felt something was wrong in the aftermath of the speech. Her father had voiced the formalities, and now those who remained had the chance to speak to the family. The guests were tentative. They offered their sympathy like a gift, of whose appropriateness and reception they were as yet unsure. Buoyed by weqa or coral tea, a few dared to meet Adelaide's eyes, but most looked at the bridge of her nose or into a space over her shoulder. She watched them hunting for the right words. They wanted to say something. Or at least they wanted to be seen to say something. Unfortunately, none of the usual phrases—*we're so sorry for your loss*—were much use. How do you condole for a missing person? How do you grieve?

Her father had managed it very well. It was a month since Axel's disappearance, and Feodor had staged this event. He named it a service of hope. The phrase was written out on a diminishing supply of cards, by hand: *the Rechnov family invites you to a service of hope for our son and brother, Axel.* There was no order of ceremony on the cards, but it was firmly established in Feodor's head. First the assembly, with a pianist providing background music. The repertoire was classical; nothing too well-known, or too sentimental. A few words explaining the situation, for protocol's sake rather than to fill anybody in. And then Feodor's speech.

He spoke adeptly, as he always did, his voice carrying to every nook of the panelled suite. The rooms were quiet and graceful, their walls striped with narrow ribbons of mirror, red cedar and sequoia. Subtle lamps drew out the natural richness of the wood, whose polished surface gathered hazy impressions of those who passed. Other than the ferns and a scattering of tables and chairs, the rooms were unadorned. They were also windowless. Adelaide's brothers had hoped that the informality of a small, intimate space would make for a more congenial atmosphere than was traditionally associated with the Rechnovs.

At the walls, security guards stood rigidly enough to be all but invisible. Only their eyes, constantly roving, revealed alertness.

Adelaide had wedged herself into an alcove. The space was wide enough to seat two people, but Adelaide crammed her legs in too, denying anyone else access. Two things separated her further from proceedings: a lace veil covering the upper half of her face, and the fronds of a metre-high fern. From her semi-hiding place, the rooms, full of figures and reflections, did not look quite real. She couldn't help hearing her father though.

Incense and cedar permeated the air. Adelaide hadn't eaten all day; the sweetish smell and lack of food were making her feel nauseous. She loosened her tie and undid the top button of her shirt, and felt a little better.

"...finally, the family would like to thank you for your continual support and your generous messages. We await news of Axel with anticipation, and as always, with hope." There was a pause. Adelaide knew that Feodor was taking a pinch of salt from a tin and throwing it, in the direction where a window would have been. "Thank you, once again."

Syncopated claps rang through the rooms. When the sound died out there was a difficult silence, before murmurs and music recommenced. The service, despite the oration, remained unresolved.

Adelaide stayed where she was and wondered what she should do next.

Feodor's speech had already triggered numerous arguments amongst the family. The idea of the service was despicable to Adelaide. Nothing, she knew, would dissuade the family, but she spoke out nonetheless.

"Nobody understands Axel, not before and certainly not now. Nothing you can say about him is worth saying."

Those words resounded only a fortnight ago, and they had all been present, sitting around an oval conference table on the nineteenth floor of Skyscraper-193-South. It was neutral ground. Beyond the immense glass window-walls, Osiris lay bathed in a clementine sunset. The city's conical steel towers were burnished gold, and as a flock of gulls swept past the scraper, their wings caught flashes of red as if they were afire. Adelaide paid no heed to the view; she had seen it all her life. Her attention flicked between her grandfather, her parents, and her two other brothers. Dmitri's fiancée was not at the table. The Rechnovs were clannish. A matter of blood was a matter for blood.

The meeting was the first time Adelaide had spoken to any of them in months, and she was wary. She seated herself at the south end of the table, deliberately facing everybody else. Her mother's eyes, the same green as Adelaide's and Axel's, pleaded with her for compassion, or perhaps for leniency. Viviana would try to use the catastrophe as a catalyst for reconciliation. Adelaide folded her arms on the table. The wood was cool on her bare skin, but sweat lined the hollows of her palms. A grain of salt for every harsh word, she thought. For every tear.

Feodor cleared his throat. He thanked them all for being there, a sentiment clearly directed at Adelaide as the estranged member of the family. Then her mother stood up. She had the blanched face of someone who had not slept in days. Adelaide hardened herself against sympathy.

"I've been thinking," said Viviana. She stopped, and for a moment it was not clear whether she would continue. Then she seemed to gather her strength. "I've been thinking about what we should do," she said. "And I think—we must have a—a service. Some sort of gathering, so that people can pay their respects. To commemorate Axel."

It was the wrong choice of word. Adelaide knocked back her chair as she stood, words feverish on her lips.

"How can you even think about saying that? We don't know Axel's dead. We have no idea where he is. You just want him gone so you don't have to worry about him showing you all up any more."

"Unjust, Adelaide," said Linus mildly.

"Is it? I don't think so. Feodor paid for just about every shrink in the city but he wouldn't set foot in Axel's home. None of you would. Deny it if you can."

After that there were tears, and shouting. Only when her accusations ran dry did Adelaide look at her grandfather, his shoulders stooped, weariness articulated by every line in his face. He was still, except for his hands, one resting on top of the other, shivering every now and then like two dry leaves stirred by a breeze. He was old, the Architect, over ninety years old.

Something about her grandfather's silence induced Adelaide's own. She returned to her seat, and folded herself inward.

The rest of the family accepted her retirement as a compromise and for an hour they tried to discuss objectively what form of service might be held. Her brothers decided that Feodor must say something. If the entire script could be reported in full, it eliminated the necessity of delivering a press statement. Adelaide listened and said little more. She felt numb. She wished she could expand that emptiness until it filled the cavern in her chest.

Viviana talked about the candles she wanted with a specificity verging on the deranged.

"We'll have a large red one directly beneath Axel's photograph, and smaller orange ones surrounding it. I'll arrange them in a half moon shape, very simple... And then the layout repeated on each table, I suppose it will have to be the same colours, orange and red, or red and orange, we must put the order in with Nina's..."

"You know, I'm not sure about having the photograph," said Linus. "It might give the impression Axel's dead."

"But how can anyone think about Axel if there's no reminder of what he looks like?" Viviana's eyes glistened. "We haven't seen him... in so long."

"That is a consideration," Feodor said. "When was the last time anyone had contact with Axel? A year ago? More?"

He did not say, *apart from Adelaide*, which would have been a concession. Viviana was incapable of replying. She buried her head in her arms, strangling her sounds of distress. Streaks of grey meandered through the deep red of her hair, almost conquering it at the roots. Adelaide wondered how much of that was a recent development. Her mother was a strong woman; Adelaide could not remember ever seeing her cry.

"I saw Axel eight months ago," said her grandfather. "After Dr Radir's last report."

"Did you? How was—" Feodor stopped himself. "Oh, there's no point."

"He was the same," her grandfather replied.

The last remnants of pink and red light infused the room, rendering its occupants unnaturally soft. The room hushed under this elemental spell, and the heavier mantle that fell with it, of guilt.

"What will you say it is?" Adelaide's voice startled her, reinserting itself into the discussion almost without her consent. The others looked at her with equal surprise.

"What?"

"What will you call it? I mean—the gathering, or however you're going to describe it."

That was when Feodor came up with the phrase service of hope. He said this was the reason they were holding it, so they might as well make their intentions clear. There was no verbal dissent. Viviana got up and went to stand by the window-wall, staring vacantly out as though the regimented rows of skyscrapers would yield the whereabouts of her son. She rocked back and forth on the balls of her feet, her arms cradled. The familiarity of the pose unnerved Adelaide. For the first time that day, she wanted to reach out and pull her mother back.

They progressed inevitably to the content of Feodor's speech. No-one could work out how to talk about Axel's life without implying that it was over, which as Feodor pointed out, would be a strategic blunder. At the same time, Viviana was adamant that her son's achievements should be mentioned. In the end they agreed that Feodor should compose the speech and send it to the others for approval.

Discussion returned to the mundane. Dates and times. Who should be invited. Where it should be held. They hammered through decisions with a rigidity of conduct, faces disciplined tight. Only at the end did anyone raise the question of the Council investigation, and then it was in passing—Dmitri mentioned to Feodor that they had been asked for access to Axel's bank records. Feodor frowned and said he supposed they couldn't refuse.

Such easy capitulation infuriated Adelaide, but she saw no profit in expressing it. The choice had been made a long time ago. She no longer warranted a say in Rechnov affairs.

Two weeks later and here she was. From the alcove, she watched the guests circulate, half eavesdropping on their conversations. The whispers made her angry. Axel had been whispered about for too long.

Adelaide's mother had chosen her candles and arranged them in small clusters on every table. Even grouped together like that, the flames they emitted seemed frail. Viviana sat at the head of one table as if she were holding court, but the glass at her elbow was untouched and she displayed no interest in conversation. A pocket-sized version of the photograph eventually designated inappropriate lay on the table in front of her. From the briefest of glimpses, Adelaide knew that this had been taken some years back. The directness of Axel's gaze was a shocking memory.

A curious mix of people had come. There were a few wild cards—she noticed Zadiyyah Sobek, head of the electronics corporation, chatting to one of the family Tellers—but most were her father's crowd, either politicians or other venerated family members. They had split into cliques. The Dumays, of Veerdeland extract, occupied one corner. The Ngozis, descendants of the Pan-Afrikan Solar Corporation, whispered in another. Adelaide's father and brothers worked the rooms, careful to acknowledge every guest.

The Rechnovs traced their own roots to the Sino-Siberian Federation. At its conception, the City of Osiris had attracted the world's most brilliant minds, rich and poor, from the northern hemisphere to the south. Looking at the assembled congregation, Adelaide felt that there was little evidence of that intellect visible today, and particularly amongst the Councillors.

With their upright carriage and pinched expressions, they were easy to spot. Some of them wore the formal session surcoat over their suits, the sweeping garments giving them the appearance of doleful bats doused in cherry juice. Linus and Dmitri had already established themselves within the illustrious hallmark of the Council Chambers. Linus's personal mission was to convert his sister. He liked to dangle words like future and ramifications under Adelaide's nose, fish on a hook she never bit. As a Rechnov, even a renounced fourth gen one, Adelaide retained the respect, prominence, and wealth afforded all of Osiris's founders: this was her inheritance.

But she had her own name now. Adelaide Mystik. She had her own set, too. They were known as the Haze. A few of them were here, distinguishable by their roving butterfly wariness and adherence to fashion. Beneath cloche hats, the girls' lips were matte in red or mulberry. Their diamond-patterned legs shifted as they tested standing in one spot, then another. The boys, usually so at ease, loitered self-consciously amongst the Council members and founding families.

Adelaide saw Jannike, one of her oldest friends, bend over to say something to her mother. Viviana did not glance up.

A smattering of reporters completed the parade. Some of the krill journalists had attempted to glam up their shabby hemlines with a belted coat or a hat, but nothing could disguise their insidious manner. Perhaps it was the proximity of these conflicting factions as much as the event itself that produced such an air of uncertainty. A Councillor bumped into a socialite and both parties blushed and fell silent, alarmed by the prospect of conversation. Under other circumstances, Adelaide might have found the interaction comical.

Her part had been clearly appointed.

"Just show up and don't cause a scene," Feodor had said.

"Fine. But that's all I'm doing."

"I wouldn't trust you with anything else."

"You're wise," she said, though she bit her tongue not to let her resentment show.

So she had stayed on the edge of things, waiting with almost malicious intent for another unfortunate to approach and offer some convoluted form of condolence. She imagined herself glittering like some hard bright object. Go on, she willed them. Try me. But fewer and fewer people did. The rest of the family were more accessible, even her mother. Her own friends seemed confused by their leader's withdrawal from centre stage. They clung together in tiny shoals, chattering over the rims of their glasses.

In the next room, the pianist picked his way through the second half of the programme. A Neon Age interlude drifted into the Broken Ice sonata. Adelaide's throat tightened. Axel loved this piece. Axel used to play it, badly. Such was the intensity of her longing that she believed, for a second, that she saw her twin standing there—and then she blinked, and the ache of missing was as vast as it had been before.

Adelaide leaned out to get a better look at the performer. It was Ruben Tallak, the composer, who had tutored both her and her brother. Standing alone by the piano was her grandfather.

He had seen her. Slowly, Adelaide extracted herself from the alcove and made her way over, straightening her collar and tie. Her grandfather, though in many ways the most lenient of the family, was meticulous about presentation. Above the lapels of his velvet jacket, his face was an intricate network; a history contained in every line. He held a glass less than half full of an amber weqa. She knew it was because of his shaking hands. He was worried the liquid might spill.

"Alright, Adie," he said gently.

"I want to go, Grandfather. Please, say I can leave."

Leonid's hand rested for a moment on her hair, as it often used to when she was a child. She felt it tremor. She wished that her grandfather could give her a hug. But they were in public, and besides, she had given up that right.

"I'm sorry, Adie. We need you to stay."

"Leonid." One of the Councillors approached her grandfather, solemn faced. Adelaide melted away. The Councillor's pompous tones echoed after her. "Such a tragedy. Barely come of age…"

She stumbled upon other conversations, each flirting sombrely around the same topic, each fading away at her approach.

"Poor Viviana, have you seen her? So wan."

"She should drink an infusion of red coral tea every night. It may not restore the spirits immediately, but it does energise the body…"

Low murmurs; a group around the canapé table.

"—can't help noticing that this is the second incident involving a founding family. Has anyone even considered that it could be the same people who killed the Dumays? What if…?"

"My dear, that was almost twenty years ago—"

"Eighteen, to be precise—may they rest with the stars."

"—and anyway, Kaat was convicted."

"Actually, she was never officially convicted because she never confessed."

"A sure sign of guilt… of course I am not saying he *is* dead, you understand, but one does fear the worst. And it might have been easy, you know, the way he was, to lure—"

Finding Adelaide's eyes cold upon her, the speaker stopped abruptly.

"Adelaide, my dear—" someone else spoke.

Adelaide turned away. She saw Linus talking to one of the krill, and watched him for a moment, wondering what he was saying. The journalist was listening intently, nodding through Linus's sentences. Then she reached out and put a hand on his arm. It might have been a gesture of sympathy, nothing more, but Adelaide saw him shrink. And something about Linus's reluctance struck her as important, as if, having listened to a song a thousand times over, she had suddenly noticed a flat note in the vocal. She continued to survey him for some time before she realized it was not her brother she should be concerned with. The discordance lay elsewhere.

"I'm sorry about Axel."

The voice from behind her was Tyr, who worked for her father. Generally they would exchange pleasantries, but today she did not turn to look at him. She couldn't.

"Why? He's not dead."

Tyr paused. "I mean the not knowing."

"Yes," she said. "Yes, that is something to be sorry about."

Through the doors, she saw her father was engaged in discussion with a black-suited man she did not recognize.

"Who is that?" she asked Tyr.

"I believe it's the new man in charge of the investigation."

Her father was tall, but his companion stood half a head above him, a thin angular streak of a man. His head was inclined politely towards Feodor.

"For Axel?"

"Yes."

She moved away before Tyr could tell her more, pushing through the mourners, or whatever they thought they were. Feodor saw her coming. She knew he was aware of her intent, half expected him to vanish the visitor away before she had a chance to speak to him. But when she reached them, Feodor made the obligatory introductions.

"This is my daughter, Adelaide. Adie, this is Sanjay Hanif, who took over the investigation when it went to Council."

There was nothing in this pronouncement out of place, other than the abbreviation, which suggested an affection entirely absent from their relationship. Adelaide contrived an equally fake smile.

"Hello. We've not seen you before. I haven't, anyway."

"How could you have, Adelaide." Feodor's voice was light in its warning. Hanif appeared not to notice. He had dark sombre eyes, a listening face. He reminded her of someone but she could not think who.

"I was only recently assigned," he said. "I read your statement."

"I hope you enjoyed it."

He looked at her curiously. "It was through you the family discovered Axel was missing, was it not?"

"Indirectly. It was the delivery girl, Yonna."

"A girl you employed."

"That's right."

Feodor interrupted before she could say any more. "It was very important to Adelaide that her brother was well looked after. She undertook a lot of organization on his behalf."

"It is very important," Adelaide clarified. "And it's alright, Feodor, I've been through these questions before. I have no objection to going over them again if it helps to find Axel."

An awkward silence followed. Sanjay Hanif glanced at his watch.

"I'm deeply sorry for what you are all going through," he said. "Hopefully we will have new information soon. But I'm afraid I cannot stay any longer. Thank you for your time." He pressed his inner wrist to Feodor's, then Adelaide's, in formal greeting. She waited as he stepped swiftly through the crowds, gauging the optimum moment for pursuit. Feodor took her arm.

"You can't go after him." The genial tone of this pronouncement did not deceive Adelaide. She had grown up in a public environment; she knew the duality a voice could hold.

"Why not? I have to talk to him."

Her skin was drained of colour where he gripped it, and there was a nerve twitching just above his left eye that she knew of old. She saw it for the first time the day Axel let out a cage of geckos at one of their parents' anniversary parties. The twins were six years old. The stunt had earned them both a beating. *Open it. You open it! I dared you first.* Old friends, these memories. She almost smiled, but a twinge of pain shot through her arm as Feodor's fingers squeezed harder. She wriggled, trying to free herself without drawing attention to her captive status.

"You promised not to make a scene. Osiris's eyes are upon the family today. You promised." Her father was struggling to keep himself in check. His reaction seemed entirely disproportionate to what she wanted. She wondered if he too was remembering the geckos.

"I didn't know Hanif was going to be here then. Let go of my arm."

He maintained his grip. "You're not going anywhere."

"Let me go!"

They stood locked in mounting fury. Words raced through her head: all the things she could and would say to Feodor, after. What right did he have!—how dare he stop her—what did publicity matter, what did the Rechnov name matter? He didn't care about Axel, never had, none of them had—

The crowds were closing in on Sanjay Hanif. In a moment the doors would do the same. It might be the one opportunity she had to catch him outside of Rechnov supervision, she couldn't follow beyond the gathering, there were too many krill. She twisted her arm once more, biting her lip to suppress an exclamation. Her eyes grew hot. She despised herself for the tears gathering there, though they were not the product of pain but of frustration. Why could her father not understand that she had to know? She blinked furiously.

Now Hanif was nodding to security. His black-coated figure was sliding away, subsumed by the closing doors. Gone.

"Why was he here?" She wrenched her arm free. Feodor nodded to a passing Councillor. "What was he doing here?" she repeated, louder this time.

"He probably thought it was as good a time as any to introduce himself."

"What about the rest of us? Why couldn't I talk to him? Axel's my twin for stars' sake!"

"Because this is a public event." Feodor had subsided into a low hiss. "And we are meant to be presenting an appearance of unity. If you can't behave yourself for us, then at least do it for your brother. Now pull yourself together."

She threw him one look of derision and walked away. The gathering did not permit her to walk far, but the gesture felt right. She wanted the numbness back. She craved its anaesthetic. How stupid she was to even attend this pathetic event. Their father was wrong, Axel would not want her to behave. Axel would scorn everything about his service of hope: the pomp, the speech, the piano. She imagined him appearing like a magician from under the instrument's lid, hopping onto the stool, striking a jaunty note whilst the guests stared, flabbergasted. "Did you miss me, A?" he'd say.

At least, the old Axel would have done.

That sense of the off-key clanged again. Even her own role today was unforgivable.

By the refreshments table, two of the Ngozi girls had given up discussing Axel and had moved on to the next prominent item of society's speculation: the execution of the westerner Eirik 9968.

"Are you attending?"

"Well, I'm not sure. Aunt Mbeke says we all should and I suppose she's right. It might be a bit unpleasant though."

"I shouldn't worry. We'll be miles away from the westies."

"I suppose. And I'm quite intrigued to see, you know, what he looks like."

"You should have said. Dad could have got us into the trial. I wouldn't have minded seeing it either."

Eirik 9968 was the last thing that Adelaide wanted to hear about. There was something eagerly nasty in the girls' fascination with the execution that told her they had been talking about her twin in exactly the same way.

Ignoring them both, she took an open bottle of weqa from the table and went to the next room where earlier she had noticed a balcony door. She slipped out. It wasn't a large balcony, only a few metres wide, a cuboid sanctuary seventy-eight floors above sea-level. She sank to the ground, knees drawn to her chest and her back to the closed door, shivering violently. The regulation strip of soil in front of the railings supported trembling plants. Autumn had arrived. It was freezing.

The veil itched her skin. She tore the hat off, feeling the pins in her hair come loose, and flicked the hat over the balcony rail. The sunshine made her blink.

Osiris lay before her, a shimmering metropolis sunk shin deep into the ocean. Before dawn, mist obscured the entire city, enveloping the thousands of pyramid skyscrapers in its damp, arcane touch. It was noon now, and the fog had mostly dissipated. Deceptive sunshine polished the tapering structures of glass and metal, turning the bridges and shuttle lines that webbed them into silver threads. The solar skins of the towers greedily reaped this bounty of heat and light.

Adelaide took a gulp of weqa. The wine had a sharp, tangy taste. She read the bottle label: seaweed farmed from the northern kelp forests. In Osiris, every possession or belonging or simple luxury was representative of an achievement. Adelaide ate avocados that germinated under artificial light. She smoked cigarillos rolled from tobacco nurtured in the green-houses of Skyscraper-334-North. Nestling in the heights of the eastern quarter, the Rechnovs lived off the produce of Osiris ingenuity, first sown over one hundred and forty years ago with the establishment of the Osiris Board in remote Alaska.

It had been drilled into her since birth: Osiris's history, the Rechnov history. She had never felt further from it.

In the distance she saw a man abseiling down one of the gardens. His yellow jacket wove steadily through the green canvas. He was probably repairing storm damage. Adelaide lit a cigarillo. The nicotine rush caught her by surprise, and for a second she had the peculiar sensation that the city was melting, its majestic horizon stretching and reforming into new, unexpected shapes. She reached for the sculpted bars of the balcony rail-ings and pushed her face between a spiral and a serpentine curve. The metal chilled her skin.

The building opposite was a tightrope walk away. Several floors down, a shuttle line fed into its belly like an intravenous tube, and snaked out the other side to continue its journey through the eastern district.

Adelaide pulled herself up and folded her arms along the balcony rail, resting her chin upon them. Ahead and behind, to left and right, the pyramids marched away in ordered lines. The sea rushed between them. From this height the waterways looked harmless, like washes of blue tinted paint. But in the sometime erratic progress of the boating traffic, there was a hint of the sea's underlying menace.

She thought, as she did at least ten times a day, about the last time that she had seen her brother.

It was midweek. Adelaide had been to a fencing class in the studio fifteen floors down from her apartment. Her muscles were stiffening after the workout and sweat still clung to her body. She was running late to meet Jannike for lunch. She didn't hurry, though. Inside, she was never seen to rush. Outside she rushed everywhere, on speedboats, on jet skis and on waterbikes. Adelaide had cultivated this image over the years.

On that particular day, the lift swished up through the core of the skyscraper and she got out on the ninety-ninth floor. When she entered her apartment, a figure was standing by the glass wall, facing out. None of the lights were on and darkness lined the flat like velvet. But she knew it was Axel because of his stillness.

She flicked the wall switch.

"You found your key then?"

That was definitely her opening line. Not said in an accusing way. By that stage, resignation had become the dominant frame of mind with her twin.

He said something odd. Have you heard about the balloon? Or maybe it was, did you read about the balloon flight? It might even have been, what do you know about the balloon?

Nothing worth paying attention to, anyway. Axel talked in riddles; he no longer made sense. Adelaide was late and the need to take a shower was pressing on her with her own damp odour.

"No," she said. "Are you alright? Do you need anything?" If he did he didn't tell her. He repeated the same question about the balloon. He did not turn. Fraying strands of denim, inches long, trailed on the floor behind his bare feet. His gaze was fixed beyond the glass, but there was no view. Osiris was held hostage by fog.

The tips of his hair, the same bright red as hers, attracted motes of light like a crown. She had a strange sense that he was smiling.

"I'm going to change," she said. "I have to meet someone. You know where everything is, A."

In the bathroom she peeled off her jogging pants and Urchin tank top and threw them carelessly on the floor. She stepped into the shower before the water had time to heat, gasping at the dousing. After, she wrapped herself in her kimono and went through to her bedroom. Carefully applying a sweep of scarlet lipstick, she almost forgot about Axel.

When she came back he was gone. He had left the front door ajar. She pounded it shut, purely for her own satisfaction, because she was sure he was nowhere near by and even if he was, the noise would have meant nothing to him. She went for lunch in the Hummingbird Café in S-771-E. Jannike was late too and had a tale about a faulty shuttle pod or some other transport problem. They ordered weqa. She remembered choosing the bottle because her staple choice was out of stock, and it was the first time she had read the wine list in several months of patronage. It was likely she had eaten bird.

That was the last time she saw Axel. A month had passed in the way that the months always passed, and sometimes she thought about him more and sometimes less, and then he was gone. It occurred to her, shivering in the glacial air, that it was impossible to say exactly when he had vanished.

She realized now who Sanjay Hanif had reminded her of: it was Dr Radir, the most recent of her twin's consultants. Radir had failed to diagnose Axel with a condition. He said he had never treated anyone like Axel.

Adelaide let the cigarillo fall. She knew the reason she was out here. It was that nameless thing people did when they felt bereft of decision: waiting, seeing. There was something about Osiris that demanded this act of looking out, perhaps because there was nothing beyond the city to find. It was the behaviour of a fool. She had unearthed a fracture and did not know what to do with it.

One other resource remained open to her.

She took her scarab out of her purse and slipped in a jewelled earpiece. Then she entered the code that she had memorised two days ago. The o'comm at the other end buzzed twice before it was answered.

The voice that responded was curt but unremarkable.

"Yes?"

"My name is Adelaide Mystik. We spoke earlier this week."

"Yes. You've decided?"

"I'd like to go ahead."

"Very well."

"You understand that this remains outside of my family's jurisdiction?"

"I guarantee discretion."

"Use this number only if you have to contact me. If I don't respond, don't speak. The funds will be with you within the hour. Start with the hospitals. I'll relay Axel's photograph to your scarab."

"There are plenty of photographs of Axel Rechnov."

"Not recent ones," she said.

There was a pause.

"Send the photograph," he said. "I'll be in touch."

"I want to meet," she said quickly. "Let's say Friday, the week after the execution. That should give you enough time. Eleven o'clock at the butterfly farm."

"As you wish."

The scarab emitted a tiny beep as the investigator disconnected from the Reef.

Adelaide brought up the last recorded image she had of Axel. He wasn't looking at the camera. The miniature screen showed his pallor, the way his cheeks caved his face. It showed what remained. She entered the investigator's code once more. Axel's face hung there for a moment in profile before the picture blinked and the scarab went dark.

Her fingers fumbled as she put away the scarab, numb with cold. Nonetheless she stayed outside, exhausting the weqa, until the guests went away and she could leave.

2 | VIKRAM

Vikram's watch ticked off the seconds with silent, calculated precision. It was nearing half ten o'clock; the appointed time of Eirik's death was eleven. Vikram had already been here for over an hour. The boats had gathered early.

His hands were shaking. He clenched them into fists, catching shreds of torn lining in the pockets of his coat. Something had changed when he woke today. A tight band squeezed his chest, constricting the airflow and his heart. He could not have said what it meant; for so long he had felt only a blankness tinged with fear.

He stood at the boat rail of a rusting waterbus anchored far back in the crowd. The Council had chosen to stage the execution near the north end of the border, where four soaring towers cornered an impromptu square. On the western side, the sea was carpeted with boats, every craft jammed with westerners who had congregated, whether to witness a spectacle or out of disbelief that it would be carried through, Vikram could not tell. Apart from a few officials and the skadi, there were no Citizens on the surface. They were all inside, locked away behind window-walls, or listening to a reporter describe the scene on their o'dios.

"Mind if we squeeze in here?"

The man was a head shorter than Vikram, his breath misting in the cold, steering a child of perhaps eight in front of him. Vikram moved along the rail.

"Sure."

What could he say? He glanced at the kid, a boy, whose expression was open and curious. He wanted to ask the man if it was right the boy should witness such a thing, but to draw any attention was risky. There was always a chance that one of the skadi might recognise him. They did as they pleased, and in the event of any trouble, Vikram's record would count against him. The thought of going back underwater was enough to bring sweat trickling down his back.

"They say he's the NWO leader," said the man. "Eirik 9968. They say he's number one. What do you reckon?"

"I don't know."

He could have said a lot of things. He could have said that he had known Eirik like a brother, once. But between the rumours and the krill speculation and what Drake and Nils had told him, he no longer knew what or who to believe.

The kid pointed to the tank, sat on the deck of a barge a hundred metres away, beyond the front line of western boats. Behind it, the border rose out of the waves, its rippling mesh wet and dripping with seaweed.

"Is that it?" said the kid.

"That's it."

"Where's the prisoner?"

"They'll bring him out soon."

Soon. In a matter of minutes, he had to watch Eirik die. Vikram thought he might cry, or shout out, or be sick. If he only knew if the man was guilty or not! He drew in a deep breath. When he exhaled the air came out loud, too loud, the woman on his other side turned her head to look. He had thought that his face was blank, but you never knew what really showed. Vikram had seen fear and horror spark in the most hardened of features: the emotion sudden and unexpected, like electric light in a dark window.

Keep yourself empty, he thought. A pebble at the bottom of the ocean. A bit of kelp. When it's happened it's over, done. Then you move on.

That was what the three of them had agreed, him and Nils and Drake. They would go to the execution, because they couldn't stay away. But they would do nothing. There was nothing they could do.

Eirik's sentence had finally been announced in early summer, eight months after Vikram was let out of jail. There had not been a public execution since the six Osuwa criminals were shot at the border twenty-eight years ago, for an alleged act of terrorism at the university. Even Vikram knew that Eirik had committed no acts of terrorism. The Citizens were going to execute him anyway.

Was the City actually scared of the west? How could they be, when there wasn't a single coherent movement or activist group? The west was in chaos, crippled by food shortages and drug trafficking and the continual power failures. The shanty towns were terrorised by gangs who imposed illegal levees and warred continually amongst themselves. Once every few months there might be a straggly protest at the border, mute and seemingly purposeless, but it didn't take a Councillor to work out that the west was in no position to threaten anyone.

Twenty minutes before eleven. The back of Vikram's neck tingled with the bitter cold. He pulled up his scarf. In a couple of weeks, he'd need two to go outside.

It was an incongruously clear, pretty day, the sky palest blue and utterly empty. Under its expanse Vikram felt the unsettling jumble of freedom and an at times incapacitating terror of losing it again, which had dogged him ever since he got out. Around the towers, waves slapped the decking with light, almost playful gestures. The waterbus he stood upon with twenty other westerners rose on the swell.

A skadi boat glided down the edge of the crowd. They had a fleet of barges and speeders, and they had strung a line of buoys to fence in the western boats. The skadi were dressed bulkily in their habitual black. They were all armed with guns and tasers. One of them had a speakerphone.

"You will stay behind the barrier. You will not move your boats. Any attempted action will meet with severe punishment."

The execution boat, anchored between the western crowds and the City, was a squat, ugly craft, surrounded by clear water and painted entirely black except for the prow, where someone had daubed two white orbs and the teeth of a shark. The deck was flat. On it, the transparent cube reflected the towers on either side and the people and the empty waiting sky.

The wind blew spray into Vikram's face and he licked the salt from his chapped lips. It stung, an unwelcome reminder that he was really here. He was alive, and awake.

The speakerphone crackled. "You will stay behind the barrier. You will not move your boats…"

Vikram was nine years old when Mikkeli first brought him to the border. From his earliest memories, he had heard people talking about the infamous waterway. It was a subject which made voices change, and sometimes faces too. In Vikram's young world, which consisted mostly of places he could not go or things he could not do, this barrier dividing the west from the City was a concept at once as solid and as transient as the sky.

On that day Mikkeli had blagged two passes on a waterbus and sneaked Vikram up to a balcony sixty floors above surface. Once they were safely installed, she unwrapped a package of fried squid and kelp. She said that someone had given her the food, which was a lie. Vikram knew Mikkeli had stolen it because he had heard the fry-boat woman yelling at them earlier as they ran away over the raft rack.

They shared the squid rings, greasy and chewy on the inside but coated with thick, salty batter. Mikkeli gave Vikram most of the kelp squares. She pointed outwards.

"Look over there," she said. "See them towers?"

"Yeah. They're all silver." That was his first impression of the City. Silver and glorious, like the morning sun on the waves.

"We can't go there," said Mikkeli. Her voice sounded strange. Vikram could not work out if she was cross or if she might actually cry. He thought about what Mikkeli had said and decided that there must be a reason for it.

"Why can't we go there?"

"'Cause we're westerners, that's why. We're not allowed."

"Why not?"

"'Cause it's the rules. The Council's rules." Mikkeli spat over the balcony rail. Vikram leaned forward to see the gob of spit fly and Mikkeli grabbed his collar and pulled him back.

"Who's the Council, Keli?"

"Stupid old gulls, Naala says. Stupid gulls who make stupid rules. You see, Vik, our mum's and dad's folks, they weren't born here. They came from some place else."

"I know that. I'm not an idiot."

"No, you're clever, that's why I'm telling you this. 'Cause it's important. And it's not fair. Why do we get left in this dump and them Citizens got heating and 'lectricity that works all the time and you know what else they've got? They've got the *o'vis*." The yearning in Mikkeli's voice reminded Vikram of hours spent waiting outside the fry-boats, smelling the smell of hot squid, knowing that it would be long past twilight before leftovers. "Naala actually saw an o'vis once. She said it's amazing. You can watch ancient filmreels the Neons made; the newsreel and animés and *everything*."

"What's the newsreel?"

"This announcer thing they got, tells you information and stuff, like if someone dies, everyone knows 'cause it's on the feed…"

Mikkeli talked on. She told him weird and wonderful stories of a fabulous world where people went to parties and wore beautiful clothes and watched acrobats and then stuffed themselves with weqa and fish until they vomited.

People didn't get sick in the City, she said. They didn't get horrible coughs and die in the night.

The Citizens did peculiar things. They kept animals in their rooms—as pets. They wore coats with bird feathers inside. They had gliders.

If they wanted to come to west Osiris, which they didn't, they were allowed to whenever they liked.

Vikram listened. He looked at the sleek, silver towers. The shuttle lines looked like jets of blue fire leaping from one gigantic cone to the next. Fire was one of Vikram's favourite things in his limited world.

"Can't we just go to look around?" he asked.

"No. Look down there—careful! Naala'd murder me… See that net coming out the water? Goes down as far as the sea mud. People say the Tellers tied it, right at the centre of the earth. But that's all lies. The Council wanted to keep us out so the skadi put it there."

"We can't go ever? Not when we're older?" Vikram wanted to be sure.

"Did you listen to what I said? Never ever. You try and cross that waterway down there without a tag that says you're a Citizen, the skadi shoot you—*zap!* Just like that. They hate us, they call us dogs. Look, look, there's a boat of 'em going past right there, that dirty black speeder. Naala told me it all. I wasn't even meant to bring you with me, it's that dangerous."

Vikram saw a gull fly past the nearest tower on the other side. The light, reflected from a window, turned the bird for a second into living gold.

Everything that was beautiful belonged to the Citizens.

"Then why did you?" he said angrily. "Why did you bring me?"

It seemed like the most unfair thing that Mikkeli had ever done. But Mikkeli was unimpressed at his outburst.

"Because Vik, one day someone's got to do something about it, and it might as well be us. Right?"

He looked from the waterway, where the low-lying skadi boat was gliding past one of the silver cones, and back to Mikkeli. Last week, she had stolen a new garment: a yellow hood. Within its furry halo her face was deadly serious.

Vikram would have done anything for Mikkeli.

"Alright," he said. "How?"

Nine minutes to eleven. Vikram shivered uncontrollably. He could not take his eyes off the boat. With its unkind mission, the vessel itself seemed to have acquired a mesmerising power. Each of its component parts was imbued with more than simple menace; the cracked graffiti eyes, the crew posed at stiff attention, gun barrels protruding from their shoulders, the waves lapping and the creak of the hull. There was something inherently wrong about the scene. The boat's natural purpose had been reversed. It would no longer protect life; it carried a tomb, clear and silent.

The kid on Vikram's right fidgeted, looked up at his father.

"Not long now," said the man.

Vikram wondered if there was anyone in the crowd who had plans to break Eirik out. He felt the tension of the crowd, really felt it, the way he'd sensed unease three years ago, the day the riots began. Who else had Eirik known? Did he have allies? Colleagues? Were there members of the New Western Osiris Front in the crowd? Had they ever been anything more than a rumour, or had all of those dissidents quietly disappeared after the riots were crushed? Perhaps everyone present today was simply relieved that a scapegoat had been found and that it wasn't them.

He gauged the thickness of the glass construction, wondering if a single shot would break it. He remembered, distantly, the feel of a gun in his hand, that sense of absolute power and invulnerability. It had proved false, like everything else.

The skadi would have prepared thoroughly. They always did.

Only another few minutes. There was no sign of Eirik.

"Maybe they'll cancel it," said the woman next to Vikram.

He looked at her properly for the first time. She was old, at least fifty, and wheezing in the cold air. She probably had tuberculosis. He remembered Mikkeli's lilting voice—*people don't get sick in the City, Vik.* He wanted to ask the woman her name, but could not trust himself to know even this tiny piece of personal information.

"It's just an act," he said—whether to convince himself or the woman he did not know.

The crowd murmured impatiently. Where was the condemned man?

Vikram had not seen Eirik since before the riots. Even if he had wanted to, prisoners were allowed no visitors. Underwater, the information that Vikram overheard came in drips and leaks. A whisper, across cells, that Eirik had confessed. Months later, in the breakfast line, rumours of the tribunal.

He hadn't been sure about Eirik at first. It had always been the four of them: Vikram and Mikkeli, Nils and Drake. Mikkeli, as the oldest, was the leader. None of them had family; they had grown up on the boat and later they lived together in a single room. They squabbled and got into fights, they tried and sometimes succeeded in finding work and eventually, when their circumstances could no longer be viewed entirely as a joke, they had talked, talked seriously, and they had founded the New Horizon Movement. Their ideas were popular. Others joined. The talks grew to meetings of fifteen or twenty people, but they were always the core.

One night, Mikkeli brought Eirik back to talk to them. Vikram remembered Eirik walking into their favoured bar for the first time, tossing his coat onto the table, drawing up an empty keg.

They had been in the middle of a heated discussion. When Eirik sat down, they all stopped talking. The silence was expectant.

"Well," Eirik said. And looked at them all. A canny, knowing look, but somehow gleeful, as though he was pleased with life and what it offered, and even how it found him. "Well."

He remembered Mikkeli, sidling forward, a shyness about her. Vikram had never seen her like that before.

"This is Eirik," she announced. "He wants to hear about Horizon."

Vikram was suspicious. He could tell that Nils and Drake felt the same way, sensed them bristling beside him.

"Show him the letters, Vik," said Mikkeli. She spoke to Eirik. "Every week we send a letter to the Council. Vik does the writing for us. He's the smart one."

Vikram was embarrassed.

"He doesn't want to see those, Keli."

"Oh go on."

"That's our business," Nils interjected. "We don't know who this guy is. No offence, Eirik."

Eirik smiled. "None taken. How about we all get a drink instead?"

Later, Eirik took Vikram aside.

"I didn't want to make you feel awkward, Vikram, but I'd be interested to see what Horizon sends to the Council. There's too much talk of violence out there. It's understandable but it won't work. We need to use our heads."

"He's a spy," said Nils, when Mikkeli and Eirik had left and Vikram relayed what had been said to the others.

"He's almost forty." Drake emptied the dregs of a tankard into her mouth.

"What's that got to do with anything?"

"Old, but no grey hair," she said simply. "Don't you think that's interesting?"

"Clearly Keli does," said Nils sourly.

"I'm not sure he is a spy." Vikram was thoughtful.

"Must be."

"But he looks like us."

Eirik had what they all had—the unmistakeable taint of the west. It wasn't just the general shabbiness and the permanent smell of salt from water travel and poor diet. It was something in the eyes. Part wariness, part resignation; a continual expectation of the worst, as though by acknowledging, almost welcoming the worst of their situation, they could somehow ward off the reality. According to the only survey ever carried out in the west, by the Colnat Initiative, life expectancy in the west was an average of forty-three. The years before, filled with sickness and unemployment, would become increasingly harsh. They all carried this knowledge on their faces, and the only time Vikram actually noticed it was when he saw someone who did not look like that. Like the skadi.

Eirik came back. One by one he won them over. Part of the lure was undoubtedly that Eirik knew how to talk.

"You people are exactly who I've been looking for," he said.

When Vikram showed him the transcripts of their letters, Eirik was visibly excited.

"These are great ideas! Joint fishing missions, that'll appeal to the anti-Nucleites, they're desperate to get further out of the city. And if you re-phrased a few things—you don't mind me making suggestions? Like here, you talk about reducing security at checkpoints—what you want to say is *border reconciliation*. It's all about the jargon."

Vikram wrote it down.

"How do you know this stuff? Who taught you?"

"You learn to pick things up. Odd jobs in the City—I always scan their newsfeed. Listen to them talking. Know your enemy, Vikram. It's the oldest rule in the universe."

Then he began asking questions. *So now we know what we want—how are we going to get it?* It was *we*, right from the start. That had made them feel good. And it was a valid question, to which none of them yet had an answer. This was what they sat around arguing about for nights on end. They had been happy enough doing that for a while, with Vikram composing the letters, and occasional suggestions that they might orga-nise a protest. Mikkeli had come up with a series of slogans. But after Eirik showed up they started noticing other things—like the fact that one electric bulb did not produce adequate light even in the summer, and that no amount of well-written words could assuage the fact that none of them had had a decent meal in weeks.

"We need to engage with the early justice groups," said Eirik. "Get right back to the start. The Western Repatriation Movement, they were good people—you know about them? They sent the first official refugee delegate to the Council, seven years after the Great Storms and the first immigrants arrived. The Council made promises, of course. The western quarter's only temporary, they said. Give us eighteen months to restructure the city, we'll find you somewhere decent to live. Eighteen months go by, the delegates return, they warn the Council that people are getting angry, and the Coun-cil places them under house arrest—idiotic move but they were probably scared shitless. That's what led to the rise of the New Osiris Affiliation, and *they* led to the second wave of riots, and what happened at the Greenhouse, and finally, thirty-nine years ago, to the border. That border's as old as I am. We've grown up together."

He sat back and held their eyes, one by one, steadily.

"Everything," he said. "Has a root."

Eirik's voice was thoughtful and inevitable like a tide. They could listen to him for hours. It seemed that Mikkeli's adulation had proved well founded. They had followed her and she had needed someone to believe in as much as the rest of them. It was only Eirik himself who seemed to wander, fleet as foam, unhindered by such petty concerns as doubt.

As the weeks passed, Vikram noticed shifts in attitude. At first it was small things. There was less attention to the letters. Instead of helping him dictate, the others might talk about an incident at the border. A man who had been detained at the checkpoint for forty-eight hours without reason. A woman, beaten up, who had lost an eye. Phrases crept into conversation: *if only I'd been there*. Vikram found himself only too happy to join in.

The lack of response to the Council missives began to feel like a personal insult. Did they even read what was sent? Was there any point in writing at all?

He started revisiting old childhood haunts, by the border. The towers on the other side seemed brighter and more blinding than ever and his hands would itch with inactivity.

He clearly remembered turning to Nils one day and saying, "If something happened this winter—if people decided to riot—what would you do?"

Nils said without a flicker of hesitation, "I'd kill as many of those skadi bastards as I could."

"Not Citizens though."

"Course not Citizens. What d'you take me for?"

And then came the morning of strange quiet, the day the riots began. The day that everything fell apart and the skadi came for Eirik. The City published findings that they said proved Eirik was NWO. He'd gone from group to group, they said, winning trust, gaining followers. Recruiting. They gave him a number.

For Eirik, after three years in a seabed cell, death might be a relief. He wondered if Mikkeli's ghost had lingered with the other man whilst he was underwater, the way she had with Vikram, presenting him with her lifeless body over and over again, the tattered yellow hood that fell back from her face drenched to ochre. Did Eirik even know she was dead?

The second hand edged past eleven o'clock. Something was happening. Birds, alert to the change in mood, began to swirl overhead. A curious gull dove low over the boats. Of course the birds would come today.

The hatch on the execution boat had opened. A skadi officer emerged. He came to stand at the rail, hands clasped behind him. Wide sunglasses wrapped around his head caught the sun as he turned this way and that.

The officer barked an order. Eirik was led out from below deck. He must have been kept there all along, in darkness. Vikram strained his eyes, desperate for a glimpse of Eirik's face, but it was concealed behind a dark hood, part of a prisoner's suit.

A frisson went through the crowd.

"That's him... that's Eirik 9968..."

Eirik seemed to move as one in a dream. His hands were manacled in front of him. The man leading him gave tiny jerks upon the chains, and Vikram could hear their clank beneath the ever present rush of the ocean and the whispers of the audience.

The executioner checked the tank. He rapped the glass on each side and on the roof. Two skadi on either side of Eirik held his arms. They turned him towards the western crowd, but his head flopped on his chest, and his face remained in shadow.

He's drugged, Vikram realized. He felt anger stirring at their cowardice, mixed with a horrible relief that Eirik would barely be conscious.

The air keened as a dozen loudspeakers were switched on. The wheezing woman next to Vikram covered her ears. The man to his right squeezed his boy's shoulders. Vikram wanted to wrench the kid away and cover up his eyes. In the next breath he thought no, he should see this. He should know what the Citizens do to us.

A voice began to speak. The tone was clipped and robotic.

"The man known as Eirik 9968 has been sentenced for his actions against the city state of Osiris. He is found guilty of the following crimes: denouncing the Osiris Council, organising collective violence against the City, inciting aggressive action in westerners, acts of personal terrorism, assault and mass murder. In particular he is convicted for his role in reviving the illegal New Western Osiris Front, the organisation responsible for the atrocities committed at Osuwa University in the year twenty-three eighty-eight, and for leading and instigating the July riots three years ago. He is judged responsible for both the deaths of Citizens and the necessary reprisals against the west."

Eirik made no reaction to this speech. His posture was bowed and defeated. It was doubtful whether he had even heard the accusations. Confronted with that small, lone figure between two cities, all Vikram could think of was Eirik sat cross-legged in Nils's room, leaning forward, gesticulating as he spoke, his face intense and serious, half illuminated by the flickering light. *Look, it's not enough to know the history—we've got to know how these people* think. *Why won't they take us seriously—why* won't *they answer Vik's letters? Because we don't use their language and we don't understand their systems. We don't know who they really are.*

The memory was so strong it made him giddy. Vikram could hear Eirik's voice perfectly; he could see that room, smell the empty wrappers of squid and kelp. His head swam.

Instinct told him the truth. In that moment he knew, with absolute and shocking conviction, that everything that had been said about Eirik was a lie. Because Eirik, who did know the language, had been a threat. He might actually have made people listen. And the City couldn't let anything threaten the divide, so the City were going to remove him.

Maybe Eirik had helped to feed the riots. Did it matter? It was not a terrorist who had thrown the first fire torch. It was an ordinary westerner like Vikram, who had been up against the border and everything it represented too many times, and in a single moment of frustration had cracked. Anyone could have started the riots.

The officer on the boat drew himself up, concluding his speech.

"For this long and atrocious history of criminal activity, the Osiris Council has condemned Eirik 9968 to death by drowning."

The kid leaned forward over the boat rail, eyes wide and eager.

Vikram felt a rising panic. It couldn't happen. Eirik was innocent. Vikram knew he was innocent. Where were Nils and Drake? If he could find them—he had to explain. It was as though he had emerged from hibernation. How could he ever have imagined that Eirik could be involved with the NWO? The idea was insane. What had he been thinking?

There was still time for a miracle. The speaker would reverse his statement. He would declare that the execution had been a warning to the west, and Eirik would be freed. They couldn't—they couldn't kill him.

He willed Eirik to look his way. A moment of contact—he needed Eirik to know he was here—

"Pardon."

The call came from the other side of the crowd. Quiet at first. Then another voice joined in.

"Pardon."

The call rose, each voice creating a new bubble of sound. Vikram added his own plea, but his throat was tight and his voice hoarse and barely audible.

"Pardon. Pardon."

The executioner stepped forward and zipped up the hooded suit, concealing Eirik's face completely.

No—

One of the guards opened a door in the tank. They pushed Eirik inside. He fell against the side of the tank and slumped to the floor. The skad banged the door shut. Vikram felt the reverberations shudder all the way down his spine. *You didn't believe him*, they said. *You didn't believe him, believe him, believe him…*

Wild ideas raced through his head. If he could get to the tank underwater—hold his breath long enough to swim—

Chatter skittered through the crowd, small sounds of distress, quickly choked, others muttering in anticipation. The people around him were faceless and alien. The man on his right had lifted the kid to sit on his shoulders and someone behind was complaining that their view was blocked. Vikram could not see Nils or Drake anywhere. He was on his own.

Two skadi went to their stations at the pumps. The executioner checked his watch, gave a curt nod. A stifling quiet fell over the crowd.

It was so still that Vikram could hear water guzzling through the bilges. The first load splashed into the tank.

He heard disjointed words behind him.

"I can't watch—"

"Don't look. Come here, just don't look—"

"Dad, the water's going in—I can see it—"

Behind the glass the water trickled, greenish in colour. It foamed and swirled with the pressure. Strands of floating kelp were sucked inside. A small fish was flung out of the pipe. Eirik lay prone against the tank wall, his hands still manacled.

Stars—

Help him!

The water gathered around Eirik's legs. At last he seemed to stir. The shock of the icy water must have jerked him from his state of comatose. He moved his head. He drew his knees to his chest. Every movement he made was infinitely slow.

"It's going to take ten minutes," said someone on the next boat.

"Ten? Fifteen at least."

"No, not fifteen. Not as long as that."

"I'll bet you on it."

A girl began to scream, a long and eerie sound, rising and falling. A skad lifted his rifle and fired a warning shot into the air. The scream stopped abruptly. The crowd rippled with alarm. He saw several people duck, some hunching protectively over their neighbours, but no one shouted; no one dared to protest. It would have to be Vikram. If he spoke up, he could incite the crowd—they must be angry enough to act—surely they must want to stop this—surely they didn't believe, as Vikram had—

His body had turned to lead. Some part of his mind knew that this was self-preservation. That there was nothing he could do for Eirik now. He could only give Eirik the dignity of a witness. Someone to remember, to throw salt in Eirik's name.

The skadi bent and straightened as they worked the pumps, first in time, then in an almost comical seesaw motion. One paused to wipe his brow before he bent to the task again.

"Get on with it!" a westerner shouted.

"Why don't they just shoot him?" muttered a girl on Vikram's boat.

The water swilled, a foot high.

The woman beside Vikram gasped and let out a long sigh as she fainted, her weight a sudden heaviness against his own too-light frame. The man lifted the kid off his shoulders to help Vikram support the woman and the kid climbed up onto the boat rail to see better and stared and stared.

The girl who had spoken before knelt to give the woman water. The woman's eyelids were violet. Her lashes fluttered as she regained consciousness.

"Is she alright?" Vikram's voice came out ragged. He cleared his throat. The noise sounded as loud as a slap.

"I'll look after her," whispered the girl. Her eyes met Vikram's and for a moment held, whilst a slight frown creased her forehead. He froze, suddenly terrified that she had recognised him. Did he look like an insurgent? Could she ever have seen him with Eirik? He turned stiffly away.

"Dad, look, the water's up to his neck," said the kid. "He's going to die now."

"They're killing him." Vikram couldn't stop himself. It was important that he said this, that this definition, at least, stayed with the kid, even if his father gave Vikram a peculiar glance and placed his hands protectively on the boy's shoulders.

Eirik tried to stand but slipped and crashed back. He tried again. His legs could not support the weight of his torso.

"Well you know… if the NWO really had come back… maybe it's better this way…"

"You think..?"

"The skadi would have crucified us… if you were old enough to remember what happened after Osuwa, you'd know…"

"Please, don't talk about Osuwa."

The snippets of conversation drifted from all sides like small feathers. Vikram could no longer tell where they came from.

The water lapped at Eirik's chin. He got clumsily onto his knees. The movement must be an exertion. Perhaps he was in dreadful pain. The black overalls hid his body; whatever previous tortures had been inflicted upon him were invisible. Vikram imagined the prison guards entering Eirik's cell, taunting him, with words at first, the jeers giving way to cigarette burns, blows, worse. He winced.

Time was winding down. The two skadi at the pumps seemed to move in slow motion. What kind of man could kill another in this way? Vikram looked around at the crowd. Every one of them was complicit. He was complicit himself, because to do nothing was to aid in the working of the pumps.

Eirik floundered on his knees. His gloved hands slipped at the sides of the tanks. He fumbled to remove the gloves and they came adrift. Vikram saw Eirik's bare hands slide against the glass, feeling to his left and right, reaching up to the top of the tank, finding this too blocked.

Vikram folded over the rail, his head buried against his clenched hands. He did not care now who saw. He wanted to cry. But his eyes remained obstinately dry, and even if the tears had come he knew that they would be for himself, for his own stupidity and his failure to believe in a friend, as much as for Eirik who in many ways was already dead. The impulse shamed him. He lifted his head; he would make himself watch the end. It was the last thing he could offer Eirik.

He heard the skadi at the pumps grunting with exertion. The water level rose and rose. It reached Eirik's shoulders. Eirik was trying to undo the hood. His bound hands flapped ineffectually around his head. He didn't seem able to bend his fingers.

The crowd, sensing a conclusion, were growing voluble. From all sides a chorus lifted, the voices louder now and more aggressive. Shouts and insults, wailing, overlapping. The skadi fired a barrage of warning shots into the water. A girl, perhaps the same girl, started screaming. This time no one stopped her. Vikram's boat rocked; the crowd was pushing at the barrier, jeering at the skadi. The man beside Vikram pulled his kid roughly from the rail and told him to keep his head down. Skadi boats sped down the crowd barrier, whipping around, racing back again. Spray hid the execution boat momentarily. The boat in front moved sideways, blocking Vikram. He had to crane to see what was happening.

The tank was almost full, and Eirik was fully conscious. His body convulsed like a bird hooked in a net. His feet thrashed the water white. He was floating on his back, head half submerged below the last few inches of air.

That's enough, he thought numbly. *Just stop now. There's still time, the lesson's learned. He could live—*

"Oh, but there's never enough time, Vik, that's why you have to take it—"

Mikkeli was speaking. No, Mikkeli was dead. Her body limp and sodden on the decking. Frost already forming on her eyelashes.

"You have to take it from someone else!"

Mikkeli's ghost laughed, that big, slightly dirty laugh. She cocked her head at Eirik and winked, once. Ice splintered in Vikram's ribs.

"That's right," said Eirik. "She's right. If you steal anything, steal time."

In the tank, the last inch of air disappeared.

Vikram imagined Eirik's mouth forced open as his lungs battled for oxygen. Water pouring in. Water like acid, water to burn away words. He had seen this in his dreams, his own body and those of friends, turning over and over. This was just a dream. It must be a dream.

Eirik's limbs jerked in spasms. His hands and feet pounded the ceiling of the tank. He was asphyxiating.

The crowd fell silent. Vikram heard dry whimpers, or was it laughter? The girl behind him, crouched by her mother. The kid had gone quiet.

A gull wheeled overhead. Its screech trailed across the bleached out sky. Eirik threshed, knocking the glass of the tank with dull thuds.

Vikram could only observe. The waves moved, and the sun shone on the water, but time had finally stopped.

The body stilled.

What floated in a tank of seawater was no longer Eirik. Eirik's spirit had been torn loose. He was out there with the ghosts now, a half thing condemned to the waves.

The body, face down, rotated half a circle, drifted slowly back again. It bobbed against the tank ceiling. The arms hung loosely down, Eirik's bare hands indistinct shapes in the subsiding water. There was nothing but silence in the two crowds. The silence pressed on the space between Vikram's shoulder blades. He hunched over the rail like an old man.

On the barge, a medic stepped forward. Two skadi slid open the ceiling of the tank with a grating noise. Some of the water splashed over and they stepped quickly back, as though it were poisonous.

The medic reached into the tank and lifted Eirik's arms. He had to tip over the body first, and the movement dislodged more water. The medic rolled up Eirik's sleeve. Vikram saw him examine a red band around the elbow. He nodded, looked at his watch, and said something to the officer wearing the sunglasses.

The loudspeakers crackled.

"The convict Eirik 9968 is pronounced dead, at oh-eleven hundred hours and thirteen minutes."

Vikram stared at the body. He felt the steel band that had gripped his chest all day dissolve at last, and with it, the past three years. He was back on the decking, holding Mikkeli's body. The pain was as sharp and as real as it had been on that day, but this time he knew that it would not disappear. It expanded in his ribs like a lungful of broken glass.

The City had won. They had won at the moment they arrested Eirik. They had won when Mikkeli burst into Vikram's room, yelling, "Vik, get out, they've taken Eirik and we're next!" He had found it so easy to believe in Eirik's guilt. Underwater, that belief had manifested as rot, slowly eroding the will to survive—and for what? So that he could watch the New Horizon Movement die with a clear conscience?

Did he know himself at all?

The skadi had not replaced the lid of the tank. Their procedure from this point seemed unclear; they were standing about uncertainly. A seagull landed on the rim of the tank and a skad butted it away with his rifle. The medic had gone below deck.

The show was over. Vikram needed to get out. There were too many people. One by one, the other passengers came into focus, like ghosts emerging from the mist. The waterbus was hemmed in on every side.

"What will they do with the body?" the kid was asking.

Vikram crouched to see if the woman who had fainted was recovering. Some of her colour had returned. Recognising him, she gave a weak smile.

"Are you okay?" he asked. "Do you need more water?"

"Thank you—I'm sorry, it was the crowds and so—so horrible—it's over now?"

"It's over."

He wondered what were her reasons for coming today.

There was a scuffle at the front of the crowd. A man had pulled his row boat a little way out, past the barrier of buoys. He was pointing at the tank and yelling. Vikram could make out one word, over and over again. *Murderers! Murderers! Murderers!*

Seagulls screeched overhead. Their cries merged with the man's—*Murderers! Murderers!*

Another boat nudged forward. Others were urging the protestor to get back. Now the skadi had seen what was happening. Three of their own boats began powering towards the barrier.

A noise like scraping metal sheets came out of the loudspeakers, before the sound settled into speech.

"All westerners get behind the barrier. Get behind the barrier now."

"Get back, you idiot," Vikram muttered.

The skadi arrowed in. A shark-faced prow rammed the rowboat. The protestor clutched the rocking sides of the boat and managed to stay afloat.

"Murderers!" he yelled.

"Get back!" Vikram wasn't the only one who called out. The shouts converged from every side. It was impossible to know who was saying what, whether they were yelling at the protestor to save himself or at the skadi to retreat.

Still defiant, the protestor raised his arm.

"Mur—"

Vikram saw a parallel movement as the barrel of a rifle took aim at the man's head.

There was a single shot.

A red fog filled Vikram's head.

He never knew who made the first move. Maybe it was him after all. Maybe it was Nils or Drake, or someone else in the crowd. He locked his gaze on the speeder where the skad was now lowering his rifle. Vikram had only one intention. He was going to get to that boat. And when he got to it—

The red fog had him. He took no time to consider the ramifications of his actions. His movements seemed ahead of him as he leapt agilely over the rail of the waterbus, landing in the stern of a smaller rower. It rocked with the impact.

A hand grabbed his shoulder.

"What the fuck—"

Vikram was already gone. Scrambling from boat to boat, he bounded across the unstable carpet. Some tried to stop him. Others joined the push forward. The weight of the crowd was all around him, no longer dormant but a physical, surging force. Gaps of sea widened before his feet. He saw the waves surge as he jumped from boat to boat.

Boats crashed into one another. He was close. There were only three rows between him and the skadi speeder.

He could see the body of the protestor, slumped over the side of the rowboat. He clambered up onto the deck of a waterbus. Over the railings. He hit the deck rolling, vaulted over the other side, dropped onto the abandoned flat of a raft. He could see the skadi faces. He could almost see their eyes.

And then he saw another figure, someone making the exact manoeuvres that he was. Drake. She was headed for the same boat, and a skad had his rifle trained on her lanky figure.

Vikram almost lost his balance using the end of a canoe as a stepping stone. He took a flying leap onto a motor boat.

The skad's rifle lifted.

Drake saw it. She faltered.

She was one boat ahead of him, on the buoy line between west and skadi. Vikram gathered all of his breath and jumped. He slammed into her. Her body flew sideways. He spun from the boat and plunged into the water.

Explosions boomed above. He opened his eyes underwater. Silvery bubble trails criss-crossed the water where the skadi were shooting freely. Drake's face was a few metres away. Her arms arrowed as she dove towards him.

A man plunged into the water. His eyes were bared. A red flower bloomed in the water from a leak in his chest.

Stars, what are you doing, get out!

Vikram followed Drake's lead, diving low, swimming underwater until his lungs were ready to burst.

They were under the boats. The dark was almost total, the occasional slice of light slashing weirdly down. His hands brushed hulls jagged with barnacles, slick with algae. They needed an exit. There was nothing. His lungs burned.

He felt a tug on his ankle. Drake, behind him. She jabbed her hand upwards. He saw the darker shadows of the hulls and understood. They were beneath two small boats, and there was a tiny gap where the sterns almost met. He contracted his body, wedged himself between the two slopes and pushed with his feet. Drake joined him. The space widened, marginally, then enough for her to slither up. He saw her boots exit the water. The boats knocked together once more.

His vision went fuzzy. The water was black.

A hand reached down and pulled his hair. He broke surface and gulped in huge draughts of oxygen. Water trickled from his nostrils. He grasped the sides of the two boats and hauled himself out. He managed to swing his legs free just as the boats collided once more. The crash resounded. His ears were ringing; above surface the noise was mayhem, gunfire, shouts, screams, crashes—

He saw one boat forced beneath another. A man was crushed to death.

He saw a skad fall backwards with a knife lodged in his throat. Other skadi were pulling masks over their faces, launching canisters into the air. Gas. There was no way of avoiding it.

Drake was beside him. They were lying side by side on one end of a small fishing craft. The other occupants took no notice of them. They were engaged in their own vendetta, pointing and yelling at the skadi. Vikram and Drake exchanged no looks, no words. We're idiots, Vikram thought. We're bloody idiots.

He had been turned inside out in a day.

Breathing in chemicals, the gas worked fast. One by one his limbs seized until he lay, immobile except for his eyes.

Drenched, nauseous with the gas, Vikram finally allowed himself to look up.

He had landed up at the other end of the western crowd. Beyond the netting, directly across the square, rose one of the City towers. It was silver and fleeced in greenery. Two floors above the surface was a balcony, and on the balcony, watching, were the elite of Osiris.

He could see the man who had sentenced Eirik to death. Vikram knew who he was. Everyone in the west knew who he was. The man's name was Feodor Rechnov, Councillor. Head of the first founding family in everything but name. His face was many metres away, disguised and protected by the faint shimmer of a defensive sonar shield. But Vikram knew those features as well as he knew his own.

Two younger men stood next to Feodor: the sons. They were slighter replicas of their father, well-dressed and rigidly postured. The daughter stood between them. Her famous red hair was covered, but her face was as white as salt.

Vikram wondered how Feodor Rechnov would feel if it were one of his own three children floating face down in the tank. Knowing, as every person in Osiris knew, the mechanics of drowning. Knowing that the body would be bloated. That if you pushed down on the chest, white foam would leak from the mouth and nostrils. The face would have swollen just enough to distort a memory that had been, until that moment, familiar as the skin on your own hand.

He wondered what Feodor would feel, unzipping the corpse of his son or his daughter. If he would grieve. If the man was capable of grief.

Sounds swept overhead—a whistle, shrill; the whoosh of a boat throwing up spray. Each separate noise seemed to arc through the air, leaving its echo like a sparkler or a yard of ribbon, so that the sky was painted in sound. Vikram sensed, throbbing distantly, just waiting for the gas's effect to fade, the scrapes and bruises that caked his body. It was the same sounds, the same aches, the same red fog from three years before.

Time was unravelling. Keli was here. Eirik was here. Everyone was talking at once, past and present and future, a collision of time. With a final effort, Vikram wrenched his eyes back to the balcony.

The Rechnovs were leaving.

For a few precious moments, his head was clear. All we were was a breeze against a cyclone, he thought. The ideals argued and laughed over, the late-night plans laid so optimistically—they had really believed in themselves. He only saw it now, when it was too late. Because without a political platform, without visibility and words, they had nothing. The New Horizon Movement had never stood a chance.

Watching Feodor Rechnov turn away, Vikram felt a current shift inside of himself. A realization, distant but imperative.

This was where it had to stop. On a strange, pale skied autumn day, the City had crossed a line. And Vikram had woken up. Really woken up. The glass shards jostled in his chest, minute needles of memory and of pain. He knew that he would carry them now forever. Eirik was the first but he would not be the last. Everything they had been through, everything they had done—the starving winters, the riots and the border protests, his best friend's death and Eirik's execution—all of that was worthless unless they could convince one man to listen.

Then he thought: this is the west. There is no we. So it's up to me. If I want to change anything, I have to start again. I have to rewrite the rules.

The chemicals in the gas seeped steadily through his veins with every breath he drew. Beside him, Drake lay inert. Dizziness overtook Vikram at last. His eyes closed, and his mind moved quietly away.

3 | ADELAIDE

S he had never seen anyone die before. Death was meant to be sudden. The condemned man clawed at the glass. He slipped and tried to get up and fell back down and the water erupted in bubbles as his hands smacked the water.

His panic was infectious. It made the air thick, the sea restless with cloud-capped waves. Overhead, colonies of birds formed dark helices as they swirled, some diving low over the crowd of western boats. Adelaide's lungs tightened. She knew it was false; she could still breathe. In a matter of minutes that man would never be able to breathe again, and anyway his suffering should not affect her—if she felt anything, it ought to be satisfaction at justice being done. She knew all of this, but she stepped back, prepared then and there to leave.

A shoulder blocked her passage. She was wedged between Dmitri and Feodor, two solid boulders. Her eldest brother's expression was inscrutable, even bored. On her other side, Feodor wore his usual faint scowl, intended to suggest burdens of responsibility far beyond the public imagination.

The man slipped again in the tank. How long would it take?

There would have been documents. Administration. The trial had been going on for years, so long that Adelaide could barely remember when it had begun. Somewhere along the line, a decision had been made to produce the showcase on the surface. Who had taken that final step—who had written *drowning* against the execution order? One of Feodor's cronies? Was it her father himself?

The thought made her shiver; a chill that was nothing to do with the cold summer air. It was sickening. She wished she could faint, she would have welcomed nausea, but her legs continued to hold her up.

"You can't expect me to watch this."

She spoke quietly, but she knew they all heard.

"You can't leave, Adelaide." Dmitri was brusque. "If you leave now, that's more of a statement than not coming at all."

"But it's monstrous," she hissed.

"It's not pleasant for any of us," said Feodor. His lips barely moved as he spoke. "Public service rarely is. You should know that by now."

"Then why isn't mother here?"

"She's not feeling well. And your grandfather, before you ask, is far too frail to stand for so long in the cold. You have no such excuse."

"Think of what this man has done, Adelaide." Linus's voice was tight. He doesn't like it either, she thought. But he's still here. He contributed to this. "Think of the lives he has taken."

"Yes," she said. "I know. I know what he has done."

She had seen the reports. Everyone in Osiris had seen the reports. Eirik 9968 had confessed to acts far more atrocious than what was being done to him today. He had killed people with bare hands and with knives; Eirik 9968 had not shown mercy. There were charges of false confessions eked from force-fed drugs; scarrings on the soles of feet.

There was a strange precision in the scene below: the four corners of the square, the buoys and the Home Guard speedboats cordoning the western crowd; a barge, solitary oblong in gunmetal water, its glass cube catching the light. The hooded figure stumbling within it.

He's guilty. He deserves this. He must deserve it.

Except that his sentence had been orchestrated by her father. Glancing once more at his set, determined profile, she was suddenly certain that the method of execution was Feodor's choice.

The Ngozis and the Dumays were grouped at the other end of the balcony. Each founding family formed a tight core. If one of them wished to leave, she could go with them. It only took an ally.

No one met her gaze.

A gun was fired and Adelaide jumped. The westerners were growing restless. The waterline was at the man's neck.

She couldn't watch any longer. She held her breath, trying to bring on a fit of dizziness. She waited for lines to split her vision, removing what was before her eyes, but nothing happened. She had to draw breath. When she exhaled, the air came out shakily.

"Adelaide?" Linus had noticed.

"I need to leave," she said. "I'm going to have to leave."

"Then do. If that's really what you want." Feodor's voice was casual, but she heard the subtext. *You know the consequences.*

She thought of the investigator and the transaction that had just been made from her bank account. She thought of the resources she would need.

I can't abandon Axel.

The water in the tank rose. She focussed on the boat, counted the teeth of its shark face. They ran in two zigzag rows, thirty in the top, twenty seven in the bottom. But the tank drew her back. She watched it the way you walked in a ground-dream, observing the phenomenon but knowing, even as your foot brushed the grass, that the scene could not be real.

Adelaide had seen live fish pulled from the water in restaurants that writhed the way the dying man did now.

In his final moments she felt oddly absent, as though she were observing herself from a long way off. The man was drowning, and there were lines being drawn before her. She felt the chalk on her back. She felt very cold. She thought of the day of the Great Silence—the day they said the world had drowned. There were connections to be made, but she would not make them. One level of consciousness, the part that would allow her to sleep through future nights, the part that allowed her to breathe when the man down there could not, closed her mind quietly down. That was survival. Perhaps the condemned man had played the same trick, the night before, sitting in his cell. Had he wanted to remember everything or nothing?

The man was drowned. He floated to the top of the tank. Where his face would have been the zipped up hood pressed against the glass.

The frothing water subsided. He drifted. The tank looked serene.

She heard his name again on the loudspeaker. Eirik 9968.

What he was—

What he isn't—

The birds circled and she shivered.

The medic pronounced him dead. She sensed a shift in the western crowd, their hostility sharpening.

A small rowboat ventured past the buoys. The rower was standing upright, shouting.

"What's he saying?" Dmitri asked.

"He's calling us murderers," said Feodor.

A rippling movement ran through the crowd. The mass altered; as she watched, transfixed, the hundreds of individual figures turned into one vast contraction, heaving and surging towards the Home Guard boats. The Guards began to fire. At first they aimed into the air. Then they sprayed the water before the barrier with warning shots.

"Shit—" Linus swore. "Tell them to stop firing."

Dmitri grabbed Adelaide's shoulder and pushed her down. She got to her feet impatiently.

"I'm alright, Dmitri—"

She was pushed back.

"Keep down, Adelaide—"

Security formed a line in front of them all, blocking everyone's view except Feodor's. Linus, still standing, strained to see between their shoulders.

"Linus! Linus, what's going on?"

"You're perfectly safe." The head of security spoke to Feodor. "The barrier is secure."

"Then move," snapped Feodor. "The last thing we want is for the terriers to think we're afraid of them."

The security reinforcements stepped aside and Adelaide got to her feet. In the chaos below, she began to see lines within the crowd. A man ran over the boats as though they were nothing more than an inconvenient obstacle course. *Go on*, she willed him. But there was nowhere for him to go. Others were making similar dashes—like rays returning to the sun, they were all set to converge on a point at the barrier. She followed, horrified but fascinated, as they drew nearer.

The Guards will kill them—

At the last moment, the man she had first noticed veered sharply to the left. He collided with another figure. They toppled into the sea and went under. She waited for them to surface, but they did not reappear. Water foamed where they had fallen. The noise of boats crashing together was punctuated by screams and gunshots.

"They'll have to use gas," remarked Dmitri. His hands, clasped behind him, were fidgeting. Adelaide could tell that he wanted to brush down his suit, but that would look indecorous. All three Rechnov men stood stiffly.

"They should have used it ten minutes ago," said Feodor irritably. "Look at that rabble—and people question my judgement over today."

The gas subdued the crowd. The Home Guard speeders continued to steam up and down the line. They had rounded up a few westerners on another boat and were systematically handcuffing them.

The mat of lifeless boats rocked as one. Vehicles at the edge gradually separated off and slunk back into the channels of drab western towers. A waterbus, tipping smaller boats aside, was trying to nudge a pathway out of the centre.

"What will they do now?" she asked.

"Don't know. Don't care," said Dmitri. "Stars, it's freezing out here. We must be done by now."

Feodor glanced across at the Ngozis, who were being shepherded back inside. He nodded gruffly.

"Goran will take you back, Adelaide."

"I don't need an escort," she said coldly. She hated Goran, and the way he crept about the family lodgings like a soft amphibian.

Feodor looked like he might hit her, but Linus stepped in. "Let her go, Father."

"Thank you, Linus."

A blast of wind hurried her inside. She collected her handbag from a carrier girl. She never came this far west; she would have to take the Crocodile shuttle line.

"Adelaide." Linus caught up with her in the stairwell outside. His tone was stern but not unkind. She gave him a blank look. There was no point in offering words. Words were ammunition.

Linus hesitated before speaking again.

"Empty threats are useless," he said at last. "I may not always agree with Father's policies, but sometimes action is inevitable. I just want you to know that I wish it hadn't been necessary."

"I see."

"And Adelaide." His voice was different this time.

"What?"

"Be careful."

"Why should I need to be careful, Linus?"

Her brother did not answer, but she did not require a reply. Her thoughts were elsewhere. The dead were dead, but the missing were still out there, waiting to be found. The investigator she had employed was even now at work. In seven days, they would meet.

The shuttle lines were busy on her way home. As the pod skimmed east through its glowing chute, Adelaide leaned against the smooth fibreglass sides, watching her reflection flicker. She wondered who else on board had been watching the execution.

She wondered what Eirik 9968's last thought had been.

I'd remember—I'd have to remember—

Axel, crouched in a myriad of broken glass.

Hiding behind a curtain, in the Domain with Axel, at the theatre with Tyr.

The Roof. The double-A parties.

Horses' hooves.

Don't think.

She knew that from tomorrow she could not remember this day. She would relive it as she drank her late night voqua and watched without taking in a reel on the o'vis. If she slept tonight, the scene would haunt her dreams. But after tomorrow, today had to go. Today had never happened.

4 | VIKRAM

Vikram woke to a morning that was almost colourless in its brightness. He stretched, gradually persuading his reluctant limbs to leave blankets that were warm with body heat. The window-wall was wet with condensation and he wiped a patch clear. His hand came back dirty with grease.

In a couple of months, ice would freeze the window-wall shut. Days would come when he barely left the flat. He had let the place go. Mould sprouted in a corner of the ceiling and meandered down the walls. The tiny room pressed on his sanity.

With a jolt, he remembered that today was different. Today he was going east. Into the City.

His heartbeat quickened even as he tried to relax.

Can I really do this? Do I even want to?

You don't have a choice, he told himself firmly. He'd screwed up the order when it was delivered by hand—reading its solid formal prose had filled him with rage. But later he'd smoothed the letter out, read it again, thought about the implications. He'd wanted a political opportunity and here it was. Clearly it was no coincidence that after twelve months of writing letters, he had been granted an audience with the Council less than a week after the execution—but that did not give him an excuse.

The mayhem surrounding Eirik's death must have struck a chord with the City as well as the west. Vikram—what was left of Horizon—was finally being taken seriously.

He made himself as presentable as he could, washing with cold water from a bucket and pulling on the best clothes he possessed. He used his knife and a sliver of mirror to shave. Brown eyes glanced back at him, a tiny scar above the right. Wariness was their resting expression. Couldn't change that if he tried. His coat was a shapeless affair that would not impress anybody, but he was damned if he would sacrifice warmth for appearance. In any case, the coat came with Vikram, or Vikram had come with the coat. Somebody once told him it belonged to his father, and it might have done, but it might have belonged to some anonymous figure who had no connection to him at all.

He wound a scarf around his neck and rooted through his bag for gloves. He found only one. It seemed impossible to have lost the other amongst so few belongings, but time was tight and he had to leave without them. On the way out, he noticed again that the lock was weak.

It was a long trek downstairs. The lower lift had failed last month and so far nobody in the skyscraper had managed to lure out an engineer. The stairwells and corridors were busy. People sat smoking on the stairs and lounged in empty door frames, idly reiterating yesterday's conversations. He smelled the distinctive aroma of manta. Eyes grazed Vikram as he passed. He kept his watch hidden beneath his sleeve. He could have flogged it for several hundred *peng* or a few City credits, but he loved the watch and he wouldn't give it up until he was desperate.

Ten floors down, he banged on an even less secure door. There was no response. He banged again, and this time heard an answering curse and someone staggering across the room. The door opened and Nils peered out. His eyes were bleary. A week-long beard shadowed his jaw.

"Vik. What are you doing here? It's morning."

"I'm going to the Eye Tower," Vikram said. "To speak to the Council. The order came through two days ago, remember?"

Nils looked surprised. "I thought you weren't going to go... I mean, after..."

Neither of them said Eirik's name.

"I changed my mind," said Vikram shortly.

"Oh. Okay."

"You coming?"

Nils yawned. "Think you might be better off on your own." There was a crash from the floor above. Nils winced and roared, "Shut the fuck up!" He turned back to Vikram, forced a laugh. "Floor twenty-six. I'm moving to twenty-nine, I hear they've got a working shower. Anyway, good luck, I suppose. You nervous?"

"Not exactly. What can they do to me?"

"Wouldn't like to guess. Send you underwater?"

"Tried that already."

The light-hearted tone fell flat. Nils's fingers curled around the door-frame.

"Well, let me know how it goes. I'll catch you later."

The door shut. Another crash came from upstairs, followed by a yell. Vikram jogged down the remaining twenty-five floors to ocean level. He thought about Nils's reaction. He wasn't sure that his friend was entirely happy with Vikram's decision—he hadn't said so, not outright, but there had been an ambivalence in his eyes that was unlike Nils.

Outside, the cold punched him like a Tarctic wind. He cinched the belt of his coat tighter; the buckle was broken and it kept slipping. The float-ing deck that encircled each tower shifted beneath his feet. A man was shouting that his boat had been blocked in, but nobody could find the owner of the vehicle responsible. Squinting in the bright light, Vikram made his way to the east side of the decking, where a vandalized signpost marked the waterbus stop.

The queue jostled around him. As the decking rose and fell on the swells, those waiting kept their balance as one. He found himself look-ing at other people more carefully than usual. They were all ages and all heights, because the majority of westerners were unemployed, surviving on handouts from the City and their wits. Under hats and hoods the odd Boreal face stood out amongst the southerners, but they were all dressed the same, bulked up with as many layers as they could beg, borrow or otherwise acquire. Could he tell the Council that people had to steal clothes in order to keep warm, or would they assume that everyone in the west was a thief?

A cry went up as the waterbus was sighted. The surge forward knocked him off balance. He suppressed the desire to shove back and used the momentum to inch his way past a mother clutching a child in each hand.

The ticket collector stood wide across the boarding gate. The waterbus pulled in with tantalizing slowness. Vikram saw a girl in a yellow scarf duck under a man's arm and sidle around an old woman. His heart jumped with the thought that it was Mikkeli, before he remembered, again, that it was impossible. The ticket collector braced himself as he unlocked the barrier.

Vikram pushed a few *peng* into the ticket collector's hand and fought his way into a place at the prow. On the landing stage, a squabble broke out among those left behind. As the waterbus angled around the circumference of 221-West, Vikram saw the man who had complained about being blocked in, crouched in his own boat, in the process of setting loose the offending vehicle. He was striking at the chain with a pickaxe.

The waterbus nosed into the main channel of the waterway. Vikram huddled over the rail watching the spit of spray. The western quarter of the city had never been finished, and when he glanced up he saw clumsily made, open bridges connecting building to building. Many of the graffitied towers were ringed by boats, homes to the very poor. On the outskirts, boats lined up like dominoes. Nobody could say for sure what was concealed within the rotting hulls. People went to the shanty-boat towns for drugs or women. They didn't always come back.

He had to find a way to describe all of those problems. For months, he'd been composing a speech in his head. Now the carefully arranged lines were void. Events had overtaken him. He had to focus on the things that could be changed. He had to ignore what they had done to Eirik.

It was Drake who had told him to start writing again. *Gotta have a purpose, Vik. Gotta have something to do.* The subject of most of Vikram's letters, and his primary focus today, was to ask for a winter aid programme. The most important thing he could secure would be repairs and insulation in the worst of the buildings. In winter, cold killed as many people as starvation. The last riots had been sparked by the City holding back food reserves. He would ask for kitchen boats too. And for restoration work to begin in the unremembered quarters.

How would the Council react? Would they deny the situation, pretend it was less severe? He was ready to argue.

He tried to recall Eirik's advice, so readily available at the time, now distant through time and suppression. Eirik would have known exactly what to say.

At Market Circle, the hub of the western quarter, the ocean was almost invisible under its cover of boat traders and traffic. Vikram ducked as a gull skimmed low overhead. It came to rest atop a fry-boat selling hot squid, where many of the birds gathered, shuffling. Their cries pierced the clamour of human voices—selling, haggling, shrieking—that pursued the waterbus as it barged a way through the congestion.

People carried on. They had no choice.

On the other side of Market Circle, the waterbus began to lose passengers. It chugged past greenhouse towers and a recycling depot. Down a waterway clustered with rusting houseboats was Desalination Plant W-03, around which the decking bobbed quietly, as though nothing had ever happened. Still Vikram imagined he heard the splash, and he kept his eyes forward. They were approaching the border.

By the time the waterbus was in weapon range, only five people remained on board. Nervously, Vikram felt in his pocket for his day pass and the letter detailing his appointment with the Council. His ID had stood up to previous scrutiny, but he could never feel quite safe.

A narrow gap in the border mesh, barely wide enough to squeeze a waterbus through, allowed a clear glimpse of the glittering City. The checkpoint jetty ran out from the base of 774-West. Skadi boots rapped the decking. The skadi cradled their rifles with the loose, easy attachment one might assign to a fifth limb. They laughed and joked amongst themselves, but when their attention went westward, their expressions lapsed into something between inscrutability and a strange taut hunger. Vikram glanced quickly around and saw that the other passengers were trying to look as blank and dull as possible.

"Papers."

There were two inspecting officers. The first vaulted the waterbus rail and strode across the deck. His coat, heavy and black, swung deliberately free, revealing both a hand pistol and patches of storm-flecked camouflage. He checked the driver's licence first. The rifle muzzle fell lazily at his side. Vikram was intensely aware of it. When his turn came, he held out his ID and the letter in silence.

The officer read it, his eyebrows raised. He let out a fat laugh.

"Council, eh?"

Vikram nodded.

"What the hell d'you think you're doing there?"

Vikram was not sure if it was a rhetorical question or not, and judged it best to keep quiet. But one of the passengers gave him a tiny nudge, and when he looked up he found the officer still staring.

"I'm giving a presentation," he said.

The officer laughed again, but with less humour this time. "Fuck presentations," he said. "And fuck the Council. Or maybe that's what you'll have to do. Fuck them." The idea clearly amused him, and this time his mirth was shared by a couple of men on the jetty. "You're wasting your time, terrier," he declared, and offered Vikram a jab in the thigh with his gun before ambling on to the next passenger, a young girl. Vikram had passed.

But there was a dispute over the girl's papers, and they were delayed for twenty minutes while the officer sent one of his subordinates to make a call. He filled the time by pointing out targets for his men—a floating crate, a resting seabird. Shots crackled sporadically. The bird rose with a squawk of alarm. The skad who'd missed swore. It was typical of a skad to shoot birds for entertainment.

Vikram tried not to look at the men too closely, wary of recognising or being recognised. There was a large part of him that wanted to. The part that did idiotic things. The part that followed naked impulse.

Witnessing the execution had been more than stupid. It had stirred up old grievances that he had barely begun to control. He folded his arms, squeezing with his fingers until it hurt. He had a chance with the Council. And they had to listen—now, they had to listen.

The man came back with the order for clearance. Frowning, the second officer, still seated in a deckchair on the jetty, beckoned him over. The two conferred. Then the second officer pointed.

"You. Over here."

His target was unclear, and the five passengers looked nervously down. He beckoned.

"You. Woman in the green scarf. Here."

"That's you, gullhead." The officer still on deck hauled the woman out of the line. "Off the boat."

"My papers are in order," she protested.

"That's for us to say."

Vikram kept his eyes on the deck.

"What's wrong with them?"

"Get off, bitch, and you'll find out. Or do you want me to throw you off?"

The woman's face crumpled. As she climbed over the rail Vikram saw her hands were shaking. The officer followed her onto the jetty and waved the waterbus on. As he turned away, Vikram saw that his scarf was deliberately wrapped low to reveal the eye tattoo on the back of his neck.

The driver let out a ripple of curses as soon as the boat was out of earshot, whilst the other passengers grumbled. Vikram watched the forlorn figure of the woman left behind growing smaller. She was arguing with the officer. He hoped they wouldn't hurt her. They always had that hunger in their eyes. As the waterbus crossed over the border, he had to fight back creeping tendrils of fear. The last time he had been at the mercy of Citizens, they'd put him underwater.

The old song came to him:

> They'll put you underwater where the sun will never rise
> And the mud will take your tongue because you've told too many lies
> The mud will eat your fingers and your toes and then your face
> And then you'll lose your head and disappear without a trace.

He knew what it was like to disappear.

"I'm half an hour late now," one man said irritably. Yet again, Vikram checked his watch.

The passengers retreated into silence. Trust was a risk: best stick to your own problems. Vikram returned to the rail. The morning's brightness had already dissolved and a fine rain was beginning to fall, dampening his clothes. The cold burrowed deep into his gloveless hands.

He watched a covered ferry glide past. The boat was in good repair, but passengers looked cross and miserable with their lot. Glancing up, Vikram saw the preferred highways: shuttle lines weaving from scraper to scraper, another network every twenty floors, all interlinking to form a vast, complex web. Within their translucent skeins, shuttle pods moved like beads of mercury on a string. He tried to imagine what it must be like to cross the city in one of those tubes, the feeling of enclosure, of privilege.

Ahead, the terminus was in sight. Vikram took a second waterbus, and within minutes found himself walking up one of the ten platforms which extended from 900-East like the points of a star.

The Eye Tower was the tallest skyscraper in Osiris and the most magnificent. Vikram had only ever seen pictures of it. Upon entering, he was thoroughly scanned and searched. Vikram showed the letter once again. Released into the building, he climbed two empty floors. It was a standard flood control device, although he saw no signs of water intrusion.

At the lobby, he stopped.

The riot of colour before him was giddying. Sunk into the floor was a vermilion mosaic, reflected many times over in the gigantic, gold-hued mirrors. Coniferous trees stretched up into the open core of the tower. Vikram stood on the mosaic tiles, under the trees, gazing up at the rough patterns of their bark, the slender needles that looked like tufts of hair. He touched one. It pricked his finger. It was real.

Surrounding the central lifts was an aquarium, two metres thick and fat with wildlife. As high as Vikram could see, the spiralling stairways and balconies looked in upon its undulating creatures.

He stepped into the lift with a bundle of people. He was the only one dressed in outdoor clothes. After initial glances at him, the Citizens averted their eyes diplomatically, one woman patting down her pale pink blouse as if it might have been dirtied by their brief proximity. As the lift swept upward he watched the fish floating in their glass jail. They were every colour of the rainbow: beautiful, darting things, but Vikram had an instant antipathy to the aquarium. It was still a cage.

He checked his watch furtively. In just under an hour he would be delivering his statement, persuading the Council that west Osiris was not just a convenient scrap heap, but a valid part of the City's society. Could he describe the daily life of westerner? How could he explain freezing to death to people who had never been cold? The question occupied him all the way to the hundred and eleventh floor, through further security checks, into reception and within eyeshot of the vast doors to the Chambers, which were flanked by four uniformed guards.

He waited for nearly two hours before they admitted him. A receptionist told him that talks had been going on since ten o'clock, but offered no explanation for the delay. She showed him to a quiet room with a bowl of fruit piled luxuriously high and a machine that pulped the fruit to a juice. He peeled an orange. Its scent filled the air. He ate the fruit slowly, remembering that the few times Mikkeli had been able to get an orange, she insisted on removing the peel in one long coil whilst they all waited for a share, intoxicated by the scent.

"They're ready for you."

The interruption startled him. A woman stood in the doorway, looking expectant. She took his arm and steered him carefully, as if she expected him to break and run.

"The speaker will announce you," she whispered. "Then you can speak. You have a presentation prepared?"

Vikram nodded. Of sorts. "I wasn't given much notice—"

"I hear you've been writing letters for quite a time! I'm sure you have plenty to say. Turn and smile, will you?"

She swung him around. There was a flash. Vikram realized he had been photographed. He winced instinctively.

"That's great, Syrah," said a young man with floppy hair. They moved on.

"After your presentation, do not speak. The Council will debate. You don't speak. Understand?"

"But what if I—"

"It's protocol. Understand? It's very important that you understand before I let you in there."

He forced a smile. "Don't speak. I get it. Thanks for the briefing."

"You're welcome." She brushed his jumper down. He was acutely aware of its fraying edges and the grease he couldn't wash out. "You look—oh well. You first." She gave him a little push.

When he walked into the Chambers, his shoes cast hollow echoes. The room was round and windowless, formed entirely of pale stone with a smooth, polished texture and darker capillaries. Slender columns supported an empty balcony running its circumference. The ceiling arched up and up into a perfect dome. There were paintings on its panels, of sirens and dark-finned fish. He had never seen anything like it, and the thought that he might never again made him sad in a way he did not recognize.

The woman hassled him forward. He was taken to a podium. Now he saw the austere faces of the Council, assembled in rising crescent rows.

The Speaker's voice boomed from somewhere above and behind him.

"This is Mr Bai, who has requested to address you on some of the issues concerning west Osiris. He speaks on behalf of pressure group Horizon."

It annoyed Vikram that they labelled it a pressure group rather than a reform group, but as Horizon's sole remaining representative, he was hardly in a position to argue. From Eirik's lessons, Vikram knew that the last group to be granted a hearing with the Council was the now dissolved Osiris Integration Movement, and their history was blemished.

As for the title, Vikram had no surname as far as he knew. He had made one up for his previous communications and for the purpose of today. In jail, like Eirik, he had been allotted a number.

"Please begin, Mr Bai," said the Speaker. Vikram resisted the temptation to turn around.

"I'm not going to speak about Eirik 9968 today," he said. When he spoke Eirik's name a flicker of distaste ran around the Chambers, but Vikram's voice remained steady. That gave him the courage to continue.

"Our opinions will hardly be the same and it seems pointless to resurrect a debate which has already been decided. Instead, I'd like to tell you about the real west—the west you know nothing about."

He found that the acoustics of the Chambers carried his voice well. After a few minutes he almost forgot that he was addressing the Council, Osiris's ruling elite. As their faces separated into individual imprints, he tried to force them out of their aloof curiosity. Primarily he spoke about poverty. He told them of diseases that scurried through the shanty towns and raced up the towers, claiming children and adults alike. The people he had seen coughing up their lungs with tuberculosis. The shortages of food and clothing. He described how a man looked when he froze to death. He told them of the hospice that struggled to care for those who had lost limbs to frostbite. He didn't linger over crime, but told the Council what they already knew, that it was fuelled primarily by the needs of people who had nothing, and would not decrease until they had something. Then he laid out his arguments: what was needed now. An emergency winter aid programme. More accommodation, repair works and insulation for the uninhabitable buildings.

Then, because Eirik and Mikkeli had taught him that unless you demanded everything you got nothing, he tossed in his firework.

"Finally, Councillors, I would like to propose what some of you might think of as revolutionary." There went the understatement of the year, he thought. "West Osiris is cordoned off from the rest of the city. We are separated from your facilities and your people by a military border. We are practically quarantined. I think the border has been here long enough, and I'm not the only one. It has to go."

The cries of outrage were rising even as he uttered that last incendiary sentence.

"Is that all, Mr Bai?" the speaker nudged. Vikram heard a few sniggers from around the Chambers.

"And as soon as possible," he shouted. He glanced back at the speaker. "That's all for now." His heart was beating fast. He sat down with no small sense of exhilaration.

"Open to the floor," declared the speaker.

Furious debate was already under way, but the Council appeared to have certain rules and now one woman stood up to speak officially.

"The very notion of demilitarizing the border is preposterous," she said. "Mr Bai may not wish to speak of Eirik 9968—indeed I am surprised he dares mention the name—but I shall not flinch from it. The execution was a warning. Why was a warning necessary? Because the west have grown out of control. They cannot maintain order within their own quarter, never mind letting their violent antics rampant on the City."

Vikram was ready to retort, but she raised her hand and her voice.

"I think one word is enough to reinforce my argument—Osuwa. Two skyscrapers blown open to the elements. And targeting the University—a place of learning, of mutual respect, not to mention those people trapped in the shuttle line where the explosion was set..."

"That was twenty-nine years ago," argued someone else.

"We learn from history," she snapped. "It has a clear enough line for us to read. First the greenhouse. Then Osuwa University and the New Western Osiris Front. The one occasion we did lower security, what happened? Alain and Helene Dumay were assassinated in broad daylight at the gliding race."

"Grete Kaat was a rogue sympathiser."

"Then we are even more at threat. If a rogue can murder a member of a founding family, just imagine what organized terrorists can do."

"What about three years ago? You can't say security was lax then, but it didn't prevent riots."

Another man stood up. "The June riots are precisely the reason we have to remain on our guard. Those attacks were completely unprovoked. Civilian lives were lost. We cannot allow any further incidents."

Disregarding his instructions, Vikram leaned forward, his hands clenched together to stop any other physical movement that might betray him.

"People were starving that winter," he said quietly. "They were desperate. They'll be desperate again if you don't help them. And Horizon is not another NWO, if that's what you're implying. Ninety-nine per cent of westerners completely condemn the NWO. So don't insult us."

"Mr Bai, you have had your chance to speak. It is now the Council's turn."

The Councillor who had spoken gave Vikram a cursory glance. "The westerner seems to be implying further violence is not only possible but probable. And he suggests we open our borders?"

"It's worth considering the root causes of the June riots," another voice said coolly. Vikram couldn't locate the speaker.

"The rioters were westerners," shouted the first woman. "What more do you need to hear? And they've had enough help from us. We have more important problems. The mining station on the north shelf, for a start. I've heard reports of serious machine malfunctions."

"Greatly exaggerated reports—"

"Not from what I've heard—"

"The west is under our jurisdiction," argued someone else. "We have a responsibility—"

"We have a responsibility to our own people, not to put them at risk."

"Exactly, do we want a repeat of three years ago?"

"I hardly think an aid programme is going to incite riots." It was the cool voice, cutting across his colleagues again. Vikram searched for its origin. The speaker was a young man sitting several rows back. He leaned forward to emphasize his point. As he did, the light caught a hint of red in his hair, and Vikram suffered a shock of recognition. He had seen this man at the execution. He had been standing next to Feodor. It was one of the Rechnov sons.

There was a brief silence.

Then someone said tentatively, "There're no spare resources for that kind of programme."

"It has nothing to do with the border anyway."

"Actually, it has everything to do with it," the young Rechnov said. "I happen to agree with Mr Bai. The border should be demilitarized. However, I would be a fool to imagine that such a move might be taken today, by this Council. Nor do I think that the time is right. First the west needs development and support, and that is where the proposed winter aid programme through Mr Bai's group comes in. Otherwise we will have another angry mob on our hands—no, Hildur, I am not talking about the NWO, seeing as we have zero evidence to support any current underground activity, I am talking about ordinary people growing angry—angry enough to act—and who can blame them?"

"And where do the resources for this aid programme come from?" A new voice, strong and powerful, spoke up from the opposite side of the room. This time it was easy to locate the speaker. All heads turned towards him. Vikram followed their direction and recognized this man instantly.

Nausea rose in his throat. Had he known, all along, that Feodor Rechnov would be here today? Probably. He hadn't permitted himself to think about it.

Feodor was an imposing figure; Vikram had seen that before. Now, so much closer, he could see the grey threads in the thick hair, the slightly sallow complexion, and eyes that settled comfortably, with a keen relish, on any opponent, daring them to outstare.

But he doesn't know me, he thought. *I'm an alien to him.*

"A simple case of reallocation," said the son again. "The resources are there, we require only a good mathematician and a little imagination."

"I see. And may I ask if you envisage the west developing further—perhaps to the same standards as the rest of the city?"

"Is there a reason why not? Is it Osiris doctrine to promote starvation and hypothermia?"

"I take your point," said Feodor. The chambers had hushed for this debate between Rechnov and Rechnov. If he hadn't known who they were, Vikram would have suspected he was observing a pair of regular antagonists. It made no sense. "Clearly we are not advocating poverty. Our city was not built with that intent—far from it. Nonetheless, Osiris has changed. We have been stretched beyond our resources, and we cannot offer the west the lifestyle of the City. False hope is a dangerous tool to employ."

"You're a defeatist, Feodor," said the young man. His tone was dismissive, and Vikram allowed himself a small smile.

"I am a realist," the other replied. "That is our job, to be realistic. To implement the feasible. East and west can never be integrated. Draw up your aid programmes if it appeases your conscience, but I guarantee the consequences will be more problematic than you imagine."

"Consequences are always problematic. That doesn't mean we should shy away from action. I tell you, we may choose to forget history, but it has not forgotten us, and nor will the west if we persist in flaunting our ignorance. We have executed one man—the threat, as some would say, has been eliminated. Now is our opportunity to show the west we can be generous."

The younger Rechnov's name was Linus, Vikram remembered. He looked more like the infamous sister than the father.

Feodor pressed on. "Do you honestly believe that any kind of integration could be accomplished without mutual tragedy?"

"If it were dealt with sensitively, I see no reason why tragedy should be the result."

Restlessness pervaded the chambers now. Vikram sensed the debate slipping away into personal territory. Evidently he was not the only one, because the woman who had first spoken stood again.

"It is pointless spending hours going over these issues today when clearly the matter requires further research. I suggest we move onto other items on the agenda?"

A cheer echoed her. Vikram dragged his attention away from the two Rechnovs.

"What do you mean, other research? How much research does it take to see that people are dying of cold?"

"Mr Bai, you have been warned once."

Half the Council were on their feet, raising their voices over one another as they argued.

"Actually, we're neglecting an opportunity here. What we really need is a larger budget for the western defence perimeter. Personally, I'd recommend a twelve point five increase."

"Twelve point five? Eleven should do it."

"Eleven, twelve. We can discuss figures later. What we've got to do is streamline entry procedures. With that kind of budget we can develop waiting zones, double the checkpoints."

"Exactly. We could even filter some of the allocation into the western task force. Surely Mr Bai will be happy with that."

"There might be provision for a few places in schools, if it were passed by the parental boards..."

"That's already covered by the Colnat Foundation—"

"No, no, no. The perimeter's the important thing, I tell you."

The speaker leaned over his podium to speak to Vikram. "Thank you, Mr Bai. Your presentation was most enlightening."

"But we haven't even started! You didn't decide anything—"

"Mr Bai—"

The tug upon his arm was light but firm.

"No!" Vikram's voice came out as a shout. The female Councillor was still on her feet. She turned to him, her face smooth and flat and devoid of emotion. Something about her complete inflexibility dissolved his reserve. "I've changed my mind," he said. "I want to talk about Eirik 9968."

"Oh yes? Do enlighten us."

Vikram did not heed her sarcasm. He was only aware of Feodor's heavy, brooding gaze. But he looked at the woman.

"I want to know why you killed him."

She gave a little shrug. "I haven't killed anyone, my poor friend."

"Then who did?"

"I think you'll find it was a matter of City justice." Her lips parted in a flat half smile. "Why? Colleague of yours?"

"I didn't know him."

"So you say."

"I said I didn't know him."

Very deliberately, she crossed her arms.

"I don't believe you came here about the west at all. I think you came about the execution. What are you after—revenge?" She glanced over her shoulder. "I take it he was searched before you let him in here?"

Vikram gripped the podium.

"I came because there was no reason for that execution to happen and there's no reason it ever should again—if you fucking do something to help us."

"How dare you speak to me in that manner!" But Vikram could see that she was delighted at his outburst and it made him angrier.

"Hildur, enough." Feodor Rechnov cut through the woman's protests. Slowly, his gaze lifted to Vikram. "I believe this debate is at an end."

Vikram didn't care any more. He felt reckless and giddy.

"It was you, wasn't it? You killed him. You gave the order."

"I sanctioned a Council decision. You may go and tell that, if you wish, to your friends in the west. And when you do, remind them that the mode of execution is in good repair and that if anyone wishes to follow Eirik 9968, they know where their path will end."

"He was innocent. He did nothing but fight for the rights of people he owed no allegiance to."

"Then he and I have something in common. How ironic."

"You have nothing in common with Eirik. You murdered an innocent man."

"He was an inciter, a terrorist and a common killer. And if you don't want to be taken as one too, Mr Bai, I suggest you reacquaint yourself with silence and leave this session. Speaker, I urge this house to order."

The tug on Vikram's arm grew persistent. He kept his eyes locked on Feodor; all of his burning rage channelled into one single focus.

"I hope your sleep is haunted by ghosts," he said.

"Remove him."

"Mr Bai!"

"I hope they come to you in your sleep and tell you how they died."

Feodor remained unmoved. Vikram's minder had an inexorable grip on his hand. Now there were other hands, on his arm, on his shoulders, pulling him away from the podium. In seconds, the faces of the Council were obscured from his view. The clamour inside the Chambers was muffled as the great wooden doors swung closed. Doors like that would never be made again. Vikram stared at this sign of wealth in mute fury, first at Feodor Rechnov, and then, increasingly, at himself.

He had been in front of the Council—and he had lost them. How had he lost them? How had he lost control?

"They never do, I'm afraid."

"What?"

His minder was still with him. A woman in a narrow suit. She smiled sympathetically. She had no reason to be sympathetic. It felt like pity.

"Decide anything. They don't decide anything. Try again next month. Persistence can get results."

"Do you have any idea how long I've been writing letters for? How long I've been petitioning, just to speak? Twelve months. That's an entire year. How long d'you think it'll take to get another hearing?"

She shrugged. "That's the way it goes. I might say you were foolish to lose your temper."

"You might say a lot of things," he snapped.

He realized she was waiting for him to leave, no doubt under instructions to ensure he did not cause a scene. He tried once more.

"I can come back later. Talk to them again. You could help."

"I don't think so. Not today."

"Tomorrow then."

She did not reply. The doormen were exchanging glances. He strode angrily away, only to hear the woman running after him. "Don't forget your coat," she said. "It's cold out."

It was a kind gesture but it annoyed Vikram all the more to have to turn around and go back to the cloakroom. The attendant returned his unsightly coat. He yanked it on and heard the lining rip.

Helpless anger rumbled in the pit of his stomach. It was a warning. He knew what that rage could do and there was a reason he had worked so hard to still it. Images he had thought long banished rose up one by one. Mikkeli with a gun. Mikkeli floating. Her body shedding water when he pulled it onto the decking.

Where had those events lead? To a green cell and a flooded tank. Mikkeli was dead. Eirik was dead. And Vikram had sabotaged his one chance in front of the Council. He had failed all of them.

A security guard was walking towards him. Anger wouldn't help now. He needed strategy. He needed time.

He turned back to the cloakroom. "I have to go to the bathroom."

The attendant eyed him warily. Vikram clutched his stomach.

"I think I might be sick…"

With a look of distaste, the attendant jabbed a finger. "It's that way."

He walked meekly past the guards to the end of the hallway and out through the secondary doors. He was back in the main corridor. There were no windows, just soft lighting and soft carpeting, his worn down boots noiseless upon it.

He went left towards the lifts. No one was about. Fifty metres along was a statue of an early Teller, and just behind it, a small cubic space with glass cabinets housing Neon Age relics on either side. It was said that back then, people had lived to one hundred and fifty years, and they looked the same as they did at fifteen, their skin fresh and beautiful, their organs plucked from their bodies and replaced with newly grown ones. In this way they had achieved immortality, until the Blackout.

He slipped around the statue. The alcove overlooked the interior of the scraper. He could see the shadow of the lifts moving up and down inside the aquarium, people trapped in a watery world. It was a bizarrely pretty parody of imprisonment.

He turned away and studied the cabinets instead.

Engraved and personalised hologrammic device, he read. *Twenty-second century, Alaskan.*

He thought of Mikkeli's precious map, pictured Alaska on it. The map had been their great secret. At night they had spent hours poring over the outlines of land, guessing where their ancestors had come from, until Naala found the map and said it was illegal and burned it in front of them. There were no maps in the cabinet.

The Eye Tower's security was surprisingly lax. He had been searched at the border and on the way into the tower and the Chambers, but for all the Councillors knew he could be part of a larger conspiracy. He could be here to scope out the building. He might have a partner armed with explosives. Evidently they felt confident that he posed no kind of threat.

They were right. He didn't. Not today.

Strategy was patience. Vikram settled on the floor, leaning gently against the cabinet. He would wait.

The City clock chimed three times on the hour; a deep, austere vibration. Vikram started. He'd let his mind wander. He heard what he was listening for: the sound of the great doors being levered open and well-shoed feet hurrying out of the Chambers.

The Councillors spilled into the corridor. Vikram watched them sweep by, oblivious to his presence in the alcove. Feodor passed, deep in

conversation, and Vikram lowered his eyes in case a sense of mutual ani-
mosity should draw the other man's gaze. He could not see the younger
Rechnov. In the rush Vikram was afraid he had missed him, but then
he spotted the sleek, charcoal-suited figure, a heavy coat slung over his
arm, the auburn tint in his hazel hair.

Linus was one of the last out and he was alone. Two pieces of luck,
which was more than Vikram deserved.

Linus turned right. Vikram waited for the last stragglers to amble pass
and hurried after him.

The young man walked briskly, Vikram following a short distance behind. The corridor curved gradually and Vikram lost sense of how far
round they had come. Linus went through a set of doors. The skyscraper
was even larger than Vikram had supposed. Within its outer ring was a
maze of tiny corridors. These too were carpeted, with wall-hung lamps
and decorations which Vikram had no time to look at; portraits and long
lists of names.

A little way ahead, Linus stopped. He put on his coat and did up each
of the buttons and a feather collar. Then he disappeared through a door.

Vikram followed, opened the door and stepped silently out onto a balcony.

He was at least a hundred floors above surface. The skyline was spectacular: a medley of pyramid tops, flat, pointed and asymmetric, swathed
in nylon mist. The wind met him ferociously. Another day, he would have
admired the view, but today he had no time for it.

Linus was leaning against the wall, his feet casually crossed. A coil of
smoke rose from the glowing cigarette reversed in one gloved hand. The
upturned collar cut sharp angles across his jaw. Vikram guessed that the
coat was lined with feathers too.

He shut the door gently behind him.

"Mind if I join you?"

Linus looked around. Surprise flickered for a moment in his eyes. Then
it vanished, to be replaced by a cool, relaxed assessment.

"Not at all," he said. He had a face that contained both strength and
delicacy; the Rechnovs were undeniably a good-looking family.

Vikram took out his own cigarettes. His hands, lacking mittens, had
become paws. The cellulose packaging of his cigarettes almost defeated
him. His fingertips skidded on the top of the first tube, fighting to extract

one from many.

"Shit."

He saw the cigarette fall before he felt it depart his fingers. It wasn't as if he could afford to throw them away. He brought the packet to his lips and teased out another with his tongue. The smell of oranges lingered on his fingers.

Linus passed him a lighter. Vikram cupped the flame and passed it back. They stood in silence.

"You must have been waiting some time," said Linus at last.

"Twelve months."

The Councillor gave him a quizzical look.

"Since I began writing letters. But that's not what you meant."

"No."

"You're wondering why I followed you."

"I could take an educated guess."

Vikram gestured. "Please do."

Linus exhaled a thin stream of smoke. In his smart coat, he was well protected against the cold, and he appeared in no rush.

"I'm sorry that your case was not considered. It would appear that the hearing today was something of a formality."

"You're on the Council."

"Yes. Well, in an advisory capacity—that's all it's really here for now."

"Maybe with more preparation—more evidence…"

"Actually, it's nothing to do with preparation. You could do as much work, amass as many studies as you like. The outcome would be the same. It always has been, ever since the earliest attempts of the WRM—the Western Repatriation Movement, back in seventy-four." *I know who they were*, thought Vikram, but he refrained from interrupting.

"Not that the NWO has helped your cause, sadly." The Councillor paused, apparently musing over the issue. "I'm Linus, by the way. And I know who you are. Obviously."

"Linus, nice to meet you," Vikram muttered. Introductions weren't really his thing; perhaps it was there that he had stumbled. Choosing the wrong name, or something. They pressed wrists anyway, his own skin fish-bone dry with the cold, the material of Linus's glove smooth and unidentifiable. "I have to ask—why do you say that? About the Council?

When you're on it, I mean."

"Oh, there's many reasons. What you're proposing—radical social reform—it doesn't really sit with the Council any more. They tried it already."

"They used to be more philanthropic."

"They used to be younger," Linus said. He must be quite young himself, in his late twenties, Vikram thought. Fourth generation, anyway. Linus seemed to sense the scrutiny, because he raised one eyebrow. "You don't agree?"

"If you mean that age affects resolution and liberality, then yes, I suppose you're right."

"You're what—twenty six? Twenty-seven?"

"Twenty-five." The age Mikkeli had been.

Linus laughed. "Young, anyway. That's the thing. You remind these people of themselves a long time ago. They know they lack that conviction now and it shames them. And just in case you're wondering, the man I was duelling with earlier is Feodor Rechnov. My father."

Vikram did not mention that he already knew the connection. He was not confident that he could keep his voice free of emotion.

Linus seemed unaware of any tension. "Then again, you have to remember what some of them have been through. What they've lost."

"That's too convenient an excuse. At least let someone else try."

"Someone like you?"

Vikram shrugged. "Maybe."

Linus retrieved a silver case from his coat pocket. He took out two cigarettes and offered one to Vikram.

"Thanks." Vikram slipped his own packet away.

"Not a problem."

Again the lighter was passed. Vikram cupped the flame and drew deeply on the cigarette. It brought on a rush of light-headedness. Evidently tobacco was rolled stronger in the City, or it had less junk in it.

Linus inhaled gently. There were no lines around his mouth. Vikram wished he could tell what the other man was thinking. There was something unnerving about the controlled politeness, as though Linus were prepared to tell Vikram anything, secure in the knowledge that if he felt the information were even fractionally at risk, he could have the westerner tossed over the balcony without a second thought.

The cold was beginning to penetrate through Vikram's thinner coat. The preliminaries were over. He would get no clues from a Rechnov.

"I need your help," he said.

"After today's exhibition, I suppose you do." There was no judgement in Linus's voice, only dry fact.

"You're a Councillor. You must have influence."

"Very little, I'm afraid."

"But you spoke up today. For the west."

"I did. As you saw, it was a futile case."

"Then tell me what I need to do. You know these people. I don't."

"Oh, I admire anyone who will stand up and take on the Council. But you're wasting your time."

"Thanks." Vikram stared moodily out. "That's really useful."

"There are other routes, of course," Linus continued. "Less orthodox routes."

"Such as?"

"Find yourself a patron; someone rich and popular." Linus finished his cigarette. He stubbed it out carefully on the rail. "Someone like Adelaide Mystik, perhaps."

"Adelaide Mystik? You mean—" He stopped, confused by the oblique reference. "Why would I talk to her? She's a—she doesn't do anything."

"Exactly. Like most celebrities, she doesn't do anything. Therefore I would imagine she has time to do many things, if approached the right way. And she's influential." Linus looked thoughtful. "Yes. Talk to her. Don't say I suggested it—just turn up as if it was your own idea."

Vikram felt wrong-footed, but could not pinpoint where or how it had happened. Instead he asked, "Why would a Rechnov support the west?"

Linus's smile was slow and closed. "An interesting question. One that would require time to answer. I don't have time. But I do have a query for you. Did you know Eirik 9968?"

"Would it make a difference if I did?"

"Not to me."

"Well, I didn't know him. Not to speak to."

The lie slid easily off his tongue. It occurred to him that if he said it enough times, he might begin to believe it, that knowledge of another person was as frail as mist.

"He was wrongly numbered, I believe. Assigned a 68. He should have been a 65, for Tasmayn. Not that it makes a difference now. Funny the way that our origins are disregarded nowadays."

The snippet of information could only have been dropped as a test. Vikram kept his face impassive.

"What's the name of that stone, inside the Chambers?"

"Stone?"

"Yes. The pillars."

"Oh. It's called marble. Rather beautiful, isn't it. Mined in quarries over a century ago. Finally shipped across from Patagonia. Quite a feat." Linus paused. "Ah yes. This might help you—I won't need it." He handed Vikram a card. "Good luck. Don't freeze out here."

The door closed on him before Vikram could reply.

Find yourself a patron. Linus's turn of phrase rang oddly in his wake. Not *someone like my sister*, but *someone like Adelaide Mystik*. As though Adelaide were a completely separate entity. It didn't sound like a recommendation. Then again, what did Vikram know about these people?

He recalled the Rechnovs, gathered on the balcony to watch the skadi execute Eirik. Their family portrait seemed even stranger now than it had done last week. There were four fourth-gen siblings, he knew. Vikram wondered if that had been calculated prescience in light of the later population control laws. Linus was evidently on the Council. There was the other brother, and then the infamous twins. Axel, the ex-jet set boy who'd disappeared. And the daughter. Beautiful, catastrophic Adelaide, who refused to use her family's name and headed up socialite group the Haze in a whirl of parties and social misdemeanours. Crazy Adelaide, mad like her brother, mad in the way that could only end badly. Last famously captured necking from a bottle at Axel's remembrance service, or whatever the feed had called it, because the kid was surely dead. And Linus was suggesting that Vikram solicit her help?

Vikram looked at the card. It sat snugly in the palm of his hand, about the size of a playing card, but thicker. The card was red with a pink rose motif, and running across it in gold type was the inscription.

Adelaide Mystik invites you to Rose Night at the Red Rooms, to be held on the second Thursday of the month, attendance after the hour of twenty-one.

The back was watermarked. It had an Old World feel to it, pre-Neon, even.

Something struck him on the cheek. He looked up. Hail. Cursing the weather's erratic switches, thrusting the card into his coat pocket, he retreated indoors.

Two guards were approaching down the corridor.

"Time's up, kid. Out with you."

They marched him back to the lift. Hands folded in front, eyes averted, they accompanied Vikram down the hundred floors, across the mosaic-tiled lobby, past the evergreen trees and down again through the flood control floors. They opened the doors for him to go outside. As he passed, one of them grabbed his collar.

"Hey—don't forget to check out your picture in the newsreel."

The other grinned inanely.

"We don't have your damn newsreel in the west," Vikram flung back. "Don't you know anything?"

The doors hissed shut. Vikram was left at the waterbus terminus, watching the next load of passengers embark in the freezing hail.

5 | ADELAIDE

The Rechnov offices were quieter than she remembered. Through doors left ajar or windows with the blinds half drawn, she caught glimpses of her father's employees. They were smartly but plainly dressed, their workstations clean, uncluttered. These days, amidst the eternal rumours that bits of the City were falling apart, she supposed the company was more concerned with maintenance than creativity.

Occasionally, seeing her shadow pass, a worker glanced up. Some dropped their eyes, others stared overtly. She hadn't been invited.

Her meeting with the investigator was in two days time. What she expected to uncover here today she was not yet sure, only that she was following instinct, and instinct was tracing a path backwards.

In an empty foyer that smelled of decomposing ideas, she passed the things that had never been built, forever imprisoned behind glass frames. Plans for an underwater shuttle network. A piece of concept art for a hotel like a bubble on the seabed, the date marked in the bottom right corner—Summer 2366. A mere twelve months before Storm Year.

It was a strange feeling to think that this image was half a century old, its creator probably dead. He might even have been born outside Osiris; walked on land and seen places that no longer existed. Axel had been obsessed with the Old World at one stage, and the idea of rediscovering it. For weeks on end he had pestered Feodor with questions. What had happened to the land? Why had everyone come to Osiris and why could no one leave?

Feodor, who liked to lecture, told them that Osiris was built because the world was collapsing. Even before the Great Storm, the old lands had been crippled by disasters. Floods, famine, plagues made by scientists, war, drought—earthquakes that ripped the land to pieces. The twins wouldn't know, but a long time ago there used to be giant discs drifting in the sky—s'lites, they called them. S'lites looked like stars. They took photographs, and connected scarabs in an enormous web spanning halfway across the globe. Back in the Neon Age, said Feodor, everyone knew everything about everyone else in the world. They had machines inside their heads. The sky was full of giant mirrors and cloud spraying monsters. Some of them were planning to live on the Moon. But all that was before the Blackout.

Now, a city like Osiris, entirely self-sustaining, was a stroke of pure genius (partly by the people on the Osiris Board, but ultimately, said Feodor, by their grandfather and his father Alexei before him, who travelled all the way across the Boreal States on the back of a grain cart so that he could enter the architectural competition). There should have been many more Osiris cities. They could have saved lives. But the city came too late, and when the Great Storm arrived, the few refugees that escaped land's terrible plagues only confirmed the worst.

Nobody has ever answered Osiris's distress signal, Feodor told them finally, because nobody is left to answer. He shook his head, a tired, resigned gesture. He only wished it were otherwise.

Looking at the faded plans, Adelaide remembered that speech very clearly. It was the only time she had ever supported Feodor rather than Axel.

She strode down the corridor, purposeful now. She was reaching for the brass handle of Feodor's office when Tyr stepped out of the adjacent room and manoeuvred himself in front of the door. He must have seen her coming on camera.

"Feodor's at a press conference," he said.

"Feeding that insatiable desire for publicity, is he?"

"He's delivering a statement on the west. They had a westerner in the Chambers this morning. Someone has to put a positive spin on it." Tyr surveyed her blandly. "He's not due back any time soon."

"I can wait. In here."

She took a step forward. Tyr did not move. They faced one another, close enough to see blemishes, lines, embryonic beneath the skin. Close enough to touch. Green stilettos put Adelaide almost on a level height with Tyr. A clump of his hair stuck out over his forehead, light brown, streaked with honey. She fought the urge to push it back into place. Her own resolution was mirrored in the set of his jaw, the slight contraction of the irises. His eyes were the colour of dusk, and held its ambiguity.

Stalemate suspended them for a few seconds. Then Tyr shrugged.

"Your call."

"Thank you."

He opened the door in a twofold gesture, pushing it ajar, and as she stepped forward holding it there before opening it all the way. Adelaide ignored the bait.

"I'll take a coral tea," she called over her shoulder. "Strong. Plenty of ginger."

"I know how you take your tea," said Tyr.

The door swung shut, cutting him off.

Adelaide looked about, remembering. The room contained the accumulated possessions of three proud and quite different men, none of them able to erase the presence of their predecessor. Alexei's bookshelves squeezed between Leonid's maps, their edges neatly aligned. The floor was dwarfed by Feodor's huge table, itself covered in architectural drawings, and beneath or in places upon them, in tea glass rings. Adelaide slung her handbag on top.

She crossed the room to the Neptune. Its oceanscreen showed deep sea beyond the submerged island and the Atum Shelf. The image was three-dimensional and opalescent. It seemed to pulse. There was no sign of the city's underworld: no plateauing pyramid bases, pipelines or energy turbines; nothing to reveal human intrusion at all.

"You old-fashioned fool," Adelaide said aloud.

She placed one hand flat against the activation strip. Nothing happened. The Neptune must be programmed to respond to Feodor's fingerprints. She tried the drawers to his desk. They were also locked.

Tyr entered without knocking. He had been working with the Rechnovs for some years now and had acquired certain family privileges. Feodor trusted him implicitly. Tyr gave her an incalculable glance and placed her teaglass on a table beside a leather armchair. He stood there until she moved away from Feodor's desk.

Adelaide lifted the glass to her nose, inhaling the steam as ritual dictated, then blew lightly across the liquid. They surveyed one another without pretence.

"Do you have a Surfboard?" she asked.

"A Surfboard? No."

"I thought there might be some reading material to occupy those of us who have to wait upon Feodor."

"I'll suggest it to him," Tyr said.

When he had gone, she seated herself in the armchair, and hooked one shoe across the opposite knee. Her foot jiggled. She waited. After a moment she grew bored of waiting, and crossed the room to the sideboard jammed against the bookcase. She relieved it of one of the more expensive raquas and poured herself a triple measure.

She went to stand by the maps, the raqua in her right hand, untouched. Most were plans of Osiris, but there was one that showed the Old World land masses. It was a beautiful and very rare object. Adelaide traced the outlines with one finger, thinking of Axel's questions.

It was stranger than she had expected to be here. She remembered when she was younger occasionally visiting the premises, feeling awed by the vastness of her father's territory and the operation he commanded. This office had seemed like a sanctum then. The twins' four feet had dangled over the edges of the chairs. The adults discussed complex matters whilst the twins whispered; the room was thick with the shadows of their long gone whispers.

Her eyes flicked to the Neptune again. Over two weeks had passed since the Service of Hope, and there was no further information about Axel. If Feodor knew anything—via Sanjay Hanif, or independently—the clues would be on that machine. Adelaide was not sure exactly what those clues might be. She was not even sure, yet, of what she suspected.

She heard noises from outside, voices followed by urgent footsteps. She ran her tongue over dry lips, suddenly nervous of what the meeting might bring.

The door opened to admit her father.

"Afternoon, Adelaide. What are you doing here?" His gaze took in her, by the maps, and the raqua, as she had known it would. "You're aware of the time, I presume."

"I was waiting. So yes."

"Impudent as ever."

She sucked in a breath. Three words and she was biting her tongue. Expressionless, she swilled the amber liquid in the glass, watching the moon-shaped tidemark left by the alcohol.

"To your continued health, Feodor," she said finally, and drank the contents. Her throat burned. Not just a cheap stunt, but that was a waste of good raqua if it did not rile him the way she needed.

She sensed her father's infuriation as he crossed the room to a chair by the table, leaning both hands heavily upon its back. He still bore the signs of a strong physique, though years and work had etched their marks. His face was lined, more than it might have been for a man his age. It was a face that took its time before succumbing to the necessity of conversation.

"You'll have to forgive my lateness." His voice, used to public speaking, sounded trapped in the office. It took on other nuances too—sarcasm, and flashes of contempt. "As Tyr no doubt informed you, I've been in the Chambers all morning. An absurdly unproductive session. Hildur Pek has been kicking up a storm about the ring-net, as if anyone is worrying about sharks right now. Then we had some western lunatic speaking. Stars knows where they got him from, I suppose it's hard to find literates over there. Practically demanded that we demilitarize the border, and Linus— Linus!—supported him, would you believe."

"I didn't come to talk about Linus."

"No." Feodor's face closed. "No, you didn't, did you. Well, Adelaide? I've had to leave a press conference because Tyr informs me you've materialized in my office. I can't just drop everything to attend to your whims."

"Here you are though," she said.

The look he shot her was half fury, half despair. Their mutual dependency filled the air, hanging like a veil between them. Feodor, she knew, would never be able to accept Adelaide's defection from the family. Whereas Viviana, much as she might pretend otherwise, had not been sorry to lose her only daughter. The rift had come as a relief to them both.

"You made me go to that hideous execution last week," she said. "Even though I hated it. Even though watching it made me sick."

"Stars, don't bring that up. I've heard enough about the damn execution for one day."

"I want the keys to the penthouse."

"Is that a property request?" he said sardonically.

"No, Daddy, it's not." It was not an affectionate term, and she knew its power. The first tinges of colour crept into Feodor's cheeks.

"Then why would you ask for the keys when you know I have handed them over to the committee?"

"All of them?"

Feodor's eyes flicked to the window-wall before resettling upon his daughter.

"Except for the set which must have been with Axel, yes, all of them."

"Don't say it like that."

"Like what?"

"As if he's not coming back."

"I'm sorry, Adelaide."

"Stop it."

"It's been over six weeks. We've consulted the most eminent Tellers."

"So?"

Feodor looked sombrely at his hands. She rallied.

"There must be another set. You would never have given up the only one."

His heavy eyelids lifted. "Accuse me of falsehoods if you wish. The keys to the penthouse are with the investigating committee, as requested when we reported Axel's disappearance. I expect Hanif will retain them until the investigation is closed. Until then, no one is allowed access, not even family."

"You're lying."

Feodor gave a faint smile. She cursed herself silently, knowing she had tripped on the most obvious of wires, unable to retract her step. She should have been used to the lies. It was a Rechnov trademark; they talked themselves into belief.

"Look," she persisted. "The penthouse is one of our properties. There's always another way in. That's one of grandfather's tricks."

"Oh, be reasonable. Even if I indulge your bizarre conspiracy theories, as if I have time to play games about locked doors—do you not think that

Hanif will have accounted for such a possibility? If he wishes to seal off the penthouse, I guarantee it will be guarded by more than a key."

"And we both know you could get past such obstacles, if you wanted to."

Her father gave her a haughty glance.

"Are you suggesting I break the decrees of the Council I serve?"

"I'm suggesting you put your son before your work."

The nerve above his eye began to twitch. "There is such a thing as integrity, Adelaide. But let's forget the practicalities for a second and talk about the premise. What in Osiris do you expect to achieve by going through Axel's belongings? The last time you were there—"

"Precisely." She leaned forward. "It's months since any of us have been inside. I need to see what's there, if there're any clues to what happened. I'd have thought you would want to see too."

"I've no desire to visit." Feodor shook his head. "It's a cursed place."

"Of course. I forgot." Her own anger was growing. "It's an embarrassment to you. My brother is an embarrassment."

The colour flooded Feodor's cheeks.

"Do you think you are the only one suffering here?" His voice rose. Adelaide swallowed. "Have you considered your mother for one second? Have you spoken to her once since the Service of Hope? You have no idea what it's like to lose a child. And if you carry on the way you are I don't suppose you ever will. You might learn something from this tragedy, Adelaide, and address your own lifestyle, instead of attacking other people's."

She was on her feet before she knew it. "Don't talk to me about my actions! You've had nothing to do with me or Axel for years. That's the way we all wanted it, that's the way we got it."

"Because of your own stubbornness, Adelaide!"

"You pushed us out—after Axel—after the incident—"

"I'm not going to dredge this up. You renounced the family name. Your grandfather's name. And not just you, you had to drag Axel along too—"

"I didn't drag him anywhere. You wanted him examined. You were going to do tests. We had no choice!"

They glared at one another. Feodor's knuckles clenched white on the back of the chair. She fought for control of her voice.

"I've come here to ask you to help. Axel is my twin. I have to know.

Why can't you see that?" She willed him to understand. To delay a verdict she did not want to make.

"There are qualified people investigating what happened. And I think, if we are honest, we both know what they are going to find out."

"No, we don't."

"Adelaide—"

"They never found his body."

"The earth is full of unburied souls." Feodor lifted his hands: a gesture of resignation. "Listen to me. It does no good to mull over these things. And besides, this is a delicate situation. Decorum is required. There are procedures. You must not—you will not—start making ripples. Hanif has everything in hand. He will inform me the moment—"

"Please. I won't take anything, I won't touch anything, I just want to look—"

"He will inform me the moment new information arises. I am sure it will not be long."

She fell still. On the Neptune o'screen, the forked tail of a fish disappeared beyond the edges of the frame. She reached out a finger, tracing its exit. Nebulous ideas, suspicions that had led her to this day and this request, tightened in her head and bound.

"How can you be so confident?" she murmured.

Feodor shifted his weight, flexing and refolding his hands around the back of the chair. "Adelaide. Perhaps this is difficult for you to understand, having been so close to your brother, but this—disappearance. In some ways, it is not, perhaps, entirely unexpected. The shock is no less, but the mind... the mind can sometimes anticipate, without knowing..."

Adelaide's chest constricted with outrage. "Are you trying to imply that he—"

"No!" Feodor looked, for once, truly scandalized. "Don't insult me. Axel was still a Rechnov, he would never—Let me finish. I am talking about accidents. An accident... Nothing more." He took a deep breath, visibly gathering himself. "Now what I need you to do, Adelaide, is give me your word you will take this matter no further. Come back. Come back to the Domain. We will survive this as a family. We must not forsake one another in our grief."

"I can't grieve for someone who isn't dead."

Even as she spoke, she felt a dull flicker of recognition within herself. Grieving was exactly what she had been doing for the past year. But there was no longer time for that.

Feodor let out a long sigh, as if to say only the deeply misguided could still have hope, and for them, he was powerless.

"Ask the stars for guidance, if you will not accept mine. And drop this crusade. It will not bring him back."

A shaft of sunlight fell across the room, whiting the image on the Neptune. The machine whirred gently.

"You won't help me," she said. The words fell slowly, hand in hand with the confirmation. If Feodor wouldn't help her, he had to be hiding something. What did he know that she didn't? Had the Rechnovs already been inside the penthouse? Had they found something? She imagined Feodor and Linus going through Axel's things, discussing their strategy, agreeing that under no circumstances would they tell Adelaide.

"Even if I did have access—which I do not—I cannot possibly let you interfere with an investigation. All Councillors are under oath to the City. You know that. We have duties beyond the personal, and you, as my daughter, are implicit in that."

She kept her face, her voice, carefully neutral. "I understand."

"Good. Your mother is holding a Council dinner tomorrow night. She sent you an invitation." The blood had drained from his cheeks. He was the politician again, calm and ordered.

"I received it."

"Then we shall see you there."

"Get me the keys and maybe I'll come."

Feodor made a sound of disgust.

"Oh, go back to the Haze, Adelaide. You make it impossible."

She made everything impossible. That had been the line for a long time now. Slowly, Adelaide crossed the room and picked up her handbag from the table. As she turned to leave there was a knock at the door.

"Yes?" barked Feodor.

She expected it to be Tyr, but someone else entered the room. A wide, bald man in a chocolate suit. He had dual toned eyes, one green and one brown. They slid towards Adelaide. On the back of his neck he had a third eye, a tattoo. Blue.

Goran was ex-Home Guard. Some of the Guard had been conscripted, in the early days, but Goran had volunteered. He was occasionally referred to as her father's bodyguard, but it was unspoken knowledge that his job extended beyond protection. The twins had always been scared of him; she was not sure if it was the clothes that did not quite conceal his gun, or the way such a robust man managed to make himself into a shadow, appearing and disappearing seemingly as he chose.

Goran stood inside the door, his hands hidden behind his back.

"Good afternoon, Miss Rechnov," he said. Some of the warmth seemed to leave the air.

"Hello," she muttered. She glanced at her father. "Thanks for the drink." Already her voice was retracting, back from the Rechnovs and their mire of lies, slowly back into what she had made herself. Another breath and she was there.

"Now don't trouble yourself," said Adelaide Mystik. "I'll see myself out."

Goran smiled. Whatever he had to say to Feodor was said after the door closed.

"Did you get what you wanted?" Tyr asked. Adelaide stopped.

"If I didn't, would you get it for me, Tyr?"

He pretended to think about this. "Probably not," he said, with a slow smile that took in more of her than was warranted.

"Then what use are you to me?" she said haughtily.

They were close again, inches, maybe centimetres between them. She ran her gaze over what was offered; the honeyed hair, the aquiline features. His face was highlighted by two days stubble and a darkness under the eyes, both of which were engineered—the one with a carefully applied razor, the other through his milaine habit. In the curve of his lips were tiny lines. Each containing a memory of all the places his mouth had grazed her body. Bruised her, sometimes. His hand drifted down to her hip, connected, pushed her hard against the door. Almost enough to knock it ajar.

"Some use," he said. "Apparently."

"No more than any other lover," she said, and this time she thrust past him with a force that was intentionally violent.

6 | VIKRAM

There were no delays on the return journey, but the waterbus paused before crossing the checkpoint, bobbing patiently in a swell. Vikram heard the music first, then the roar of the engine. A patrol boat streaked down the waterway towards them and he averted his eyes. The patrol boat bombed with music. Within its beat he heard the sound of laughter, present and past. He shut his ears against it. The boat flashed past. Its noise faded. The skadi would be joyriding up and down the border all night.

When the waterbus crossed the lane into the west, the squalor struck Vikram with something akin to surprise. Graffiti looked stark and lewd on structures that must once have shone. The clamour of traffic was phenomenal: Boat horns, collisions, gulls screeching, yells of abuse. Even the sea smelled saltier. For a few seconds his head swam with sensory overload and then it was normal once more.

In normalcy he saw, stretching out like the sea itself, the dreary march of the days ahead. Each washing over him as relentless as the currents. He saw how every day would be a new fight; to keep free of the gangs, the manta wars and the insurgent games; to find food enough to survive the winter and clothes to keep from freezing. He saw the riots that would come as surely as would the storms. He saw friends beaten by the skadi. The tank towed back to the border packed with swollen corpses. He saw the winter freeze ravaging the old, children hardened into crime until they wore unkindness as a resin on their skin. He saw the slow thick bleed of anger. He saw that it would take him apart, bit by bit, until he was an alien even to himself.

The outline of the invitation was sharp in his pocket. They were leaving the City behind. There was no sign of the woman who had been detained earlier.

The air seemed to quake. When he looked back, a twelve-year-old Mikkeli was perched on top of the border net. She weighed less than a tuft of pine and her voice was a fingertip brushing bark.

"Truth is, Vik, I come back here a lot," she said. "All the time. Just like you used to, over and over and over again."

She stuck her ankles through the mesh and hung upside-down, pulling faces.

About fifty metres away, the brown curve of a human arm broke the water. As the waterbus grew closer, the hump of the body was discernible under the wash of the waves. It had long been stripped of clothes. Not far from the body, a seagull rested, wings furled. It eyed the corpse speculatively. Each time the sea brought the bird closer, it uttered a squawk, as though fearful the dead thing might suddenly spring to life; a cheap trick for a hungry gull.

Just over a week ago, whilst the gas dispersed through the western crowd, the skadi had drained the execution tank. They dragged out Eirik's body by his feet and stuffed it into a plastic sack. Then they took the body away.

Vikram watched the seagull coasting on the waves. As though sensing his surveillance, the bird cocked its head and seemed to look directly at him. He would have ignored the look, except that many gulls were the carriers of dead souls, the souls of sailors and sea folk. They were all sea people in this city, and he felt in that moment the shiver of a connection across the gulf. Were the dead reprimanding him now?

He thought of Linus's feathered coat, wondered how it felt to keep the birds so close, and if they minded. The gull's head swivelled. Its beak dipped, pecking at its own feathers. It was still a bird, and it had to eat. A wave moved it within a metre of the corpse. The beak snapped up. Vikram turned away, unwilling to see the moment where it conquered its fear.

7 | ADELAIDE

Adelaide chose a secluded spot off the main pathway. She sat on the end of a stone bench, careful not to disturb a dozing Admiral. As she settled in, the butterflies swarmed about her, their minute feet brushing against her arm. Light poured from the glass dome of the roof and filtered through the tropical foliage.

Her contact was due on the hour. She waited, moisture collecting on her skin from the hot, damp air. The farm was quiet today, but there were always a few wandering visitors. A man in lightly tinted glasses was walking down the path towards her. Adelaide checked her watch. A minute before eleven and no one else was nearby.

The man was Patagonian, his hair substantially flecked with grey. Dressed in a casual shirt and well-tailored trousers, he looked like a family man, respectable, with a professional occupation—perhaps a doctor or an engineer, out for a stroll on his day off. It was possible, Adelaide mused, that he really did have a wife and children—then she put the idea aside. The line of work must be too obscure.

The investigator sat at the other end of the bench without exchanging a glance. He took out a Surfboard. For a minute or so, she heard only the sounds of his fingertips manipulating the screen. Palm leaves rustled; a little way away, a stream trickled over veined pebbles.

"Ms Mystik, I presume." His gaze was fixed on the Surfboard. His lips barely moved.

"Yes."

"You can refer to me as Lao." He took off his glasses and polished them on a square silk cloth. "A favourite place of yours, this?"

"My grandmother used to bring us here as children."

"Did Axel come here often also?"

"Not lately."

Lao focused on his screen.

"Your brother is not in the hospitals."

She followed Lao's lead, pretending to examine the butterfly that had alighted on her wrist. Its underside was tricoloured, a striking pattern of red, white and black. Red Pierrot. Adelaide loved them because Second Grandmother had loved them, and for their own ethereal beauty. Perhaps, too, it was their immaculate symmetry that she loved, two sides of the same, like Adelaide and Axel.

"Did you speak to the staff?"

"I have checked admissions records and spoken to all of the receptionist staff in the accident and emergency units. None of them recognises the image that you sent."

"I suppose that's good news."

"I also checked the morgues. I should ask you, at this stage, Ms Rechnov—"

"Mystik."

"As you wish. Ms Mystik. I should ask you exactly what your suspicions are regarding your brother's disappearance?"

"At this stage, I should say that I'm not sure."

A small girl in a polka dot frock ran past, followed by the mother at a more sedate pace. Lao waited for them to disappear down the pathway. He gave a little cough.

"Let me be blunt, Ms Mystik. A full-scale search operation has already been mounted. I understand that it cost a substantial proportion of the Council's security budget. The sea has been searched. There have been raids on suspected gang members in the west. The public operation, in short, has been intensive. This leaves us with three possibilities. One, your brother is hiding. Two, he is hidden. Or three, he is dead and it has been engineered that his body will never be found. Do you suspect murder?"

"Murder is a dangerous accusation, Mr Lao." Her voice, surprising her, came out as calm as his.

"A large part of my job is to find lies. My experience of working with high profile cases is that the perpetrators do not like to dirty their hands. If certain acts have been committed, someone—somewhere—will have seen something. They will have been paid, or intimidated, to keep quiet. You need to find out if your family are lying."

"They are lying. At least, my father is lying. I asked him for the keys to Axel's penthouse. He told me they have all been handed over to Hanif."

"And you have proof that this is untrue?"

"I know my family, Mr Lao. We have more sets of keys than we own greenhouse shares. My father would never have relinquished access so easily, which means he is lying."

Lao nodded. "Tell me about your brother. His state of mind."

Adelaide stared at a flower with large, velvety petals, twined about the trunk of a lemon tree.

"I'm sure you've read more than you need to know."

"I prefer to hear from the client directly. Please try to be as objective as possible."

"Very well. My brother—Axel—he's not himself. That is—he's ill, but the doctors can't agree on a diagnosis. Some days he's perfectly lucid, they say. Other days…" She watched an insect crawl inside the flower head. "He can be paranoid. Delusional."

"He is unpredictable?"

"Yes."

"Is he violent?"

She hesitated. "No."

Lao had finished polishing his glasses. He put them back on. "You don't have to be defensive, Ms Mystik. I am not here to judge character. I just need the facts. If your brother is the type to become embroiled in an argument, for example, that might have a bearing on the case."

Adelaide let out a shaky breath.

"He's never intentionally violent," she said. "Not to people. But he sees things. He thinks he sees horses. And—hears them."

"He hears them talking?"

"I don't know." She didn't want to discuss the horses. She wished she hadn't mentioned them.

Lao tapped his Surfboard. He was waiting.

"Sometimes his behaviour is compulsive," she allowed.

"Such as?"

"He does things—like—I don't know. Once he told me to come to his boat and he had this basket full of white cloths. He said we had to fix them to the towers. We went all through the quarter, tacking up these stupid white cloths. It started raining but he wouldn't let us stop. He said it had to be done that day. He was adamant."

She remembered the glitter in Axel's eyes, the puzzled expressions of those they passed.

"He's not well," she repeated.

"What about habits? Routines?"

She shook her head.

"Superstitions? Does he visit Tellers?"

"Not any more. He's always been dismissive of them."

"What about his regular contacts?"

"Very few. In the last few months he's hardly left the penthouse. There's myself, the cleaner, and a girl that does his shopping. But he has been known to wander, you see. Sometimes he appears in my flat—he has my key. But he might have visited anyone."

"And the last time you saw him?"

She thought of that quiet figure waiting in her apartment.

"Nothing remarkable."

Behind their glasses Lao's eyes flicked about, scanning the leafy pathways where the butterflies spun in the artificial light.

"Are there any other conflicts within the family? Tensions? Grudges?"

"There are conflicts in every family," she said, although she did not know that this was true, having had little enough exposure to other families. Her own set, the Haze, was mostly composed of those who had spurned their families, like herself. Lao gave her a sharp glance, as though he knew this, though he couldn't, of course. She collected her thoughts.

"Feodor—my father—and Linus—they've had their differences. But only over political agendas. They're all in league when it comes to family status and loyalty. Myself and Axel are estranged from the rest—not that it makes a difference to Axel these days."

"But your family continue to bankroll you." The investigator's tone was bland. She mirrored it.

"Yes. Under the condition that I attend public functions like the one

last week. Call me frivolous, Mr Lao. I daresay I am. But I like my lifestyle
and I know when to compromise."

"Your mother? I've heard it said she's an intelligent woman."

"She is. And completely allied with my father."

"And your oldest brother—Dmitri?"

"Similarly. His fiancée is proof enough of that."

"What are the Rechnovs' relationships with the other venerated families—the Dumays and the Ngozis?"

"We didn't all play together as children at midsummer, if that's what
you mean. The families are politically aligned but there are no strong
personal ties. The Dumays keep themselves to themselves since the assassinations. My grandfather was very close to the other elders, Celine
Dumay and Emeke Ngozi, but since they died the links have been purely
strategic. Forgive me, Mr Lao, but surely this is information you can
acquire equally well elsewhere? I try to spend as little time as possible
thinking about my family."

"As I said, I prefer to speak to the source. And if we are to succeed,
Ms Mystik, you may have to devote a little more time than you are accustomed to thinking about your relations." Lao put his Surfboard away.
"I suggest that we proceed as follows. As the hospitals have yielded no
leads, I will commence with further enquiries into those who last saw
your brother."

"Sanjay Hanif has done the same."

"Hanif will not be paying them. I don't doubt his ability as a detective,
Ms Mystik, but results are always better with a little financial encourage-
ment."

She gave a half smile. "That is why I employed you. You will, naturally,
receive a bonus payment in the event of a successful conclusion."

"And what do you class as a successful conclusion?"

"Finding my brother. Alive."

"Then I hope I shall locate him speedily." He rose. "I'll be in touch."

/ / /

The bath rose out of the black tiles like an island, round and white. Adelaide dipped her fingers into the searing water, then plunged both feet

in and stood, gasping. Tropical scents rose with the steam. Breathing in slowly, she lowered herself into the bath until she was submerged to her neck.

She loved her monochrome bathroom. Like her bedroom, it faced east. Her apartment was on the very edge of the city and in daylight, the view from the bathroom was the wilderness beyond Osiris; endless sea merging into endless sky. It was evening now. The window-wall was darkened and held only the room's reflection.

After a few minutes she leaned over and flicked the jacuzzi setting. She shifted to rest directly over a stream. The bubbles rippled up around her thighs and between her legs. She let her head fall back, sinking into daydreams. The water sloshed gently. She might not need company, but everyone needed physicality. Denying that urge was as foolish as believing there was life outside Osiris: it demonstrated only a basic disregard for fact.

Her hand drifted down, lazily, absently, and her breath snagged. It was not really her touch, it was Tyr's. Their liaison had spanned some five years, but the forbidden meetings, restricted by time and place, still had an airless excitement. Sometimes she felt as though he was stitched into the fabric of her body, her responses a preordained thing. But nothing more than sex would ever lie between them. They both took other lovers; that way they averted suspicion.

The last time it had been at the theatre. With only a red curtain and the distraction of the play to cover them, he had kissed her mouth, her neck, the border of her backless dress. Her fingers lingered on the same spots. She felt every place his tongue had touched tingling again, as though the hot, scented jacuzzi tide had the potency of renewal.

In public, they used the studied banter of two rivals. Tyr worked for her father, and Adelaide hated him, so it was not a hard script for either of them to enact. She enjoyed their coded battles. But she was wary too, of the power folded into the layered phrases, the potential each of them held as a wrecker of the other's life. Tyr would be in attendance at the Rose Night, which Adelaide traditionally held on the second Thursday of February. Her mind straddled the various possibilities of a rendezvous. Which stage in the evening might she slip away. Where they could fuck.

She slid down into the bath, out of the bubble stream. With the loss of sensation she felt her mind pulling back. She closed her eyes and remembered the theatre; the audience hushed, the sumptuous velvet of the curtain, the frisson when they kissed. She wanted the moment back. It was too late; her mind was roving now, tomorrow morning already panning out. A series of tasks. She needed to order the rose stock. In the afternoon she had a tasting session with the owner of Narwhal, who was devising the cocktail recipes.

The invitations for Rose Night had just been sent out. She imagined the squeals of delight from those receiving them. Adelaide's guest list was the most envied publication in fourth gen Osiris. To have your name on the list was a statement: it linked the owner with dynamism and charisma, with Adelaide. In the early days, the era of the Double-A Parties, the twins had done the list together. Now it was just Adelaide.

The bath was beginning to cool. Not quite ready to depart, she leaned over and unleashed a gush of water from the taps. The hot current engulfed her feet before it bled into the rest of the pool and the temperature evened out into a pleasant shawl. Adelaide scooped up a handful of foam and held it to her face, listening to the bubbles popping against her skin.

She mulled over the meeting with Lao. The things he'd said. The things he'd implied.

Could she trust the investigator? Lao had no reason to lie to her, unlike her father. She could not escape the issue of the keys. Why would Feodor deny her access? Regardless of the press attached to Axel's disappearance, it was hardly beyond his capabilities to find some way of sneaking her into the penthouse. No, she decided. There was more to it than public appearances. There were things he wasn't telling her.

Adelaide had long thought her father capable of anything. But thinking a thing was not necessarily the same as believing it. Her mind skidded down the turbulent paths of suspicion. She must force herself to examine all angles. Lao had said there were three possibilities: Axel was hidden, in hiding, or dead. It was hard to imagine who would benefit from Axel's death—if he had been killed for political reasons, the assassins would have brandished his body in public. Axel had long been a source of embarrassment to the Rechnovs, but murder—she let out a shaky breath—she could not bring herself to believe that they would murder her twin. Incarceration was more the family style. Secrets and lies. They could have locked him up in some anonymous Rechnov apartment.

Or he could be hiding. Axel was—she had to be honest with herself—not in a clear state mind.

If only she could get into the penthouse. There were no friends or confidantes to whom Axel might have entrusted a spare set of keys. Even in the old days, his relationships were superficial. He had never seemed to need people, except for Adelaide. Before.

She slid further under the bathwater, until her hair swilled around her shoulders and only her face remained above. It felt cold and exposed. She remembered Axel, hiding in a similar fashion under the bedclothes, because he was afraid of the storms. Adelaide was afraid of birds. She'd mocked her twin, they'd mocked one another, until their grandfather came to Axel's rescue. Tell us a story, she'd begged. Tell us about the storms. And through the wind and the rain outside they listened to the slow resonant timbre of his voice as he told them about the year of the Great Storm, and how the refugees came to Osiris to escape the doomed, poisoned lands, from Patagonia, from Afrika, from India and Zeeland, even from the far flung Boreal States in the north, and how disease flew through the city like a dragon so they had to stay in the west, in quarantine. What then, she asked, what then? And he said, after the Great Storm came the Great Silence. We lost contact with the world. The people who left the City never came back. They were lost.

All of them? Asked Axel.

All of them.

When Adelaide got out of the bath it was dark. The water swilled away in languid spirals. She thought of the tank being drained the day Eirik 9968 was executed and she closed the door on the bathroom so as not to hear the noise.

She walked barefoot around the window-walls of her apartment, switching on lights, remembering something funny Second Grandmother said once about her old land-house having square rooms. *How boring*, said Adelaide. *How functional*, said Second Grandmother.

Adelaide was seized with a sudden longing to hear Second Grandmother speaking. She called on her o'musaique and selected an excerpt at random from the transcripts. The machine glowed pale violet and Second Grandmother's light, softly accented voice filled the room.

We knew, that day, that the end of the world had come. We read it in the sands and in one another's eyes. The Neon Age (as they used to call it on the beam, when I was a girl) was truly over.

Adelaide sat on the edge of her futon. Her skin was still damp under her kimono and between her toes. On the glass-topped table before her was a ceramic bowl with her keys in it, and a silver pot. Adelaide drew the pot towards her, frowning as she noticed signs of tarnish on the lid. She used a corner of her kimono to polish the metal.

And that's when we got on the boats. I had nothing with me. No belongings and no people. My family were dead. I was leaving behind fire and ash. As we crowded onto the boat, the beach was ablaze. I remember the sky—yellow, like malarial eyes. There were deaths. There were so many deaths. Some bodies had been desecrated, others were still fresh and ripe with blood. Not just through sickness, there were killings too, of course. I had spent much of the last two years in hiding. Even now I will not speak of those things.

I was terrified of the ocean. I knew that the sea sunk many more boats than the precious few it allowed to pass. I might be hurled from the boat and drown. I would be alone, in the vastest plain on Earth—the saltwater. But my terror of land and all it contained was even greater—so I fled, as we all did, with death in the surf beside us.

I did not imagine what I would find.

There was a slight cough, and Second Grandmother said, *Autumn seventy-two, end of transcript fourteen.*

A shadow made Adelaide glance up; a night bird sweeping past the window-wall. She tensed, hunched over, until it had passed. Even then she could feel its presence, as though those sharp avian eyes were fixed upon her, watching.

She thought of Second Grandmother, speaking carefully into a microphone. She thought of Axel standing at the glass, his back to her, watching space. He always had questions, her twin, so many questions, could never accept that some things just were. His later visitations might have spooked anyone else, but Adelaide had grown used to the intrusion. She came to expect it. The person that came into her apartment and stared out of windows was not really her brother. They shared the same constellation of freckles, and they had the same calibre voice, but there the resemblance ended.

It was only since he disappeared that she had felt the tug again. Before, there was the gap. What had been and what now was. As though while he was physically present, she could ignore the strange thing that had happened to him. But now he was gone, the old connection had ignited once more. Its flame was tiny. She had to shield it in both hands. Blowing gently upon it, watching the baby fires curl and evolve into dragon shapes, that suspicion, as fragile and nebulous as a bubble, hardened into certainty. Axel was alive. He might have been taken, hidden, locked away—but she was certain her twin was alive.

She just had to find him.

A distant whirr of machinery caused her to glance up at the ceiling. The three floors above her apartment were home to a private scientific facility that housed an array of sensors and telescopes trained on the stars. Sometimes she heard noises in the night. Occasionally, she caught a glimpse of someone passing in the lift, coming down from, or travelling up to the final floors.

The noise stopped. The apartment was silent once more. Adelaide gave the silver pot a final wipe. From it she took a pinch of salt, and threw it at the window to ward off the dead. Each night, out by the ring-net, the ghosts gathered in their millions, keeping silent vigil over the city.

But not you Axel, she thought. *Not you.*

PART TWO

8 | VIKRAM

The recruiting officer gave Vikram's and Nils's papers a fleeting glance. "Sign here."

His eyes never left Vikram's hands as he wrote his latest pseudonym, then passed the list to Nils to do the same. When they had both signed the man pulled the piece of paper back, smearing the ink.

Their new employer typed a few words, presumably their names, into the ancient Neptune chained to the desk. "What's that, an h? You dogs illiterate or what?"

Both men looked steadfastly at the mouldering wall behind the desk. Strips of plaster were peeling away. The wall might have been a colour once, although what hue it was impossible to tell. Now it looked like a jigsaw of damp clouds. Vikram continued to stare at it, finding shapes, patterns, anything to distract him from the dismal tap-tap-tap into the Neptune. He wondered how many other westerners had passed through here before them, standing on the same worn floor, staring at the same square foot of wall.

The officer stamped two fifteen-day passes to the City and grudgingly handed them over.

"Eight o'clock start. Be early." He waved them out of the door. "Next!"

"Parasite," muttered Nils.

At eight o'clock, when Vikram began work, the mist swaddled the world in milky white. From the moment he abseiled from the magnetized scaffolding to the morning's site, he could see only his own limbs and the indistinct figure of Nils, a few feet away. When the fog lingered longer than it should, Vikram was jolted by fear that he was lost or had been left behind. The city had vanished; there was only this smooth glassy surface, on which he must crawl forever, with nothing but the tap and scrape of his tools for company. Then his nerves tingled. He looked to left or right and felt, rather than saw, another man passing up or down the scraper.

There were twelve of them on the project, all westerners apart from the foreman. They were repairing storm damage in the southern quarter. The cold gnawed through Vikram's two scarves and his muffler; the scaffolding felt flimsy and unsafe, but it was paid work and the pay was in instant credit. At the end of each day their chips were topped up, no questions asked. He could use the credit to buy City goods, or exchange them for the western *peng* notes which continued to prove lucrative for the ex-skad profiteers who had invented them. He thought what a joy it was to choose something and buy it without haggling. Maybe he'd get a bag of oranges.

Once, through the window-wall, he caught the curious eyes of a child on the other side. Her fingers were gripped firmly in an adult hand, a father, perhaps, bringing his daughter into the office for a day. When she turned the other way, Vikram saw a red bow in her hair and he thought of the invitation to the Rose Night, discarded in a corner of his room. Westerners with workpasses were allowed to spend their evenings in the City, but few of them did. The one time Vikram had gone to a City bar he'd been stared at all night.

On the third afternoon, six of them were on a break for lunch, wedged in a row on the scaffolding. The men drank hot soup and rubbed their hands to revive the circulation. Vikram and Nils checked each other's reactions. Vikram held up his hand. Beneath the glove the webbed skin was already cracking; by the end of the week it would be raw.

"How many fingers?"

"Four. No, I'm joking. Three."

"Are you sure?"

"I'm sure," said Nils.

The rest of the group exchanged few words to start with. Vikram had been on similar projects before, and he knew the location was dangerous not only physically but mentally. Everywhere he looked he was confronted with evidence of the divide. This side of town, skyscrapers were softened with sweeps of vertical garden. Window-walls gleamed. As the shuttle pods streaked through glowing tubes, it was impossible not to imagine where they were going, all those sated stomachs in the surrounding towers, glutting on electricity.

It was only a few days, but already his visit to the marble Chambers seemed like months ago.

The lunch break was almost over. The soup had gone, and someone passed around a flask of steaming coral tea laced with raqua. Vikram took a grateful sip. The drink flooded his throat and warmed the pit of his belly. He handed the flask along to Nils.

"Looks like it's going to rain," said the man who had brought the tea. There was no direct response to this. It had been threatening to rain for the past three hours. Then another man said he had heard if you could find full-time work in the southern quarter, they would find you a room, or at least put you on the waiting list for one.

Nils snorted. "Sorry, but that's bullshit. They'll never give you a room, Stefan."

"It's worth a try," Stefan answered defiantly.

"Anyway, what would it be, work like this? You wouldn't last a year."

"One year over here might be better than one year in the west. What with people getting restless and all."

There were a few surreptitious glances inside, though the foreman could not hear them through the bufferglass. The man with the flask said, "Keep your noise down."

"Maybe they're right to worry," Nils muttered.

"Why, have you heard anything?"

"Tell you what I heard." Someone else chipped in before Nils could respond. "I heard Juraj is dead."

"Dead?"

"Murdered. Ripped apart, I heard."

"You'd hear anything," Nils retorted. "If Juraj was dead, everyone would know. The rest of his people would be out nailing feet to boats. You heard anything about this Vik?"

"News to me."

The other man shrugged. "Might want to keep it quiet. Might not want the Rochs to know, not with the manta trade."

"The Rochs aren't interested in manta, they're buying up guns," said someone else. "Friend of mine had a pistol. Kept it secret for years—well you don't advertise you've got something like that, do you. So a few weeks ago he's out, has a few too many drinks, and next thing he knows he's handed it over for a few *peng* and a thermal jacket. The buyer was a Roch."

"Well I don't know about the Rochs or Juraj," said Nils. "Been a cold spell though. Getting colder."

Vikram glanced at his friend, but nobody replied, because they all knew what Nils meant. The last riots had been foreshadowed by an unprecedented period of cold weather.

Of course, he thought, whispers like this were always abound. Talk was not a precursor to violence; talk was everywhere. Silence was the sign. Three years ago, it was the silence that had warned Vikram to leave his room carrying a knife. He remembered the sound of quiet. It had rung louder in his ears than thunder.

In the afternoon, Vikram and Nils were stationed on the scaffolding with Stefan and his partner Ilan. Vikram began to talk to Nils about the hearing. He wanted Nils's opinion. They could only just hear one another over the shree of the wind and the conversation was laborious.

"Probably just asked you there to make them feel good about themselves," shouted Nils.

"That's what I figured," Vikram yelled back. "They'll report it and it'll make them look like they're actually doing something. I told you they took my photo?"

"You're probably on their newsreel."

"Stars only knows."

"So what are you going to do now?"

"Don't know. They'll never let me inside that place again. Honestly, Nils, I've never seen anything like it. This huge, stone circle, like an acrobat's ring, you know? And all of them sitting around—"

"Like circus clowns."

"Yeah."

"There's a fire-eating troop this weekend down at Market Circle. Drake reckons she knows one of the guys."

In spite of the wind noise and the delay in hearing, Vikram felt as though the change in subject had been deliberate. But maybe it was just the wind.

"Drake reckons she knows everyone," he shouted. His throat was growing hoarse.

"Probably does. You in?"

"Long as I don't get sling-shot."

"Yeah, those kids are little shits."

A scream cut them off abruptly.

"What the hell—"

The cry came again. Vikram leaned over the edge of the scaffolding and saw Stefan dangling, twenty metres below, his mouth gaping in his face. He wasn't wearing an abseiling harness, only a short line, and he couldn't winch himself up.

Stefan's feet scrabbled on the skyscraper wall. Impulse told Vikram to move, but it was impossible to move quickly along the icy structures without risking the same accident and Ilan was closer. Vikram and Nils started to climb anyway, gingerly moving down the scaffolding ladders.

Vikram saw Ilan reaching down to the other man. Their hands were over a metre apart. Ilan began to haul, hand over hand, grunting with the effort. Other men, realizing what had happened, were abseiling back up the tower towards Stefan. Ilan and Stefan's fingers were almost within grasping distance. Their hands strained toward one another.

Something snapped. Stefan's scream sounded for a second, horribly clear above the wind. Then he was gone.

Vikram and Nils, still two levels of scaffolding up, stared at each other in horror. All the colour was leached from Nils's face.

"I cursed him," whispered Nils.

Vikram felt a cold deeper than anything the wind could contrive take root inside of him. "Nils, don't—"

"I said he wouldn't last the year. I did it."

After that, one of the men kicked up a fuss and said they weren't being paid enough to risk their necks. The foreman said Stefan hadn't secured his harness properly and the man who had complained was sacked. Nobody else said a word. They couldn't afford to. The next day at break, there was a distance between Nils and Vikram and the rest of the workers. No more coral tea was passed around, only darting looks of fear. Vikram told himself Nils's words were simply that: words, but guilt had recomposed his friend's features and Vikram was contaminated by it. They never mentioned Stefan again.

The following evening, keen to drink and to forget, they shared a bottle of raqua and talked deep into the night. They discussed Drake's new job on the ice-boat, the girl Nils had decided to stop seeing, possible work gigs, the unpredictable mood of the west. They mused over the things they wanted. Nils's ambition was to own a bathroom. It was going to be lime green with bronze taps and a walk-in shower. And a spa, Nils said, relishing this prospect as he held in a lungful of cigarette smoke. And a mosaic ceiling, he added, exhaling. With a tiger in it.

"I just want somewhere with heating that works," said Vikram. He was leaning against one wall of Nils's room, which like his was little more than a nest of things to keep warm with. Boots kicked off, blankets at his back, his three pairs of socks were steadily thawing. "Think of walking out of the cold into a blaze of warmth. Imagine if you could have a fire."

"You'd never leave," said Nils. "How many rooms would you have?"

"Three would be good."

Nils nodded. "Room for a bed, room for a bath, somewhere to eat. Nice."

Already, Vikram could see Nils creating such an apartment, furnishing it with objects and colours. Vikram wished he had his friend's certainty, the power to envisage the exact thing that he desired. But when he tried to imagine his own version, all he saw was the shadowy forms of unused furniture: a bed never slept in, cupboards with empty shelves. He changed the subject.

"Do you remember the time Keli went over the border with a fake pass?"

Nils roared with laughter, his blue eyes almost disappearing into their crinkles.

"Said she'd been in a shuttle line."

A deck of playing cards littered the space between them. Vikram gathered them together. "I don't believe her, do you?"

"Not a chance."

"Bet she tried to talk her way through, though."

"Well, that's Keli for you. Never gives up beating a dead fish."

They always talked about her like this, as if she was still alive. It was respectful. Vikram passed the pack of cards from hand to hand. Something occurred to him.

"What do they do with their dead in the City?"

"I think they have special bags. Pump them full of air so they float, and send them out to sea and then they burn."

"I heard there's a tower where they burn them. It's called a crematorium."

Nils looked dubious. "How can they join the ghosts if they burn under a roof?"

"Maybe they don't become ghosts. Maybe it's just people from our side."

They both fell silent. Vikram thought of Stefan, and wondered if he had been given the burial rites, or if he had been sent to a crematorium, or if they'd found his body at all. He glanced at his friend and saw the shadow of guilt there, and felt guilty himself for leading Nils into this macabre contemplation. He tried to think of a way to change the subject. But it was too late. The larger shadow was already in the room. Eirik. Eirik's body. What the skadi had done with it. What they hadn't done with it.

When Nils spoke, his voice was quiet. "I saw you and Drake. We agreed we wouldn't act."

"I know. I'm sorry."

"But when I saw you, I thought maybe you were right. We had to do something."

"No, we didn't. It was stupid."

"It was too late for me then. I was too far back."

"Good, or you'd be dead like me and Drake nearly were."

"Then the gas got me."

Vikram thought once more of the invitation. Perhaps if he went to the party, Adelaide Mystik would agree to help, and neither he nor Nils would have to rely on weak harnesses, and the skadi would stop using gas, and Nils could get his lime green bathroom.

The raqua must really be taking effect.

Hammering on the partition next door jerked them both awake. No one replied. More hammering. There was a brief quiet, then the sound of repeated blows as a door was kicked in. A woman screamed.

Vikram and Nils were on their feet, both tensed, each of them with a hand to their knives. Nils put his finger to his lips. Through the thin walls they heard a man shouting and the woman pleading.

"Who lives there?" Vikram's question was soundless.

"Still Ari," Nils mouthed back. "She's got that kid. Her man walked out weeks ago. He was bad news."

They heard the child crying, Ari trying to comfort it, then yelling at the intruder. The yells ceased abruptly.

They ran out into the corridor. Other people were gathered there, shapeless figures in the gloom. Eyes peered from behind doors pushed ajar. The door next to Nils's had been kicked closed. Vikram glanced at his friend. From inside he recognised the bangs and crashes of systematic destruction. He stepped towards the door.

"Don't—" said someone.

"What?"

"It's one of Juraj's men. We don't want trouble round here."

"I don't care who it is," said Nils. "That's my fucking neighbour."

Vikram shouldered the door. It collapsed immediately, swinging open on one hinge. Inside, the intruder had Ari by the hair. The child cringed against the boarded window-wall.

The intruder barely glanced at Vikram.

"Get out."

"Leave her alone."

"She owes Juraj. This isn't your business."

"The man who used to live here owes Juraj." Nils spoke from behind Vikram. "He cleared out six weeks ago. She doesn't have what you want."

"Makes no difference to Juraj," said the man. The knuckles were white where he gripped the woman's hair. His face was obscured by greasy tangles. Vikram couldn't read the man's eyes but he saw the outline of a knife at his belt.

"I heard Juraj was dead," he said evenly. The man stiffened.

"I guess you heard wrong."

Vikram's hand went to his own hip.

"Look, there's no need for this to get ugly."

The man did turn now, assessing Vikram, seeing Nils poised behind him. He gave the woman a last shove against the wall and walked out, kicking the broken door viciously behind him.

Vikram looked around. The room was in chaos. The child watched him with mute, swollen eyes from behind a thick dark fringe. Tear trails had made streaks in a dirty face.

Nils was helping Ari to her feet. A trickle of blood ran down her neck where her head had hit the wall.

"You're hurt," said Nils.

Ari pressed her fingers gingerly to the back of her head, and then her face. A bruise was coming up on her temple. "I've had worse," she said.

Vikram set a table upright. "We'll give you a hand with this."

"I'm alright. Really." As they lingered, unsure, she added, "I just want to sort this out. Please, leave me be."

On the way out Nils pulled the door back into its frame. There were low mutterings from the spectators.

"Think you should stay at mine for a few days?" Vikram asked.

"What's the point? If anyone bothers coming back, it'll take them all of two seconds to find out where you live."

"Alright. Keep an eye out though." Back in Nils's partition, the cards were still on the floor in a neat brick. Through the wall they could hear Ari rearranging the room, dragging things into place.

"What do you want to play?" Nils asked eventually.

"Start you with a hand of piranha."

Nils scooted over the pack. "Juraj and the rest are getting out of hand. Soon they'll be trying to impose tariffs on every quarter in the west."

"If he is alive. More likely than not it's his underlings cashing in before the news is out."

"Makes no difference if he's dead or not. There'll be someone else in his place within the week."

"Won't stop with the gangs though. We'll all get caught up in it." He paused. "What was her boyfriend running?"

"Soft stuff, soap and sugar, at least publicly. But judging by the argument before she kicked him out, that was a cover. Sounded like he was dealing in weapons."

"Through the skadi?"

"How else? The bastards aren't incorruptible."

Vikram shuffled, distributed, reshuffled. As game followed game, the inanimate faces of the cards took on strange personalities. The Jack of

Spades fell into Vikram's hand three times until he began to see its presence as an omen. Signs and portents were everywhere in this city. Some people said the sea itself was a judgement. That the city was cursed for its sins, past and present. And it was easy, when the lower levels were flooded for the fourth time in a month and children drowned in their own beds—it was easy, he thought, to wring your hands and blame the heavens, because nobody else was there to listen to your woes.

"Your deal," said Nils.

"Yeah. Sorry." He shuffled with a snap and cut the deck.

Now there was shouting from upstairs. Human clamour sounded loud to Vikram now; it used to be nothing to his ears. Naala's boat, where he'd grown up, was both a refuge and a morgue. The first winter he could remember, three kids had gone to sleep and in the night they'd died. The others had woken to find them, curled up like shells, a greyish tinge to their hardened skins. After that he was afraid to go to sleep.

He remembered the first night he had spent in a building, feeling sick with stagnancy and wide awake. Through the night he heard the breathing of the other three more distinctly than ever before. Nils's smokers' rasp. Mik's gurgles. Drake's long clear inhalations.

Mikkeli never said what stunt she had pulled to get the room, but Vikram suspected it had to do with the packages she sometimes delivered for a man named Maak. She collected the packages from the shanty towns. She took them to locations whose owners never had names, only yellowed eyes and mouths that liked to argue over previously negotiated bargains. Mikkeli didn't like Vikram coming along. He understood why the first time he saw a man pull a knife on her.

He had a feeling, looking back now, that Mikkeli's packages had probably contained weapons too.

It was shortly after that Vikram began his stints on the illegal fishing boats. Decisions and answers came easily then. He realized, as time went on, that things had degrees. Degrees of hurt and degrees of shame.

The Jack of Spades was in his hand. It was his turn. He had no idea how long he had been lost in contemplation, but Nils said nothing and Vikram suspected his friend was similarly absent tonight. You make your own luck, he thought. He played the Jack. It was a reckless move. He lost the game.

The bottle of raqua was almost dry, and they gathered up the cards for the night. Then, because it was late and he was a little drunk, Vikram asked, "You ever think about getting out of here, Nils?"

"Out of where? Six-fourteen? 'Course I do."

"I meant out of Osiris."

It was a question each of them had posed to the other, a number of times, over the years. The sea got inside your head. Its currents pulled you, this way and that way. That was why you had to keep people around you, at least one—to act as ballast when the tide got too strong. Nils glanced at him. His forehead creased.

"Now that is crazy talk. You want to start fishing again? Not all those boats come back. Dangerous business, fishing."

"Maybe they don't go far enough."

"They're looking for fish, Vik. Anyone who went looking for land got eaten by sharks or drowned. Nothing out there to find."

"They might've ended up on land, for all we know. What if it's out there, what if it's there to find… just waiting for us. Waiting for us to be brave enough."

"And what if it is? What do you think you'd find? Rocks? Sand? You can't eat sand. Can't eat wind, either."

"But you'd know. You'd know."

He had a vision of wind blowing across an empty plateau. Not a creature in sight, just desiccated rock stretching on and on. Why was it so alluring?

"Wouldn't you like to see the land your folks came from?" he asked.

"Vik. I know what it looks like. Everyone knows that whatever land is left, it's toxic. Fire. Corpses. Plague and insects, man. Hell on Earth."

Vikram nodded. He knew, but sometimes he couldn't believe it.

Nils reached across and gave his arm a friendly shake.

"You're drunk."

Vikram couldn't deny it. His limbs felt like cotton wool. Neither he nor Nils could afford to build up a tolerance to alcohol. Vikram reached into his pocket and pulled out the invitation.

"What's that?" Nils asked. Vikram passed him the card. The Rose Night was two days away, he couldn't keep it to himself any longer.

Nils looked at the card. He grinned.

"Where did you get this?"

"Linus Rechnov."

"That guy you followed?"

"He's Adelaide Mystik's brother, isn't he. Well, estranged brother. The other one's most likely dead, if you believe what the krill say."

"The twin was a nutter. Family probably did away with him. Why would Adelaide Mystik's brother give you an invitation to some random party?"

"He said I needed a patron."

Spoken out loud, it sounded even sillier than it had in Vikram's head. Nils looked suitably dubious.

"It was you that followed him, right? So you caught him unawares. He probably thought you were out to assassinate him. He didn't know what to do, so he's palmed you off on his sister."

Vikram shook his head. "No. It wasn't like that. He's—" He sought for a way to describe Linus Rechnov, but suitable words eluded him. "He's too smart," he concluded lamely.

"Smart? He's a Citizen. Defective at birth."

"Fine. So what if I go? And what if it's a trick? Or a weird joke, I don't know. At the time I thought he sounded genuine, but now…"

"No, you're right. Citizens have reasons for everything. Still." Nils turned the card over in his hands. He scratched the watermark with one nail. "It's one hell of an opportunity."

"To get myself chucked in jail?"

"More to spy," said Nils. "Maybe this Linus guy, whether he realizes it or not, has a point. If we can't beat them with guns and letters don't get through, try something else. Try infiltration."

"I'm not sure that's what he meant either," said Vikram.

"What does it matter? Go along, have a laugh. Eirik would love it." Nils fell silent for a moment, but quickly recovered. "If you're lucky, you'll get to meet the mad bad Adelaide herself. Well worth a spell in jail."

Vikram raised his eyebrows. Nils shrugged.

"Worth a day in jail?"

"Clearly you've never been underwater," Vikram said dryly. Nils said nothing in response. He could not. The cell, with its green light and clogged porthole, was one memory they did not share. Time in a cell had made Vikram calm, dangerously calm. He had beaten down his anger so successfully that it had become an alien thing to him, unknown, and now unpredictable.

As the last few weeks had demonstrated. Perhaps, he thought, it was a warning. That for every hurdle put before him, there would always be a greater one behind it. At that moment, he knew that he'd always intended to go to Adelaide Mystik's party.

9 | ADELAIDE

"So tell me, Adie. Why exactly did you want to meet here?"

Tyr had to stoop to see into the mirror. He twitched the points of his collar carefully into shape, frowning slightly as he did so.

"Bit too dirty for you, is it?"

"I would have thought it was filthy by your standards."

Tyr's hair was sticking up in spikes. He scooped some water from the sink and smoothed it back. Each gesture made him a fraction more her father's man. Adelaide hated the transformation. She stretched out languidly on the bed, aware that he could see her in the mirror.

"What a peculiar idea you have about me, Tyr. Seeing as you won't come to my apartment—"

"Because it's too much of a risk—"

"And as I can't come to yours—"

"Similarly. Which is why we usually meet in dark bars or the back rooms of reasonably classy clubs, not dingy hotel bedrooms."

"Are you complaining?"

He scratched distractedly at a bit of stubble. "Just commenting. Because I know the way your mind works."

Adelaide offered him a brilliant smile.

"And that confirms it," he said dryly.

"Alright," she allowed. "We're here because I have it on good authority that Sanjay Hanif's office is across the water."

She didn't tell Tyr that she had grown impatient waiting for results, legitimately or via Lao. Nor that she had been calling Hanif's office persistently for the last week. Each time she had met with the decided tones of Hanif's secretary, and each time the secretary refused to tell her where the offices were located. Adelaide's assurances of discretion had been unpersuasive, so she had recorded their last conversation and persuaded an acquaintance to trace it. The voiceprint located Hanif in a suite of low key, thirty-ninth floor offices in the industrial northern quarter, surrounded by greenhouses and factories, and directly opposite the Anemone Hotel.

She didn't tell Tyr that she had already walked across the bridge four floors above and back down the stairwell of the scraper on the other side, gone to the floor above Hanif's, worked out where his offices were, stood there imagining the discussions going on below, almost convinced, once, that she heard the burr of Hanif's voice. She knew it would sound ridiculous. She didn't know how to explain that she could not stay away; she had to do something, even if something was nothing.

Tyr went to the window, twitched aside the curtain, and looked across at the tower opposite.

"Shit."

"Don't fret. They have no idea I've found them."

He let the curtain fall and turned back to look at the room with new eyes. She saw him register the supplies of Coralade and poppy-head crunches stacked on the bureau. A pair of Haakan binoculars propped on a chair. She half expected him to be angry. She had already prepared her response, but she saw only worry in his face.

"Adie, how is this helping? What can you possibly learn from sitting here watching them?"

"I don't know yet. That's why I'm here."

Tyr sat on the edge of the bed. "Look. Everyone says Sanjay Hanif is very good at what he does. And equally as important, he isn't corrupt. You have to trust him to do his work."

"Tyr, I just want to know what he's doing. I want to help. I'm the only one who believes Axel is alive, I know that. I can see it in your faces. Even you. But you're wrong, you're all wrong. Because I'd know if he was dead." She pressed a hand between her ribs. "I'd feel it—here. You couldn't understand unless you had a twin."

Tyr's hand came to rest, warm, on her ankle. She took his wrist.

"Maybe you're right," he said. "But Hanif can't operate on a hunch."

"Unlike Tellers, I suppose."

"Unlike Tellers."

"And why should Hanif get access to the penthouse? What right does he have to go through Axel's things? He doesn't know Axel. I hate the idea of them going in there, touching things, when they haven't even spoken to me—to anyone..."

"You think they'll judge him."

"They won't understand him."

"Can you blame them? Adie, he threw you out of your own apartment."

"He didn't know what he was doing."

"Because he was ill." She glared at him until he corrected himself. "Is ill. Alright, let's say he's alive. What's happened to him? Where do you think he is?"

"Maybe something scared him, maybe he's gone into hiding. What if someone kidnapped him?"

"What for? There'd have been a ransom demand by now."

"They might be playing a long game."

"They couldn't get in. The security on that tower is impenetrable to outsiders."

Outsiders, yes, she thought. But not to someone who knew him. Or to an aerialist.

"What if they came in through the balcony? Abseiled, used a glider?"

"Now you're in animé territory."

"Am I?"

Tyr put his head in his hands. "I don't know. But you'll drive yourself mad wondering. You've gone through enough over Axel already, Adie, I don't want to see you hurt any more."

She placed her hands on his shoulders, massaging gently.

"Has Feodor said anything about the investigation?"

"You know I'd tell you if he had."

"You could ask how it's going."

"It's better if he confides in me. Trust me, I know your father well enough by now."

She knew they were both thinking about the day she had come to the offices. The strange middle ground that Tyr walked between her and her father. She was suddenly afraid that the day might come when he had to choose, or when she had to choose. The truth was that all liaisons were a transaction at heart. With every intimacy gained, the ground was paved for what could be lost.

She leaned forward and pressed her lips to his temple. "You don't have to go."

"I wish I didn't."

His tone was sombre and there was something in his expression that she wasn't sure she liked. She took his face in her hand and turned it towards her, forcing him to meet her eyes. Her tone when she spoke was playful.

"Don't say you're feeling sorry for me, Tyr."

He responded in kind.

"How could I? You're a spoiled, selfish—shall I go on?" Adelaide threw a pillow at him. "—ruthless, soulless, grouchy bitch."

"Grouchy?"

"Maybe not grouchy. But the rest."

"Don't forget it."

Tyr brushed a strand of hair from her face.

"Believe me," he said. "I won't. Now I really have to go."

After the door closed Adelaide listened to his footsteps fading down the corridor outside. Her bare legs felt cold. The hotel's heating probably hadn't been serviced in years. Adelaide pulled on her trousers, tucking in the candy-striped shirt and cinching the belt tight. She didn't trust the shower. Besides, she enjoyed the feeling that they had marked one another; that each carried the other's imprint. She liked the feeling of secrecy as she went back into the public world, on the shuttle lines, into the shops, the restaurants, wearing Tyr's sweat on her skin.

She opened the curtains and picked up the binoculars once more. The Sobek Electronics logo blinked innocently from the top of the adjacent factory. Across the waterway, a blonde woman sat at a desk with a headset. Adelaide tried to decipher the glowing display on a large notice board behind her, but the zoom function on the binoculars was not quite powerful enough. She caught a brief glimpse of Sanjay Hanif. He was wearing black again. What were they discussing in there? Shouldn't Hanif be out searching for Axel?

It had been fun, tracking down Hanif's office. Fun inviting Tyr over.

But Adelaide was angry with herself. Here she was acting as if her twin's disappearance was some kind of game, a game that he himself had instigated. But it couldn't be. The Axel who had disappeared was not the Axel she had lost. That man—that boy—was long gone. All she could hope to recover was his shadow.

She had to start thinking like Axel. What would her twin do? What had been going through his head in those last few weeks? If he had run away, then why?

The Rose Night was two days away. She would give Lao another week. If he had no further information, he would have to help her get into the penthouse. There, she would find clues that Sanjay Hanif and his secretary had no chance of deciphering. After all, Adelaide knew that apartment better than anybody. She used to live there.

10 ¦ VIKRAM

The doorman's eyes flicked from the invitation's inscription, to Vikram's face, to his clothes and his shoes. He turned over the card and held it up to the light, examining the watermark. At last he straightened, and opened the door. A wave of music spilled out.

"Welcome to the Red Rooms, sir," said the doorman.

"Thank you."

He'd passed. Hoping his relief did not show, Vikram stepped inside and found himself in a hallway lined with mirrors and roses. At the end on the right was an archway. The music pulsed from the other side of it, the floor thrummed beneath his feet. Without pausing to check his reflection or allow himself second thoughts, Vikram walked through.

He was assailed by red, smoke, bodies and chatter. There were more flowers than he had ever seen in his life, all of them roses, all of them perfectly crimson. They were everywhere. On the walls, hanging from the ceilings, twined around furniture and plants and in sprays protruding from heads and corsages. Their scent infused the air, a light but sinuous perfume. The women's costumes were also red, and so, he realized, was all the decor. Behind the people there were plush red backless sofas, soft red rugs, red meshing screens.

Adelaide Mystik's legendary set, the Haze, were busy with drinks and cigarettes, their lips with newly chartered gossip. The women looked like an exotic breed of bird, encased in beaded corsets, flame-coloured feather skirts, shimmering stockings and jewelled sandals. Plumes erupted from their heads, making them taller than most of the men, who were a sleek contrast in black and white. Heads swivelled; they were continually looking over each other's shoulders to check on new arrivals. Vikram edged to a corner.

Already he could feel sweat on the back of his neck. The room was vast but it was intensely, tropically hot. There were no air vents open. Near the entrance end, several people clustered around a large piano, their glasses resting upon its shiny black lid. At the other end was a mezzanine and beyond the mezzanine he could see an open doorway, where the apartment opened into other rooms. The prospect of so much space for one person was incredible.

"Olga! Darling! Been to Ilse's yet?"

"On Tuesday, sweetie."

"The opening was so charming, very select."

"Oh? I was at the Weedy Seahorse."

"That little nook Mino found? How is she? Still dallying with the Ngozi boy? Naughty."

He listened a little longer but it was all names; who had done this, who had been there, who had taken that new lover. Vikram recognized faces he had only ever seen on display boards. There was the acrobat Lilja Aapo, chatting to the guy who had won the biking championship. A girl with blue hair whispered to another girl wearing a tiara of thin blossom branches that she'd found messages on Jokum's Neptune. Of course she wasn't meant to be looking, but she was sure he was seeing another mistress and did Idunn think she should confront him? Idunn didn't.

Adelaide Mystik was nowhere to be seen.

For a few minutes he played the old game: guessing which Old World land each guest was descended from, imagining the landscapes where their ancestors had lived. He wondered if Citizens even cared about those places, or if it no longer mattered to them.

There was a relentless, kinetic energy about the party. Near the mezzanine, people were dancing. A DJ was up there. Vikram imagined these people would die rather than allow silence to fall between them. He lit a cigarette, because everyone else was, and almost ashed in a glass bowl before he realized there were petals and a ladle in it. A few glasses with the dredges of liquid were stacked beside. He looked about for a new one.

A red jacketed man appeared, refilled the bowl with a pale pink liquid, replaced the used glasses with clean ones, and retreated.

"Thanks—"

The man had already gone. Vikram took a glass and ladled himself a drink. It was strong and very sweet. Heady too, or maybe that was the rose perfume, twining about his senses.

Now armed with the two essential accessories for the party, he made his way across the room. He knew that it was important to look purposeful. All of these people were actors; they might be Citizens, but Citizens had things to hide too. He found himself looking out for cats, remembering Mikkeli's old tales about the City. She would have gone crazy to see this.

Under the mezzanine, a couple were entwined upon a sofa. The woman's eyes met his over the man's shoulder, thick lashed, boldly inviting. Imperceptibly, she patted the seat. Vikram moved on.

The next room was much smaller. A table made out of shiny dark wood was in the centre, and along the wall there were shelves lined with paper books and scale mosaics. At the table, a man shook out a line of milaine.

"Hello." He nodded easily to Vikram. His pupils were dilated.

"Hi."

The man cut the line with an invitation card identical to Vikram's.

There were two doors leading out of this room. Vikram tried the first. It was a bathroom. The bath was full of ice and bottles. Vikram retreated.

The man lifted his head, sniffing. "There's another bathroom through there."

"Thanks."

The man frowned. "Not seen you before. What d'you do?"

"I'm a biker."

"Ah. Probably seen you at the races. From afar."

"Probably."

The second door took him into a sparkling chrome kitchen. A few people were leaning against the counters, smoking and chatting. Potted herbs lined the window wall. Vikram could not imagine Adelaide as a cook.

He passed straight through into a dining area, empty this time. Vikram exhaled shakily. It was the layout of the place that was making him nervous. With each room, he took himself further away from the exit, and escape.

He forced himself to survey the room rationally. Like everything else in Adelaide's apartment, this space was elegantly beautiful. He counted eight chairs pushed in under the glass-topped table, but it was laid, inexplicably, for two people.

There was one more door. If Vikram's judgement was correct, he must have made almost a complete loop of the tower. Which meant there should be only one room left.

He turned the handle cautiously. It gave onto a corridor. The corridor went off to the right and bent around a corner, presumably skirting back along the rooms he had just passed. Vikram was facing yet another door. This time, he was certain he would meet with a lock.

He glanced down the hallway. It was empty. He put an ear to the door he had just closed, and then to the door facing him. He could hear the muffled sounds of the music and people shouting over it. Nothing extraneous. When he tried the door it opened easily. He held it just ajar and peered through.

Adelaide's bedroom glowed with faint, violet lighting. He listened again, wary that she might be inside. But the room was still. He slipped through and pushed the door shut.

It felt like dusk. He waited for his eyes to adjust. A subtle scent hung in the air, not floral, something more exotic. The bed dominated the space. The wall facing it was mirrored from floor to ceiling. The window-wall was bare and black—she looked out on the open ocean, a bleak view. There were no paintings. There were no roses either.

The table beside her bed was empty except for a lamp and a bottle of medication. He read the label with little surprise; they were sleeping pills. When he put them down his arm brushed against the lampshade and the bulb lit up, making him jump.

On her dresser was a teapot in the shape of a dragon. He picked it up. A thin trickle of green powder spilled from the spout. Hastily, Vikram replaced the pot and dusted off the dresser.

There was only one photograph. He had to angle the frame under the light to see it properly. The photograph was of Adelaide and her twin, aged about twelve. Their grins and their freckles were identical. Inside her hood, Adelaide's hair was longer than Axel's, but otherwise it would have been difficult to tell them apart. They were on a rooftop, and it was nighttime.

The picture was out of focus. It seemed an odd choice to have framed when there must be so many of better quality, but maybe that was the point. Vikram put it carefully back on the dresser. He opened a couple of drawers. They contained cosmetics and lingerie. He shut them. He looked around again at the bed. Its covers were pulled perfectly straight. He supposed she had a cleaner to keep the place in order.

For a girl who could have bought anything in the city, it was a curiously impersonal room.

Voices the other side of the door alerted him. He crossed the room silently. Laughter sounded in the hallway outside. The handle turned. Behind the door, Vikram froze.

A rectangle of light spilled onto the pale carpet.

"Oops," a girl giggled. "Looks like we've found Adelaide's boudoir." She rolled the last word around her tongue, loading it with innuendo.

"Not a bad pad, is it?"

"We could…"

A set of painted fingernails curled around the door frame. Vikram shrank back.

"Not if you want to be invited again."

"Mm, maybe you're right. Where shall we go?"

"Down here. I know the place better than you."

The hand withdrew. Vikram's heart was thudding. He waited for their voices to fade, then stepped outside.

"Hello."

A girl was standing in the corridor, observing him. Her arms were folded. Her jet black hair shone almost blue and a pink feathery tail fell between two curious eyes.

"Hi." His throat was as dry as sand.

"It's okay. I'd want to see it too, if I hadn't before." When he didn't answer, she let her lips part in a mocking smile. "What's the matter, catfish got your tongue? I'm Jannike Ko. Adelaide's best friend. You can call me Jan."

Vikram tried to speak casually.

"Where is Adelaide? I haven't seen her."

"Oh, everyone wants to know where Adelaide is. Hiding somewhere, you know what she's like. Forever mysterious. Wouldn't you say?"

"I suppose so."

She laughed. The pink feather tail bobbed up and down.

"Why don't you come with me instead? I don't bite you know. Actually I'm sapphic. I should say, I'm dying for your outfit. It's so ironic. And pioneering, I don't think anyone's done western rag yet. You should talk to Mino. What was it you said you did again?"

"I'm a biker."

"A biker? You must know Udur then?"

"Not really. We're at different levels. Excuse me, I must find the bathroom," he said quickly. "It was nice to meet you."

He made his way back through the apartment, fuelled by an urgent desire to be near the exit.

In the main room, the noise and the scent of roses were overwhelming. He looked for Adelaide but could not see her. Now he wondered if he had missed an opportunity—could that awful girl have been his way in? Why hadn't he gone with her?

He refilled his drink and headed back towards his original observation post. A man and two women were grouped in intense conversation around a table. A low-hanging lantern cast shadows on their faces, giving them a slightly furtive air. Vikram leaned against the wall and sipped casually at the pink stuff.

"—done well this year, hasn't she?"

"Of course, she always does."

"Yes, but I mean, considering the *circumstances.*"

"Bound to be difficult."

"The not knowing—"

"Yes, my dear, but the *suspicion* is something else again. After all, people talk." The woman speaking looked pointedly at each of her companions and gave a little laugh. The others joined in self-consciously but then the other woman, who was younger, said in a hushed voice,

"Why, what have you heard?"

"All sorts of things. Speculation, I dare say. But one can only imagine there is a reason dear Adelaide split from the Rechnovs…"

The man unhunched his shoulders in a slight shrug. "Can't be too big a rift if she's living in a place like this."

"Yes, but can you imagine the scandal if they'd cut her off? It was already bad enough with… well, you know…"

The younger woman looked at her in slight confusion, and the man mouthed something.

"Did you know him?" she whispered back. He shook his head. The older woman checked over her shoulder, before saying, "I did."

"What was he like?"

"Oh, he was a funny one. Bright, I suppose. Almost too bright—he'd walk off right in the middle of a conversation, terribly rude. The family said it was a health issue but I was never convinced; there was something odd about the whole affair."

"I've heard people say he might have—" The man made a circular motion with his hand, as if he did not want to be any more explicit. The older woman raised eyebrows elongated to the edges of her face. "You know," he muttered. "Done it—*himself*."

The woman responded sharply. "That's a filthy lie and you tell anyone that says so."

"Alright, alright…"

"I heard they had fifty boats out looking for him," the girl chirped. "Fifty! Viviana Rechnov must have pulled every string in the Reef. And that's not all. They had entire squads of divers."

"That may be. But we shouldn't really talk about him at all—*she* doesn't like it."

They all shared a private smile. The young woman leaned forward to take a sip of something violet, and Vikram found himself in her line of sight. She stared at him curiously.

"Hello?"

The other two turned around.

"Hello," he said. "I'm Vikram."

"Vikram…" The man ran the name over his tongue as though he was testing it for toxicants, then finding it clear, shook his head in bafflement.

"Vikram who?" the older woman asked. Her eyes darted all over him.

"Vikram Bai," he said.

"And you are here for…?"

He was thrown by the question for a moment, and then wondered if she thought he was with Adelaide's staff.

"For the party," he said, and waved his invite, the magic talisman.

"Oh!" Her expression did not quite clear. "Adelaide's taken you up, has she?"

"Not exactly," Vikram said, remembering he had promised not to mention Linus's name, and now seeing that might be problematic. "I hope she will," he said.

"We all hope for that," said the man fervently.

"Don't be silly, Kristin, you've been on Adelaide's list for months. Oh *Tyr!* I didn't see you arrive." The woman's greeting, directed over Vikram's shoulder, was suddenly girlish.

"I was here early, Gudrun." The newcomer turned to Vikram, who saw the reason for Gudrun's change in tone. The man was classically handsome and perfectly streamlined in features and physique. Unlike the other guests, the shirt beneath his jacket was red. He wore the clothes with easy, nonchalant grace. His eyes were a surprisingly deep shade of grey beneath hair the colour of dry sand. They travelled over Vikram, searching. Vikram knew with absolute surety that even if he had the same access to credit as one of Adelaide's crowd, he could never look like that. The man was wet with money.

"Hi," the newcomer said finally. "My name's Tyr. Don't think I've seen you before?"

"No. It's Vikram."

"Would you mind coming with me? There's someone who wants to meet you." Tyr slung an arm around Vikram's shoulders and was leading him away before he had a chance to say goodbye. The group looked momentarily surprised, and then reformed as though nothing had happened.

Tyr steered Vikram expertly into the mirrored hallway. It was quiet compared to the fracas inside.

"So, this is the first time you've been to one of Adelaide's parties? What do you think?"

"Good party." Vikram stayed neutral.

Tyr laughed. "They always are. Now do tell me, Vikram. Which of the krill are you working for? Because you sure as hell don't belong in here."

Vikram glanced back through the archway. Two girls had climbed onto the piano and were swaying from side to side as they sung, the weight of their headpieces threatening to unbalance them completely. No-one was paying any attention to him and Tyr.

"I'm not here for any newsreel," he said. "I'm here to see Adelaide."

"That's funny," said Tyr. "Because you're not on her guest list."

"I know that," Vikram said, wary now. He didn't know Tyr's background, but nor did he doubt a stranger's capacity to throw a punch. He felt his own body tensing in anticipation. There was a growing part of him that would love to get in a fight. "Look," he said. "I'm from a political reform group. Horizon. I spoke at the Council recently. I just wanted to see Adelaide. To ask if she could help us."

Tyr stared at him as though he was crazy. "I don't know who you are, or who you're working for, but you're leaving right now."

"It's alright, Tyr. He'll go quietly."

The voice was at once layered and laden, cold and charged, honey and steel. Composed as it was of so many disparate keys, it had no right to be any one thing. Vikram looked to its source and caught his first glimpse of Adelaide Mystik. She was wearing a dress the colour of clotting blood. It rippled around her body as though she was a strand of seaweed caught by the waves. In her hair were black roses and black lines ringed her green eyes, brilliant in a pale, pointed face.

"Adelaide," he said. The words clustered on his tongue. He was ready, at that moment, to tell her everything. About Mikkeli, about Stefan, about the other people who were going to die this winter, about the fishing boats and the unremembered quarters, the coldest he'd ever been, and the way the sea sounded at night with the window open in the summer months, fierce but strangely comforting, even about the underwater cell. He was ready to tell her all of this, and despised himself for the impulse, but he could not stop. "I need to talk to you—"

"Yes," she said, and now her voice was sanitized: stripped of all pretence at kindness. "Thank you for coming. Goodbye."

The door opened. The doorman beckoned. Adelaide turned away. Vikram glared at the velveted figure, furious with himself, furious with Linus and Linus's bitch of a sister. Tyr stood with a smile which Vikram could only construe as amusement. With every second that passed he felt his options dwindling. He could fight. He could rage and swear at them. He could get arrested, and spend another few months in jail underwater. He could walk away. Once again, he could walk away.

They were encouraging him towards the latter. It had been so neatly done. Extracting him from the guests, Adelaide bidding a cordial farewell. He wanted to rob them of that victory, to make a mess and a scandal, bring blood to these exquisitely papered rooms. He was longing to break Tyr's jaw. He saw the other man's face as a mangled pulp, and was almost shocked by the intensity of his desire to make it happen. Even that would only give them more meat to feed off. He had lost all around.

Outside, he read the gold plated sign on the closed door: *Adelaide Mystik, The Red Rooms*. He vented a fraction of his frustration on the wall, denting the panelled corridor. The doorman took a step away from his post.

"Don't," said Vikram. Something in the expression on his face halted the man, and Vikram walked away.

11 | ADELAIDE

From her hiding place up on the mezzanine, Adelaide surveyed her party critically. The room was full. Hired barmen moved subtly through the red-dressed guests, replenishing cocktail bowls where the tidemarks fell low. Beside her, the DJ was brewing a potent cloud of sound to fuel the dancers. But Adelaide was distracted. There was a man present at her party who was not meant to be here. She knew he was not meant to be here because he was talking to Gudrun, a veteran member of the Haze, and Gudrun looked bemused. Gudrun was never bemused.

Loathe to create an unnecessary scene, she found Tyr chatting to Freya Kess, a tiny girl with a pixie face and hair that descended in corkscrew curls. Adelaide surveyed them dispassionately before interrupting.

"Do you have a minute, Tyr?"

"Nice to see you, as always, Adelaide." His tone, as usual for their public meetings, was just short of sarcastic.

"Now?" she said imperiously.

"Excuse me." Tyr turned to Freya, rolling his eyes. He followed Adelaide into the crowd. "What is it?" he said in an undertone.

"We have a gatecrasher."

"Where?"

"Behind me, by the interior wall, two o'clock."

His eyes flicked over her shoulder. "Black shirt, terrible hair? Talking to Kristin and Gudrun?"

"That's the one," she said. "Do you recognize him?"

"No. You?"

"Not a clue. Do you think he's dangerous?" With her back to the gate-crasher, Adelaide felt her sense of intrigue rising. The breach in security took her aback though. Her invitations were watermarked like pre-Neon banknotes. They weren't just quaint; they should be impossible to forge.

"No idea. Looks oddly familiar though. Stay here, I'll deal with it."

"Thank you."

The second that Tyr moved away her attention was claimed by Lilja. Adelaide gave the acrobat a full half of her attention. The other half shadowed Tyr as he approached the stranger and escorted him through the archway. Adelaide excused herself and moved to where she could listen without being seen.

"I'm not here for any media. I'm here to see Adelaide."

The gatecrasher sounded strange. It was a gruff voice, but hoarse too, she thought. It wasn't an accent as such—what was an accent nowadays anyway? Everyone spoke Boreal English. Even her grandfather had forsaken his childhood Siberian; she had only ever heard him speak it on those occasions when Axel had asked. She edged closer.

"That's funny," Tyr was saying. "Because you're not on her guest list."

"I know that." There was a pause. A new track started and Adelaide strained to hear over the music. Why did this man want to see her? She knew most of the krill by voice if not by sight. She was forever changing her scarab code to evade them.

"Look," the gatecrasher said. "I'm from a political reform group. Horizon. I spoke at the Council recently. I just wanted to see Adelaide. To ask if she could help us."

This was unexpected, and disappointing. Of course, it was possible the man was lying, but she sensed not. That was what was bothering her about the voice. It held the unusual ring of truth.

"I don't know who you are, or who you're working for, but you're leaving right now." Tyr evidently had no such concerns.

Adelaide judged it time to put an end to the intrusion. She stepped out.

"It's alright, Tyr. He'll go quietly."

The opposing walls of mirrors multiplied the two men's reflections, producing the illusion of spectators on either side. Tyr, calm in his red shirt—only Adelaide would know that his body was tensed in apprehension. And the stranger—up close she was surprised by his appearance. He was younger than the sandpaper voice suggested, perhaps not much older than herself. His eyes were the colour of cocoa, almond shaped, striking, but the whites were bloodshot. His hair was dark and shaggy. She ignored the clothes, her gaze stripping away the cheap layers of clothing to the sinewy physique beneath. Tall, and thin like wire. No, she thought idly. Not unattractive.

But still. Too still, as if he had practised. Even his blinking was slow, each sweep of the eyelashes seeming to reinforce some careful screen. It was a little unnerving.

"Adelaide," he said.

I must put a stop to this, she thought.

"I need to talk to—"

"Yes. Thank you for coming. Goodbye."

An odd expression crossed the man's face. There was anger there, clearly, but it was more than that. It was accusatory. Almost a look of hatred. For a moment she thought he was going to do something wild, and wondered if her assessment was way off track and he was dangerous after all. She let her smile drop into that tension, leisurely, the way he had looked at her, before she turned her back.

Behind her, quick footsteps marked the stranger's eviction. Nobody had noticed anything. She waited, aware that Tyr was at her shoulder.

"We'll have to find out who he is," she said.

"I know who he is. The westerner who went to Chambers—I saw his photograph on the newsreel. Stars knows how he got in."

"Stars indeed." She frowned, but put the gatecrasher aside. "Balcony?"

"Five minutes."

She moved away and was instantly claimed by a newly blonde Minota. It was a lucky collision. Minota was diverting but so caught up in her own cleverness that she paid little attention to anyone else. Over Minota's shoulder Adelaide saw Tyr disappear into the next room. Minota was relating a story. She gave it little glosses, doll-like hands gesticulating. There was a pet goose in the story, and the conclusion was something to do with the goose attacking one of Minota's lovers in her bed. Adelaide laughed and calculated the mental time for Tyr to make his way through the study, the kitchen and the dining room, and from there into her bedroom. Minota looked pleased with herself.

"Really, though, you should have been there. It was too brilliant."

"I can only imagine."

Minota caught her arm, eyelids stretching. "Oh honey, I hate to ask, but do you have anything? I'm so dry, I can barely afford a line."

"There's a brass pot in the drinks cabinet." Adelaide gave Minota's hand a conspiratorial squeeze. "Why don't you help yourself?"

Minota giggled. "You're so generous, Adelaide."

Minota's discovery was met with shrieks of delight and delving into handbags for suitable paper. Masked by the commotion, Adelaide slipped back into the hallway. She checked over her shoulder, then arranged her fingertips in a pattern against the glass. There was a little click, and a panel of the mirror slid across. Adelaide eased through the gap. The panel slid back behind her. She was in her private bathroom.

It was abruptly quiet. Adelaide smiled to herself. Her grandfather had incorporated some useful innovations into the Rechnov properties.

She opened the door into her bedroom, knowing Tyr would already have entered from the other side. She took a slip of milaine from the dragon pot and a thick, heavy coat from the wardrobe. Heat rose to her face with the additional layer, evaporating the moment she opened the balcony door.

She shut the door behind her, and stopped, mesmerized by the cold. The emptiness. There was nothing out here but the occasional light from a passing patrol boat, and beacons shining seven miles away at the ring-net. Just the dark, endless ocean. Another world.

Tonight especially she felt that dislocation. The night was acute with absence. Absence of wind, rain, absence of everything except the hiss of her lungs, the thud of her heart, and Tyr, breathing, a few metres away.

"You escaped," he said.

"I told Minota where to find the milaine."

"Good diversion."

They moved at the same time. At once he was kissing her, her back pressed against the glass wall, their lips the only warmth in a frozen world. She was stunned, as always, how much she wanted him. In five years of illicit sex they had never spent a night together. She knew disparate parts of him, could bind them together to make the man he might show to other lovers. But it was an imaginary picture; a concept of boundaries that she would never know. And so it was new every time, dazzlingly, incredibly new. She felt these moments in the marrow of her bones.

"Wait," he said.

"Wait?" She put a bite of anger into her voice. He responded at once, swinging her around and pushing her against the balcony. She grabbed the railings. Vertigo collided with adrenalin. She was dizzy with altitude. The hundred floor drop and the crashing waves. Tyr against her, inside her, only Tyr's hands to save her if she slipped. This was world's end, a sight to drive you mad. That madness was vented in their need for each other, in its heady savage haste. When he pulled away she felt almost sick with it.

"You could stay," she said.

He shook his head. "Too risky."

One of them always held back. She shook a fat line of milaine onto the rail and they raced to snort it before some disturbance in the air dissipated the fine green particles. Their heads collided in the centre; she met his eyes and giggled. He grinned back, sniffed.

"Hang on…"

She brushed a trace of powder from the stubble of his upper lip.

"Okay," she said.

"Okay?"

"Yes. You go back first."

"Don't fall off."

"I won't."

She watched him go with a kind of wrench, as though he was already back in her father's office. He had never admitted it, but she knew Feodor had sent him to the Haze to spy on her. Tyr bridged two worlds.

For a few moments she let herself surrender to the strangeness of the night. Scorpio and Lupus glimmered brightly. She imagined the scientists upstairs training their telescopes. The dryness in her throat, heightened by outdoor air and milaine, reminded her that she must return to her guests. She was no longer worried about getting caught; quite the contrary, she knew that she and Tyr were too clever for that.

When she got back to the party Minota was in the middle of recounting the same anecdote about the goose and the lover to a giddied circle. A mirror was on the table. Tyr lounged on the other side, his long legs stretched out, laughing. There were new arrivals. The apartment was heaving, most people now standing, many dancing.

"There you are, Adelaide!"

It was Jannike, with two glasses of pink punch. Jan's hair supported a spectacular headpiece that curled over her forehead in a furry cerise tail. Adelaide had a flashback of Axel two years ago, solemnly fixing a dried seahorse to Jan's head and assuring her it was the latest trick.

"Darling, the most incredible party!" said Jan. "You really have surpassed yourself this time, absolutely everybody's here. I met this rather handsome but most peculiar boy outside your bedroom. Said he was a biker, but Udur doesn't know him. And Linus! What a surprise!"

The mention of her brother distracted Adelaide from Jannike's previous comment.

"Linus? He's not here?"

"Yes, over there. How on earth did you lure him out?"

"He never said he was coming." Adelaide scanned the room until she found her brother. He had clearly come straight from work, dressed in a formal suit with no flair to it at all. People moving in his direction swerved away when they clocked who it was. Adelaide was not surprised. Linus was hardly stimulating conversation and besides, everyone knew the siblings shunned one another. "What does he think he's doing here, Jan?"

"Well, darling, he was chatting away—maybe not chatting exactly, but when I asked him something he responded with words. Maybe there's hope for him yet, what do you think?" Jannike pursed her lips, assessing the situation.

"I suppose I ought to talk to him." Adelaide stared at her older brother with equal fascination. Yes, she had sent him an invitation, but that was a long running, only half funny joke between them. She could not work out whether to be angry or amused.

"Give him a line," Jannike suggested. "Say, he doesn't even have a drink. I'll get him one, what does he take?"

"Get him a Rose Infusion. He needs sweetening up."

"Never fear, angel. Janko will come and save you in a minute."

Skirting the window-wall, Adelaide managed to cross the room unmolested. Linus caught her eye as she reached the halfway point. His eyes creased with amusement. She reminded herself that the Rechnovs were game players; his presence must be approached as a challenge.

"Evening, Adelaide. Made it through the hyenas?"

"I'd prefer jaguars, if Osiris had any," she said. Reaching up to his collar, she undid the necktie, pulled it off, and tossed it onto a nearby plant. "Better. Don't you know it's cabaret night?"

"I thought it was rose night."

"Rose night, cabaret theme. Anyway, this is a rare sighting. What brings you to this end of town?"

Linus looked bemused, perhaps by the disappearance of his necktie. "You sent me an invitation, didn't you?"

"Yes, but you chuck my cards in the recycler."

"Not always. Sometimes I find a more appropriate use for them."

Adelaide gave him a suspicious look.

"Tell me," said Linus. "How much does it cost you to host these things? Or should I say, how much does it cost us?"

"Why, does the bottomless pit of family bank have a previously undiscovered floor?"

"Not as far as I know. Dmitri guards the accounts. If he gets in touch, you'll know bankruptcy is imminent."

"I've not seen Dmitri for months."

"Then I dare say you have a few more parties' worth." Linus retrieved his necktie from the plant. He rolled it into a neat snail shell and tucked it into his jacket pocket. Adelaide frowned.

"I hope you aren't going to be admonishing tonight. I'd have to effect your removal."

"I promise to behave," he said. "If only because I'm too scared of your security detail."

"I thought I sensed a latent air of terror about you."

"I like the decor, by the way. Very dramatic. Although I can't help feeling a little sorry for all the women getting second-rate flowers, now that you've used up a month's worth of rose stock."

Adelaide scoffed. "Old World values."

"So why did you choose roses for tonight?"

She looked at him. Was he serious? "Aesthetics."

"Your Rose Infusion, sir."

Jannike stood before them, grinning. She held aloft a selection of cocktails balanced enticingly on a tray. The tray was angled, with the pink concoction sloping towards the rim of its glass and Linus.

"Oh—thank you, Jannike."

"You're welcome." Jannike performed a curtsy. The tray skidded away, skimming over the tops of heads like an adolescent flying saucer. Adelaide and Linus watched.

"So. Did you like your gatecrasher?"

"You heard about him? Did you, by any chance, send him?"

Linus smiled. "Now why would you think that?"

"Nobody else would give away an invitation."

"Well, I might have."

"Rude of you, dear brother. But he was evicted quickly."

"Did you listen to anything he said?"

The sudden switch in conversational direction annoyed Adelaide. She had been rather enjoying their backhanded banter. Now she had a strong urge to put Linus in his place.

"Why would I want to listen to one of your spies?"

Linus extracted a rose petal from his cocktail and looked for somewhere to put it. Crossly, Adelaide held out her own glass. He dropped it in. "Don't be absurd. Vikram is trying to encourage the Council to put through a few reforms for the west. You have influence, I thought you might help him."

Adelaide's laugh rang out. Several people glanced over as if they might approach, then seeing Linus, retracted the impulse. His presence was beginning to dampen her party. She needed him gone. "Linus, you have a very odd idea about my priorities."

"You wouldn't like to annoy the Council?"

"Even if I did, I have other things to think about right now." They were talking without looking at one another, but his next words changed that.

"Like getting into Axel's apartment?"

Her eyes narrowed. "So now we get to it."

"Get to what?"

"Why you're here. Did Feodor send you?"

"Nobody sent me, Adelaide." Linus dropped his voice. "I decided to come and talk to you. This investigation is a delicate thing. People are making accusations. The *Daily Flotsam* has even suggested we've done away with Axel ourselves because he was an embarrassment."

"For all I know you might have done," she said distantly.

Linus's eyebrows drew together. "It would be a mistake to think I don't care, Adelaide. He was my brother too."

"He was nobody's brother by the end of it."

"In any case you can't go around establishing your own private battleground. You've got to let it go. We all have."

She bestowed an insincere smile upon him. "Anything you say, Linus."

"You're impossible." He kept his voice low but it was strained with anger.

"It's been said before."

"And you should stop screwing around with Tyr as well."

She saw the regret flash over her brother's face a second after he had spoken, but it was too late. Her eyes flicked involuntarily across the room. They were playing poker at the table now. Tyr had a stack of chips in front of him. He was toying with them, letting the disks slip through his fingers in a series of clinks. It was chance, perhaps, that made him catch her eye at that moment. But it might have been something more elusive and unqualified. Understanding sprang between them. Tyr looked away.

Linus lit two cigarettes and passed her one without speaking. The first inhalation grated on her throat. He smoked something different to her. It tasted grey. She drew twice, deeply, before allowing herself to speak.

"How long have you known?"

"I've suspected for a while. Tonight confirmed it."

A cloud of laughter floated up from the poker table. Jannike had appropriated one of the barmen's jackets. She bent over in mock imitation of a waiter, cocking her head so that the crimson tail dangled over her ear. "Raise you five hundred," said Kristin. Minota stripped off her bracelet and threw it down. In the corner, one of Adelaide's musician friends had opened the piano and was playing pre-Neon baroque, oblivious to the DJ or anyone else in the room. Olga was lounging across the top, blowing smoke rings.

There was something awful, she thought, about the idea of prolonged wondering, of surveillance. She would almost rather have been caught in the act.

"You know if our father finds out he'll be fired," said Linus.

"I know."

"You're selfish."

"I always have been."

"There's too much on the line."

"For me, too." She hardly knew what they were saying.

"For everyone. This is an unstable time politically." Linus lowered his voice. "Adelaide, you must know that the City is on the verge of a resource crisis. Bufferglass and solar skin reserves are all but gone, now we're having problems at the mining station. This is not a time when the family needs distractions. Now please—if you aren't prepared to reconsider, let's just go back to how things were. We'll stick to our business and you stick to yours."

Not trusting herself to speak, she stared directly ahead. Linus sighed.

"I have to go. I've got a meeting at nine o'clock in the morning and I need to be awake for it."

"Of course. Thank you for coming."

Many hours later, when the party was over and she was sitting alone in its debris, Adelaide would have to admire the finesse of Linus's attack. He might have played his trump card too early. He had played it well nonetheless. But watching him leave, all she felt was sick, as if every last gasp of oxygen had been squeezed from her body.

12 ¦ VIKRAM

"**S**o Vik does his spiel, tells her how we're all living in shit, dying of cold and drowning down here, and Miz Adelaide Mystik goes, get this, she goes, *thank you for coming*. Thank you for coming! Can you believe it!" Nils laughed until it turned into a spluttering cough. He tapped the passing bar girl on the shoulder. "Get us another jug of that, will you?"

The boarded-up den was packed and beginning to get rowdy. Vikram, Nils and Drake hunched on either side of the makeshift table: a door propped over empty kegs. Drake had her feet up. She was wearing her prized boots, huge and chunky, their soles two inches thick and ridged like a series of fins. A naked electric bulb swung overhead, casting wild shadows, making the drunk feel drunker.

"Stuck up cow," said Drake. She drew luxuriously on a skinny roll-up and sighed out an equally emaciated trail of smoke. "Surprised you didn't punch her, Vik."

"I was tempted," Vikram said.

"*Thank you for coming.*" Nils put on a high pitched, whiny voice. "What a bitch." He shook his head admiringly. Nils's reaction was predictable. He was disappointed Vikram had seen so little of Adelaide, but she was exactly as Nils had imagined.

Drake elbowed a man who was trying to inhale the smoke from her cigarette. "So, did you get a good look at her apartment? I bet it's massive, right?"

Vikram shook his head. "You can't imagine."

"Oh, I can imagine. I can imagine the whole thing." There was a derisive, bitter tone to Drake's voice. Vikram understood it completely, but he wished suddenly that it was not there.

"I talked to this one girl," he said. "She seemed alright."

"Alright?" Drake gave a snort of disbelief. "How alright?"

Vikram couldn't say that Jannike hadn't given him away without explaining that he'd been in Adelaide's bedroom, so he just shrugged. Now he thought about it, perhaps she had given him away.

The bar girl came back with a cracked jug and dumped it in the middle of the bench. Some of the contents splashed over.

Nils jumped to his feet. "Hey, watch what you're doing!"

Vikram reached up and put a hand on Nils's arm until his friend sat down. The bar girl stalked off without a word.

"That Miz Mystik could take a leaf or two out of her book," Drake commented.

"Maybe she already did," Vikram tried, half-heartedly, to join in on the joke. He had given his friends the bare facts. He'd told them about the extravagance of the Red Rooms, his brief conversation with the guests, what Tyr had said at the end. He hadn't told them about *western rag*. He could not explain the chagrin he had felt. For Nils, Vikram's expulsion was a great escape, to be recounted and exaggerated in company. It was not an unflattering version, but every time Nils retold the story, it echoed falser in Vikram's mind.

The wind banged against the boarded bufferglass. Above them, the light bulb flung back and forth.

"Whipping up a ghost-grabber," Drake said, hooking one ankle over the other. She widened her eyes spookily. Vikram glanced at the window-wall. Watch out, the orphanage boat-keeper used to say, or the Tarctic will get you.

"Better not be," Nils grumbled. "We'll be stuck here all night."

"Better get another jug." Drake stuck her arm into the air and twisted her face into an expression of mild pain. "Oy, waiter! Are you there?" She and Nils convulsed.

A heavy-set man in a woollen hat paused by their table. His face was familiar but Vikram couldn't place him.

"Drake. Thought I heard your voice."

"Hey, man, good to see you. Working the Friday shift?"

"Maybe, maybe. You?"

"Same as always."

The man nodded to Nils and Vikram and moved on before they had a chance to return the greeting.

"Who was that?" Vikram asked.

"Rikard. You remember Rikard? He was with us three years ago."

"Think Keli knows him," Nils added.

Rikard. The face sharpened into memory; their paths must have crossed. It was possible he had never even spoken to the man, but there had been so many people back then.

"I didn't realize you were still in touch with that crowd," he said.

"I'm not. He's started crewing the boats occasionally, I ran into him a few weeks back."

Vikram looked at the soles of Drake's boots, the ridges packed with waterproof wax and fish scales. He was terrified that one day she would be caught on an illegal fish run and either killed or flung underwater, but it was pointless voicing that fear. Instead he asked, "What happened to your tooth?"

He thought she had lost one of the front ones, but when she grinned he saw that the tooth had turned entirely black.

"Some bastard tried to nick my boots while I was asleep."

"I'll buy you a gold one for midwinter," Nils offered.

"You're so generous, you. I'll have a pair of ruby earrings while you're at it. And maybe a bunch of, what was it, *roses* too—for my hair." Drake screwed up a handful of wiry curls. "What d'you think?"

Vikram drained his mug.

"Yeah, yeah, very funny you two."

When they left the den, much later, the wind had dropped and they had finished several jugs. Vikram stepped outside ahead of the others. The first bridge, thirty floors up, was a rumpled construction lashed together out of planks, boards, squares of fibreglass, broken bufferglass panes, metal sheets and whole and partial boats. Dirty water welled in the pit of a kayak, dripping erratically down.

Vikram climbed easily over the treacherous walkway. The bridge rocked beneath him, regularly, like a pendulum. He sensed movement in the sky above, the clouds scudding away on high winds. A glimmer of light drew his gaze south. He followed it, found clear sky and there, on the horizon, a phenomenon. Ribbons of gauze undulated in the stratosphere: green and yellow, flickering, shimmering. The lights always meant something. Sickness. Death. Was that where his failure to engage that lofty girl would end? He was afraid, but the strange evanescent beauty drew him in spite of his fear. He could have sat on the bridge for hours, with no company but the sea hissing somewhere below.

The others came out, giggling. Drake couldn't walk properly. She had her arms out wide. She was flapping them. Nils steered her.

"Stars!" Nils stopped, gazing up. "Look at the lights!"

"Aura Australis," said Drake expertly. She hiccoughed. Only an innate sense of balance was keeping her upright.

"How d'you know that?"

"Someone told me."

Drake misjudged a step. Her boot stuck in a hole. Nils hauled her out.

"Who?"

"Dunno. Someone… educated."

She moved close to Nils and whispered something in his ear. Nils shook his head. Drake whispered again, more urgently.

"What's up?" Vikram called.

Nils cupped a playful hand over Drake's mouth.

"She's pissed."

They reached Vikram. He took Drake's other arm and they progressed slowly along the bridge. Behind him, the Australis lights pulsed. But the dizzy laughter of the others swept him onward, pulling him back into the mesh of the group, where he belonged.

Vikram lay awake for the rest of the night, listening to the wind and thinking about the three of them, bound together by strange layers of history. They had once been five; they should always have been four. He tried to imagine what Mikkeli would have done. Keli wouldn't have accepted defeat, and nor could Vikram.

"Now you know what you're up against," she'd say. "So work out how to fight it."

He had thought, in the first bewildering days when he was released from jail, that he would miss her all the time. But it didn't happen like that. She intruded on his thoughts at specific times, with specific actions. He found that he missed her more outside. In boats, always, and when he caught a glimpse of a mismatched, roguish face. Sometimes he told himself that it really was Keli, and as long as he didn't follow her, she would stay alive. He realized that the dead didn't go away. They lingered.

Vikram had made her a promise. He had done it with rites, made an incision in his own skin and sealed it with salt. As much as to himself, he owed it to Mikkeli to pursue every avenue.

In the dirty bufferglass reflection he saw her nod approvingly. "That's right," she said. "You're not going to let that bitch get the better of you, are you?"

When the labouring work came to an end Vikram began his research. He went first to the recycling depot. The caretaker was old, with soft indoor skin and a frostbite scar where one ear was missing. He was mostly deaf, but insisted on taking Vikram on a tour of the depot. They looked into room after room full of City junk, the old man mumbling things that Vikram could not understand, pointing at the piles of unsorted plastic and broken parts that were waiting to be disassembled, melted down and returned to the Makers that had produced them.

When they reached a room of discarded Neptunes, Vikram stopped. Some of the machines still worked. He pulled up story after story about the Rechnovs on the cracked screens. The old man peered curiously over his shoulder. He touched a creased fingertip to the fuzzy picture of Adelaide, stroked the line of her hair.

"They call her the flame."

His voice was like crackling paper.

"Yes. Yes I'm looking for stuff on her. Can you help me?"

The caretaker grinned, showing blackened gums, and beckoned. Vikram followed his shuffling progress to a room where discarded paper newspapers and pamphlets, which had been a fad for a few years in the City and were still used in the west, were piled high in precarious stacks. The caretaker let him take what he wanted.

Back at 614-West, he holed up in his room. The papers were thin and had curled with the damp air. Some were full of holes where small creatures had chewed through. He ran a finger down columns of print, marvelling as always that something so flimsy could come from something as solid and compact as rock.

At first Vikram tried to organize the information, making notes in the margins of articles, scribbling ideas on a patch of the wall. The krill loved Adelaide: she was a tabloid goldmine. Vikram couldn't say exactly what he was looking for, but he wanted to extract some nugget of truth from the speculation. The cuttings grew too many; soon they made an overflowing pile on the floor.

He wanted to dismiss her. She had everything. She was clever though; she had all but renounced her family without losing any of her inherited privileges. Then she had established her reign as undisputed leader of the Haze. The parties grew bigger and wilder and still the city forgave her. The media chronicled her exploits in tones of indulgence, the *Daily Flotsam* with a more malicious glee. She never gave interviews.

He found a ten-page feature on the Rechnov family. Here they were lined up in a formal portrait: the Architect and his wife, now deceased, Feodor and Viviana Rechnov, the four children. The same proud, haughty faces, an extended version of the representation at Eirik's execution. Vikram thought this quite naturally, and realized with a shock that he was able to consider the execution almost abstractly. It still enraged him, and the guilt remained, but Eirik's death had become part of a sum; immersed into a greater mission.

In the older pictures, Adelaide was always beside her brother, identical with their oversized shades and their smiles full of open confidence. Here they were at some party or other. Getting out of a shuttle pod, late at night and drunk. Axel in a hang-glider. Adelaide jet-skiing. The pair of them on the roof of the Eye Tower, preparing to abseil past the Council Chambers. Vikram thought of the single photograph in Adelaide's bedroom.

Something very odd had happened to Axel. Vikram had never paid much attention: these people were fairy tales to him. Now he examined the pictures with renewed interest. In one photo, Axel's eyes were averted from the lens while his sister stared directly, accusingly ahead. Was there something protective in the way she stepped forward before Axel, her fingers at his elbow as though she'd just let go his arm?

Vikram tossed the photo aside. He was forgetting his original mission: to find Adelaide's weaknesses and work out how to use them. He settled down with yet another article and began to read.

Hours later, the window-wall had drained of light but he had gathered several pieces of information that he could assume were factual. His eyes strained. Lost in thought, he had barely noticed the onset of dusk. He took a pinch of salt from his tin and threw it at the window.

What to do? By all accounts, Adelaide Mystik was particular in her habits. She opened her flat once a year for the Rose Night. Other than that, the Red Rooms were closed off to visitors. As an honorary member of the Gardeners' Guild and a sporadic landscape designer, Adelaide was occasionally seen on botanical sites. For lunch, she frequented four or five select restaurants, and she dined late at night from an equally exclusive list. She was glimpsed in the famous bars and nightclubs of the Strobe. She took a lot of milaine and she drank.

Crucially, Adelaide was inaccessible without the aid of credit. Vikram didn't have credit, so he was going to have to tackle her at home. There was one detail that had caught his attention. It was in a magazine interview with one of Adelaide's alleged rivals.

Adelaide's an insomniac, he read. *That's why she parties all night, because she can't sleep. It's nothing to do with stamina.*

The by-line was attributed to a journalist called Magda Linn. The rest of the interview was useless; if Vikram hadn't seen the sleeping pills beside Adelaide's bed, he would have ignored it.

The next morning, when he reviewed his plan in the light of day, it seemed flimsy. Tangling with Adelaide Mystik was getting into political games; games whose rules he did not know and whose outcomes he could not predict.

He did not confide in Nils. He was probably wasting his time anyway. Linus's idea was a good one but impractical, exactly the sort of thing a Citizen would suggest. Maybe Vikram should stop trying to decipher the bizarre world of the Rechnovs and go back to what he knew: to protests and waterway violence. He understood violence. Its mechanics, its randomness. Its lack of mercy. He thought of Drake's casual hello to Rikard and wondered if there might be anything more to the connection than she claimed. He dismissed the idea. They'd known a lot of people back then; it was impossible to avoid running into a face from the past.

He began to work out the practicalities of the plan. His pass had expired, he would have to sneak across the border. By Undersea or by boat? Either way he'd have to bribe someone.

Night, then. Night held his best chance. From a practical viewpoint, there would be fewer people about. But he also reasoned that Adelaide, on some level, must be like everyone else. At four or five in the morning, furthest from the warmth of the sun, her body would be at its lowest ebb. Her heart would slow, her lungs shallow. In those hours, dark thoughts often invaded the mind. This was the time to find her, when she was vulnerable.

13 | ADELAIDE

The curtain, a waterfall of white velvet, was lifted at one side by an invisible hand. The assistant extended his arm silently, inviting them to go through. Adelaide folded her arms and gave Jannike a pointed look.

"Off you go."

"Come on, Adie. I paid three hundred *lys* for this appointment."

"Three hundred *lys*! For a single consultation! It says here she's only been Guild ratified for the last five years." Adelaide pointed to the Teller's certificate, prominently displayed on a stand. "You've been conned, Miss Ko."

"I haven't, she's the best. She has contacts outside Osiris."

"Who with, the ghosts?"

"No! Anyone can contact the ghosts. She finds living souls, on land."

"Then she's definitely a fraud."

"What if she could contact Axel?" Jannike said boldly. Adelaide stared at her, so intensely that she might have unnerved another woman. Jannike's brown eyes gazed back, unperturbed. There was little that could rattle Jan. The hidden hand holding the curtain jostled it, a reminder that time was booked and bookings were money.

Adelaide and Jannike stared at one another for a fraction longer. Then both girls ducked under the curtain. It swung back into place behind them. Adelaide blinked, surprised by an intense brightness.

There was only one visible source of light. It was star-shaped, sunk into the floor, and emitted a silvery glow that steeped the tent. As Adelaide's eyes adjusted, she realized they were in a triangular enclosure lined with the same velvet drapes. Sitting on the other side of the star-light was the Teller. Her legs were crossed. She was clothed in a pyramid of folds.

"Sit," she said.

The two girls perched obediently, echoing the Teller's pose.

"There are two of you," said the Teller.

"I've just come to watch," Adelaide said.

"Your hand," instructed the Teller, and Jannike put hers forward promptly. The Teller reached for it. Her hand brushed past Jan's before connecting with it. As she leaned forward over the star-light Adelaide saw her eyes. They were milky white, blank inside of blank. Adelaide had an unnerving sense of pitching forward into water. Her vision grew cloudy, as though she had swum into the unplumbed depths of a kelp forest, chasing the tail of a fish which each time she neared it shot further away into the weed.

The woman was blind. She was young, too, without lines or wrinkles, the youngest Teller Adelaide had ever seen.

Beside her, Jan tensed as her hand was enclosed.

"There will be deceit," said the Teller.

"Tell me something I don't know."

"Look to those close to you. Your friends shall become stronger but so shall your enemies."

"How about me?" said Jan. "How about all the beautiful sirens out there waiting for me to swim into their lives?"

"You are impatient," said the Teller.

"Yes I am."

Adelaide half listened as the Teller predicted Jannike's near future; read her palm lines and the channels of her wrist veins, then handed her a salt vial and told her to scatter the grains. The whited out tent was soporific.

"And you, my sister." The Teller's hand trembled, midair, seeking what her eyes could not. "You have already been told your fate."

Adelaide realized she was being addressed.

"I've been told many fates," she said. "None of them match."

"It has been spoken, sister, spoken in the salt. The place you shall go to. Not yet, perhaps. It cannot be forced. But when you are ready, you shall go willingly."

"Where's she going?" Jannike asked. The Teller's head bowed.

"It has been spoken."

"What about Axel?" Jan nudged Adelaide. "Go on, ask!"

"For the boy, nothing."

Adelaide was taken aback by the abruptness of the response.

"What do you mean?" She leaned forward, eager now, and gripped the woman's hand. It was incredibly thin. She could feel the web of bones shifting in the scoop of the palm. "Can you see where my brother is?"

The Teller's eyelids lowered in a mockery of demureness.

"Has Axel left Osiris?"

"Nobody leaves Osiris." The Teller's voice took on a chanting quality, and a higher harmonic pierced the low hum, eerily, so that it sounded as though two voices emerged from her swathed throat. "Osiris is a lost city. She has lost the world and the world has lost her. Thus it was ordained, thus it is."

"That old rant," said Jannike. Adelaide knew that Jan's eyes were rolling upwards, although she also sensed the other girl's interest in what had not been said. Adelaide was equally annoyed by the retreat into seer speech.

"If he hasn't left, then where is he?" she pressed. She turned to Jan. "I want to see her alone."

"I thought she was a fraud?"

Adelaide stared at her. Jannike got awkwardly to her feet. Adelaide waited until the white curtain had descended behind her friend's back.

"I'll pay you double what she did. Triple. A thousand *lys*, untaxed credit. Tell me what you know about my brother."

"My knowledge is no greater than yours."

"I'm a Rechnov. I'm ordering you."

"Tellers obey a higher order."

"Just tell me if he's alive, at least tell me that. Please, I need to know."

But the Teller would say no more. She shook off Adelaide's grasp with an irritated gesture and her hands disappeared into the folds of her garments. The curtain lifted behind Adelaide. The brightness inside the enclosure diminished and she had a brief glimpse of the Teller under normal electric light, the shadows of tiredness on her young face. The man who had ushered Adelaide in beckoned her out.

Adelaide's scarab was glowing. She checked the screen, looked for Jannike and spotted her friend browsing salt tins at a craft stand. Adelaide walked over to the opposite side of the hall where a plasma display depicted the history of Tellers through the ages.

"Yes?" she spoke into the scarab.

"I hear you've been staking out Sanjay Hanif's office."

Adelaide spoke sharply. "I've been trying to contact you."

"At first I thought you were being extraordinarily stupid, but then I decided it may work in our favour. After all, if they know you were camping out across the way, it detracts from any possible connection with me."

"Have you been following me?"

"I'm aware of your movements."

"How thoughtful of you. And do you have any information about my brother, or did you just contact me to explain how you've been misusing my funds?"

"At this stage I have no concrete evidence to report. The witnesses' stories all corroborate Hanif's versions."

"So there's nothing."

"I said nothing concrete. I have a potential lead. The maid you employed—Yonna—she mentioned seeing an unfamiliar woman leave the penthouse one day before she started work. She was able to give a rough description."

"A woman? What kind of woman?"

"Unlikely to be a sexual liaison, if that's what you're thinking. The maid said it was a plain woman who looked to be in her forties. Possibly an airlift."

"And you think you can find her?"

"I'm looking. If she is an airlift, it will make it all the easier. Ex-westerners are distinctive whether they wish to be or not."

"Call me when you do. And whilst you're talking, there's something else." She lowered her voice. "We need to get into the penthouse where my brother lived."

"Can't do it. Possible crime scene, Hanif's put high security on the entrance. His people won't be bribed."

"I'm sure in your line of work, Mr Lao…"

"Absolutely not. Forget this idea."

"But I need to—"

"I'll be in touch."

The line went dead.

"You'd better be," she muttered. Masking her fury at Lao's insouciance, she stood in front of a looping documentary about Seela Nayagam, the first official Teller to work in Osiris. *Footage from 2372*, read the caption. The images were forty-five years old. Everyone visited Tellers, whether they heeded them or not. Axel used to wind them up. Adelaide had always felt more ambiguous.

Jannike was haggling when she returned. She held out her prize for Adelaide to examine; an oval tin with crocodile pattern etchings.

"Nice," Adelaide agreed.

"So did she say anything? Why did you ask if Axel had left Osiris?"

Adelaide thought of Axel's last words, of the balloon. "Just a whim," she said. The Teller's words echoed in her head. *Nobody leaves Osiris.*

"You never talk about him, not even to me. I know you miss him, I know you must be miserable. And he was my friend as well, you know. Remember when we used to sneak out to the Roof and drink Kelpiqua? Remember when we stayed out in that crazy storm for a dare?"

"Axel was furious."

"Of course he was, that was a proper Tarctic. We could all have died."

"Or one of us." He was afraid of us being separated, she thought. More than the storm. "There's no point in talking about it, Jan. There's nothing to be done."

Jannike sighed. She took Adelaide's hand and squeezed it and let go. Briefly Adelaide considered telling her about Lao, and what she had paid him to do, before dismissing the notion. She loved Jan, but her friend was a liability.

"I'd rather drink," she said.

"Come on, then. I'll take you to a new place."

They went to the neon emporiums of the Strobe. The towers threw out light and noise and the whole was cut by laser lines from the Rotating Towers central to it all. Every night, packed with frantic pulses, the Strobe's towers vibrated with renewed intensity. Hour after hour, from east to west, they branded the darkness until the grey light of day stripped it of all effect and nudged the ravers home. From boats, even from beyond the ring-net, people said you could see it beating like a great cold heart. They said it woke the ghosts.

Autumn lingered. The ice season was drawing near. They danced, and they drank. They split a bag of milaine along the length of the bar, made patterns in the jade green powder, took turns to imbibe. More people came. They danced, and they drank; they drank and they danced some more. By midnight, the world had become an inchoate place. Neither Adelaide or Jannike could stand straight. Adelaide knew that it did not matter. They were young, and they cared for nothing, because nothing in Osiris cared for them.

14 | VIKRAM

He heard the door handle twist. In the second the door swung open, anticipation dried his throat.

Adelaide Mystik's face was clean and angry. She was wearing a see-through kimono over something made out of silk and lace. Both garments stopped at her thighs. She did not look like someone who had just woken up, although Vikram had been knocking persistently for the past ten minutes.

"Hello," he said. "Is this a good time?"

"Who the hell are you?"

She did not look especially vulnerable either.

"My name's Vikram. I met you once before. Well, not met exactly. Actually you threw me out."

Her eyes narrowed into mossy crevasses. "Rose Night," she said. "Linus's spy. I thought you'd got the message. Now fuck off before I call my security."

She slammed the door.

Vikram waited. The corridor was impossibly quiet. He could hear his own breathing. He reminded himself that it was almost four in the morning; on this side of the city, people were sleeping, and silence the norm. The twist of apprehension loitered nonetheless.

He plunged his hands into his coat pockets to stop himself fidgeting with a new rip. It was not an unpromising start; it looked as though his insomnia theory was correct, and Adelaide had given him an ultimatum before actually calling for security. He assumed. Noise distracted him, a faint progression of clicks like the second hand of a watch magnified tenfold. It seemed to come from the ceiling. He looked up. The chandelier shone dimly. Who lived above Adelaide Mystik?

Five minutes later he banged on the door again. This time it flew open immediately.

"Who the hell do you think you are? I said fuck off." She glared at him.

It was the aggression of the girl which convinced Vikram he was safe. Brazen, but theatrical. It lacked the edge of promise.

"Aren't you curious about why I'm here?"

"No. Double fuck off."

The door started to shut. Vikram wedged his foot to block it. Through the gap, Adelaide stared down at his dirty boot. Her attitude changed. She arranged herself against the mirrored wall of her hallway, delivering an evil smile. Her lack of fear was almost insulting. He supposed it came hand in hand with her arrogance—as the Architect's granddaughter, she'd never had to be afraid.

"Have you ever been in jail, what was it—Vikram?"

"For a number of days. And yes, it's Vikram."

"What's it like down there?"

He ignored this. "Contrary to what you might think, I'm not a spy. Not for Linus, or for anyone. I'm here for my own reasons."

"To be arrested?" she enquired.

Vikram remembered Linus's reaction the first time Vikram had sought him out. There were similarities between brother and sister, and not just their looks. Confidence rose from them like a costly, seductive perfume.

"That's up to you," he said.

"You're right," she agreed. "It is."

She surveyed him speculatively. Something had given him the edge of advantage. She had not called for backup, as he had thought she might. There was a reason for that; she might be unafraid, but presumably she wasn't stupid. Perhaps she did not trust her own people.

Perhaps she was just bored.

"I'm here because I think you're the only one who can help me," he said.

Adelaide cocked her head.

"That's entirely possible. But you're missing one crucial element. Why would I want to help you?"

He shrugged, following instinct. "Because you'd be doing something you've never done before."

"Oh?"

"Yes. You'd be helping people."

She looked unimpressed.

"And it would make you look good," he added.

"I don't have an issue with the way I look, do you?" she said sweetly, and if he did not meet that gaze he had to look at the rest of her, which was no doubt what she intended. There was only one way to play this game. He stared at her openly for a good ten seconds before replying. The posters did not lie: she was that beautiful.

"Not especially," he said.

"Good." There was a pause, and he wondered if he had read her right. Then she said, "Two minutes then."

Vikram looked past her into the apartment. A lone red petal wilted on the floorboards of the mirrored hallway.

"Can I come in?"

"I'm fond of the doorstep."

"Fine. But I don't think you're very hospitable."

Adelaide's eyes snapped with apparent delight at this game. "You've lost a good twenty seconds already."

Inside his coat pockets, Vikram crossed his fingers.

"Listen," he said. "This city has everything. It wouldn't take much to give some aid to the people who need it. I know it doesn't affect you now but one day it might. People are angry, over there, in the bit you forget about. But we do exist. There will be more riots and one day the violence will come here and then you'll wish you did something about it before. But if you used your influence like Linus said you could—"

"Leave Linus out of it," Adelaide interrupted. "More. Seconds. Lost."

He looked at her for a moment, not as he had before, but as though he was searching her out. Testing her. He doubted anyone had ever looked at Adelaide Mystik this way before, and he was not sure how she might react. But she seemed to lean into his gaze. She did not break the silence.

"Have you ever seen anyone dead?" Vikram asked.

"Yes," she said. "My grandmother."

"Did you see her die?"

"She died in her sleep. I saw her afterwards."

"It's different when you watch them die."

"Is it."

"You should know," he said. "You were at the execution."

She stared back at him in a way that should have been frank, if she had been capable of frankness. He sensed catacombs beneath her expressions.

"You knew that man?" she asked. "Eirik 9968, you knew him?"

"Not personally." Once again, a flutter of guilt accompanied the lie. It was impossible to tell whether she believed him.

"Then who died on you? Death seems important to you, so who was it?"

"I've known a lot of people who died."

"It's never about the many. Nobody's that philanthropic."

"Her name was Mikkeli," he said blankly.

"Ah. A girl." Adelaide twirled a strand of red hair between two fingers. "And is that why you want to help your people, for this dead girl?"

Her words were probing fingers, digging through his hair and his skull to root around inside. Vikram told himself it did not matter what he said now. Adelaide could have what answers she wanted as long as she helped him.

"Something like that."

"Something like that," she repeated. Her gaze idled up and down him. Vikram matched it.

"Yes."

"And what exactly do you want to do for your westerners?"

"Food. Warmth. Jobs. Hope. Is that concise enough?"

"I'm not sure," she mused. "I suspect it might turn out to be rather more complicated than that."

"I could tell you more, but it might take longer than your two minute allocation."

"You are insolent." Adelaide toyed with the lace of her nightclothes. "What are you going to do for me in exchange for my voice?"

"What do you need?" He kept his face expressionless. A smile lit up her beautiful, flawless features.

"I'm sure I can find something. Let's just call it an i.o.u. for now, shall we? Meet me at The Stingray on Friday. Fourteen o'clock. Don't be late."

"I'll be there," he said.

She reached out, past the doorway for the first time, ran her finger lightly along the edge of his jawline. Her face was close to his. She looked incredibly young; only the traces of lines in their making showed she had left her teens behind. Perhaps it was that that made her so unreadable, like a slate yet to be written.

"You know it won't bring her back," she said.

It wasn't a compassionate line. He wondered why she had said it.

"I think I know that."

"Goodnight then."

"Goodnight."

The door shut. There was no sound from the other side, or from upstairs. Vikram stayed for a minute, memorizing the patterns of the wood, and those of the girl behind it.

He waited another hour before the first Undersea train of the morning. He had bribed a man to smuggle him over the border by barge, a quarter of the credit from the two weeks work. The man had hidden him in a cupboard-sized compartment, and when they reached the checkpoint, Vikram had heard skadi guards banging up and down the length of the barge and his heart had leapfrogged. It irked him that Adelaide hadn't asked how he had got to her, hadn't cared, even if it was better she didn't know.

The Undersea was dark and virtually deserted. Vikram had earmarked a hiding place in his carriage, but no one checked the train going back west. When he finally reached 614-West it was still dark and he was burning with a low exhilaration. He debated banging on Nils's door. Nobody liked to be woken before dawn, though, and he hadn't decided what to tell Nils when he did see him. Out of habit he tried the lift. Its OUT OF ORDER sign had been graffitied long ago. Vikram was tempted to add his own mark: an affirmation of the night's work, but he had nothing to scratch or spray with.

He ran up the first couple of flights, then slowed, stopping every few floors to catch his breath. After thirty-six floors he felt leaden with tiredness. He fumbled with the key in the lock—still weak—and collapsed onto a stew of rugs and clothes. He pulled everything over him. He expected to sleep instantly, but his brain thwarted him, spinning into action. He replayed each moment of his conversation with Adelaide. Was she lying awake now, or was she sleeping? If she was sleeping, what was she dreaming? Did she have ground-dreams like everyone else?

Vikram's dream was always the same: a stretch of golden sand. A beach. He walked along it, at first near the surf where it was damp, and then inland, past tufts of vegetation. The vegetation gave way to waving grasses. Where the grasses grew through the sand there were pebbles, smooth and white. In the dream he picked one up, one by one, and dropped them into a bucket that never filled.

Vikram lay awake a little longer. Sounds dulled by memory now crept back to taunt his hope of sleep. An itinerant banging from the floor above. The stamp of footsteps up and down stairs. Shouting. Always a dispute somewhere that could only be resolved when one throat grew too hoarse to continue or a raised fist brought an end. Beneath it, the ever present chatter of a city that had not known unconsciousness for a long time. Osiris articulated itself in waves of vocals, rising, falling, meandering through his subconscious like the disparate moods of the sea.

He was woken by persistent hammering. Dozy with dreams, he stumbled to the door. A flashlight temporarily blinded him, then dispelled the darkness of the room. Behind the torch he made out the faces of Nils and Drake. Drake's wayward hair was squashed beneath two woollen hats and a hood. She was grinning.

"How d'you fancy collecting an iceberg?"

Vikram stared at them both.

"What time is it?"

"Dunno. 'bout nineteen o'clock?"

"Shit." He'd slept right through the day. He rubbed his eyes, replaying Drake's previous words. "Iceberg? You mean?"

"I mean there's a space on the boat if you want…"

She wiggled the flashlight helpfully. Vikram located the water bucket. It was still a quarter full. He splashed his face, pulled his own coat out of the bedding and slung it over his shoulders. "I'm in."

Twenty minutes later, they were aboard a motor boat in pursuit of three industrial barges. Above them, the Moon moved in and out of its cloud cover. The sea was calm and dark. Vikram stayed by the rail with Nils, keeping out of the way of the crew. There were six of them including Drake, but no one else he recognized.

"Can you hear it?" Nils whispered.

Vikram listened. Beyond the engine motor, he heard a metallic susurration, like the sound of pooling chains. Ahead of them, high above sea level, a line of green lights stretched to left and right. He nudged Nils and pointed. It had been years since either man had passed the ring-net, but Vikram knew that Nils was thinking the same thing as him, that those were no lights: they were the glowing eyes of the dead.

The net was invisible in the darkness, but the windows of one of its watchtowers shone. The fleet of barges approached. Heavy clanking told Vikram that a curtain of the ring-net was lifting. The barges slid past the watchtower, slipping under the gap in the net. The smaller western boat followed in the swell. As they passed beneath, Nils's and Drake's faces were bathed in the green glow from the capping beacons. Vikram held up his hands. His gloves were tipped with the same green. The chains clinked in a tug of wind. Then they were through, the other side of the boundary.

Osiris waters lay behind them.

Vikram felt suddenly hollow. Who knew what had really happened to all those boats that left the city and disappeared? If only they had left a trail, a length of string that could be followed, hand over hand, by those that might wish to go after. Vikram leaned forward, straining his eyes. The Moon had gone behind a cloud.

The boats drove out for twenty minutes before they began to slow. Everyone on board fell silent. There was no noise except the sea, the humming motor, and a dull creaking.

Ahead, the sea turned entirely white.

"Is that...?" Vikram murmured.

"Yeah," said Drake. "That's it."

The phosphorous island stretched away beyond the barges' searchlights. The boats continued cautiously and came to rest at a point where the ice cut away smoothly, a sloping three metre cliff rising from the waves. Searchlights trained upon it. The air filled with the whirr of gears and engines.

Two platforms extended horizontally from the first of the boats. They were crowded with men and machinery. When the platforms reached the ice field, the workers clambered onto it, unloading their equipment with practised efficiency. Against the ice they looked like busy black insects.

Vikram watched in fascination as the process he had heard explained but never seen began. The crew dragged giant lasers into position. Through the night they would cut the ice sheet into many separate pieces, then tow them inside the ring-net. The freshwater bergs would relieve the load of the desal plants, which guzzled energy.

The lasers began their work, with a noise like metal plates scraping together. A shout went up on Drake's boat.

"That's it! That's our bit!"

Everyone on board ran to the rail. The boat keeled. The deck juddered underfoot as two small harpoons, trailing cables, fired across the water and embedded in the ice.

"Who's first?" yelled the skipper.

Drake gave Vikram and Nils a harness and a head-torch each. "Go on," she said. "I've done this before. Don't let go unless you fancy a dunking."

They exchanged grins. Vikram fastened the strap of the head-torch and switched it on. A pale beam illuminated the rail and the cables. Another member of the crew showed him how to hook his harness onto the cable. Vikram climbed over the rail and pitched forward.

A shove sent him swinging across the gulf. Air rushed at his face; he was flying. The head-torch picked out the wave trenches and the foam-flecked caps. His boots dipped the water. He brought his knees to his chest. The ice loomed. He stuck his feet out in front and landed with a crunch.

Nils's boots thudded down a second later. Vikram reached over and grabbed his friend's hand. Holding onto the cables, they clambered up the remainder of the slope, and stopped.

It was as though they had stepped onto the surface of the Moon. The ice was pitted and cracked, sheer blank slates giving way to hillocks and gaping craters. Fifty metres away, the laser beams were working their way across the sheet, a flicker of lightning marking their progress. The noise was phenomenal.

Vikram stamped on the ice. It was rock hard. Beneath the groan of the severing pack, he heard water lapping against its edges. Land must sound like this.

Others had joined them. Drake took a running leap and skidded eight metres before landing on her arse. Vikram whooped. They moved, at first cautiously, then throwing themselves around the ice. Their head-torches made peculiar shadows of the uneven surface and their own figures. They twisted to make even weirder, eldritch shapes. The ice glinted pale blue. The Moon came out from behind a cloud and turned it greenish yellow. It smelled raw and new, of the untouched and the untouchable. It had never held human imprints before.

Nils shouted. He'd found a long, sheer slope. The three of them sat in a row at the top, Vikram in front, then Drake, then Nils. They yelled a countdown.

"Three—two—one—go!"

They flew down the slope, as one, then as three, as Drake lost her grip and Vikram shot on ahead. At the bottom they curled up, toppled on their backs, helpless with laughter. The sky above was a jigsaw of cloud and stars. They regained their breaths slowly.

For as long as Vikram had known, since the beginnings of Osiris, the ice had come. Legend told of a land beneath it, a land free from storms and safe from flooding. It had a name, so rare, so precious, it was never spoken above a whisper. 'Tarctica. The southern land. It would cast off its frozen shell and one day, when all the ice had gone, the Citizens of Osiris would find a new home. So the legend went.

The laser rays continued their work. At last, with an ear splitting crack, the segment claimed by Drake's boat broke away. A fissure yawned, then it was a chasm, then a valley of ocean. Drake's boat was already towing away the section of ice, heading back inside the ring-net and leaving the flotilla of barges to continue their dismantling work until dawn.

The ice was moored between two towers on the outskirts of the western quarter and that night there was a carnival. Westerners came out in droves. People danced and performed theatrical charades. A band of acrobats tumbled, stood on their hands, and walked across a tightrope that had once been somebody's clothesline and still had a pair of leggings pegged to it. Statues, crude and artistic, were sculpted out of the hillocks. Fry-boat kitchens chugged out of the city to set up shop around the edge of the ice. The vendors leaned out of their hatches, shouting their wares of squid or saufish in amicable rivalry. Other westerners arrived in tiny skiffs, hacking off blocks of ice with pickaxes and towing them back into the west.

Nils produced a bottle of raqua and the three of them wandered about the ice, passing the bottle back and forth and admiring the spectacles. They settled at the edge of a crater where a crowd had gathered around a group of musicians. In the centre, a heater was wedged into a small pit. The smell of frying saufish and kelp dispersed through the foreign scent of the ice and skinny dogs came to lap at the meltwater.

Through the remainder of the night and the daylight that followed, Vikram almost forgot about his private mission. Sometimes, whilst they were laughing at each other's drunken antics, he felt the pang of a missing part, because Mikkeli should have been there to complete their quartet. And then Adelaide Mystik drifted back into view, her green eyes becoming the lights from the ring-net, the gaze of the dead.

"Look out!"

They had been on the ice for twenty-four hours when Vikram saw a man at the edge of the field hurl himself to one side. A moment later, a harpoon sunk a foot deep in the patch of ice where he had been standing. A second harpoon struck the ice five metres along, then another.

Nils got unsteadily to his feet.

"Fucking hell, it's the fucking skadi."

They could see the boats crouched a little way from the ice field. Struck by panic, other revellers leapt to avoid the deadly spikes. Some fell into the water. Hands reached down to rescue them but some were pulled in after and washed away from the field, caught by invisible currents. In the darkness, Vikram heard their cries growing fainter and fainter.

"Come back! Come back!"

In the confusion, it was a minute before Vikram realized that they were moving away from the towers. Already a stretch of freezing water lay between the ice field and safety. Some of the revellers refused to move, or were too intoxicated to perceive the danger. They leapt and cartwheeled, hurling fire beacons into the air. Dogs barked, small bodies racing up and down the field. The skadi fired a second wave of harpoons. Beneath the yells and clinking chains and the noise of straining ice, Vikram heard something new: a deep, rhythmical thudding.

"Drake! Where's your boat?"

"I don't know! I can't see it!"

The fry-boat kitchens were unhitching and pulling away. A man threw himself onto one of the roofs. He slipped and crashed into the sea with a shriek. Other than the abandoned torches subsiding on the ice, there was no light. But Vikram could hear the sea. The gap between ice field and towers was widening.

A figure lurched towards them, arms whirling overhead.

"It's the end of the world! Swim, swim, the ghosts are coming, swim for your lives!"

Vikram turned to Nils and Drake.

"Come on, we need a boat."

They ran towards the nearest fry-boat, whose vendor was clumsily packing away her wares, catching one another as they stumbled over abandoned bottles or melt holes. Again Vikram heard that deep, rhythmic thudding. It sounded like drums. The sound was metallic, a clanging, resonant thunder, accompanied by throaty cries.

With no warning, the sky lightened. The sea and the ice turned to shimmering gold. Instinctively all three of them dropped. Belly down, Vikram peered out across the water.

From between two towers emerged a monster of fire. Its flames shot three storeys high into the air. Smoke spewed from its core. The fug billowed before it, reaching over the ice. As it moved forward, ash rained down on the ocean.

It was a boat, and it was entirely aflame. From the prow of the thing protruded the effigy of a colossal shark fashioned from wires. The wires glowed white with the heat. Flames jetted from the gaping mouth.

"Lights of australis," whispered Drake. "What is that?"

"Its Juraj's gang," said Nils softly.

The burning barge had an escort. On either side, nine rafts rode low in the water. Each platform was stacked with drums upon which their crews hammered out a relentless beat. Vikram felt each boom in the ice beneath his stomach.

"That's not all," he said. "It's Juraj. What's left of him."

Mesmerised, they could only stare. As the blazing craft drew closer, Vikram saw that the carcass of one boat had been dragged on top of another.

At its peak, the gang lord's body was strapped to a crudely erected mast. As the flesh shrivelled and peeled away, Juraj's skeleton emerged like a warped chrysalis, the bones black and distorted.

He had no limbs. They had been removed. In place of limbs he had crude prosthetics, longer than arms and legs could be, and spouting fire.

Tapers of flame fell upon the raft drummers. They kept beating. The rest of Juraj's gang were dancing maniacally on the rafts as they accompanied their dead leader to his final grave. As they approached the ice field, their yowls filled the night. The drums grew louder and louder, faster and faster.

"They're catching up," said Nils.

Vikram swore. "They're sending it at the skadi."

The skadi, at last realizing their danger, began to shoot. The pyre glided forward. The rafts let out a shrilling chorus of *ai-ai-ai!* The drums pounded. Now the skadi were frantically trying to retract their harpoons. But the spears were embedded and the tow ropes were metal chains. The skadi barges were tethered to the ice field. The pyre was moving faster than they could tow.

The drummers whooped.

Ai-ai-ai! Ai-ai-ai!

Almost leisurely, two crafts drifted towards one another.

Juraj's pyre ploughed into the first skadi barge. The flames reached out. Vikram clapped his hands over his ears.

The explosion was deafening.

Debris rained on top of them. Burning embers sizzled where they hit the ice. He curled into a ball, arms protecting his head, feeling the sting as something struck his back.

Vikram was the first to recover. Ears ringing, he helped the others to their feet. Drake was bleeding. Vikram led them to the edge of the ice field, ducking the sprays of gunfire. In a matter of minutes, the sea would be swarming with skadi boats.

He saw a stray shot catch one of the fry-boat vendors still struggling to unmoor. The woman was flung backwards in a spray of blood. Bent double, they ran towards her boat.

Nils started up the motor whilst Vikram and Drake hauled the dead woman out onto the ice. There was nothing they could do for her now. As they steered away from the ice floe, he heard bolts striking the boat roof. The night blazed with fire and searchlights. The drums and the cries grew ever more frantic. The ice, gleaming yellow beneath the flames, was spotted with inert bodies.

As they pulled away from the battleground, Vikram saw something like a comet streak through the air from the rafts and explode alongside another skadi boat.

Drake was visibly shaking.

"Oh shit, oh shit, oh shit."

They were drawing near to the first tower when dazzling white light blinded Vikram. A speeder lay directly in their path. Vikram veered the boat sharply right. The searchlight followed. He increased their speed. The light lost them momentarily, then switched off.

He could hear the drone of the smaller, higher performance motor as the speeder approached.

Grimly, Vikram began to lurch the boat in a zigzag pattern. It was large and unwieldy and he could hear its sides groan with the strain. The sea was getting choppier too. Bad news for the speeder and worse news for them. The fry-boat was not designed to be out on open water, and now they were a good half kilometre from the towers, moving further away from the fire fight.

Nils swore as he leaned out of the hatch, watching for the speeder. Shadows scooted past. He thought it was the other boat, but now it had vanished entirely. The noise of the waves masked the two motors. He could sense the other boat out there. Waiting. Listening.

"Vik, I can't see them." Nils whispered this time. He came to stand beside Vikram. Drake took up position at the hatch.

"Where the hell are they?" muttered Vikram.

He reduced the engine power. They were almost drifting now. So was the speeder.

Residue noise from the fire fight echoed across the water. From a distance, it looked like a strange ritual, a dance between flames on the water surface. Vikram could not tell who was winning.

"Why don't they just open fire?" hissed Drake.

"They want prisoners," said Vikram. "Juraj's gang are so crazed they won't stop until they're all dead. The skadi need examples."

"What are we going to do?"

"Run for it."

Nils nodded. "It's our best chance."

"Hang on tight."

He took a firm grip himself as he swung the boat back towards the city and hit full throttle. Instantly the searchlight flickered back on, some hundred metres away, and began roving the waves.

The boat lurched forward, jamming into the encroaching waves. Vikram wrested the craft first one way, then the next. Crates of kelp and fish shunted from side to side. His elbow cracked against metal, sending bolts of pain up to his temples. Spray dashed in his face. In seconds he was drenched.

"Where are they Drake?" he yelled. Drake hung precariously out of the hatch.

"Right on our tail, seventy metres," she yelled back.

"Watch out now, you're coming into the city." Nils, clinging on beside him, could see a little better.

"You'll have to direct me."

He was steering blind now. He could only trust Nils's directions. He sensed the first towers looming up on either side as they barrelled back into the maze of the city. A shot glanced off the roof.

"Fifty metres!" Drake shouted.

"Shit."

Vikram began to weave. Their only chance now lay in using the towers as cover.

"Listen. You two have to get out. I'm taking this over the border."

"You're what?" Nils hung on as the boat lurched.

"I have to get over the border tonight. I can't explain."

"It's that bloody girl, isn't it? That Rechnov woman?"

"This is the best chance I have. All the skadi are back there, the border will be as close to unguarded as it ever is."

"Vik—"

"Just do it, will you? They won't follow you."

"Yes, they'll follow you, you idiot—we should stick together!"

"Come on," said Drake. She staggered up the boat. "Nils, come on. Tell us when, Vik. And good luck."

Nils was shaking his head, plainly furious, but Vikram had no more time. As they approached Market Circle, he choked the throttle, slowing the boat just enough to skid past a decking. Nils and Drake leapt from the hatch and dropped flat to the decking. Vikram powered ahead once more. He risked a glance back and saw that the speeder had followed him. Nils and Drake were safe.

Now it was just the two boats. Vikram's only advantage was that he knew the western waterways. He closed his eyes momentarily, allowing instinct to take over. Through Market Circle. Out the other side. This part of the west was quiet. He was following the route taken by the waterbus on the day he went to the Council. As he approached the border, the speeder was hard on his tail, but his assumption had been correct—there were only two skadi boats stationed at the checkpoint.

Setting the boat on a direct course through the gap in the border net, Vikram ducked low. The shooting came late; the border guards had not expected his clumsy vehicle to charge. He hurtled straight through, searchlights sweeping overhead.

He was in the City.

The speeder was chasing him, and now one of the border boats as well. He kept the fry-boat straight. He had to get out fast, but they would not be able to shoot so easily deep in Citizen territory. He chose a residential tower—swung the boat in close and leapt from the fully powered vehicle. He hit the decking hard, hurting his ankle, and rolled. Jumping to his feet, running to the doors, he pounded the open button. The doors slid apart and Vikram darted inside. He heard a shout as the skadi spotted his exit, and then the doors slid shut.

He was inside a clean, low lit lobby with four lifts. He ignored them and ran into the stairwell. The skadi would be following.

He raced up the stairs until he heard the sounds of them entering the building. Now he had to be silent. He removed his dripping shoes and socks and carried them. He moved on up in bare feet, as quietly as possible, unaware if his pursuers were doing the same. His heart was pounding so fiercely he was sure they must hear it. There was no shortage of electricity in the City; every floor had the same low night lighting. No dark corners to hide in.

Ten floors up, he came out of the stairwell and ventured into the corridors. He limped past the numbered doors of apartments. He was acutely aware of his appearance, tattered and soaked. He had a fresh cut on his temple which he could feel now was bleeding. His only hope was that at whatever time of night it was, the Citizens who lived here were all sleeping.

And then he saw it—so simple, so easy. The fire alarm.

He kept going, through the heart of the tower, looking for a stairwell on the other side. First he needed somewhere to hide. With every step, he felt the fear of capture heighten. Sweat lined the inside of his clothes. He didn't dare look back. What if there were cameras? What if they were lying in wait?

He kept going up until he found what he was looking for—a cleaning room, full of mops and buckets, with enough space for a skinny man. He limped back into the corridors. The fire alarms were posted at every level. He took a deep breath, glanced once around the silent corridors, and smashed it with his good elbow.

The noise was shrill and instant. Vikram ran back to the cleaning room and slipped inside, pulling the door to. From his tiny prison, he listened to the sounds of the tower waking up. Running footsteps pattered on the carpets as people evacuated their rooms. Their voices were groggy and confused.

"What's happening?"

"Where is it, where's the fire?"

"Orla, get back here now, don't run!"

They streamed past him. An age seemed to pass before they had all gone. When the noise had faded, Vikram slipped out and continued back up the stairs. He had no doubt that the fire fighters would be investigating that floor within minutes. The skadi would guess who the culprit had been, but the confusion had bought him time.

He kept going, fighting a great flood of weariness, until he saw the sign for a bridge. He urged himself on. Just as far as the next tower. Walking across the closed, windowless bridge he felt trapped and nervous, and hurried through the tunnel as quickly as he could persuade his exhausted limbs to move. In the morning he was going to have to find himself some clothes that would pass in the City, and track down Adelaide's restaurant—but for now all he wanted was a bolthole to curl up in for the night.

He took the lift. When it reached the first level underwater he felt the hairs raising on the back of his neck, but he doubted the skadi would expect him to go down; they knew the horror underwater held for ex-prisoners. The Undersea station was silent and deserted. Vikram ran down the giant escalators, feeling the damp chill of tunnels blasted out of rock below the seabed. Salt trails ran down the cracks between display boards flashing up taglines for skating exhibitions, electro recitals, gold-level Guild ratified Tellers, the annual gliding race. They were all months out-of-date. On the dusty screens, the letters scrambled themselves and fingers beckoned. Adelaide Mystik's virtual eyes followed him as she lifted a Sobek scarab in the palm of her hand, her lips o-shaped to blow him a kiss.

The dripping walls of the platform were streaked with lichen. The weight of the ocean bore down upon him, and his head pounded. The idea of spending more than a few minutes here was terrifying, but he needed to hide. He jumped onto the tracks and walked into the tunnel.

15 ¦ ADELAIDE

I t was after midnight, and everything outside the penthouse was the same except for the yellow security bar bisecting the wooden door. Adelaide reached past it and deliberately twisted the handle. It was locked, as she expected. She took out her old key and pushed it into the keyhole. It didn't fit. Axel had changed the locks. She sat down in front of the door and waited for someone to come.

Two years had passed since she had stepped out of the lift to find this same door, her own front door, wide open, a gateway for the landslide of her possessions. The way in had been blocked with a cabinet. When she clambered over one heel snagged and her foot slipped out of the shoe. She grabbed the door frame for support. The trail continued into the penthouse: shoes, clothes, pictures, cosmetics. She heard glass smash.

"A?" she shouted. "Is that you?"

The tinkling sound reverberated on and on. Then there was silence. Adelaide abandoned her shoes and wriggled into the hallway. Not knowing who she was about to meet, she padded through the ransacked rooms. The door to her bedroom was ajar. She pushed it cautiously.

Her twin crouched in a myriad of broken glass. Shards winked at the ceiling and each other and Axel. He was sucking on one finger. A line of blood ran down his wrist and his shirt sleeve was scarlet. Adelaide looked at the wall where her mirror had hung. The rivets that had held the glass were still there, with clinging fragments of silver.

"Axel?"

He stared at her. Scratches marked his face. For a moment she thought he didn't recognize her. Then his features bunched.

"What are you doing here?"

"What?"

"You don't live here."

She almost laughed. "What are you talking about, A?"

"I said you don't live here." Axel raised himself slowly. A shower of glass fell from his clothing.

"You're bleeding," said Adelaide.

Axel glared fixedly at the ground. He began to trace a deliberate circle around the room. Each step destroyed another remnant of the mirror. On the floor near the bed, Adelaide saw a hammer.

"I think you'd better go to the bathroom," she said, louder this time. "Axel. Come on. Get cleaned up, I'll fix us a drink and you can tell me what happened."

He stopped pacing. His eyes flicked up. "You shouldn't be here," he said.

"This is our apartment, Axel," she said carefully. "Not yours. Ours. Neither of us had a problem with that before. If something's changed, now's the time to tell me."

He barged past, slamming her into the wall. Anger flooded her. She chased him to the kitchen. He began to pull pans out of the cupboard and throw them onto the tiles in a discordant opera of noise. Adelaide put her hands over her ears.

"For fuck's sake, what are you doing?"

Utensils and machines followed. A bottle opener flew past her head. The blender cracked on the floor. Axel opened the glass cupboard. Adelaide darted forward and grabbed his wrist. She felt his blood on her skin, wet and slippery.

"Oh no, you don't."

Axel shook her off and reached for the nearest glass. She moved—an amalgamation of leap and unkind embrace, pinioning his arms to his sides. They fell to the floor together. Metal struck her elbow. Her entire body twanged with the pain. For whole, excruciating seconds she was paralysed. Axel was struggling to get up. Gathering her strength, she tackled him. They fought viciously, a tangle of limbs, childhood tactics made newly cruel. He yanked strands of hair from her scalp. She got both hands on his arm and twisted. They scratched and kicked. Pots and pans skidded over the floor. Then his hand struck her forehead. The blow sang inside her skull. She grabbed the nearest utensil and thrust it between them in panic.

"I'll do it, A, I'll really hurt you if I have to—"

His body went slack. His head fell to one side as though he was listening intently, and his fingers drummed the ceramic tiles. A repeated tattoo, like hooves. Then he got up without looking at her and walked out of the kitchen. She lay gasping on her back. Her face and body smarted with bruises. She stayed there for twenty minutes, listening to the sounds of her twin evicting her. Second by second, her courage seeped away.

"Miss Rechnov?"

Adelaide opened her eyes. The door was obscured by a pair of black trousers, neatly ironed. The shoes beneath them were highly polished, but looked worn-in, comfortable. Sanjay Hanif.

"It's Miss Mystik," she said.

"I apologize. According to official records your name is still Rechnov. Would you care to explain what you are doing here? This is an investigation scene."

"I'm not on the investigation scene."

Hanif crouched, bringing his face closer to her level. He had dark eyes. Intelligent eyes, she thought. He was a man used to making quick assessments, yet now he was forced to take the long slow path of unmatchable clues. How could anyone make sense of Axel?

"You tried to get in," he said, and pointed to a high corner behind her.

"I knew it was locked," she said. "And I know you have a camera there. I'm not stupid."

"I don't think you are, Miss Rechnov. Which begs the question once more, what are you doing here? Some might consider trespassing on Council territory an act of extreme stupidity."

"I was looking for you," she said.

Hanif clasped his hands, resting them upon his knees. He balanced easily in such an awkward position. She wondered if this was how he interrogated criminals.

"You have my attention," he said.

"Axel's my twin. I have a right to know what you have discovered."

"I understand. But as I have already explained to your father, the family must be excluded from the investigation until we have ruled out the possibility of foul play."

"You mean murder."

Hanif's face remained still. She wondered if he was aware of the underground activities of people like Lao. If he had any inkling that Adelaide had hired her own man. She wondered whether Hanif knew about the airlift.

"It is customary to explore all avenues. In my experience, well-known people do not go missing for no reason. When was the last time you saw your brother, Miss Rechnov?"

"You've seen my statement. A month before Yonna found him gone. He came to my apartment."

"And you're positive you did not see him again?"

"Of course I'm positive."

"Did you come here?"

"No."

"Did you make any effort to see Axel?"

"No, I—no."

"Did you ever feel angry with your brother, Miss Rechnov?"

"Are you interrogating me now?"

His mild expression did not alter.

"We both have our questions, Miss Rechnov. You have yours and I have mine. If you do not believe that I wish to solve this riddle because I care about what happened to your brother, at least believe I will do so because it is my job."

She stared at him. "Everyone gets angry with the people they love."

"Of course."

"You should trust me," she said. "I knew him. The rest of my family had no interest in Axel after he changed. He was an embarrassment to them. A problem."

"It's late, Miss Rechnov," he said quietly. "You should go home."

He called the lift. She understood that it was for her. Not far above them, the huge wheels started to turn and the cables rushed through their bindings. They waited, each intent on the incalculable drop beyond the glass doors. People said Hanif was a good man. His quiet manner, his level tone, all were suggestive of a man of integrity. But everyone was corruptible, and the Rechnovs had more money and influence than anyone in Osiris. How far could she really trust him?

The roof of the lift swept up. The doors parted. She stepped inside. As the lift started its descent his calm unhurried face vanished, then his torso, and finally his polished shoes.

/ / /

Adelaide curled up on the futon. The wall opposite flickered with a continuous projection of black and white films, but the sound was off, and she did not really see the images.

A week after her eviction from her home, Axel turned up at Jannike's apartment where Adelaide was staying. He was distracted. He asked her to come back but she refused; she was scared of him. Axel could not understand why she wouldn't come back, and she was too humiliated to tell him. After that, the visits stopped. The rift cut like acid.

The Red Rooms were her home now. So she kept telling herself.

Four in the morning and Osiris was quiet. She knew the night's fluctuating dynamics, the grace notes that marked a creaking machine from the floor above or the generators shifting to beta mode. By four o'clock, Osiris was always quiet.

She refilled her voqua glass. Clean, clear, uncomplicated.

In less than twelve hours, she was due to meet Vikram. Although she had made the appointment with no intention of keeping it, something about his face, his stillness, lingered with her. He was the angriest and the calmest person she had ever met. It was like stumbling upon a ticking device; the horror of what might happen was only equalled by her desire to see the mess. She imagined him waiting at the restaurant tomorrow. Today, now. Had he drawn up a plan of action? Was he running through the arguments he might use?

He'd lost someone too. Mikkeli. The name burned, as though Mikkeli's vibrancy in life had passed into a flame that needed no oxygen, only a vessel. Adelaide did not know how tall Mikkeli was, or the colour of her hair, but the girl was present with the ghosts circling the city. She hid behind wave crests. She lay supine in troughs.

Axel is alive, Adelaide told herself. Otherwise I would see him like I see that girl. With salt in his lungs and frozen crystals in his hair.

Occasionally, when she was very drunk, Adelaide wondered if other cities had been like Osiris. If other great metropolises ate away at sanity by hurling people through their gates, more and more people, an overdose of life, until the crowds became drugged with their own gluttony. She studied photographs of lost civilizations and touched the imprints of the people in them and in her head she moved them to Osiris and watched their faces change. And sometimes she moved herself from Osiris to those long gone places and watched a different Adelaide walking on streets. That Adelaide had the same eyes, lips, hair. She had the same indolent walk. But the ground was different. It pressed onto her feet and sometimes it tripped her and sometimes it hurt. But she felt it. She knew it, with the witless intimacy and the trust offered only to a stranger.

Ground-dreams. Everybody had them. Adelaide poured herself another splash of voqua. Osiris was clever. Osiris made you think too much.

She sank back against the cushions, her eyes half-closed. The projection played out its muted scenes. Vehicles with silent wheels and boats that flew. Moving stairways held rivers of people. Their eyes forward. Their eyes all-knowing, knowledge in every part of them, injected into their blood, in the machines that lived in their heads. Now steps lead to a door: a house with four walls. *How functional.* Trees leaning out of the ground. Wind moving the arms of the trees, the vehicles rushing past them, careless of the ground, of roots or earth.

The whirrs and tics of everyday life in some other world. Worlds, she reminded herself, that had failed.

Out in the ghost-sea, the girl Mikkeli breathed. She had a message for Adelaide. Don't give up. Keep looking. Follow the silver fish.

/ / /

In the morning, a whim sent Adelaide across the city to see Linus. He was in a meeting when she arrived. She busied herself reading the news headlines on her Surfboard. *Home Guard arrest key Juraj gang members in all night fire battle. Council announce budget increase for western perimeter reinforcements...* The moving text made her dizzy. She stopped reading.

After ten minutes her brother appeared. He escorted her directly to his office, glancing around the reception area as though she might have inflicted unmentionable damage in the short time she had been waiting. The room was smaller than Feodor's, but meticulously organized. She supposed this was the impression Linus wanted to create: geometric and clinical. His walls were covered with incomprehensible graphs.

Linus sat behind his desk and indicated the chair opposite.

"To what to I owe the pleasure, Adelaide?"

"Sarcasm already? You know I am still very angry with you, Linus." But she didn't want to talk about Tyr, and added quickly, "Any Council gossip?"

"We steer clear of that."

"Oh." The chair had wheels. Adelaide used one foot to propel her in circles, aware that he was watching her. "I wonder why you do it," she mused.

"I'm not going to explain myself for your entertainment. You have no idea what's going on in Osiris."

She paused spinning. "Have you and Vikram formed some sort of conspiracy?"

"You've met him again, have you?"

"I had a visit."

"And?"

On the Neptune, a long-finned angelfish swam forward until it filled almost the whole of the oval oceanscreen. Its mouth opened and an envelope floated out.

"You have Reefmail," said Adelaide.

"So I see."

The angelfish swam back and forth.

"Seems important," Adelaide commented.

"It can wait. When did you see Vikram?"

"Doesn't matter. I'm not going to help him."

Linus propped one arm on a filing cabinet. "He's right, you know."

"Of course you think that."

"Look, you and I have grown up with this divide. But that's not an excuse to accept it. Our parents' generation won't talk about it, they feel too guilty. It's up to us."

"They're the ones that did it, Linus, let them sort it out."

"They're tired, Adelaide." His voice was earnest now. "They can't imagine a way to reverse that decision without a massive backlash. And they're right, it won't be a smooth transition. But that doesn't mean it shouldn't be done."

"What, you want to integrate now?"

"I think we should demilitarize the border, yes."

"And get us all killed," she scoffed.

"I didn't say it's not a risk. But we're sitting on a time bomb. Remember the riots three years ago, all those people killed at the desalination plant. A plant, I might add, which is now functioning at forty per cent."

Adelaide looked ceiling-ward. There was no dust here, no places for small creatures to hide. "Are you trying to scare me, Linus?"

He sighed. "Maybe I am. But there's an even bigger issue at stake. Even you must know what it is."

She fell quiet. The Neptune hummed. The angelfish still swivelled around the flashing envelope. She could not resist a glance at the window, where misty rain sheened the glass.

"You mean this idea that the weather's changing," she said finally.

"So you have noticed something." There was a shift in his voice—surprise? Satisfaction?

"People talk. I'm not convinced. Anyway, grandfather hasn't said anything and he's been here longer than anyone. He'd know."

Linus rapped the wall graph behind him. "Facts, Adelaide. This proves it. We've been experimenting—making forecasts. Not far ahead—but it's often accurate. That's a sign that the atmosphere is settling."

"Is that what they're doing above my apartment? Weather telling?" She looked away. "Doesn't seem right."

"Right or wrong, it's going to happen. It has to, for what must follow. What I was telling you before, at your Rose affair—no, don't sigh, it's not a joke. Osiris has a very real problem. There are many things in this city we can make—we can grow foods and medicines and bioplastics, our Makers produce complex parts—but there are crucial things we can't. Like bufferglass. Solar skin. Those are Afrikan technologies, and we've used up our reserves. Now there're reports that the water turbines are breaking down. Next time a hyperstorm hits, it could do terrible damage, not to mention making a serious dent in our energy capacity. Our only option to repair this damage would be to leave the City."

She turned back, shocked.

"Leave the City! Are you insane?"

Linus looked pleased with himself. Perhaps he was just trying to rattle her.

"On the contrary," he said. "I have never been more serious. We will have to renew expeditions."

"What about the storms?" she countered. "Even if you designed this amazing weather teller, how would a tiny expedition boat escape the storms? It would be ripped to pieces."

"As I said before, Adelaide, the climate is adjusting. It's a natural process. Besides, Teller portents favour journeys. The political time is right, and the necessity is there. Sooner or later, the Council must acknowledge it."

"But there's nothing out there. There's nothing to find."

"You've taken Osiris doctrine too much to heart. This is my contention with Council policy. Education should be about stimulus, about questions, not rote. We shouldn't stop asking. Or hoping."

"Hope is a fool's errand, Linus. You'll only alienate people when you can't deliver what they want."

His lips curved. "You sound like Father."

"Don't be ridiculous, I couldn't be less like him."

She was thinking of the last communications ever recorded before the Great Silence. They had arrived by boat. A refugee had carried the images all the way from the northern hemisphere, on a Neon Age hologram that now sat in the Museum. It might be upsetting, the teacher had warned them. But every pupil has to see. Otherwise you will never understand.

It wasn't the images of destruction so much as the last radio broadcast that Adelaide always thought of: the voice, quietly desperate, speaking knowingly to people that would never come. Everyone in the class cried. The teacher was crying. Even Axel, if he wasn't a boy, would have been crying. Everyone except Adelaide. She had suspected then that something was wrong with her. She couldn't cry; she could only watch the images of those doomed people unfold one by one and feel hollow inside. Something had died in her that day. Maybe Linus was right—it was hope.

"Adelaide? You must see my point."

"You're deluding yourself, Linus. Everyone loves the idea of land. But it's only an idea. It's—what did Second Grandmother used to say—over the rainbow."

He looked at her sympathetically, and she knew they were chasing different shadows.

"We have to find out," Linus said. "It's imperative that we know what is left. We must think ahead."

"No-one will listen to you."

"They will. Maybe not today, or tomorrow, but eventually. Because unlike you, a lot of people share my hope."

"Poor fools."

He laughed. "You'd fight me all day. I wish you'd understand how influential you could be. If you only converted that cynicism, people would follow you."

"You want me to lie."

"No." Now he sounded troubled. "No, I don't want that."

Idly, Adelaide tapped the desk. "It wouldn't be a problem. Technically I'm a very convincing liar."

"Incorrigible." Linus fell silent, as though he had reached the end of his persuasions, and yet they had not quite achieved the conclusion he had sought. For a moment Adelaide felt sorry for him. She had never considered his belief in an outside world to be quite so integral to his character, but there it was, in blunt appeal, inextricably woven into the fabric of his political career. It struck her as odd that he might spend years campaigning for something so dreamily insubstantial.

She felt the same, nudging impulse that had brought her here.

"I'll meet Vikram," she said. "But I make you no promises."

"Don't underestimate what you're embarking on."

Adelaide stood and sent the chair wheeling under the desk with a backward kick of her heel. "Brother dear. When have you ever seen me in over my head? We may have different methods, but I'm quite as capable as you. If not more so."

He gave her a crooked smile. She saw a flash of Axel in his face. Something in the way the eyes creased. She was so accustomed to warring with

Linus, she tended to forget they shared a genetic code.

"As always, that alarms me more than anything else," he said.

"I'll send you an invite to the next soirée. I don't expect to see you there."

"I'll ensure that my schedule is full."

She nodded. Linus, at least, understood that collaboration was not reconciliation. At the door she paused.

"One thing, Linus. If you're so worried that we're running out of buffer-glass, why would you support repairing towers in the west?"

He smiled. "Think about it. The thinner our resources are spread, the sooner the crisis looms…"

"And the sooner you can push for your expeditions." She thought about it. "Yes. Clever. But it won't work, you know." It had been a successful whim, she thought. Linus thought she was doing something worthwhile, so he would keep quiet about her affair with Tyr. Neither had he guessed Adelaide's agenda. What with Lao's refusal and her abortive meeting with Hanif, she had realized it was impossible to get into Axel's apartment. Impossible without help, that was, and if necessary, someone who could take the fall.

She checked her watch. If she hurried, she'd only be forty-five minutes late for Vikram.

16 ¦ VIKRAM

"**G**ood afternoon, sir. Do you have a reservation?"

"Yes, it's under Adelaide Mystik—or Rechnov, it could be Rechnov."

"Ah, Miss Mystik," said the waiter, drawing out the syllables as if there were many things he could impart about Adelaide. "Yes, she's reserved for two o'clock. She isn't here yet, but if you'd like to come through?"

If Vikram's dishevelled appearance perturbed the waiter, there was no trace of it in his face. It had taken all of Vikram's nerve to walk into the changing room of the watersports centre, and walk out again wearing a mishmash of stolen clothes, expecting at any moment to hear a shout of discovery at his back. He checked his watch, looked back once at the entrance to *The Stingray*. No sign of Adelaide.

"Sure."

He followed the waiter through a stone archway. Inside, the restaurant opened out into a glittering cave. The tables were scattered a discreet distance apart, round with turquoise cloths and almost all of them occupied. A female pianist was playing something light and fluid. The waiter led him to an empty table with a single rose laid at each of the two places. He pulled out a chair and took Vikram's coat. Vikram sat awkwardly.

In this place he felt every minor injury with ten times the intensity he would have anywhere else. The previous night was a blur of fire and drums and the distant rumble of engines which he had woken to in the tunnels. His head ached. He was covered in bruises whose origins he could not recall; even his face was scratched.

"Is this the first time you have visited us, sir?"

"Yes."

"I trust you will find everything to your satisfaction."

"Thank you."

Was he supposed to say anything else? The waiter bore his stolen coat away. Vikram looked about him. The walls and ceiling of the restaurant were covered with mosaics depicting fish of every imaginable size and shape. The mosaic was beautiful but he barely saw it because in between the tiles were large portholes with external lights that revealed the real ocean.

The hairs rose on the back of his neck. His nerves were so frayed he almost jumped up and fled; he had to press his hands against his knees to stay put. He reminded himself that Adelaide had never been in prison. She could not have known about the portholes. Even if she did, she did not know what they meant to Vikram.

The waiter returned with a menu and a glass of something green, which he said was complimentary.

"While you're waiting, sir. We always look after Miss Mystik's guests."

"Is she usually late?"

"I'm sure you know better than I do, sir."

There was no answer to this, so he perused the menu in silence. It was, as the decor suggested, primarily a seafood restaurant, but Vikram hadn't heard of most of the dishes listed. He tasted the green drink. It tingled, hard and bright down his gullet; he imagined he was swallowing diamonds.

He glanced at the other diners under pretence of studying the menu. He didn't recognize anyone from the Rose Night, but his time there had been limited. The clientele seemed less effusive than Adelaide's set. Conversation was quiet and intimate. Vikram felt like an impostor. He touched the gleaming set of cutlery before him. It left a smeary fingerprint. He put his hands beneath the table, feeling guilty for ruining the aesthetic perfection, and then guilty for feeling guilty.

A woman at the table opposite was talking earnestly about the Colnat Foundation. Vikram hid a smile. He had never read Colnat's report, but he knew that it described the standards of living in the west as poor (an understatement but a statement at least), and that it had sparked off a minor "save-the-west" movement in the City.

Eirik had spoken enthusiastically of Colnat. The Citizen was an idealistic man, a man Vikram had admired at the time. Colnat had had visions of redeveloping the west. He wanted to set up schools. For a year or so he was a common sight, crouched in the prow of a boat, scribbling notes with industrious fervour. He was accompanied everywhere by his dog, a great scruffy animal. The dog contracted a disease and died; it was said that Colnat never recovered from the loss. At any rate, he went back east not long before the riots and was not seen again.

The woman opposite was talking as though the initiative was still running.

"Of course schooling is the key to it," she said. Her voice was low, urgent. "If Palenta could just be persuaded to support the motion, we might have a chance of pushing it through…"

"Under what clause?"

"I don't know. The Aek Amendment. Even the Ibatoka."

"Have you heard Palenta speak?"

"Oh, I don't know him personally, darling. This looks delicious, doesn't it?" The couple's knives and forks clinked, and their conversation reverted to trivia.

Vikram didn't have any education; it was Mikkeli who had taught him how to read and write. Now and then, those days adopted his thoughts like driftwood. Hazy recollections of Naala's boat, with its fumes of alcohol and icy sweat. Keli hoarding books, her index finger running under the lines whilst the letters loomed large and slowly familiar.

A fish swam past the porthole. Where the hell was Adelaide? Was she even coming? His stomach was rumbling with hunger. He felt more and more ill at ease. He found himself checking for exits, wary of a trap.

The couple opposite had reached dessert. The woman was lingering over a concoction in a tall glass, dipping the spoon with delicate, precise movements.

"Loviisa wants gliding lessons, but I think water-skiing is more beneficial, don't you? Gliding's such a hassle. But she will go on."

"I know. Toi's been nagging me for a waterbike since last midsummer." The man leaned over and tapped her hand. "But let's not talk about them. It reminds me of her."

They weren't really a couple, Vikram realized. Not officially, the way people did things this side of town, where relationships were ratified by

Tellers and salt. And something else: they were in love. He supposed guilt and grief were common luxuries here. He thought of the girl with the red bow in her hair. She was part of it. So was Adelaide Mystik. He could not condemn the City as false outright, but none of it seemed real to him. It was too brassy, too effusive. How could you trust the sadness of someone who had never seen that cold could kill? Who had never seen a gun fired, never been afraid to sleep?

He checked his watch. Adelaide was already twenty-five minutes late. Vikram drained the green drink, and as the waiter passed, held up his glass. He might be here for a while.

17 | ADELAIDE

Vikram was putting on his coat, about to depart. Adelaide congratulated herself on her timing.

"The waiter said you'd be late," he said. "Personally, I'm amazed you showed up at all."

She heard, subdued but not quite disguised, the note of contempt. She refused to be bothered by it.

"I wasn't going to," she said.

"What made you change your mind?"

"I have my reasons."

A waiter appeared at their table. "Good afternoon, Miss Mystik. Will you be dining with us today?"

Adelaide scanned the menu. "Yes, I believe we will. I'll have the rainbow-fish. With karengo squares on the side. Vikram? I've kept you waiting, I owe you lunch."

"What do you recommend?" he asked the waiter.

"The chef's special is excellent, sir. Marinated swordfish fillet."

"That sounds great."

"We'll take a bottle of my usual," said Adelaide. "But first, aperitifs."

"Octopya, madam?"

"Exactly."

With a slight bow he moved away, taking several empty glasses of Vikram's with him. Adelaide placed one hand on top of the other.

"Now," she said. "Business. I assume you can break into an apartment?"

"What makes you think that?"

"If I remember right you've been in jail."

"Not for breaking and entering."

"What for?"

"Assault," Vikram said.

The waiter arrived with two conical glasses containing blue liquid and a metal appliance. Over each glass he balanced a slotted spoon with a sugar cube. Spigots from the metal appliance dripped water slowly through the sugar. Adelaide watched, silent, until the process was complete. She pushed one glass toward Vikram and sipped her own. It was the hit she needed. Fire and ice in one gulp.

"I love the first taste," she said. "The doorway to possibility."

Vikram tried a mouthful and made a face of disagreement.

"You were saying about your conviction," she prompted.

"I was involved in the riots three years ago," Vikram said. His voice was chilly as a Tarctic wind. She had never met anyone so unforgiving. "I did a lot of things like a lot of other people and I hit one of the Guards."

Adelaide nibbled on a crystallized apricot. "How did it feel?"

"Like the beginning," he said.

"How long were you in jail for?"

"Two years."

"That's a long time underwater."

He leaned forward. Shadows made his eyes dark. A nerve flickered in his throat. "Why does this matter to you?"

She smiled. "Just curious."

"I don't care for your curiosity. Where I come from there's no place for it. Tell me where you need to get into."

A thought occurred to her.

"You're not an Osuwite, are you?"

He looked at her coldly.

Adelaide's plate slid neatly in front of her. "The rainbow-fish, madam." The fish, belying its name, was a warm rose colour. "And the swordfish."

The waiter filled both their glasses with weqa and placed the bottle on a stand, withdrawing discreetly.

"It's wild swordfish, by the way," she said. "They catch their seafood fresh every morning. Probably confiscated from an illegal fishing boat."

She prised a segment of rainbow-fish from the delicate spine.

"My grandfather told me that when Osiris was first built, these fish were all they ate. But they were vastly overfished. And now, they're exceptionally rare… you have to stalk the shoals for hours. But you know how they catch them?" She waited, but Vikram did not offer a guess. His fork was poised over his plate. "Their tails glow in the dark," she said.

"That's ridiculous."

Adelaide's reaction had been the same the first time she heard the story. Now she shared some of her grandfather's indignation. She took a bite.

"Delicious. Enjoy your swordfish."

"I will."

He cut into the fillet with quick, precise movements. Adelaide lingered over her fish, watching him surreptitiously. His dark hair was overlong. The ascetic planes of his face seemed inadequate for those whirlpool eyes. Haunted eyes? She wondered. Or just wary?

"So where is it?" Vikram asked.

"Top floor of three-zero-one-east."

"Sounds expensive. Who lives there?"

"Nobody, at the moment. My brother used to," she clarified. She sampled the weqa. It tasted saltier than usual and she pulled a face. Vikram sighed. He sat back and met her eyes squarely.

"Your twin brother, right? The one there's a huge investigation about?"

"Axel. Yes."

"A crime scene."

"He's not dead."

"But you get my point. I'm guessing it's somewhere secure."

"Otherwise I wouldn't need to break in, would I?" Adelaide squeezed a lime quarter over her fish. "Would you like a karengo square? They do them well here."

"I'll pass."

"On the karengo, or the break-in?"

"The seaweed. As to the break-in, I think you're fucking crazy. You know it's instant jail time if we're caught? Are there cameras?"

She nodded. "And a security bar. I can bribe someone for a swipe card and to cut the cameras, but I need you for the locks."

Vikram shrugged. "Your money."

"My family's money," she agreed.

"Fine. I'll do it. In exchange, you're going to get us a second address with the Council and persuade them to start a winter aid programme." He paused. "I'm assuming you'll want your part done first."

"Of course," she said serenely.

"In that case, I want your word that you'll keep helping me until I've achieved my own ends."

Adelaide speared her few last flakes of fish.

"Let's be honest with one another, Vikram. My motivations are selfish, and I don't care about your people. You certainly can't trust me. On the other hand, I'm probably the best chance you've got."

He was silent, but his fingers tightened around the stem of the weqa glass.

"There's a song in the west about prison," he said eventually. "They'll put you underwater where the sun will never rise. And the mud will take your tongue because you've told too many lies. That's how it starts. And in the end, you lose your head."

She looked at the untreated cut on his right temple and thought, *what in hell's tide am I getting myself into?*

Vikram hadn't finished.

"I could never explain what underwater's like to someone like you," he went on. "But I do promise you, if we get caught, I'll drag you all the way with me. So do we have a deal?"

Adelaide met his eyes, those watchful eyes. Below the chink and chatter of the restaurant, the pianist spilled her rippling chords, notes like surf and jetsam. She thought of her grandfather's piano, out of reach in the brocaded rooms of the Domain. Out of reach, like Axel. But the penthouse would hold the answers she so badly needed.

"I believe we do," she said.

Vikram clinked his glass to hers. Neither of them blinked.

PART THREE

18 | VIKRAM

The hallway outside the penthouse was silent. It was four minutes past three in the morning, and the lifts were still, poised on different levels of the skyscraper. Vikram crouched in front of the yellow-barred door, his eyes level with the second keyhole. He selected a slim metal pick from a set and inserted it into the lock. He liked to think of this as a skill rather than a profession, but there had been enough occasions where he'd helped Mikkeli on the break-ins of her later career.

Just busting a lock was enough to push the memories forward. The dripping green cell. The porthole. He felt too large for the door and its frame, as though he had grown and the corridor had shrunk. He closed his eyes, used his ears instead. Metal scraped on metal. Now he began to feel the personality of the lock, its strengths, its lines of weakness. Gently he manipulated the pick this way and that.

"Will you hurry up?" hissed a voice behind him. "We haven't got all day."

Vikram sucked in a breath and told himself, very sternly, not to respond. It had taken precisely forty-four seconds to break the first lock. That wasn't quick enough for Adelaide, who had moaned and cursed and once, poked him with the plastic sheathed toe of her shoe. Anyone else pestering him like this would have received a black eye for their pains. Today, he had no choice but to be with Adelaide.

He had told her that if they got caught, he would take her down with him. Realistically, he knew there wasn't a chance. If they got caught, Vikram was as easy a scapegoat as ever she could find. That was the only reason she had agreed to the deal.

He twisted the pick twelve degrees left.

"I mean, really, how long does it take?"

Her impatience was a physical scald on his back. He sensed her fidgeting behind him. He twisted around and scowled up at her. She was practically on top of him, arms folded across her chest and both eyebrows elevated. Her red hair was tucked under a woollen hat. He supposed this was her idea of a criminal outfit.

"It's a science," he said. He tapped the deactivated bar. "Your money might have got us the swipe card for this, but it won't buy you a picklock. So shut up and give me some space."

Adelaide's eyes narrowed but she took half a step backward. Vikram returned his attention to the lock. Twenty seconds later he heard it—a whisper of a click. The door popped ajar. Vikram sat back on his heels. His satisfaction was tempered with a stab of fear; he'd done it now. Second offences sent you plummeting toward the seabed without a trial.

"Aren't you the clever one?" Without waiting for him to move Adelaide ducked under the yellow bar and disappeared inside.

"You better hope that alarm doesn't work," he said.

Her voice floated back to him. "It's disabled."

"I hope you're sure."

"I told you. There was a code to change the code. Only me and Axel knew it." Vikram heard the sound of a cupboard door opening all the same. Then Adelaide's smug tones. "I was right."

For about the fifth time that night, Vikram wanted to strangle her. He didn't bother telling her that if she'd been wrong they would have known by now, just glanced back at the empty corridor behind him—the final curl of the stairway rail, the red carpet, dimly lit, and the security camera trained on Axel's apartment. It was off. Adelaide's bribe had given them fifty-nine minutes to get in and out. They had about fifty-four of those left. He'd assumed she'd got some minion to do the actual bribing, but she had reacted to this implication in amazement. I'm *hardly* going to trust anyone else, she said. It made sense. She had a cajoling voice; with the additional seduction of money it was no doubt irresistible.

He slid the set of picks back into his jeans pocket, feeling a rush of gratitude towards Drake, who had sourced the tools for him without asking any questions. He followed Adelaide inside and shut the door behind him.

He was in a rectangular hallway. A row of identical pot plants marched along the right hand wall. They were ordered in ascending height, with about an inch between each. Their withering leaves pointed in the same directions. Vikram counted: there were twenty-two. A watering can sat at the end of the row. He peered in. Any water had evaporated.

Stacked against the other wall were columns of shoeboxes. Each had the same label, neatly aligned in the bottom right hand corner. Vikram checked his gloves a final time and eased the first lid open. A pair of stout brown boots rested inside. He checked the soles. They were unworn. The next box contained the same shoes, also unworn. He prised out a box from the middle of the stack and raised the lid, knowing by now what he would find. He pushed the box back again.

"I've set the window-walls to one-way," called Adelaide. "So we can turn on the lights."

"Great," he mumbled. The *we* was anything but reassuring.

He expected to find more neurotic ordering in the next room, but instead walked into a scene resembling traders' day at Market Circle. The room was crammed with cabinets. There were open shelf units, cabinets with glass doors, trunks with metal bolts, sets of drawers and a wardrobe with the doors thrown open. The wardrobe bulged with bolts of material, stacked in alternate reds and yellows. Adelaide was on her hands and knees, peering underneath it, her trousers stretched over the seat of her pants. Vikram allowed himself to enjoy the spectacle, and the silence, for a moment. He had no idea what she expected to find.

"What's all the material for?" he asked.

"How should I know?"

"Well, what are we looking for? We haven't got much time."

"I told you. I don't know yet."

Vikram tried a few drawers. Their contents varied. One was entirely full of cans, the same fizzy Coralade, crushed to flat silver disks. Another contained thermometers. He found a third brimming with model horses; wooden, plastic, stone, even cardboard. He showed it to Adelaide. She picked up one of the horses and turned it over between gloved finger and thumb, frowning slightly. Then she put it back and shut the drawer. Vikram's curiosity was piqued. He wanted to ask what was special about horses, but did not expect to be graced with an answer.

"When were you last here?" he said instead.

Adelaide prised open a drinks cabinet and cursed as a landslide of rubber bands poured out. Vikram went to help her pick them up. She didn't thank him but after a minute she said, "It was a while ago."

"So you won't know if anything's changed. Since Axel's been gone, I mean."

"I'm not assuming anything has."

Vikram gathered up the last of the rubber bands. Between them they eased the cabinet shut.

"Then why are you here?" he asked.

"Because I can read what they can't," Adelaide said. She uncurled her hand. A miniature plastic horse was in her palm, legs gathered up as if it was galloping.

"Horses," she said.

The penthouse was similarly structured to Adelaide's apartment, with room collapsing into room like a pack of dominoes. Vikram walked into a room containing only a table, exactly centred. There was something about its solitary positioning that reminded him of the table he had seen in Adelaide's dining room, beautifully laid but unused.

He didn't switch on the light but went over to the window-wall, checking out the view. Despite the hour and the haziness, Osiris was a network of light on black. A shuttle streaked through its glowing shell, reminding him of the traces left by sparklers on midsummer night. The ocean was invisible and the city felt rootless. Vikram rapped the bufferglass with his knuckle, taking some comfort in its tensile strength.

He found the kitchen, and then the bathroom, which were both cleaner than everywhere else. The bathroom cupboard was full of medication. The bottles were organized in order of label colour. He took one out, tossed it in the air and caught it. The bottle rattled. It was unopened. So were the rest.

"Your brother had a lot of doctors," he called to Adelaide, who was in the next room. She appeared sharply. She ran her index finger along the rows of prescriptions.

"Well, that has no effect... haven't tried that. Interesting, nothing from Radir..."

Vikram had already learned that the best time to interrogate Adelaide was when she was distracted, and was therefore more likely to volunteer information. It meant pretending you weren't really there, but since Adelaide was so self-obsessed this was remarkably easy.

"Who's Radir?"

"His last shrink."

"How many did he see?"

"Just about everyone in Osiris, I think... I never knew they gave him *that*... My father insisted."

He didn't push the issue any further. Whatever illness Axel had suffered from, two things seemed clear. The doctors did not agree on it, as none of the prescriptions matched, and nor did Axel, who had not been taking any of them. He left Adelaide peering at labels, mouthing their formulas to herself.

In the next room there was a broken clock on the wall. He stood looking at it, trying to decide why anyone would keep a broken clock. He checked his own watch. They still had over half an hour. If he listened, he could hear the watch ticking.

He found himself straining for noise. The twins' reputation might have been wild, but the penthouse was not somewhere he could imagine holding a raucous party. It was easier to imagine his own friends here than it was Adelaide's Haze. He wondered what Nils would say about it. Shake his head and laugh, Vikram decided, then remind Vikram that the penthouse's owner was, after all, related to "that celebrity bitch." Laughter was Nils's reaction to most things: defusing agent and first line of defence. When Vikram finally told him about the deal he'd cut, Nils's laugh was there. He'd had a warning, too. Watch out for her, he'd said. Don't worry, Vikram had responded. I've not lost my head yet.

A laugh would sound strange in here.

The weirdness of being in a dead man's home was steadily seeping into his consciousness. When people died, they were found and somebody mourned them and then their living space was recycled. What came with loss, unacknowledged and unspoken, but still there, was continuity. The penthouse held nothing of renewal, only endings. Death of the body. Worse than that, he thought. Death of the mind.

Adelaide strolled out of the bathroom with the sound of rushing water. She was doing up the buttons of her trousers.

"What?" she said. "I needed a piss."

Vikram had a feeling the vulgarity was for his benefit.

Then she saw the clock. Her hands stilled at her waistband. He was going to ask its significance, but he saw her face, just for a second, succumb to something like fear.

She began her examination of the rest of the room. Her methods were erratic. She pressed her hands flat against the walls. She listened, with the shell of her ear close to the wallpaper, her face expectant. There was a white strip of skin between her glove and the sleeve of her shirt. She didn't wear a watch. The foolishness of relying on one timepiece struck Vikram at the same time as he noticed how thin her wrists were.

When she twisted her head to look at him he thought of all the images in those paper magazines. A few strands of hair had escaped the confines of her hat and stuck to her face. He smiled to see the plastic sheaths over her feet, her long legs cut off so abruptly by the blue bags. Now he had to laugh.

"What's funny?" demanded Adelaide.

He pointed. Adelaide frowned, then gave a reluctant smile. She raised her knee and extended her leg sideways in a slow motion kick. He imagined her muscles flexing beneath the loose black trousers.

"Sexy, aren't they," she said. She balanced for a moment, at once athletic and comic, before dropping her foot. For the first time he saw the charm of the girl. But he wasn't going to tell her that.

"C'mon," he said. "Let's get going."

They came to the last room. The lock was broken, presumably the key was with Axel. Adelaide turned the handle and stopped. Vikram peered over her shoulder.

The room smelled, not damp exactly, but chill, like old ice. It had been papered. Every inch of wall, floor and ceiling was covered in hot air balloons. Even the window-wall had been claimed. Repeated over and over again was the upturned pear shape, the coloured segments of the balloon envelope. There were prints, photographs, technical drawings, mathematical formulas. Here and there were swatches of yellow and red material. They were glued, taped, nailed or tacked, but they fluttered from their moorings as if stirred by an invisible breath. Vikram looked at the ragged edges of the cuttings. Axel's handiwork was evident in illegible scrawls. He imagined the frenzied tearing, the hammering in the night. He felt cold.

He tapped Adelaide's shoulder. She jumped.

"Do you want to go in?"

She shook her head and motioned to the floor. A minefield of nails stuck out of the dust.

"Looks like your brother was planning to skip town."

"What kind of person thinks about making a hot air balloon?"

Vikram did not reply at once. He was thinking of an old western story, a legend about a balloon.

"Maybe the sort of person who thinks there's something worth finding," he said slowly. They were speaking in whispers. Vikram forced himself to raise his voice.

"We should go," he said. "The hour's almost up."

All the same they stayed. Vikram could not dispel a niggling sense of premonition. By stepping into this man's apartment he had crossed another border with it, one of obligations and no returns. He glanced at Adelaide. There was no doubt about it this time, she looked scared. Her hand bumped against his. She did not immediately move her arm away.

Noise startled both of them. First an erratic, then a regular drumming. Adelaide's head snapped up. Vikram turned silently. Then he realized it was just the rain, rain breaking on windows covered in paper trails.

He looked at his watch.

"Shit, we've got three minutes, come on!"

Adelaide didn't move.

"Come on!" he repeated. He took her arm but she thrust him off. He ran back through the penthouse. He thought she was right behind him but when he turned she was dawdling, opening a drawer, a cupboard door. They had two and a half minutes.

"Adelaide! Get out!"

The porthole loomed once more. He saw the skadi banging on his door in the middle of the night.

"Adelaide!" he yelled.

Still she lingered. He saw her touch a broken rivet on the wall.

"Fuck!"

Tiny but ominous on her finger, Vikram saw a bead of blood. His eyes snapped to the broken glass, which now carried the indelible mark of Adelaide's DNA.

"Wipe it off! Use your sleeve, clean it!"

She obeyed. He hauled her forcibly through the domino rooms of the penthouse, past the broken clock, the cabinets, past the plants and the stacks of shoeboxes, out the front door into the hall. Adelaide slammed the door shut. He checked his watch. Sixty seconds.

"Lock up!" hissed Adelaide. "You have to lock up. Otherwise they'll know!"

A string of expletives exploded in Vikram's throat. He ripped the picks from his back pocket and with fumbling fingers shoved the first into the lower lock. He couldn't see it. He could only see the porthole. His hand shook. Adelaide ran. He heard her footsteps clatter down the first ten steps and knew she was safe. At that moment he hated her.

Forty seconds. The corridor was shrinking again. He closed his eyes and listened to the lock. Tiny movements. Forget the porthole. Forget Adelaide. Forget everything but the way the metal works.

Listen. Just listen.

The lock clicked. He whipped the swipe card through the yellow bar and threw himself into the stairwell. Out of camera range. Six seconds. He counted, slowly, as the slender hand completed its circuit. When it reached the twelve he looked up at the buried mole of the camera in the ceiling. A red light blinked, just once, as if the tiny machine was waking up.

Adelaide crouched further down the stairs, her face electric. Their eyes connected. The tension between them was like the trembling space between polar magnets.

She ran.

That's right. Run. Because if I get my hands on you now—

The thought prompted his body to move. It was only in motion that he realized the full extent of his rage. He hurtled down the stairs, chasing after her. In their efforts to make no noise they moved in contortionist shapes, half flying, half falling. Above his own straining lungs he heard the intake of her breath, the faint squeak as she grabbed the banister rail and vaulted a corner. Her blue overshoes landed with a crackle of plastic.

Thirty-one floors down she skidded to a halt.

"I thought we weren't going to make it," she said. Her face was pink with exertion.

"We?" he repeated.

Adelaide was bent double, breathing dramatically. Her face stretched in a grin. It was a game for her, he thought. He kept a deliberate metre away, trying to slow his own breathing. Cross that border and he might not be able to stop his hands from fastening around her neck.

"You ran," he said. "You fucking ran." His throat ached with the effort of keeping his voice down. If anyone came out and questioned him, he had fake ID and no City pass. He had to get somewhere safe.

"Of course I ran," said Adelaide. "I'm not going to get caught."

"Except for your blood." That shut her up, but only temporarily. He could see her mind working, figuring out how to turn the situation around. He didn't give her the chance. "*We'd* better get out of here."

"There's a storm started, genius. I can't take the boat back to my scraper now."

"Great. We're stranded."

His temples were splitting. Adelaide stretched up again, hands over her head, her spine arching.

"You might be," she said. "I'm going to the tea parlour on floor sixteen."

"Fine." He didn't care where they went as long as it was down, as far away from the penthouse as it was possible to go. "Then we're taking the lift."

"You can go home if you want," said Adelaide.

Vikram jabbed the call button. Deep in the belly of the skyscraper, he heard a distant rumble as the lift started its journey.

"I'm not going anywhere until my side of the bargain's settled," he said. "I've risked enough for you today. How the hell do you think I can get over the border at four in the morning?"

Adelaide shrugged.

"The Undersea?"

"The Undersea doesn't stop here. If you'd ever taken it you'd know that."

"Why would I want to take the Undersea? Anyway, you can't stay at my apartment."

Vikram gave her an insincere smile. Clearly she hadn't thought things through. The mechanics of it. What she was going to do with him in the lag time between her side of the bargain and his. For his part, he'd had no intention of spending any more time with her than necessary. But if he could bear it, an opportunity presented itself: to get even.

"Afraid I'm going to have to," he said.

"Nobody stays at my apartment."

"Then I'll be the first. Don't worry, I won't rob you."

There was a low ping and the lift doors slid open. Vikram stepped inside. Adelaide stayed still, her mouth set.

"You getting in or not?" he asked.

She got in. Once again they stood side by side, repeated in the mirrors. Their faces echoed the rigid stance of their bodies. He was a head taller than her. This small, biological victory gave him some satisfaction.

Perhaps noticing the same thing, Adelaide's scowl deepened.

"Don't think you've won," she said.

"I wouldn't think anything so childish," he shot back.

/ / /

Adelaide's tea parlour had the dreamy, slow-motion atmosphere of a daylight facility still operating in the middle of the night. Purple lanterns hung in clusters, illuminating the low level tables, cushion seats, ink paintings on silk and the dividing mesh screens. Around a corner was an adolescent girl, folding paper napkins into a menagerie of birds. Adelaide gave the girl a wide berth. The old man near the entrance wore a full tuxedo, and glanced up nervously at every clink of a spoon. A woman in a large green hat, ostensibly reading a newspaper, would now and then recount some portion of it to the rest of the room. On the other side was a man with a cat on a lead. The cat had its own glass.

Vikram and Adelaide sat opposite one another in one section. Nobody seemed interested in them.

"The red coral tea, sir."

The deferential did not go unnoticed. Vikram smiled his thanks. Adelaide fixed the proprietor with cold eyes. The proprietor, a tiny Asian woman with her hair in a chignon, ignored the look and placed a tray carefully on the table.

The teapot was flat and heavy with an s-shaped spout. It was accompanied by a small bowl of powdered ginger. Adelaide, very deliberately, took the pot and poured tea into one of two round-bottomed glasses. The liquid was pale amber. She blew ripples across the top of it before allowing a tentative few drops over the barrier of her lips.

Vikram poured and gingered his own tea. The scorching temperature did not affect him; hot beverages had kept him alive on many nights. Despite himself, his anger was fading under the dual influence of warmth and relief. They hadn't been caught. The aroma of fresh tea, the soft drifts of rising steam and the intermittent sounds of human habitation relaxed him. He was safe. Even Adelaide's pettiness with the tea seemed trifling. It was good tea too, the sort that would find its way onto the black market in the west.

"Me and Axel used to come here," she said. "It was our local. Axel loves the Chinese because they keep their Mandarin, and he's always been into Old World languages. Do people keep their languages in the west, Vikram?"

"Some do. But it makes it harder to get by." And why make it harder than it already is, he thought.

"Axel used to speak bits of Mandarin with the servers and then we'd sit and make up stories about everyone else. You get some right crazies in here. You know, I can't help wondering if he's ever come back without me. Where would you hide, Vikram, if you wanted to escape?"

"Depends what you mean by escape."

"Disappear, then."

"When people go missing in the west they turn up dead or not at all, which generally means they're being eaten by fish. I guess that's one way to disappear."

He spoke without thinking and expected an angry glower, but Adelaide was looking up at the misty windows. The rain still pounded on the exterior walls. Her cheeks were flushed.

"No, he's alive."

The question was too obvious not to be posed. Besides, Vikram was curious. He had made up his mind even before the break-in that Axel must be dead; seeing the penthouse had only confirmed his thoughts.

One way or another, the boy had found his way to the sea.

"Why do you think he's alive?"

"I don't think. I know."

She was staring at him now with an air of expectancy, almost as though she wanted evidence of his disbelief. Something to pounce on. Her fixed gaze was like that of the cat on the lead. She had a cat's detached nonchalance, he thought, a curious immunity to violence. She put her associates unquestioningly in the position of the mouse.

"How can you know?" he said. Adelaide clicked her tongue.

"Intuition. He's my twin, so I know. We have a connection. It isn't like a connection that you have with other people. You just—know."

Vikram thought of the photograph in her bedroom.

"What's he like, your brother?"

Adelaide smiled. For the first time, it was a genuine smile.

"He was clever," she said. "Really smart. Maths, oceanology—he was great at those things. And he was smart when it came to people too, especially the family. I used to get angry with them, but Axel always calmed us down. He'd know before I did when I was about to flip. He was always there. The two of us, it needed two of us, really, against the rest of the tribe."

She ran a restless hand through her hair. The woollen hat was tossed aside on a cushion. She seemed embarrassed, almost cross about what she had said, and he suspected that she did not often talk about Axel. Strange that she should choose him—but it had been a strange night. "Anyway," she said lightly. "He changed."

"What happened?"

"He forgot things. Small things at first. He started mixing up names, and dates. Then it was bigger things. People. Places. Oceanology. It all seemed to happen very quickly. But it stemmed from the Incident."

He looked at her questioningly. "The Incident?"

"Oh... It was my mother's birthday party. A big, public, Rechnov event, on an extremely large boat." She rolled her eyes. "I'm sure you can imagine. We were sixteen. We always hated those events, but we tolerated them, I suppose. But this time, Axel was acting oddly. He was making no effort to be polite. He kept staring at people in a very fixated, very intense way, as if there was something wrong with them. I thought it was funny to start with, but he kept—staring. Then just walking off when someone was talking to him. And later—there was the speech."

She sighed. Not wanting to deter her, Vikram said nothing. Adelaide stirred her tea for a moment before continuing.

"Feodor was about to make one of his pompous speeches. He was standing at the head of the boat, my mother at his side, the picture of respectability. He never got the chance to speak. Axel leapt up in front of all these people, pushed our parents aside—it was almost comical, in a way—'Ladies and gentlemen', he began. Very proper. He winked at me, and I laughed. I remember, I did laugh. But then he started talking about all of these other things, things that made no sense, things even I had to admit sounded crazy… it was awful. When he finished, he bowed, three times. You can imagine the silence. Finally, he took this running leap, and he jumped off the boat."

"He jumped off the boat?"

"Into the sea, yes. It was so cold. We could hear him, whooping, splashing the water. They had to send someone in to pull him out. He was drenched—that beautiful suit, completely wrecked—shivering all over—and he was still laughing. He came and hugged me. It was like hugging an ice sculpture. 'Oh A,' he said. 'Look at their hopeless, broken faces. Did you ever see such a desolate sight?' I took him home. He was hospitalised with pneumonia the next day." She frowned. "I shouldn't be telling you this."

"So why are you?"

"I don't know." She took a sip of tea, and set the cup back without a clink. "What about your girl? Mikkeli, wasn't it? What was she like?"

He felt indebted to answer. "She wasn't my girl," he said. "Not like that. We grew up together. She looked out for me. She was smart, too." He smiled wryly. "Not like your brother. She was a thief."

Adelaide smiled back. "I like that."

"Anyway, she died." Vikram almost said *too*, but caught himself in time. He stretched out his legs under the low table and realized that both of them still had the plastic sheaths on their feet. He removed his and discreetly stuffed them into his boots.

The girl with the origami was taking her booty from table to table, depositing a napkin bird on each polished surface. When she reached them, Adelaide spoke sharply.

"We don't want that."

The girl ignored her and placed a bird on a saucer. She moved dreamily onto the next table. Vikram picked up the offering. Its folds were clean and crisp. "What's wrong with it?"

"I don't like birds."

"You don't like—" He glanced at her and grinned with the realization. "Oh. You're scared of them."

Adelaide scowled blackly.

"It's alright, you're not the only one I've met with a phobia." He tucked the origami into his pocket. "I won't tell."

The girl, having finished her rounds, paid for her tea and left.

"Where do you think Axel is?" Vikram asked bluntly.

"He may have gone somewhere. Somewhere he feels safe, until I can find him. That could be anywhere, with Axel." Adelaide hesitated. She checked around them and lowered her voice. "But I have to consider the possibility that he's been taken somewhere. By someone who wants him out the way."

Stars, he thought, the girl's deluded.

"Then I hope it's the first option," he said.

Vikram's certainty was equally strong. The way he saw it, Axel's death could have been accidental or deliberate. If it was deliberate, presumably the Rechnovs had decided the boy was too much of an embarrassment, and had him removed. They were an important family with a big reputation at stake. Vikram had no doubt that they were capable of it. Or, Axel had chosen to die, in which case it was better for all the Rechnovs if his body was never found.

Osiris was not a kind city, but to choose to opt out was the strictest of taboos. In the severest cold spells, Vikram had spent the nights with friends, talking through the long dark hours, pinching one another at the first sign of drowsiness, because if sleep came there was no guarantee of ever waking up again. Every sunrise was a miracle. On days like those, you didn't think about why, or what for. You just clung.

Perhaps that was why Adelaide was so adamant that her brother was alive. To avoid the shame if he had taken his own life.

"You saw something in the penthouse." Adelaide changed the subject. "Not about Axel. It was the balloon room. When you saw that, you thought of something."

He was surprised that she had noticed.

"It's not important," he said. "You'd think it was silly."

Denial was a sure way to catch Adelaide's interest. She poured herself another glass of tea and then topped up his, absently or on purpose, he wasn't sure which.

"Tell me," she said.

"There's a story about a balloon flight." Vikram shrugged, trying to impress upon her its insignificance, although the tale resonated with him. "When I saw that room, I was reminded of the story. That's all."

"Go on."

She wasn't looking at him but he sensed the beam of her attention, bouncing off the windows and lancing him in the chest, where another voice was stirring. He felt Mikkeli sit up, shake her spiky mess of hair out of its hood.

"There's a legend," he said. "When the rain began in the year of the Great Storms, a balloon set out on a journey to Osiris. There were two passengers. One of them was a girl—an important girl. Some people say she was a ruler or a princess. Others say she was some kind of star."

A smile flitted over Adelaide's face.

"Like me." She raised her coral tea to her lips and sipped without looking at the glass. He had earned her concentration.

"Well," he said. "More like me, actually. They'd be refugees, wouldn't they? Anyway, she has different names. She's also blind. The other passenger is a man. Her guide."

He heard Mikkeli's voice in the quiet parlour. *Come on, Vikram, you can do better than this! Where's the drama?* He couldn't do her exuberant speech, her exaggerations, but they were both speaking as he continued, because Keli had loved this story and narrated it many times, whispering to Vikram from the bunk above his on nights when the orphanage boat rocked on frightening waves, and Naala's off-key, drunken singing was drowned by the wind.

"The girl relies totally on the guide. He flies the balloon. He has promised to take her to a safe place—to Osiris, he says."

"Where did they come from?"

"Nobody knows. Some say south where the ice is, others say deep in the deserts, far up north. It doesn't matter. What matters is, the man isn't who he says he is. He's an assassin."

Adelaide made an *ooh* shape with her mouth. Vikram paused, making a show of sprinkling a finger-and-thumb full of ginger into his tea. The tiny grains floated for a second, then sank.

"Well? Does he kill her?" Adelaide demanded.

"He poisons her. And then he discovers that she isn't who she says she is either. She's a double. An illusion of the real target."

"So who wins?"

"Nobody wins. He poisons himself in remorse. The legend says there is a cure in Osiris, but they haven't got here yet. The balloon is still flying. That's why it's called the last balloon flight."

Adelaide licked her index finger and dipped it into the ginger. She sucked thoughtfully.

"They'd be dead," she said. "Or old. Ancient, by now." She fell quiet.

"It's a story, Adelaide."

"I know," she said quickly.

"People talk about it mostly when they're thinking about getting out. You could say it's like an alarm bell."

"Maybe Axel heard it."

"I don't know. It's a western thing."

"He might have thought he could take that flight."

He did not reply to that because her words rang uncannily close to Mikkeli's. His best friend, leaning forward over the oars of a rowboat as they scuttled from tower to tower, lit only by the moon. *Just imagine, Vikram, that it was true. Would you take that flight?* Keli would have. She'd have jumped on board without a glance back, just to get that close to the clouds. And then they'd hop out the boat and bust a lock.

"I said your tea's gone cold," said Adelaide.

She was staring at him. He wasn't sure why he had told her the story. It felt like a betrayal. As if he had given away a piece of the west, its fragile, ethereal psyche. He wanted to take the story back, to tell Adelaide that she wasn't worthy of their superstitions. Her side of the city had safety; they did not need hope.

Vikram looked at the windows. "Doesn't matter," he said. "The rain's stopped anyway."

19 | ADELAIDE

A delaide reached across and groped on the bedside table. Her fingers closed around the plastic body of the stolen horse. It was no more than a few centimetres long, a child's toy, crudely made. She moved it up and down, emulating the motion of waves, the way she imagined a real one might run. Shadows of her hands and the horse rippled over the walls and ceiling. It was dark outside; the light within the colour of a bruise.

She turned the model over to look into one of its black eyes. Dr Radir, last in a long line of Axel's psychiatrists, had been the first person to mention horses. According to Radir's assessment, the hallucinations had begun months, even years before. He said Axel had theories about the horses; elaborate hypotheses about storm omens and contact from outside Osiris.

Rat-a-ta-tat. Rat-a-ta-tat. The music of drums: Axel's fingers. *Sounds like hooves, A.* Adelaide sat up. She saw him in the room, standing by the dark pane of the mirror, a shadow in a pool of shadows. He didn't move. He never moved. He was looking for the balloon.

Where are you, A?

The balloon was gliding through cumulus clouds. Adelaide was back on the balcony, high above the sea, staring over the edge. The sea below fell into a giant crater. At the bottom, so far away she was no more than a speck, Mikkeli was a chromium mermaid. Her tail swished and clicked in the mud. Adelaide looked for Tyr, but he wasn't there, only Vikram was. She reached for Vikram's hand. His eyes were murky whirlpools. She wanted to tell him that Mikkeli was there, down in the crater, but her tongue would not work. She had never felt so cold before, and she wasn't sure she could stand it.

Her eyes flew open. She must have been dreaming. Her skin was tight with goosebumps; the horse was imprisoned in her linked hands.

"Where have you gone?" she whispered. "Damn it, Axel, where have you gone?"

On the other side of her apartment, Vikram was sleeping on the futon under the mezzanine. She imagined his breathing as a tiny hum that ran through the woven rugs, under the doors and along a crack in the floorboards to her ear. What would Feodor say if he knew she had a westerner under her roof? *Reduced to terriers, Adelaide? That's scraping the seabed, even for you.*

She hadn't locked the door. She didn't like locked doors, and she wasn't worried by Vikram's presence. Vikram assumed she thought all westerners were scum, but he didn't know her. If he did, he would know she never thought about the west at all.

Best, though, to let Vikram think he had won this round. Sometimes impulse led down strange avenues; she had learned to accommodate herself to life's twists and forks. She heard movement. Perhaps Vikram was still awake, or the scientists were at work upstairs. Then she realized that it was not an interior noise but the rush of rain against the window.

She curled deeper under the duvet, listening. Some people, like Linus, said the rain was changing. They said it sounded more consistent than it used to. When people were desperate they found omens in the blue, pulling boats from the horizon and now balloons out of the sky. Vikram understood this; he had told her the story of the balloon.

Adelaide had lost count of nights passed with only the rain for solace. She knew every version of rain: ice-bound rains and fresh bold showers, rattling hailstorms, delicate snowfalls. It gave her a feeling not of fear but of safety and enclosure. Axel had never understood this snugness, and perhaps in truth she only felt it now, since he was gone, and the rain had become her companion.

She thought of the Roof, frying saufish, drinking Kelpiqua, meeting

Jan. She and Axel, drenched and shaking on a towertop after a storm. When they were still living at the Domain, the twins used to go there every night, until Goran caught them. They'd been happy there.

The rain was passing. Linus and the anti-Nucleites were wrong; it came and went according to its own whimsy.

The little horse lay in her upturned palm. She imagined Axel locked inside in his balloon room, sewing bolts and bolts of material. He would have spent hours studying the paths of the winds, devising instruments for navigation; some part of him must remember his love of science. Axel had been preparing for a journey, but to where?

20 | VIKRAM

He lay on Adelaide's futon, a rug pulled over his body—not because he needed it for warmth in her apartment, but to feel the soft luxurious weight of the material. The lights were dimmed, the glass walls darkened, but he could not sleep. He was hot, conscious of a thin sheen of sweat. There was a decanter of water on a table beside him. He poured himself a glass and choked when he discovered it wasn't water at all, but voqua.

He thought of the coldest he had ever been, trapped in the unremembered quarters on the very edge of the west, certain he was going to die. The towers had fallen into such disrepair that they were more of a sea barrier than a living space. No electricity. Broken bufferglass. Ghosts. One of the towers leaned sideways; monolithic, charred. It had burned once and people had burned in it. It was said that something nameless lurked in its depths, gorging on the foundations.

Stars knew what he'd been doing there; he must have been about twelve. He remembered a tarpaulin. Huddling under it, shaking, his fingers blank with cold. He remembered the rivulets of water that eased their way through the cracks, only to halt as the molecules contracted and froze. The floor inside a maze of glittering snail trails, outside, the sky sagging. It had been too cold to snow.

Snow, in Adelaide's world, was nothing but a pretty white blanket.

Vikram knew the layout of the apartment. There were only three rooms between himself and the Architect's granddaughter.

He made himself recall the day Eirik was drowned. He remembered seeing Adelaide and her father, closer than a westerner could have imagined but impossible to reach. Adelaide was unprotected now. He could take her hostage. He could, if he wanted, go into her room, put his hands around her neck, and throttle her. He could strike a fatal blow to Feodor Rechnov right now, here, tonight.

Stop it.

He shoved the idea away in horror. It was as far from Horizon's ideals as the stars; he could hardly believe the thought had crossed his mind.

But it was an opportunity—he could not deny that. He would never have a chance like this again. Now—while she was sleeping. It wasn't what Horizon had been about, but hadn't that all changed? And he couldn't trust Adelaide, she had told him that herself. Now she'd got what she wanted, what guarantee did he have that she would carry out her side of the bargain?

She almost let you get caught tonight. She could turn you in just because she feels like it. Sticking with her isn't worth the risk.

For all you know, the skadi could be on their way over right now.

Eirik, Mikkeli—they would have thought about it. There was no doubt that to many in the west, the act would make Vikram a hero.

Stars, what was he thinking! And yet...

Go on, another part of him urged. *Do it. It's what they all want.*

He pushed aside the rug. He could feel his knife sheath where it lay against his thigh. It could be done bloodily or it could be done with bare hands. For a more poetic justice, he could drown Adelaide Rechnov in her own bath.

That would be the best way. A clear signal to the City. Explicable, and understandable.

For a moment his own coldness froze him. And then he saw Mikkeli in her yellow hood. She came in through the window-wall and she walked across Adelaide Mystik's floor and sat on the piano lid. She was still twelve.

"You're not going to let that bitch get the better of you, are you?" she said. Foam dribbled from her lips. Her voice was as dead and as empty as surf.

You know it's what they all want. And it's so easy.

He sat up and walked silently through the study into the kitchen, closing each door behind him to block off her escape route. Moonlight fell across the white tablecloth and crystal glasses in the dining room. The outline of the next door was a grey line around its pale panels.

He stood looking at it. The only sounds he could identify were the thud of his heart and the drumming of his pulse in his ears. If he went through that door, he would be taking a step that could not be reversed.

The door opened. Adelaide came out, one hand rubbing her eyelids. When she saw him she stopped.

Their eyes met for a long time.

"Can't sleep?" he asked.

"I need some water."

He saw Eirik, in the tank, his mouth open. Perhaps she did too.

She said, "Do you want a glass?"

"Yes, please."

She walked around the table. She passed within a few inches of him. He recognized the effort it must have cost her, because she had seen his face. He turned and followed her into the kitchen, watched her bare legs crossing the tiles. She opened the fridge door. The light flooded her slender body, crouching naked beneath the slip of lilac. She took out a jug and poured two glasses of chilled water. Face averted, she placed one on the sideboard for Vikram.

"Sleep well," she said. She took her own glass of water and went back through the empty dining room and shut the door.

21 | ADELAIDE

She slumped against the bedroom door. Her legs shook. Five minutes passed before she could stand, walk to the bedside cabinet, take out the gun, and go back to sit by the door.

He was going to kill me.

She kept the thought there, wrapped with her the way her fingers wrapped around the grip of the gun.

He was actually going to kill me.

And he's still here, in my apartment, right now.

22 | VIKRAM

Silently he opened the door that Adelaide had just shut. He knew that she would not hear him. He stood barefoot outside her bedroom. It was so quiet that on the other side he could hear her breathing, long and shaky.

Minutes passed. He stood there, motionless. He took out the knife. He turned it over, noticing the network of scars on his hands and forearms, old and recent, in places overlapping.

Adelaide, and people like her, had given him those scars. Whether she knew it or not, she was guilty.

He sensed the west behind him, urging him to revenge. It was a simple emotion. He could not deny that he wanted it. Gently, he closed his fingers around the door handle.

There was a tiny tremor in the metal, as though, sitting against the door, she was shivering.

He hesitated. It was the briefest flicker of concentration, but within that second he felt his resolution slip away.

Putting the knife back, he padded back through the apartment to the futon. He lay down and pulled the rug up to his neck. The soft fleece gathered at his throat like a noose.

He let out a long, muted sigh. His heart was beating wildly. He was covered in sweat. The relief that flooded his body only mirrored the horror at what he had almost done. The footsteps made to Adelaide's door and back felt like those of a stranger.

"It was me who found you in the unremembered quarters, Vik. Nils dared you, remember? It was a stupid dare."

Mikkeli was waiting for him, hunched over, her feet skimming the piano keys.

I'm sorry, he thought. *I forgot.*

It was true; Mikkeli had found him. She'd shone a torch on his face. Or maybe that was a different occasion. There were so many other times, anyway; lying on the edge of starvation, his body sabotaged by hypothermia. Time losing all logic whilst he waited for warmth.

Mikkeli climbed off the piano and stalked out of the window-wall, back to wherever she had come from. He remembered hugging her to him, trying to press some warmth to that lifeless body, but he'd had none to give, or she had taken it already.

Lying on Adelaide Mystik's futon, staring at her ceiling mural, Vikram promised himself he was never going to be that cold again.

23 | ADELAIDE

"**S**o the first thing you have to understand is how the Council works."

It was late morning. They sat on opposite sides of the table, the polished lake of wood between them. At one end, a pot of coral tea on a ceramic base steamed gently. Outside, heavy fog obscured the city entirely. The apartment felt like an oasis.

Adelaide's eyes were sore with tiredness, but the day's agenda was full. She had people to see. She tied back her hair as though she was preparing for hands-on work. The action focused her mind. If she was going to help Vikram, and for today at least, that illusion must be maintained, then she had to dive deep into the recesses of memory. She must recover incidental conversations between her parents, old lectures from Linus. She must listen once more to her grandfather's calm unhurried voice.

When the dawn came she had dozed for an hour or so, the gun still resting in her hand. She thought about barricading herself in until Vikram went away. But it was light. He had let her live. She put back the gun. This morning Vikram was uncommunicative; both the strange intimacy of last night and the nightmarish tension in the kitchen had all but vanished.

Adelaide reached behind her neck and unclasped a string of onyx beads. She arranged the necklace in a half circle. Then she took a ring off her middle finger and placed it under the arch.

"Here we have the Council, and here—" She touched the ring. "Is the Speaker. You probably stood on the podium just in front of him, right?"

Vikram nodded.

"The Council is like any other group. It has factions." She unhooked an earring and put it at the left end of the beads. "Here sits my illustrious father Feodor, and his cronies."

"Yes, I remember your father. I think he might remember me too."

Abruptly Adelaide recalled the day she had gone to see Feodor. Hadn't he said something about a westerner? The idea gave her a turn, almost as if they had met before, unwittingly. She tapped the earring with her forefinger.

"Feodor doesn't like anything to disturb the perfect order of his world. And he has to think about saving face. When the Council first established the border, Feodor was one of the Councillors who spoke out strongly for it. Any step towards unification, however small, will be an admission that they, and he, made a mistake."

Vikram's eyes were watchful. She knew that he wouldn't miss anything.

"Why did they do it?"

"What, divide the city?"

"Yes."

Adelaide kept her tone brisk. "You know why, Vikram. The west got too violent. After what happened at the Greenhouse, the City didn't have a choice. Harvests decimated, working citizens stabbed—I mean, there were children in there for stars' sakes. Only three of them came out intact."

Vikram scowled. "Conveniently."

"What do you mean, conveniently?"

"I mean it's convenient that when the 'seventy-seven riots started, the Council decided it was a great idea to let school parties wander round public buildings. Don't you think?"

She stared at him. "You can't accuse—"

"I'm not accusing."

"What are you saying then?"

"I'm saying that it was a long time ago. You can't know what really happened at the Greenhouse."

"And I suppose you can't know what really happened at Osuwa University, either. Perhaps that was allowed to happen too?" She strove to keep the anger out of her voice. Who was he to be lecturing her?

"No," he said. "That was a few individuals in a militant group called the New Western Osiris Front, which got out of hand. But I can tell you exactly what happened afterwards. The sk—the Home Guard let Citizens into the refugee camps. They even loaned them some guns. And your people used them. Like toys. I don't suppose anyone noticed if there were children around then."

She picked up the onyx beads and let them clatter back, pointedly.

"Well, as you so rightly pointed out, I wasn't there. You can't blame me for what other people did. You asked me why the border was created and I told you."

Vikram's expression was almost mocking now.

"I know the official line. I'm interested in why your father came to that decision."

"That depends upon who you ask," said Adelaide. She was happier discussing her father. Feodor was easily culpable. "According to my brother Linus, there was a huge debate over the issue and Feodor felt some glimmer of guilt about it—they were refugees, after all, it wasn't like the Council could ship them off somewhere else. But if you ask me, it was easy for Feodor. He was doing what he always does—protecting his interests. Now I'm telling you this, Vikram, not because I care, but so you know what you're up against."

"We're," he insisted. "What we're up against." He grinned. The expression was slightly startling. "You'll be the next Grete Kaat."

She dismissed this as too idiotic for words. "Grete Kaat was a criminal. She conspired to assassinate Alain and Helene Dumay. The parents of my compatriots." Not that she had anything to do with the Dumay offspring, but Vikram did not know that.

"Grete Kaat was never proved guilty."

"You believe she was innocent?"

"Do you really believe she was guilty?" he countered.

Adelaide gave him her blandest look. "Kaat is celebrated every year in the west for what she did."

"I'm sure that's what they tell you. Actually she's celebrated for what she didn't do. Kaat died in jail of pneumonia. The only reason she was locked up in the first place is because she'd expressed sympathies with the west in the past—the perfect scapegoat. That was the so-called evidence."

Adelaide decided not to comment. She had better weapons at her disposal.

"I'll tell you something ironic, shall I Vikram? My grandmother was a refugee. Second Grandmother that is. The first one died when Feodor was a child."

Vikram's face contracted. She had rattled him at last, although she was not sure now that it had been her intention. This kept happening with him, she thought. Things slipping out that she had not meant to say at all.

"Is that some kind of secret?"

"I'd hardly tell you if it was a secret. Don't forget, west and City wasn't an issue then. But imagine when Grandfather's son grew up and joined the segregation movement. I think it broke his heart. Having said that, I didn't see him jumping to live on the other side."

"Didn't he contest it? Your grandfather? Surely when his own wife—"

"No, no. My grandfather is the Architect, he was never on the Council. Feodor started that little dynasty. And besides, I don't suppose Grandfather felt there was much choice, if they wanted to preserve anything of Osiris. Quite funny, really, isn't it?"

She was speaking faster. It must be lack of sleep. After all, she had spent the night with a gun in her hand, it was hardly surprising if she was a little on edge.

Vikram looked at her straight on.

"Answer me something," he said. "Do you honestly believe the border is right?"

"It doesn't matter what I believe."

"Humour me."

"I'm helping you, Vikram, because you helped me. But I'm not getting into discussions about morality with you." She conjured her best mocking smile. "That's not my style. Now, moving on from Feodor's section—"

She slipped off a bracelet and laid it further along the beads.

"Here we have what I call the Executors—the departmental heads. Always look at the second row. That's where the Board of Four sit, the top Ministers. First Security—supervises the Home Guard and the ring-net and the civilian police. Then Finance—responsible for maintaining the credit system, including the anon cash chips given to westerners, seeing as you're not properly registered. After all, you can only get so far on *peng*."

"Which is another thing that could be sorted out if the border went."

"Are you listening to me or not?"

"I'm listening. I was just wondering how long you'd last if you had to barter for your fancy jewellery, that's all."

If he was trying to rile her, he was succeeding. But she refused to show it, and replied in her sweetest voice. "Luckily for both of us, that's unlikely ever to be an issue, is it? Getting back to the Executors—after Finance comes Resources, who looks after greenhouse production, parts manufacture, and the mining operations." She had an uneasy flashback to Linus's speech, cast it quickly aside. "And then there's Health and Science—self-explanatory. But also responsible for the meteorological facility up there." She pointed to the ceiling. "You'll notice that these four Ministers always get the people in the front row to speak for them. They don't like getting their hands dirty."

Vikram raised his eyebrows, pointedly.

"What?"

"Nothing. Just, coming from you…"

Was that a joke? She wondered.

"Actually, I don't mind dirt. It's people who piss me off."

"You should come to the west some time," he said.

"Maybe if we win."

"Deal."

"I think we've made enough deals, don't you?" One look at his face told her this time he was definitely joking. "Oh. Very funny. Anyway, the Executors tend to be the ones to suggest any new laws, but it doesn't happen often. They'll be violently against you."

Vikram rested his chin on one hand, looking at the beads.

"Do Citizens hate the west that much?"

The question surprised her. "Not hate, no. We don't really think about you." She considered for a moment. "I suppose it's seen as a lost cause. We'll have to pull out a few sob stories, Vikram, get the newsreels on side. Maybe you should tell them about Mikkeli. Do you have a photograph of her? A drawing?"

Vikram looked uneasy. He shook his head. His silence indicated her transgression more clearly than any words would have done. Adelaide took off another ring and placed it next to the bracelet.

"The liberal set. But rivals of Linus. They're Nucleites—they believe we're the last city on Earth," she explained. Her other earring went beside the ring. "And Linus and co. Who are anti-Nucleite. They believe—"

"In survivors outside Osiris." Vikram looked at her. "What are you?"

"Pro, of course. It's only Linus who's gone on this wacky spiritual kick. Why, aren't you?"

"I suppose I don't see things quite so black and white. Things are different in the west."

Adelaide thought about Linus's strange weather experiments. Less than a year ago she would have said he was mad, without question, but she knew better than anyone that madness could not be qualified.

"I suppose you think we should renew expeditions too."

Vikram picked up the earring she'd just set down, toying with it. "That's an interesting idea. Is that what your brother wants?"

"I don't know what Linus wants," she admitted. "But I can tell you one thing. Whatever he says or does, there's an ulterior motive behind it."

"How do you know all this, anyway?"

"It's amazing what you hear once you've become an alcoholic." Adelaide spoke flippantly, although she thought once more of her grandfather, and his patient, determined explanations to the twins. They used to have lunch once a month. But Leonid had grown frailer, he ventured out less, and then everything with Axel… their lunches had become infrequent.

She missed him.

"Can I have your watch?" she said.

Vikram undid the clasp and handed it over wordlessly. The steel links sat heavy in her palm. She placed the watch at the other end of the arch.

"My grandfather's contemporaries. Old and mostly deaf, or they only hear the bits they want, which is my personal theory. They saw the City finished. They built it, really. And they don't like it threatened." She paused. "Have you thought about what you're going to call yourself?"

"Yes. The New Horizon Movement."

He said the name hesitantly, with a hint of shy pride. It must be important to him.

"Very ambitious," she said. "And are there more of you?"

"There were. There will be." He did not explain further. "How will you get me an address?"

She smiled serenely. "I have a plan."

Vikram sat back and folded his arms, clearly appraising her. His watch ticked gently amongst the glittering collection of jewels. Neither of them had touched the tea.

"Are you helping me to get at your father?"

Adelaide was getting used to his directness. She thought about confronting him about his intentions last night, but did not quite dare. Today he needed her, but who knew how he would feel tomorrow?

"Sadly, getting at him usually means helping out Linus in some way. So it's a catch-no-fish situation."

He nodded, smiled to himself as though he found something funny. "Should have figured."

/ / /

She set up an account for Vikram on her Neptune and showed him the o'vis catalogue for when he got bored of working on his presentation. He displayed some signs of interest in that, asking her if she had Neon Age filmreels and what she would recommend. She found his enthusiasm oddly touching. She left him in the apartment and went to see Radir.

On the shuttle journey she thought about what she had uncovered so far. Axel was not in the hospitals; according to the official investigation, he was nowhere to be found in Osiris. A westerner had come to see him, an airlift. Axel had been planning something. He intended to make a balloon. She thought of Vikram's story about the last balloon flight. A western thing, he said. Her brother must have heard the story from the airlift. No doubt the horses had told him to do it. Axel had gathered all the resources, but something had interrupted his plans.

Radir was the next card in the deck.

The psychiatrist's office was in the northern quarter, on the tenth floor of a low rise scraper. It was a surprisingly industrial area for a private practitioner. The squat, adjacent pyramids housed on one side botanical gardens which grew the plants for cosmetics and anaesthetic, and on the other a reef farm.

The reef farm had been Adelaide's favourite haunt as a teenager. She used to go there when she was angry. Axel used to go with her, although he would inevitably wander off to talk to one of the wardens or marine biologists. Not for the first time, she considered the irony that his last psychiatrist had been there all along, seeing patients in the tower next door.

The receptionist was easy. After a sharp knock on Radir's door, Adelaide announced herself. "Good morning, Doctor."

The psychiatrist, a large man with an arched nose and fair hair who had so far repelled all of Adelaide's efforts to flirt with him, looked up and sighed. He did not seem surprised to see Adelaide. On the contrary, he had the expression of a man resigned to his fate.

"Good morning, Miss Rechnov." His voice was mid-range, the sort of voice you trusted without asking why, although if Adelaide had been asked, she would have said she trusted his eyes. They were blue and turned down at the corners. Seeing him again in the flesh, the lack of resemblance between Radir and Sanjay Hanif could not have been more marked.

Adelaide slid into the seat opposite him with a charming smile. It was not returned. That was another reason she trusted Radir. She had no effect on him.

"You can call me Adelaide," she said. "I told you that before."

"Miss Rechnov," he said implacably. "I must remind you that I have patients to see."

"I'm aware of that, Doctor. I'm also aware that this is your lunch break. Now don't think me amiss, but your receptionist was kind enough to get me a glass of water and I confess I did take a look at your appointment book whilst she was gone. You're free until half fourteen."

Radir tapped the activation strip of his Neptune with an air of finality, abandoning whatever he had been working on.

"I should also remind you, Miss Rechnov, that in light of the current investigation, I'm not sure you should be speaking to me."

"Right," said Adelaide. "Now we've got the formalities out the way. You may be wondering why I've come."

"I have an inkling."

"Well, Doctor, I suppose I want your opinion as to what has happened to my brother."

She sat back casually, as though she had just remarked on the rising price of raqua, and crossed one leg over the other, waiting.

"I cannot possibly conjecture. My sessions with Axel were cancelled six months before he disappeared. Over that period, his state of mind may have undergone a drastic transformation, or none at all. You will remember our last conversation."

Radir had said he felt sorry for her, a statement she had viewed as unforgivable at the time. The psychiatrist watched her, his face contemplative above his steepled hands. Adelaide found she did not care any more. He could think what he liked. He could pity her, if it would make him answer.

"Axel's last session," she said. "Were there any signs that he might be planning something?"

"You've had the report, Miss Rechnov. Your entire family has had the report, albeit via five separate requests."

"It's not the same as hearing about it. He came to see you here, didn't he?"

Radir swivelled slightly in his chair so that he faced away from her. He might have been recalling the visit; he might have been absolving himself of responsibility for what he was about to say.

"Your girl, Yonna. She brought him. He exhibited no signs that it was under duress, appeared willing to be here. He was—as he always was with me—at times lucid and capable of maintaining a conversation. He called me Doctor, but did not know my name, or if he did, he chose not to use it. And then, as if a switch had been pressed, he would become completely absent for minutes at a time. Lost in his own world. Unresponsive."

"What did you talk about?"

"Ordinary things, never specific people. The weather. The ocean. He often talked about the ocean, he said he liked to listen to its voice late at night."

"Did he mean the horses?"

"I suspect it may have been one and the same to him."

"Is, Doctor. It is."

"My apologies, Miss Rechnov."

"Did he ever mention a balloon?"

"Not that I recall."

"You're frowning, Doctor."

"The balloon... Something about that word rings a bell. But not from my sessions with Axel. Perhaps another patient."

"Did he—did he ever talk about leaving the City?"

"Not directly. I would say that Axel was aware of the City's limitations, even in an abstract capacity. Osiris is too small, he said once. We think we're free but we're not."

"What do you think he meant by that?"

"Feelings of entrapment are a common theme among those I see, Miss Rechnov. But I might add that we live in a quarantined city. Human beings are not designed for confinement, however vast and exquisitely made the prison; the explorer in us will out."

She sat for a moment, considering this. What if Axel had met the airlift through Radir?

"Doctor, do you ever see airlifts? Ex-westerners?"

"I cannot give you information on my clients."

"You know my family think he's dead."

Radir looked at her. She could see him selecting his words.

"Miss Rechnov, I am—saddened that I could not help your brother. As I have explained in the past, I could offer no diagnosis; Axel fit no specifications. Over the years I have seen patients who have, through various causes, withdrawn in some way from typical social interaction, for a longer or shorter period of time. Those who suffer post-traumatic stress, for example, following injury or a shocking incident, but sometimes there is no obvious trigger. The condition is a more common occurrence than you might expect, though it is rarely spoken of. Citizens of Osiris are survivors, are we not?"

His tone as he uttered that final sentence was gently ironic. Adelaide looked at the single picture on his wall, a swaying kelp field on the edge of the Atum Shelf.

"Is that not a positive trait, Doctor?"

"For some, doubtless. There are others who find it a source of pressure. In any case, whatever happened to Axel seemed to be an extreme form of this kind of internalization, and that, I feel, was a loss. To society as well as to the family."

She nodded. In spite of the formality of his tone, she believed Radir was genuine. She folded her hands tightly.

"I know he's alive. We have a connection, you see. Do you understand that, Doctor? Do you think it's possible?"

She hated the plea in her voice, but she could not hide it. Radir showed no signs of sympathy. She was grateful for that.

"I believe that there are things which will never be mapped by science," he said. "There are many that were once mapped and are now lost. But I also think, Miss Rechnov, that our society can be harsh, perhaps more condemning, of certain acts, than might be fair."

Adelaide's face went hot and her body chill.

"If you mean to imply, Doctor, that my brother might have committed—" She forced herself to speak the taboo. "*Suicide*—you are very much mistaken. Axel would never humiliate himself in that way. And he would never leave me."

She sensed that there was a weight of things behind Radir's blue eyes. Things that he might or could have said, if pushed. Those unspoken words chased her as she scraped her chair back, got up, stuck out a formal hand and pressed her wrist to his too hard for politeness. They followed as she walked out of the office. They followed her into the lift where she punched in level twenty-four, stood rigid for the fourteen floors up to the Obelisk shuttle line, and stalked onto the platform.

Why not? said the voice. *You left him.*

/ / /

She felt muddled and angry all the way to the Southern Quarter. In transit it seemed that the shuttle pod stood still and the city itself was rushing towards her, pyramids, steel and bufferglass all flying upon the ocean surface, but the speed was not enough to abate her turmoil. She took out her anger by sending Lao an o'voy.

Any news? Am I not paying you enough?

She did not expect a reply but to her surprise, her scarab flashed almost instantaneously.

Paying me to be discreet. Therefore will contact only when news. I'll be in touch.

She replied:

Been to see Dr Radir. Check his client list. He might have seen a westerner.

There was no return message. Moving her bag to accommodate another passenger, Adelaide struggled to assemble her thoughts. This next negotiation required careful handling. She had to put Axel aside, for now.

"Excuse me?" It was the woman who had sat next to her. "Can I have your signature?"

Adopting a gracious smile, Adelaide signed her name in green ink.

"I loved that garden you designed for the medical school," said the woman. Adelaide was tempted to tell her that the garden had come from a series of doodles on restaurant napkins whilst she was waiting for Jannike, nothing more, but if the woman wanted to think of Adelaide as a land-scape designer, so be it. Adelaide liked plants. She liked the feel of earth crumbling in her fingers; she liked its dank alien smell. Plants behaved as you expected them to.

/ / /

The *Daily Flotsam* offices were undersea and windowless and smelled of perspiration overlaid with heavy perfume. At sixteen o'clock, the place was a tip. Dirty Neptunes balanced on desks overflowing with Surfboards, wrappers, BrightEye pills and mouldering tea glasses. A screen on one wall showed the latest feeds from rival press groups. Nobody recognized Adelaide when she first walked in, then the whole office reacted towards her; a sea of sunk conversations and swivelling heads.

"I'm looking for Magda," she said.

One of them moved. Over the years their faces had changed, but the avaricious hunger had not. Adelaide no longer cared what they wrote about her. She only cared about what they had done to her twin. Odd lines—the things she hadn't been able to avoid, still stuck. *Is Axel Rechnov sick in the head?* That was one of Magda's. Looking about, she was able to match each headline to its creator.

Silence endured until the door to the inner office opened and Magda Linn looked out. When she saw Adelaide a smile spread across her face, slowly, like clotting butter.

"Well, well, well," she said. "Little fishy's come to play with sharks."

Magda's office was surprisingly clean. Her Neptune had a bright red frame and was unadorned. The editor sat at her desk and waved an arm at the chair opposite. Both women crossed their legs.

"Adelaide."

"Magda."

"What can I do for you?"

For a woman with a penchant for character defamation, Magda Linn looked remarkably innocent. She was small and neat, with straight black hair and low eyelids. Her right hand sported a scratched glass ring with which she toyed incessantly. Adelaide hated every inch of her neatly proportioned features. It was difficult to look Magda in the face without conveying this, so Adelaide examined the wall behind her.

"I heard you wanted access to a few events."

"And I dare say I'll get it."

"I don't know. The Haze has had enough security issues recently. This season we're really clamping down."

"My reporters will have to become more ingenious."

"Maybe so. But they'll have to be remarkably wily to get into Jannike Ko's twenty-second." Adelaide paused. "Private party," she said blankly.

For a brief moment, Adelaide felt bad about offering up her friend as bait. But Jan could handle it.

"Jannike Ko's twenty-second," Magda said slowly. Her smooth face could not help but flicker at the thought. Adelaide knew she was imagining the newsreel, constructing, already, the headline copy. Jannike Ko, last of the Haze to come of age, could supply Magda with enough subreels to keep her afloat for the next year. Then Magda's face closed down again.

"What do you want, Adelaide?"

"I want you to do what you are best at, Magda. I want you to lie."

"I see. And what type of lying might you require?" Magda tapped her ring against the edge of her desk. "Some light slander before breakfast? How about a nice little libel case?"

"No, that doesn't serve my purpose. I'm after something simpler. The Council will be holding a convention next week to discuss the implementation of western aid schemes. I'd like you to announce it."

Magda's expression was pure disbelief.

"The Council?"

"That's what I said."

"Since when have you been interested in the Council?"

"Since today, Magda."

"And why would you be interested in aid schemes?"

"I don't see why that would concern you. The request is simple enough, is it not?"

"You'd give me access to Jannike Ko's twenty-second in exchange for a little article on aid schemes?"

"A big article, Magda. A headline article. I'll be invoking the Ibatoka Clause—you can say that too."

Magda laughed. "The what?"

"Why don't you look it up?" Adelaide suggested.

"If I don't know what it is it's not headline material," Magda shot back. "You coming to my office asking for help, now that's headline material."

"Come on Magda. You know you love the Council. Miserable old octopuses, promoting unprecedented aid schemes. You're telling me you can't make something juicy out of that? Spin it whichever way you like, I don't care."

Magda scraped the ring against her front teeth.

"Jannike Ko only turns twenty-two once," Adelaide mused.

"Well, I suppose we could run with a riot containment theme. There have been… flickers. A profile of one of the Home Guard might of interest."

"No Home Guard. How about a neglect and sob story piece?"

"Yes, thank you, I don't need you to tell me how to do my job."

"Do excuse me. I've been the subject of your job for so long, sometimes I feel I know it as well as you do."

Both women sat back, assessing one another.

"What guarantee do I have that you'll keep your word?"

"I don't give guarantees," said Adelaide.

"I could turn this whole industry against you."

Adelaide pretended to give this a second's thought.

"I doubt that. On the other hand, I could get you fired in the time it takes to do this." She snapped her fingers. "Still a Rechnov, Magda. Now. Do we or do we not have a deal?"

Magda gnawed on the ring.

"Make sure you check the morning feed."

"Good." Adelaide stood up. "I'll see myself out, shall I?"

/ / /

The knock at the door was insistent. She went to answer it, muttering to herself about people who couldn't wait. Axel stood grinning in the corridor. He strolled into the apartment, a half-smoked cigarillo dangling from his lips.

"Is that the time?" he said. The cigarillo waggled comically in his mouth. "Must have been gone longer than I thought."

"Months, actually," she said. "Where were you, the western quarter or what?"

"Oh, this and that. Baiting Linus. Annoying Dmitri with my expenses. Why, A, did you miss me?"

She woke with a jolt and found herself on the futon, fully dressed. For a minute she thought it was raining again, but it was just the noise of Vikram's fingers on the activation strip of her Neptune.

"Evening," he said.

"Did I sleep?"

"Yes. You got about halfway through telling me about going to the *Daily Flotsam*. Linus called, by the way."

She rubbed her eyes. They were prickly with sleep.

Hell's tide! She was beginning to wake up. Last night this man had wanted to kill her. Today she was falling asleep in the same room.

But she wasn't scared any more. She sensed that a line had been crossed.

"What did Linus want?"

"To let you know he'd had a message from some woman called Linn asking about a conference."

She smiled at that. "Good. We're going to force their hand."

And why are you trying to help him, Adelaide?

"There's some fresh coral tea if you want."

"What's the time?"

"Twenty-one thirty."

"Shit. Said I'd meet Jannike for dinner. You coming?"

"I've got a presentation to write."

"It's your call."

Vikram hadn't woken her for Linus's message. She could not decide if that was a good thing or not. She perched on the futon to pull on her boots, sneaking surreptitious glances at his thin angular figure, tensed over the Neptune. Her laces were tangled and it took her a few minutes to work out the knots.

There was no time for tea so she took a shot of voqua, aware that

Vikram's eyes were on her, nervous in a way she could not pin down. If those eyes held a different light, they might draw her right in.

Better pull yourself together, girlie. You might not be as strong as you think you are.

The lift came almost immediately when she called it, from the floor above. The man inside held the door for her.

"Good evening, Miss Rechnov."

She noticed a funny motif on the collar of his shirt; a white winged insect. One of the facility crowd. What the hell did they do up there, anyway? Was it really astronomy, or some kind of dubious experimentation? She felt the voqua burn down her gullet and wondered if the man could see it, like a red streak down her neck.

"Evening," she acknowledged.

"Please, give my regards to the Architect."

She nodded. The lift plummeted. It was a good thing Vikram wasn't coming. He was too unpredictable. She would have to babysit him all night and besides, Tyr was going to be out. She was conscious of an overwhelming desire to have Tyr's arms around her while he told her that all would be well, that everything would work out, as he had the day after Axel evicted her from the penthouse. She felt as though she was carrying the weight of a colossal secret, and yet the truth was she knew nothing at all.

24 ¦ VIKRAM

Vikram stretched his arms above his head, relishing the solitude and the peace. A week had passed while he worked in the Red Rooms, preparing for his presentation and watching Adelaide's magical filmreels. Adelaide had just left, slamming the door of her apartment shut with a small implosion. It was not an aggressive sound; she always slammed doors. Vikram had got used to her. On this day of the Council address, though, he was glad of these last few minutes alone to prepare for the debate ahead.

He lifted his gaze from the Neptune to the window-wall. The sleek silver towers stretched away like sentinels. If it weren't for the year of storms, the entire city would have looked like this, and Vikram might not have been here at all. The sight stirred up a rare well of nostalgia within him. He examined the feeling, turned it over, tested its value toward today's proceedings. Once more he read through the notes he had made.

Adelaide had been surprisingly, even shockingly useful. She knew all the intricacies of the Council. The more they talked, the more he realized that as an ally she would stretch far beyond this initial appeal.

There had been times when working with the girl was actually fun. They ran ideas past one another, tentatively at first, but grew increasingly frank in their discussions. Together they had pored over legal documents. They looked at records of previous appeals to the Council, from the Western Repatriation Movement's first address, to the threats issued by an emerging NWO. Adelaide was quick to spot the inconsistencies in a piece of legislation. With her caustic commentary, she made him laugh more than once, and if she wasn't expected at some soirée or other, they could quite easily sit arguing late into the night. Her energy reminded him of Eirik, although he could never tell her that.

Neither of them ever mentioned that first night.

A knock at the door interrupted his thoughts. He did not register the noise at first. Nobody ever came to Adelaide's flat. Then it sounded again. He raised his head. Definitely a knock. It had occurred to Vikram, before now, that his and Adelaide's cavalier attitude to the Council might well have made them enemies.

His hand went to his ribs but he was not carrying a knife. He went to the kitchen, picked out a paring knife from the block and slipped the blade into the back of his belt.

In the hallway he listened. The knock was not repeated. There was no other sound. He caught a glimpse of himself in Adelaide's mirrors, a bundle of tensed muscles camouflaged by a suit. He opened the door.

Standing in the corridor, a good metre back, was a short woman in a bulky coat. Her hair was flecked with grey. She had a scarf around her neck and her cheeks were flushed, which told him she had probably travelled by boat. Vikram knew instantly that she was a westerner. As always, it was the eyes that gave her away. She was good though; the expression almost but not quite repressed.

"Hello," she said. "I'm looking for Adelaide Rechnov." She spoke quickly, a gruff voice.

"She's not here at the moment." Vikram kept one hand on the door. "Can I help?"

The woman brought her hand up to her hair, as though she might smooth out the frizz, then dropped it again.

"No—no. I need to see her directly." She did not move, all the same. Vikram's apprehension evaporated; he was caught between irritation that she might delay him, and curiosity. What connection could another westerner have to Adelaide's glamorous life? Perhaps she was—what did they call it over here, an airlift.

"Can I take a message?" he persisted. "What's your name?"

Her eyes wavered. He thought she might bolt. With the speed of sudden decision, she removed a haversack, unzipped it, and took out an envelope.

"I was told to bring this here if Mr Axel went away. He's not here now so I guess that means he's gone away. So here I am." The last words were almost incomprehensible, her voice trailing downwards with her lashes.

"Would you like me to deliver it to Adelaide?" he asked. She hesitated, still a metre away, the envelope gripped tight in her fingers. Instinctively, he knew if she left now, she would never come back. Vikram recognized that fear; he knew the effort it must have cost to come. "I'm going to see her very soon," he said gently. "In about an hour, in fact. If you want to leave it with me I'll make sure she gets it."

"Alright," she said finally. "You'll tell her what I said. I—meant to come sooner. But I don't want anything more to do with it—with them. These people. You understand."

He knew then that she had recognized him as well.

"I'll tell her," he said.

She held out the envelope abruptly. He stepped forward to take it. The smell of outside was on her. Her fingers clasped the paper for a moment longer, then yielded. She zipped up the haversack and settled it firmly across both shoulders.

"Thank you," she said.

She hurried away down the stairs and he guessed she would call the lift a few flights down, out of sight. As soon as she had gone, Vikram realized how much he had failed to find out. He hadn't even asked who she was.

He shut the door and looked at the envelope in his hand. The letter A was written in green ink. The envelope was bumpy. There was something more than paper inside.

He put the envelope under the bowl where Adelaide kept her scarab o'comm and her keys, and went back to the study. He read through his notes a final time, enunciating each word clearly in his head before some part of his nervous system admitted he was taking in none of it and his legs took him back to the main room.

Fifteen minutes before he needed to leave. He glanced down at the bowl. The keys were there, the big brass one and the smaller silver, on a large metal ring with a red enamel rose. Vikram bent to pick up the keys and straightened with the letter in his hands.

That's more like it, he heard Mikkeli saying. *For a minute there I thought you were going to leave it.*

The ink on the envelope was blurred, as though the writer had scratched the A hastily and the nib of the pen had snagged, spattering bright green gobbets. *No*, he thought. *I can't read this.* In the same moment he was walking towards the kitchen, knowing exactly what duplicitous trick he was about to perform, and unable to summon the willpower to stop himself. He filled the teapot with water and put it on the heat. When it began to whistle, he held the envelope over the plume of steam and carefully prised apart the seal. Inside was a letter, intricately folded, written in the same green ink. Something else fell out: a necklace, with a charm, smooth and ivory coloured. It looked like a shark tooth.

He read the letter twice.

A.

I'm taking advantage of an afternoon's rare lucidity.

That is to say, there are times when the clouds clear, and I know that I have been walking in clouds—because once I am in them, I forget they are really there and assume that this <u>fogginess,</u> yes, today I'll call it fog, is real. So I was surprised to find blue sky today. You understand.

Listen. I think, A, that I have been taken away. I'm not sure where, or how, or even what for, though I suppose there's some design in it. Or not. That's the way Osiris—the name just came to me, this is a good day, A, a productive day!—the way <u>Osiris</u> works. Not with wheels and bolts and mechanisms. With yarn and threads. There is a big web of knots and sometimes you put your finger on one and know the answer but mostly you don't, and in the fog you have to trust your instincts, Adie. Always trust your instincts.

This Osiris appears to be a maze. I have gone along some of the walkways but not today. I haven't felt like exploring for some time. There are too many people. I look for you often, though. I search all the windows. (There are many of them, and they are like eyes. It takes time.) Today you are clear, but often you make yourself indistinct, as if you are hiding. Then I remind myself that you are playing a game, and it is my mission to find the rules and then you will become like crystal.

The horses were back earlier. They still don't speak, but they're running, secretly. I'm waiting for them to stop. I know they have something important to tell me—something about Osiris. I'm not alone, Adie. <u>We're not alone.</u>

The white horse will talk first. I am sure of it.

Now, there is an event, a slide of what they call memory… it's not focused, because it hasn't been out in the sun long enough… I'm jumping in water, A. It's very cold. It's cold here, as well. I think it's a test. I have to turn to ice before I can be warm again. The ocean calls and I will have to dive deep to discover its purpose.

I am going to tell you a secret, Adie. That is why I am writing to you, because when the hour comes I will have to leave very quickly and will not have time to say goodbye. I am making a balloon. <u>Don't tell anyone.</u> It's just between you and me. I was going to tell you before, but I knew you were angry, and I thought the horses might not like it. Don't be cross, A. It's for the best. And when I come back we can find the sand. You'll like that. No more mazes, no more clouds.

I'll find you soon.

A.

The teapot was screeching. Automatically, Vikram moved it and switched the electricity off. Steam lent the windows a temporary mistiness. It was misty outside too and his own vision seemed to slide out of focus. He refolded the letter back into its original shape. It looked to him roughly the shape of a horse's head. A conversation with Adelaide flashed into his head. *What was he like, your brother? He was clever.* It was the only time he had heard her refer to her twin in the past tense.

Even as the implications of what he had read settled upon him, Vikram realized he had no time to ponder the consequences. It would be insanity to give Adelaide such material minutes before they appeared before the Council. He slipped the envelope and the necklace inside his jacket pocket. He would reseal it later.

In the hallway he paused, catching his reflections once more. A young man in a smart suit met his gaze, clean shaven, his dark hair combed neatly back, a necktie at his throat. Vikram stared at this stranger. The clothes had done their work; he did not appear, at first glance, like a man with a history of violence. Truth was in the eye, wasn't it? He moved closer to the mirror. His breath, quicker than usual with nervousness, made a patch of condensation. He looked deep, but found no history there. The belief that you were able to see a person's soul in their eyes was false after all. The eye was only matter. Axel Rechnov had known that, once. Just another example of human frailty.

25 | ADELAIDE

She looked at all the fish in the elevator aquarium and chose the angelfish. It was an old game. If it followed, they would have good luck. As the lift doors closed, the nose of the angelfish edged up. It looked for a moment as though it might launch, then dived suddenly down into the depths of the scraper. The lift began to move.

At level fifty-four a man intent upon his Surfboard got out and a young woman in a long skirt got in. Her glance took in Adelaide's costume, then floated, as those dull, earnest types always did, up to Adelaide's face. Adelaide stared blandly back.

She knew why she was helping Vikram. It was because she was bored. And boredom in Osiris was dangerous, boredom was a one-way ticket to insanity. Liaising with a westerner, on the other hand, could not be described as anything other than reckless.

As the lift rose she was overwhelmed by a sense of vertigo, a sense that her involvement was about to become far bigger, far wider than she had accounted for. Level eighty-one. The lift doors paused, the doors parted. There was still time. She could get out now. She could walk away.

But she didn't. Adelaide had been accused of many things, but no-one had ever said she was a coward.

26 ¦ VIKRAM

He waited in an aisle approaching the podium, just out of sight. The Chambers looked different today. The viewing balconies bulged with noisy spectators whilst below, the crescent rows of seats were unoccupied and expectant.

In his jacket pocket, next to Axel's letter, was a pine needle. He had taken it from one of the conifer trees in the lobby, for luck, and he could still sniff the aroma of the trees; the scent of mystery and far away places. Adelaide stood beside him. She was wearing a white trouser suit and tinted glasses and she'd done something to her hair, a new fringe that fell to her eyebrows. Vikram could not have imagined a more unlikely partner.

She pointed to the balcony.

"Your new fan base, that's the Haze, are installed up there. The Council will be shuffling in shortly. So tell me, Mr Bai, how does it feel in the green room?"

Vikram grinned in spite of himself, and the tie at his throat felt a little looser. Today, Adelaide's irreverence was a tonic.

Behind the podium, a gowned man was enthroned in a circular turret about two metres high. The Speaker, Vikram thought.

Three long, sonorous notes flooded the Chambers. There was a rustling as everyone on the balcony got to their feet. The great wooden doors of the Chambers swung open. One by one, the Councillors filed in, silent and solemn faced. They wore purple surcoats over their suits which swished on the pale marble floor.

"These public events are so theatrical," whispered Adelaide in Vikram's ear.

He nodded, nervous, but his eyes were more astute now. He looked around the filling rows and he could divide the Council into their five, distinctive segments. On the left, the reactionary heavyweights, second generation, responsible for implementing the border thirty-nine years ago. He found Feodor Rechnov straight away and studied him closely. Feodor's face was entrenched with lines, but there was Adelaide's perfectly straight nose, her strong brows, the set of her shoulders. It was a predator's face, but not a reckless predator. Feodor Rechnov was like a high soaring bird, manipulating the thermals to scan all possible territories. Vikram knew he had to emulate that clear sightedness.

Taking his seat, Feodor leaned over and muttered something to the man next to him, who nodded. Next along were the Executors, as Adelaide called them. He located the Board of Four in the second row, where their position enabled them to lean forward and whisper the things they wished to be announced into the ears of their subordinates.

"That's Security on the left," murmured Adelaide. "After her it's Finance, and after him Resources, then Health and Science at the end."

Behind them gathered other departmental heads. Adelaide pointed out Climate, Education, and Estates. The Executors were not communicating much between themselves, but each of them looked ready to do battle. Opposite and over to the right were the two factions of liberals, the Nucleites and the antis. Vikram spotted Linus speaking very quickly to the man and woman behind him.

"There's Dmitri," Adelaide said. "In the second row, wearing a redstriped necktie. Doesn't look much like the rest of us, does he? If I didn't know my mother, I'd say she'd had an affair."

"She never wanted to join the Council, I take it?"

"She was too busy designing invitations. Actually, she's a better politician than any of them, but she prefers to exert her influence over raqua and dessert."

"That might not be such a bad idea," Vikram said drily.

He had forgotten the way the pale stone of the Chambers whispered. Scuffles and muttered words chased one another around the indoor amphitheatre. As the Council settled with a flurry of surcoats, his gaze was drawn to the final faction on the far right. The first generation Councillors were stooped, always one of them shaking, like so many pine needles disturbed by a breeze. Their hair was as white as snow. The women's coiffeurs were cropped short or drawn into wispy buns. Their earrings were bright chandeliers against the soft folds of their necks. The men had jackets under their surcoats in moss green or mulberry red. Many wore glasses that both magnified their eyes and disguised them. Adelaide had warned Vikram not to be fooled by their antique appearance; a lack of sharpness, she said, only increased their obduracy.

Despite their inevitable antipathy towards him, it was these veterans that interested Vikram the most. As their hair had gained streaks of grey and finally was bleached of all colour, they had watched their city change. They had witnessed it pass from elite, technological masterpiece, to benevolent rescue centre, to reluctant tyrant. Finally they had seen it become two cities. Perhaps that wall gave them the illusion that the thing they had created retained its beauty and its integrity, but Vikram doubted it.

The three notes sounded again. Only when the entire Chambers had hushed did the Speaker begin.

"On the second Thursday of the month of Mae, I declare witness to the gathering of the Osiris Council, guardians of the city of Osiris, one hundred and forty-five years after the founding of the Osiris Board, the city being now in its seventieth year as an independent state. This session opens at the hour of two minutes past eleven hundred. This session is held in the domain of the public eye, although the public shall not contribute to the issues discussed today which are for the consideration of the esteemed Councillors and them alone. As Speaker, I invoke the Eleni Clause which orders that all words spoken in this session are words of truth."

The Speaker drew a long breath and continued. Up in the balconies Vikram saw yawning faces. Even the Councillors looked peevish and uncomfortable under their purple robes. Finally, the Speaker introduced Adelaide.

"Miss Mystik has invoked the Ibatoka Clause. I remind all present that the Ibatoka Clause may be used by Citizens to speak on a matter which they feel, if not addressed, shall have detrimental consequences for the future of Osiris. Miss Mystik represents the New Horizon Movement."

Adelaide gave Vikram's hand a tiny squeeze before she stepped up.

Cheers and whistles from the Haze accompanied her progression to the podium. First generation members of the Council shushed disapprovingly. Feodor Rechnov's face was rigidly neutral.

"Hello, esteemed members of the Council." Adelaide's voice was a river of milk. "I thank the Speaker for his words. I, however, am not so good with speeches, and I therefore present Mr Vikram Bai, who has addressed you once before, to present the matter of my grave concern." She gave a little bow. Vikram noticed her glasses slipped a fraction down her nose as she did so. She turned to step down, then turned back. "Regarding the west," she added.

A murmur ran through the Chambers. Adelaide winked at Vikram. They exchanged places. As he climbed up he felt more than ever like an appearing puppet. Then he looked around the sweep of Councillors. *I can name you now.* There was muscle in a name.

"Esteemed Councillors," he began. "I am exceedingly grateful to have this opportunity to stand before you once again." He waited a beat. "And I hope it shall prove a more profitable exchange of our time than on the last occasion. Forgive me if I reiterate a few things. I feel it is important that the facts stand fresh in our minds, and I hope also to enlighten those who were not present at my last address."

He glanced up to the balconies, where curious faces crowded at the rail. He glimpsed surprise there, and smiled to himself. They had not expected a westerner to sound so formal. Vikram wanted to remind the Council that they were under surveillance. Public debates were rare, and he was certain they did not like it.

"This is a very beautiful room," he declared, now letting his gaze roam the marbled walls, the elegant pillars. "It is also a very warm room. Nobody on this side of the city has much occasion to dwell on warmth—and why should you? Our city was built to make such day-to-day necessities invisible. And yet, on the other side of a line that a past Council has decreed a boundary, people die daily from cold. I've seen it many times. It comes when you're long past shivering, long past feeling the pains of frostbite, past recognizing the threat. You freeze, quietly, into a quiet sleep. So quiet, that there isn't going to be any waking up." Vikram paused. "How many? That's a difficult question, because as you know, there is no accurate census in west Osiris, no way of telling how many deaths. The informal numbering process affected by the Home Guard—" He almost said skadi, but caught the word in time, "—is inexact, not to mention clearly delineating westerners as different from yourselves, who after all are only one or two generations further from your own Old World origins. But I can assure you that the number of deaths is certainly in the hundreds, and more than likely in the thousands."

He let this figure resonate. With so many present, the Chambers were growing increasingly hot. A couple of first generation Councillors flapped ineffectual hands to try and stir the air. Vikram focused on this odd sight: the elderly weakened by heat.

"It is unforgivable," he said. "*Unforgivable* that this is still happening in our city. The potential for electric heating is here, at our fingertips, in the very fabric of the buildings, and yet we lack the necessary connections to access it, whilst the connections we do have are temperamental and unreliable. How many of those thousands of lives could be saved by the flick of a switch?"

Vikram sensed the fickle sway of his audience's attention, now present, now absent. The spectators listened keenly, the Councillors grudgingly, aware that they were on display and unable to retract too far into their private worlds. He judged it was time to push.

"But these things, these apparent feats of engineering, are for the future. I come before you today with a simpler request. Winter approaches. Many citizens of the west will spend the coldest months of the year on boats, with no protection from the cold or the storms. The young and the elderly are particularly at risk, if not from hypothermia than from starvation. Complete catastrophe could be averted with the establishment of a number of overnight shelters and boat kitchens. These are very basic things, ladies and gentlemen, but they require good will and funding. We need insulation works. In the future, we will also require an investigation into the undersea levels, many of which are flooded and uninhabitable, depriving the west of further accommodation.

"A few words on health and sanitation. The single hospital in the west is overcrowded, understaffed and unhygienic, no surprise as we have one to your five. It serves as little more than an accident and emergency unit. There are no provisions for those with long term illnesses, many of which could be averted if vaccinations were available. The most basic vaccinations, which I believe Citizens receive at the age of two, would save further lives."

Vikram looked slowly around the room, trying to catch each Councillor's eye.

"It seems logical to adopt a two-stage programme. The first stage, that is, shelters, boat kitchens and vaccination centres, to be implemented immediately, whilst structural repair works should be investigated in the spring. Councillors, the choice is yours. Act now, or condemn thousands."

He made no appeals. He offered no vote of confidence in the Council's humanity, or in their ability to make the right decision. Guilt was best eked from silence. It came out of the gaps and the spaces, the things not said, the things left hanging. He took a step back, and gave the Speaker a nod to show that he had finished.

"Thank you, once again, Mr Bai. That was, again, enlightening." The Speaker's voice erred just the safe side of sarcasm. The Councillors were keeping quiet. Only a small susurration of whispers indicated unrest. "Are there any questions for Mr Bai?"

A woman from the liberal camp stood to speak.

"I have a question for Miss Mystik."

Vikram moved over to allow Adelaide space on the podium. Pandemonium on the balconies greeted her second appearance; Vikram was certain that most of the press had come in anticipation of an Adelaide show. The Speaker's hammer banged furiously. The Councillor raised her voice.

"May we take it, Miss Mystik, that you speak on behalf of this group, this—"

"The New Horizon Movement," Adelaide supplied.

"Yes, yes. Are you, in fact, an active member of the group?"

"I am," said Adelaide serenely.

Exclamations flashed around the balconies. Journalists tapped frenziedly into their Surfboards. The Speaker shouted for silence. Vikram looked at Adelaide and found her perfectly composed, her lips curved in a slight smile, the sheared fringe brushing her demurely lowered lashes. He did not care, at that moment, what her motives were. She had given her name to the west, knowingly and absolutely. Glancing across to Feodor Rechnov, he saw that the Councillor's cheeks were tinged with red.

"Then do you have anything to add to Mr Bai's statement?" the woman pressed.

Adelaide's smile blossomed.

"I feel Mr Bai has explained the situation clearly enough. I only hope that the subject matter is not too distant for our esteemed Council. After all, many of you do not step outside over the course of twelve months."

Vikram saw the Minister of Resources lean forward and tap the shoulder of the man in front. The man got to his feet.

"I can hardly imagine that the cosseted lifestyle Miss *Mystik* enjoys includes outdoor excursions in adverse conditions."

"On the contrary," said Adelaide. "I regularly waterbike as far as the ring-net. Without the insulation of my bike-suit, I would probably die of hypothermia. As Mr Bai has explained, there are no such suits in the west, in fact, there is barely any heating. It does strike me as somewhat unfair."

"Forgive me if I say this is a very abrupt demonstration of concern," said the man. Adelaide was unfazed.

"Indeed it is, Councillor. I confess until I met Mr Bai, I was entirely ignorant of these circumstances. Now that I have been enlightened, I am compelled to support his cause."

Vikram stifled a laugh. There was shuffling amongst the Councillors, and the Minister of Resources tapped her spokesman on the shoulder again.

"May I request we open to the floor, Speaker?"

They don't like dealing with Adelaide, Vikram thought. She disarms them; she knows the language. He looked for Linus. Adelaide's brother's face was serious, but Vikram had no doubt that beneath the calm exterior lurked a satisfied smile.

"Granted," said the Speaker's voice overhead.

This time, there was no rush to stand. Then the woman Linus had been speaking to earlier rose.

"It seems a reasonable request," she ventured.

The word reasonable was the spark. At once the left side of the crescent were on their feet, arguing over what could be considered reasonable, questioning the criteria for the demand, the lack of available resources. It was difficult enough to keep the City in good repair. Where would the money, or the materials, come from for the west? The liberals jumped up in response. Dmitri Rechnov said nothing. Linus was vocal. The demands, he argued, were so basic as to be almost unreasonable in their conservatism.

They should be doing far more. Through the debate, the voices of the first generation Councillors sounded like thin, disconsolate reeds.

An elderly woman turned to the podium.

"Mr Bai, I recall that the last time you were here there was some incendiary talk of demilitarization. May we assume you have dropped that aggressive stance today?"

Vikram leaned both hands on the podium. "I hardly consider it an aggressive stance," he replied. "Rather the opposite. I won't say that my opinion has changed, but today I am here purely to request funding for a winter aid scheme."

"You have not mentioned costs in all of this, Mr Bai," said a balding man who Vikram recognized as the Minister of Finance. "I assume you have some form of budget in mind."

"A figure of fifty thousand credits would comfortably encompass the schemes I have mentioned. Thirty-five thousand would be the absolute minimum required."

Exchanges fired through the ranks of the Executors. Vikram exchanged a glance with Adelaide. They had agreed the asking price should be high, but now he wondered if they had pushed too hard. Adelaide clasped her hands and brought them to rest upon the podium, her white cotton sleeve brushing against his arm.

The Chambers quietened. Feodor Rechnov was rising. His eyes were riveted on Vikram. He did not spare his daughter a glance.

"Mr Bai," he said, and the Chambers hushed further. "You have made an impressive case, an—emotive, case. I congratulate you on the almost inconceivable improvement. You must realize, however, that you are asking this Council to supply you with a large sum of money on the basis of your word—and your word alone."

There were murmurs of approval from the reactionaries. The Councillor of Finance was nodding.

"I take your point," said Vikram calmly. "The reason I am standing here today, is, very simply, because there is nobody else to represent my side of the city. There are no westerners, ladies and gentlemen, in your assemblage. The labyrinth of administration with which this Council surrounds itself makes it almost impossible to gain a hearing. As to my qualifications—I can only tell you my own experience. I am, however, happy to escort any Councillors who wish for further proof on a tour of the west, and there I can show you all of the disease and poverty of which I speak. I'd advise you to wrap up warm."

A ripple of laughter from the liberals.

"Perhaps you'd like to go, Councillor Rechnov," called out a girl from the balcony. Vikram recognised the voice as Adelaide's friend, Jannike Ko. Feodor's face remained impassive, although Vikram thought that the red spots in his cheeks intensified.

"I believe the Council would prefer a more scientific assessment of the situation," Feodor countered. "Rather than the rhetoric of a westerner."

There was a collective gasp from the balcony, purely theatrical, as Vikram doubted there was a single person in the room who was not secretly thinking what Feodor had voiced. Vikram crushed his own anger. He even smiled. Adelaide had already supplied him with all the ammunition he needed, and now Feodor had given him the incentive to use it.

"Councillor Rechnov," he said. "Forgive me if I have my facts wrong, but didn't your own father, the Architect, remarry a refugee? Surely you feel a degree of responsibility towards the west, even if you do not feel compassion?"

Uproar followed. Vikram saw Feodor's jaw clench, and the red spots burned brighter for the paleness that infected the rest of the Councillor's face. Vikram did not take his eyes off the man, but sensed, at his side, Adelaide's initial surprise melting into expectancy as she, too, sniffed the resolution that had to follow.

The Speaker asked for a vote. Vikram watched the hands raise and hover in midair, swaying in an impossibly complicated semaphore whilst the Speaker took his count. There were too many hands, a hopeless number. The hammer rapped. In the commotion from the balcony, the Speaker's words were swallowed. Councillors were on their feet, imperial surcoats swinging. Vikram's heart went numb. We've lost, he thought.

As he stepped down from the podium a surge of people gathered around. Hands clapped his back, pummelled and tugged at him. He was aware of voices, offering congratulations, hollering questions through the clamour. He blinked in a barrage of camera flashes. *How did you meet Adelaide, Mr Bai? Adelaide, why are you helping the west?* He heard his lie of a surname repeated over and over, and thought dizzily that in the last half hour he had managed to become someone he was not.

Vikram turned to his accomplice. Her face was ablaze. He realized, finally, that they'd won, and he felt his face split in an answering grin. A wing of pure joy trembled in his chest. It rose to his throat, filled it, had to fly out. He grabbed Adelaide and lifted her shrieking off the ground. As he spun her around she was pressed against his smart new jacket and her brother's letter. He put her down. Her smile was a solar beam. Then, in full view of the Chambers and the krill, she kissed him.

27 | ADELAIDE

Her eyes opened. It was not yet light, and she was very still. At first she thought she'd had a nightmare that had frozen her muscles. But then her lungs expanded and she realized the restraint was physical. A pair of arms wrapped around her upper body, pinning her against the hard heat of the man's chest. Her heart beat faster, in confusion, and anger, that she had allowed this to happen. The hands that were not hers were nonetheless familiar; she had seen them manipulating her Neptune, peeling an apple with a penknife in one long strip, unfastening the strap of a watch. And now they were warm on her skin.

Vikram's breath fluttered on the back of her neck. She shifted, hoping the movement might dislodge him. He only paused between inhaling and exhaling, and his grip tightened as his breath trickled out. Adelaide thought back to yesterday. She remembered the victory afterparty, the Haze running rampage over the Red Rooms, the dancing and the octopya. She remembered kissing him at her bedroom door. She remembered locking the door. After that, memory failed her.

She twisted her head to look at Vikram. His head, pressed against the top of her spine, fell into the alcove just below the pillow. She prised his arms away and turned to study him properly. Dim light and sleep had softened him. Tiny veins tracked the half moons of his eyelids. His lashes shivered, betraying his subconscious, active in dreams. She traced a finger down the length of his back. His mouth twitched. She wondered what he was dreaming.

Fuck. They must have had sex.

She sat up and pulled the sheets around her shoulders, exposing more of his naked body. He was so thin. There was nothing beneath his skin but lean muscle and bones. She examined every blemish, every flaw, as though she could read last night's actions in the history of his skin. There was a nick above his right eye. A long scar bisected his side. The white streak ran beneath the ribcage and into the shadow where his stomach met the sheets. She could not help imagining the quick silver slice of the knife and her eyes widened with the shock of the idea. She reached out to touch, but withdrew. She'd probably done that already.

Her head heaved with recollection. Stars only knew how many people remained in her apartment. She cast aside the sheets and got up to find out. At the door, she stopped. She did not want to know. She stood there, fingers on the handle, her next move perilously unclear, when the man on the bed moved. He yawned, stretched, and rolled onto his back.

"What time is it?"

The question threw her completely.

"It's—before dawn."

"Come back to bed then. Nobody else will be awake."

Adelaide complied, to the point of coming to sit on the end of the bed. Vikram scratched at the stubble just beginning to darken his jaw. His eyes were bleary.

"You're not meant to be in here," she said.

"You didn't leave me much choice."

She glowered at him. He met her scowl with a smile. She opened her mouth to tell him not to, but he pre-empted her.

"You fell asleep on me." Now he sounded smug.

"What?"

"You fell asleep," Vikram repeated. "You were very tired. And exceptionally drunk." And when her lips parted again he added, "I've got no reason to lie."

"I never sleep," she said.

"Alright. You passed out. Drunk, a dead weight, soon as we lay down and your head hit the pillow."

It was possible. It explained, at least, the lack of memory. Adelaide felt the cold sting of humiliation.

Vikram yawned again, and flopped back onto the pillows. His face was unlike any man she had ever known. There were lines in that face that would never be erased, lines made by the early tiredness of poverty. But they had faded beneath the light of a new expression.

"You look happy," she said accusingly.

"I am happy. We won."

She had almost forgotten the events that had lead up to last night's fiasco. They came back in a flood of sound and image. She saw Vikram standing in the Chambers, his face arrested, his voice pooling into the basin of their scepticism. Suddenly she smiled.

"Alright."

He reached out a hand, and when she took it, he pulled her back against him, hugging her. They lay in silence. The windows were tinted with violet, the world outside a shadowy place, as though without the distinction of time it must remain embryonic. She thought of another face and another man. Possibilities gathered on the edge of her brain, things that could or might or should have been. She thrust them away from her.

"How did you get that scar?"

"Which one?"

Adelaide turned over, resting her arms and her chin on his chest. She traced a tentative finger along the disfigurement. It felt like embossed lettering. "This one."

"My friend—Mikkeli—she used to take these deliveries to people." His voice was low and reminded her of summer rain. "She worked for a dealer called Maak. It was dangerous work. The sort of thing where your luck only holds out for so long. One of the jobs went wrong. The buyers came after Keli at home. There were four of us living there. Only two of them but six people with knives in a small room... it was messy."

It was the most information about himself he had ever volunteered. She kept her eyes on the scar, away from his face, not wanting to discourage him.

"Why did only two of them come?"

"They didn't think we'd protect her. Loyalty in the west is—pretty easily compromised."

"And you didn't compromise."

"No."

"So what happened?"

"We killed them. Then we left the tower and we never went back." He gave her a twisted smile. "This is my souvenir from that night."

Once more she heard the whisper of knives in the dark. She bent her head and gently kissed the scar. She left her face buried. How much time passed whilst she stayed there, she could not tell. Vikram's lips brushed her shoulder. She met his mouth in sudden haste, overcome by pity, and her need to block out that other face.

28 | VIKRAM

The waterways were quiet. It was an achingly cold but clear night, and Vikram could hear the motor hum as his boat cut through the waves, uninhibited by other traffic. He ran a hand over its sides. He'd had the boat for six weeks and he still felt a frisson of ownership with the touch.

As he steered through the western quarter, graffiti-covered slopes loomed and receded, the vivid images bluish in the moonlight. From the far side of the city a cheer went up, followed by the crackle of fireworks. Vikram looked up, trying to find the umbrellas of light amidst the sky's star-studded pane, but he saw only a fading glimmer over to the east. The race must have begun.

He fumbled in a pocket for his Sobek scarab. It was slippery in his glove as he switched it on and spoke Adelaide's name for the second time that evening.

"Hey, it's me. Look, sorry I can't make it—but enjoy the show."

These small appeasements had become regular. They were for him, not her, although she did not know that. Axel's letter haunted him. Right now, it was concealed beneath the lining of a locked drawer, and Adelaide, unaware of its contents, unaware even of its existence, was urging on her favourite glider with no notion that her brother waited for the white horse to speak.

He would tell her. When it was right.

The quiet struck him again. A lone gleam of light in the distance became a single tower, lanterns glowing at the window-walls. Vikram peered ahead through the shadowy maze of scrapers, and found what always followed such a display: fire on the water surface. They were committing the tower's dead to the deep.

He switched the motor off and let his boat drift. He could see the bodies piled upon rafts, some already ablaze, others drenched in oil, their foreheads banded with salt so that the ghosts would recognize them as Osiris's people. There must have been a power-cut, or a flash epidemic.

The mourners threw torches onto the pyres. Flames leapt high. When they were all alight, boats would tow the pyres to the ring-net and cast their cargo out to burn. Vikram had always thought that would be the most terrible of duties, escorting your loved ones to their unsettled grave, the stench and smoke of their passing rich on your tongue.

Now a chorus of voices echoed over the water, keening their grief without words. Heard from afar, the singing did not sound entirely human. The wind was in it, the waves. Out at the ring-net, the ghosts would be gathering.

The pyre blaze grew smaller. Vikram let out a breath he had not realized he was holding. He switched on the motor, welcoming the mechanical hum.

The shelter covered three floors of 307-West. The bunks were eight or ten to a room, narrow with thin mattresses, but they had pillows and blankets, and the rooms were warm. The second floor housed a medical room and the canteen. When Vikram arrived, no one was eating, but the lights were on and he could hear dishes clattering behind the serving hatch.

He found Shadiyah sitting on the end of a bench, both hands around a steaming mug, talking to their single security guard. The Resources division said they could not spare anyone else, although Vikram had noticed an increase in the skadi on the border over the last month.

"What are you doing here?" Shadiyah said. "You're not on call tonight." He thought she looked pleased to see him nonetheless.

"Nothing better to do," he joked. "How's things?"

"Alright. We had to break up a fight earlier and that raving old dear turned up again. Took offence to one of the nurses, decided she was a Council spy. Calmed down now. We're full for the night but we just had two kids come in. Brother and sister, I reckon. Boy's got a nasty knife wound."

"Shanty kids?"

"Likely as not. I'm going down to the med room now, want to come?"

"Sure."

They walked down the corridor together, filling one another in on the minutiae of the day. The corridor walls had been painted pale yellow. They were still peeling, but they were cleaner and brighter. Disinfectant masked the underlying stenches brought in with the very poor.

A door to one of the dormitories opened and an old man shuffled out. He had rags wrapped around his feet.

"Osuwa," he mumbled. "Bright lights—over again. Was the searchlight caught him in a dark hole."

"Alright, Mr Argele?" called Shadiyah. "Are you looking for someone?"

He peered at them from under bushy eyebrows. His face was a garden gone wild; hair, beard, even his eyelashes seemed overgrown.

"Turn off the searchlight, young woman," he ordered Shadiyah. "They'll be here soon. Don't you know your discipline?"

He retreated and shut the door. Vikram and Shadiyah paused, listening for signs that he might have disturbed the other men. But there were no sounds from inside. Just the muffled rumble of the laundry room a few doors down, as the dryers turned in their final cycles.

"Young woman," echoed Shadiyah. "First compliment of the day."

Vikram had found his colleague on a boat frying up kelp toast for hungry kids. It was her hands that struck him first. She had been wearing fingerless gloves. Her fingertips were rough skinned, their nails short and slightly yellowed, a blister on her left thumb from the spitting fat. Her hands brought back a jumble of memories: hours spent in line at soup kitchens or fry-boats, waiting to beg for scraps at the end of the day.

Shadiyah told Vikram her story whilst smoke from the grill drifted out of the boat window. She received a negligible amount of funding for her tiny charity. It was a tough business. Her fry-boat was raided every month for its stock. Shadiyah had a sharp mouth and a discerning eye; she was able to distinguish the hungry from the starving.

"And sometimes it's a fine line," she'd said, leaning out to hand down a sizzling, paper-wrapped kelp square to one of her beneficiaries. "After all, who this end of town ain't hungry?"

She turned down his offer of a job instantly. He hadn't thought that his exposure to the City would show so soon, but perhaps it had already begun to tint him. He came back the next day, and the day after. It took time to persuade her.

It was time well spent. Once she had agreed, Shadiyah took practical charge of the shelter, creating a model on which future projects would follow. Walking through their allotted floors, they had planned everything together from the layout of the building to an information campaign. They printed flyers and people handed them out on the aid scheme boat kitchens.

Shadiyah knocked before entering the medical room.

"It's only me and Vikram," she said briskly.

The children's heads snapped up. Their faces were wary and hard as ice. The boy was perched on the single bed, his toes grazing the floor. In one hand he clutched what looked like a bundle of rags. Vikram realized the medics had cut his jumper away. A clump of t-shirts were peeled back and one of the doctors was applying stitches to a ten centimetre gash across his shoulder, whilst the other held a tray of needles and gauze. The sight of the pinched flesh brought back Vikram's own knife injury in a flash; he struggled not to avert his eyes.

The girl slunk back against the bed curtain. Her hair was chopped as short as the boy's. She had a bowl of soup at her mouth and her tongue poked out, mid-lap. Her eyes darted; Vikram, the doctor, the door, the needle, the door, the boy. There was a fading bruise on her cheekbone and scratches on her neck.

"Hey," said Vikram. "Everything okay?"

At the sound of his voice the girl jerked backwards. The soup slopped in the bowl.

"We're alright," said the doctor holding the tray. "It's a nasty cut, but it'll heal. Just make sure you keep it clean," she told the boy. "We're going to give you some pills and an antibiotic spray. I want you to use it twice a day. Okay?"

There was no reply. All of the muscles in the boy's shoulders were tense as the other doctor hooked his needle in and out, gradually knitting the exposed flesh together. Anaesthetic must have curbed the pain but not the desire to bolt. Vikram could see the outline of a knife at the boy's hip. He knew that if anyone tried to take it, the boy's hand would snap to his side in a second.

"You give it me," said the girl suddenly. Her voice was a tiny rasp like a match being struck.

"What's that, puffin?" said Shadiyah.

"Gimme the anti-whatsit. They won't find it on me."

Vikram caught the subtle interplay between brother and sister; the boy's quickly masked glare, the girl's concealed shrug.

The female doctor, Marete, spoke to the girl. "It's very important. Don't give it away, you understand? And don't sell it. Not to anyone. Or your brother will get really sick."

For answer, the girl held out her palm. Marete hesitated a moment and looked at the other doctor, who gave a curt nod.

"We'll go get it," said Shadiyah. "Standard issue, Hal?"

"Please."

Vikram and Shadiyah went next door and swiped into the medical supplies room.

"How old do you reckon they are?" he asked.

"The boy says thirteen but I reckon ten or eleven."

"Did he say how he got the cut?"

Shadiyah raised her eyebrows to suggest what a ridiculous question this was and Vikram nodded. She was right. He could guess—he could even ask, but he would not find out. They were shanty town kids, by the half-starved look of them. Somebody owned them—one of the dealers, one of the pimps or the gangs. They were lucky to have survived this long.

Vikram opened the medicine cabinet but did not immediately take out the prescriptions.

"I saw a funeral, on my way here."

She nodded. "Bad business. The skadi raided a tower last night. Suspected insurgents, you know the lines. People resisted. It got messy."

"No one told me."

"They wouldn't, would they."

He checked the list supplied by the doctors.

"Do you remember Osuwa, Shadiyah?"

She gave him a quick, measured glance.

"Of course I do. I was twelve, I was on the waterbus. I heard the explosion first. Then boats started speeding past. By the time I got to Market Circle everyone knew what had happened." She sighed. "And that it was only a matter of time before the reprisals. I'm not surprised Mr Argele raves about it, a lot of people went mad after those few weeks."

"Worse than the last riots?"

Shadiyah leaned against the work surface, her hands wrapped awkwardly around the edge of the bench. "Different. Because it wasn't just the skadi, and it wasn't just violence. To give citizens guns, that was a terrible, awful vengeance. The corpses we saw hadn't just been killed, they were barely people." There was a brief silence. "I suppose you want to know if I agreed with Osuwa."

The room seemed a little darker, a little narrower.

"Do you?"

"No, Vik, I don't condone arbitrary killing. But I won't deny that there was a part of me, whilst they were hunting us like rats, there was a very large part of me that said they deserved everything they got."

She straightened, adjusting her headscarf with her usual deft touch.

"They is such an elusive term," she said.

Vikram found the prescriptions and made a mental note of what they were running low on. After they had delivered the medication, Shadiyah made up two bedrolls in the laundry room whilst Vikram checked the dormitories. In each bunk he made out the hump of a sleeping body. Snores and rattling breath filled the rooms, but tonight everyone was still. Vikram heard Mr Argele mutter a few blurred words in his sleep. He was one of the shelter's regulars.

They left the children alone to settle in their bedrolls. In the canteen, Vikram reconvened with the doctors. Marete was filling in the record book. He peered over her shoulder.

"You can't record them as brother and sister."

"Why not?"

"Population control laws," said Shadiyah.

"Shit, yes of course." Marete tore out the page and started again.

"Only one of them is legally entitled to aid," Vikram reminded her. "We've got to be careful. They'll slash our funding if they know we're supporting multiple offspring."

/ / /

When he left the shelter, the sky was pitch dark with cloud. It felt late, but his watch told him it was only twenty-two thirty. The tarpaulin over the boat was covered in frost. It shimmered like a half-submerged iceberg. He hauled off the tarp and folded it, noticing a man observing him from the window of a tower across the water. The surveillance was unapologetic. He sensed other eyes too, hidden in the darkness of waterways and decking. He knew in that instant that he had become that incalculable thing: an airlift. Something to be watched.

As he turned the ignition key and the boat purred into life, he decided to do something he should have done a long time ago.

/ / /

The decking around his old tower was thick with boats. He circled until he found a gap to park, secured the boat and because he did not intend to linger, stuffed the tarp into the storage space under the seat. The tower doors parted and a man staggered out, holding his arm and cursing. Two others followed.

"Want to say that again, mate? To my face?"

Vikram slipped past them into the unlit passageways of the building. The shouts and blows of the fight were cut off as the doors slid shut.

Inside, a rancid stench crawled up his nostrils. He tried the lift. There was a clanking sound. He thought at first that it had been fixed, but realized the sound came from another lift much further up. As he began the familiar, gruelling climb, he felt the hierarchy of his senses shifting. He had become too dependent on sight. The smell separated into parts: fish, wet kelp, cigarettes and manta, dirt, mould, old blood, placebo chemicals. Every couple of floors he passed a shadowy form going in the opposite direction, or the backlit tableaux of two people talking in an open doorway. Kids shrieked as they chased one another blind up and down the steps. Vikram moved instinctively, one hand brushing the walls. He could not tell if the bodies he stepped over were catatonic or dead.

Floor thirty-five was dark and quiet. He stepped up to his old door with the key, before he realized that it was ajar.

He pushed the door. It swung open, slowly and noisily. He saw bodies lumped in the gloom, heard the hiss of breath. A figure scrambled to its feet, pale steel in one hand. Cold sliced along his old scar.

"Get out." The voice was female.

Vikram stood still.

"I said get out," she repeated. She levelled the knife.

"I don't mean any harm," he said. "I used to live here. I left some things."

He caught a glimpse of white eye, smelt the fear on her. She would not hesitate to sink that knife.

"I never saw you before," she said. "And if you wake my kids I'll see no-one else does, either."

"Okay," he said softly. "Okay. It's your place now, that's fine. There's just one thing I wanted—my salt tin."

There was a pause. He saw movement in the sleeping forms beyond her and he sensed her dual attention on them and him.

"Weren't any salt tin when I got here." The knife shook but she did not drop her wrist.

"It was a silver thing, about the size of a fist."

"I said it weren't here. Think I'd lie? Not likely to be angering the dead when I've got four mouths to feed, am I? You get out of here now."

He backed away, hands raised. She pushed the door to. He knew she was waiting on the other side, listening for his departure.

The door did not close properly. He never had repaired the lock. The woman had broken in, or someone else had before her. She was entitled to the room.

Ten floors down there was a glow under Nils's door. For several minutes Vikram stood in the corridor, uncertain and not sure of the reason for it. Finally he knocked. The door opened and Nils gave a roar of surprise.

"Vik! Wondered when you'd turn up. Come in, come in. Meet Ilona. Ilona, sweetheart, it's Vikram, I told you about him, remember?"

Nils's room was a pool of warmth. He had a heater burning, an unusual extravagance. Vikram realized it must be for the benefit of the girl. She was enveloped in one of Nils's jumpers. A bleached wing of hair fell across her face.

"Hello," she whispered.

"Hey," he said.

Nils hauled him into the room and shut the door by leaning on it. Vikram realized his friend was on the way to being drunk.

"Have a drink, have a drink. We're celebrating tonight, aren't we Ilona?"

Ilona did not say anything more, and exactly what they were celebrating was left unclear. Vikram sat on the floor and took the proffered bottle. Greasy papers were balled up in the corner, but the smell of food couldn't quite mask the stale ash and human reek beneath. He had never noticed those things before. He had a sudden desire to join Nils in his inebriation. He took a draught from the bottle.

"I just went up to the old place."

Nils gestured to a corner.

"Your stuff's there. Figured you might not be back for a while so I broke in before anyone else did."

Vikram looked at the little bundle. His salt tin was there. He felt a flush of guilt.

"Thanks," he said gruffly.

"Don't be stupid, you'd have done the same for me."

"I should have been round weeks ago."

"Been busy, from what I heard. I knew you'd be along sooner or later. C'mon, have a drink, tell me how it's been going."

Seduced by the rough edge of the liquor and the heater's warmth, Vikram filled Nils in on the past six weeks. Ilona maintained her silence, watching him from behind the dyed curtain of hair. There was something about her, something obvious, that was eluding Vikram.

"What do you think?" he asked, when he had finished. "Have we made any impact?"

He was eager to recruit his friend. Straddling two communities was a lonely position; he needed allies. Nils, with one arm draped around Ilona's shoulders, looked thoughtful.

"It's early days."

"That doesn't sound positive."

"No—it's just... It's going to be a hard winter, Vik. Of course people need food and shelter. But there's so many of them now, I mean, where do you even start."

"I think people are scared to ask for help."

"And Adelaide Mystik—that might have been a good thing and a bad thing. She's a bit of a joke this side of town. I mean, you know that, right."

"Nils, I needed her."

"Sure, it was the only way." Nils leaned forward, his eyes glittering. "But there's talk, Vik. First the fishing bans. One of our boats got gunned down by fucking skadi last week for so-called illegal hunting. They didn't even have any fucking fish. Skadi raided a tower last night, said there was a threat to the gliding race but we all know that's bullshit. Now there're rumours of another kelp shortage. You've got contacts now, you tell me Vik, is it true?"

"I don't know. I haven't heard."

But if it's true, he thought—then we're already too late.

"You want to help? I could use a good man, Nils."

Nils hesitated. "I've got—a few things to take care of." Vikram waited but Nils did not elaborate. Instead, he reached forward to punch Vikram on the arm. "Keep a hotspot for me, though."

"I will." Vikram was disappointed. He glanced at Ilona, who dropped her eyes. "I should be getting back. You have company."

Nils squeezed the girl's shoulder affectionately. "I do."

They stood up. Vikram noticed, at waist height behind Ilona, a large hole hacked into the wall. Copper wires dangled from it. Vikram pointed.

"What—"

Nils waved a hand. "Oh, that, that. Trying to find a vein."

"Well don't fucking electrocute yourself."

"No." Nils scowled at the hole. "Got the wrong damn spot. Current's to the left." He put a hand on Vikram's shoulder. Vikram felt his friend's weight, too light for a drunk man. Nils's eyes were beginning to glaze.

"Anyway. We won't abandon you. If it all goes wrong, there's backup. You should know that, Vik."

A tremor crossed Ilona's face. It was so fast, Vikram thought he might have imagined it. Her hair obscured any expression.

"Backup?"

His friend offered only a lazy smile.

"Always," he said. "What d'you take us for? Night, Vik."

Vikram angled the water directly onto his face, powered drops battering his eyelids and cheeks. He turned the temperature up one setting, then another, until it was almost too hot to bear. He emerged ready to embrace what remained of the night. Adelaide had called and he'd told her to come over.

A Sobek o'vis lay in its box. Linus Rechov had sent it to him as a home warming gift. Vikram poured himself a mug of chilled water and settled down to unpack its mysteries. He had unrolled the screen and attached it to the wall when Adelaide arrived. The flickering images provoked a squeal of excitement. Vikram swilled out his only other mug and opened a bottle of raqua whilst Adelaide settled on the lone square of carpet.

She pointed to the animé; a human diver with scaled skin undulating through still water.

"They asked me to do the voice for that."

"Why didn't you?"

"It was when Axel—when he started forgetting."

Vikram sank into the sofa and muted the o'vis. They clanked mugs.

"How was the race?"

"Oh, predictable. I won some money. It might get you another boat."

There had been one collision, she said, the wings got tangled but nobody died. She gave a little hiccoughing laugh when she said this, and he wondered if she was ever scared going to the races, after what had happened to the Dumays. As she talked her eyes roved the room, checking for changes.

"New salt-tin?"

"Old salt-tin," he corrected, and in answer to her raised eyebrows, "I went back to the western place."

Adelaide clapped her hands and drew her legs into a lotus, her attentive pose. "You went back! That explains it. I knew you were preoccupied."

"Mm."

"Was it strange? Ghosts of the past?"

"A few," he acknowledged.

"You never did tell me what happened to her."

"Who?" Vikram stalled.

"Your friend," she said. "Mikkeli."

It sounded odd, Keli's name, on Adelaide's lips. She pronounced it like a talisman.

"She was shot," he said. "The skadi killed her." He glanced at Adelaide. The lamp's shadow bisected her face. He was inclined to talk, but he looked away again. "It was towards the end of the riots. The Guards were driving us back tower by tower. They'd cut off the lines to a desalination plant. Everyone was worn out, we knew they'd won, though nobody wanted to admit it."

He stared at the folds of the curtain.

"Anyway, Mikkeli said we'd try one last thing. If she could sneak in and turn the supply pipe back on, we could make a final push. It was a mad plan, but Mik was like that. Me and Nils both said we'd do it, but she insisted she had the best chance, and she was usually right. She got inside the control tower. The rest of us were nearby, waiting for her signal. I was meant to be getting her away. It was before dawn so everything was grey, you couldn't see much. I waited, but no signal came. And then she appeared."

He saw it again. The way he saw it almost every night in his dreams. He watched Mikkeli exit the tower and walk to the edge of the decking. Her yellow hood obscured her face. In one hand she had a gun. She stayed there, motionless. Why didn't she move? She was exposed.

Mikkeli's hands lifted, very slowly, to her head. She still clutched the gun. He realized what was happening. Someone else was on the decking. They had Keli hostage, but she wouldn't give up her weapon. What was their plan? To flush out the rest of the rebels? But Keli would have a plan too; she always had a plan. Vikram urged his boat closer.

It was the music he heard first—an assault of bass driven metal. A motor boat skidded around the corner. It was thronged with skadi. Their guns were a fifth limb. In the predawn light they seemed to dance, all five limbs contorting in crazed shapes. The music splintered the cold, cold day, like breaking glass. Gunshots cracked. Mikkeli dropped instantly. She toppled into the water and gunfire peppered the sea and her body. The skadi hurtled on with whoops and cheers.

Vikram threw himself over the side of the boat. The cold was shocking. The waves fought him as he splashed through the freezing water. He reached Mikkeli at last, wrapped his arms around her body and hauled both of them onto the decking. He put both hands on her chest and pumped. Blood and seawater leaked from her mouth and nose. He put his mouth to hers and forced his breath into her. For an incredible second he heard her gurgle, but it wasn't her, or if it was it was the last sound she made.

A gun clicked at his head and he willed the skad to shoot before rage and grief ignited and he moved so fast he caught the man behind him by surprise. Punched him hard across the temples. They fought briefly. More figures spilled from the tower. Hands seized Vikram, wrenched his arms behind his back, shoved him forward until his chin struck the decking. Handcuffs nicked his skin. He heard the words *western* and *scum* and he felt their kicks, each a fresh pool of acute pain but he was beyond it, so far beyond.

Silver bars of frost were already forming on Mikkeli's lashes.

"I got her out of the water," he said. "But she was already dead."

Adelaide's face was intent. Her eyes glistened with tears or reflected light. She leaned forward to put her hand on his knee. "There was nothing you could do."

"Maybe."

"Sometimes you lose people and there's nothing you can do."

"It was a stupid plan. We should never have agreed to it."

Adelaide was shaking her head.

"Ifs," she said. "Ifs are no hope. They are the things Osiris has decided cannot be, and yet we dwell on them as if they were ever possibilities."

"You talk about this city as if it's the world."

"It is the world."

"Your brother didn't believe that." He spoke without thinking and Adelaide looked at him sharply. "Why else would he want a balloon?" he said quickly. "He wants to leave. He must do."

She said nothing. He felt the weight of Axel's letter. *Tell her. Now's the time.* He needed to ease his mind of at least one burden. On the brink of speech, he paused. But when he spoke, the words altered.

"I promised Mikkeli, you know. That other people wouldn't have to die…" He broke off. "I think she might have preferred vengeance."

The look they exchanged, a ghost of a smile, was neither happy nor sad. Vikram reached out and pulled her to him. He slipped his hands

under the silk of her shirt, over the contours of her ribcage. Her head
fell back and her eyes closed. He unhooked the clasp of her bra. It was a
body that had never known hunger, had barely known cold. Sometimes
he despised her for its ignorance. He kissed the hollow of her throat, her
navel, the boundary of lace at her hips. Whilst their limbs tangled and
her body shuddered he wondered if his hate might show. In eyes or touch,
or distance. In the air between their lips. Only when she was still did
he embrace her. He was wide awake and he suspected that she was too,
though her eyes remained closed. Neither of them moved.

The animé had finished. An archive reel played out on the o'vis in black
and white.

Later, when Adelaide had fallen sleep, he carried her to the bed and
pulled the covers over her hips. She mumbled something and rolled over.
She hated to be held. If he fell asleep holding her he would wake to find
she had shrugged him away, as though she feared the slightest and most
human of constraints would cage her indelibly. He admired her resolution; he scorned her for not knowing the value of physical warmth.

Adelaide's hair was screwed up under her cheek and against the bed.
Looking at her, Vikram realized what had been bothering him about
Ilona. It was her hair. Bleached, sheerly straight, it had been deliberately
cut and coloured. The only place where girls wore their hair like that was
on the shanty town boats. Which meant that Ilona belonged to somebody
and Nils was playing a dangerous game.

Vikram rolled onto his side and gazed at Adelaide's squashed, sleeping
face. Now he felt a rush of tenderness. She lay on her front, limbs akimbo,
stomach caving into the muddled sheets. He pressed his ear to the hollow
between her shoulder blades and listened to the stubborn pulse of her
heart. Adelaide was like the rainbow-fish whose tails she said glowed in
the dark. The bright things were always hunted in the end.

/ / /

"Morning, Vikram." His assistant popped her head around the office
partition. She was bulked up in coat, earmuffs and hat. Her eyelids were
heavy with sleep.

Vikram glanced up from the Neptune and caught sight of the clock.

Nine already. He had been in over an hour. "Morning Hella."

"Did you see the race?"

"I missed it, actually."

"Oh." Her expression faltered. "It was interesting," she settled. "You want a tea?"

"You're a mind-reader."

"Aren't I?" she said. Still a bit shy.

He heard her putting the pot on in their cupboard of a kitchen, and the clink of a spoon as she prepared the glasses with ginger. Hella was another airlift. They were both nervous to begin with. The first week there was a major misunderstanding over transport arrangements for the boat kitchens. Seven crates of squid were lost to raiders. After blaming one another and shouting it out, they seemed to be settling into a rhythm.

Vikram stretched his arms over his head and felt his bones click. The figures on the Neptune gazed blandly out. He had never dreamed the Council would want so much administration. It seemed pointless in light of what he could be doing; scouting a location for the next shelter or recruiting staff, even handing out kelp rations on one of the boat kitchens. Adelaide said that this was their way of keeping him in check. She was probably right.

Hella entered with two steaming glasses. She gave one to him and cupped the other.

"So how was your evening?" she asked.

Last night's events seemed unreal. Even Adelaide, whom he had left sprawled on his bed, sex and raqua lingering on her breath.

"It was a long night, actually. I dropped by the shelter. Mr Argele was there."

"Oh, Mr Argele. What did he have to say for himself?"

"He called Shadiyah 'young woman.'"

Hella giggled. "Bet she loved that."

"I think she did, actually. How were the gliders?"

After they'd dissected the race from start to finish, Hella with hindsight, Vikram with imagination, his assistant went back to the other side of the partition. She took off her earmuffs, put in the earpiece, and put the earmuffs back on. The o'comm did not buzz that often. Most of their calls were outgoing.

He had an inkling that Hella had applied for the position because she could not quite reconcile her good fortune in escaping the mire. It was guts and hard work that had got her out, but that was not enough to shift the guilt. He knew because he felt it too. Every morning, they crossed the border to this cramped fifty-ninth floor office just inside the western quarter. Every evening, they could return to safe ground. Hella led a quiet life. She told Vikram she never saw her old friends.

Shadiyah called him mid-morning.

"Your birds have flown."

"At least they came."

"I hope they don't get punished for it. Someone's going to see the stitches and ask questions. If they take those antibiotics away, he'll die within weeks. That's if frostbite doesn't do for him. Or pneumonia. Or hypothermia. Or the flu."

Vikram leaned back in his chair.

"Shadiyah," he began. "Why—"

"Don't," she said.

"What?"

"Don't ask. I know what you're thinking. I'll end up alone, frozen to death, or drowning in some flooded cell. But there's community here, on our side, if you make it that way."

The morning edged onward. One by one, lights in the opposite tower winked off. Vikram thought of Nils, who would probably be curled up with the girl, sleeping off his hangover. He thought about the choices he had made in Mikkeli's name, in Eirik's name, and wondered who they were really for, what they really meant. But they were past choices. This was his life now.

29 | ADELAIDE

Her father's man Goran was waiting for her in the hall of the Domain. His huge, pudgy hands were folded in front of him. When he smiled she felt every patch of her exposed skin prickle: shoulders, face, the small of her back. That same smile used to curl Goran's lips each time he discovered the twins' latest hiding place.

"Welcome home, Miss Rechnov." His voice was as soft as ever.

"It's not home," she said.

"Home is where the heart is, isn't that the Old World saying?"

Goran held out a hand to take her cape. She repressed a shudder as his fingers folded around its velvet weight. He led her up the main staircase, past her grandfather's rooms, and up again. She was struck anew by the richness and secretiveness of the Domain. It corridors were low-lit and full of real wood. They passed alcoves housing shell lanterns, doors with ebony handles, Afrikan sculptures, chandeliers, paintings from Veerde- land and Alaska.

There were hidden passages too, crawling under and over other rooms like a subterranean maze. It was a mysterious place. Once it had been a magical place, but the twins had promised one another they would never set foot in it again. Adelaide had not been back in six years. She would never have answered this invitation if Vikram had not been there when it arrived. *You're not scared of them are you?*

Of course not, she'd said haughtily. She could have said that the relation- ship between herself and her family was more complicated than simple fear or estrangement. That it was tied up with a history and a hatred of lies; that the bad blood between herself and her father could not affect her love for her grandfather, but neither could that love compel her to reconciliation; that of all the Rechnov children her mother had always and only adored Axel, and the Incident had only hardened her further against the rest of them; that Adelaide did not quite understand herself the tenuous links she had forged with Linus, and that all of the above was now tempered with far more frightening suspicions: she could not have said with certainty that any one of them was incapable of removing Axel to preserve the family name. She could not say this to Vikram. He did not have a family. The only person who understood the Rechnovs as Adelaide did was Tyr, and she could not tell Vikram that either.

In a passing mirror she glimpsed her reflection: pale skin in an emerald dress. Goran stepped quietly ahead, the third eye on the back of his neck watching her all the way. Every instinct was telling her to run. I'm not afraid, she told herself. I can do this.

At the greeting room, Goran moved aside, then put a hand on Adelaide's back and propelled her through the door. Her skin crawled.

"Miss Adelaide Rechnov," he announced.

Conversation died away as they all turned to look at her. A satin clad lady raised an eyeglass to inspect Adelaide more closely, her wispy brows knitted as she peered through the silver disk. One by one they came up. Some Adelaide recognized from childhood events, others were new recruits to the Rechnov clan. Each guest extended their arm, presenting the inner wrist upward so that she could press her own against it. Her wrist tingled horribly.

"Delighted to meet you at last."

"My, how you've changed!" The woman with the eyeglass had pale gums and a quavery voice. "I remember you as a little girl, playing the Steinway at Viviana's birthday. Such a sweet child."

"She's divine, Viviana." A man spoke over her head. "Really, quite exquisite."

Her mother came forward, placed her hands on Adelaide's shoulders and dabbed her lips to each cheek. Adelaide smelt her cloying lavender scent. Viviana's eyes were searching. It felt as though her mother were running a flannel over her face, softly the first time, but gradually peeling away layer after layer of skin until she unwrapped the flesh beneath.

"Welcome home, Adelaide," Viviana said finally. There was something formidable about the easy elegance of Viviana's stature. Adelaide was aware that side by side, they made everyone else in the room look plain, but there was no pleasure in the knowledge.

"Where's Grandfather?" she asked.

"I'm afraid that he is unwell." Feodor joined the growing throng around mother and daughter. "And unable to join us tonight. Adelaide."

He put a hand on her waist and steered her towards the windows. The familiarity of the action unnerved her. Both of her parents were treating the situation as though she had just returned from a week-long holistic retreat in the northern quarter. She felt sweat forming under her dress.

Viviana approached, carrying a stained-glass container, the shape of a lantern, with a steepled lid. She placed the pot in Feodor's hands. He removed the lid and handed it back. They exchanged subtle, not-quite smiles. The room hushed.

Feodor took a pinch of salt from the pot. He drew a deep, slow breath, then he flicked his wrist and scattered the salt. It was quiet enough to hear the grains skitter against the glass.

"To the dead," said Feodor.

"To the dead," the guests intoned solemnly. A theatrical shiver ruffled the room.

It was the melodrama that Adelaide despised above all. The way that everyone present conspired in the act, dressing it up as philanthropy, as though they were above such fundamental fears as ghosts at the window. Then they turned away, huddled over their grape-crushed wines.

Adelaide went to stand where the salt had fallen. Vikram had thrown a pinch over her shoulder earlier, to give her luck. She had met his eyes across the salt tin. Brown eyes should be warm, but Vikram's eyes were too complicated for pure warmth. They swirled with other things, with sadness, and responsibility. She'd had a fleeting urge to take his face in her hands and tell him he must not be so sad, he must not let Osiris work its deep, malicious magic.

Did the ghosts feel abandoned by the salt ritual? Did it hurt them to be thrust away into the night? The windows gave no answers, only her flimsy reflection.

"Adelaide. Enchanted. My name's Ukko."

It was the man who had called her exquisite. He gave her a glass of grape-wine and started to talk about next year's Council elections. He was running for a seat in Resources. She could tell by his pitch, nasal and overly confident, that he expected to get it. She sipped at the wine. She remembered the taste, rich and mellow, but sweet too, overly sweet, and she found that she no longer cared for it.

On the other side of the room, Tyr was engaged in discussion with Dmitri. They had to be careful tonight, more than usually careful, especially with Linus present. Her brother was chatting to Zakiyya Sobek. Her parents networked. Feodor's most expansive smile was in place. Every now and then she sensed his surveillance, but there was no sign of the telltale tic. In fact, her father seemed remarkably at ease.

A nasty idea seeded in Adelaide's mind. Was it possible that the twins' great escape might have been less of an escape than she had believed? The Rechnovs had foreseen this day. They had let her and Axel go, always assuming that they would have to come back.

Viviana clapped her hands.

"And now, dinner!"

The guests murmured their appreciation as they entered the banquet hall, footsteps ringing out on the chequered floor. Feodor and Viviana took their places at the head of the oval table. Each place was laid with a symmetrical display of crystal and cutlery. Adelaide's grandfather should have been opposite, but in his absence Dmitri took that chair. His fiancée, a banker, sat next to him. A chair was pulled out for Adelaide. She sat, strangely aware of the air and space at her back, the nebulous movements of the servers. She found herself directly facing Tyr.

They had first met at a banquet like this, weeks before she left. They kissed behind a tapestry, giggling, each caught by surprise. She had run at Tyr like any other obstacle, unafraid of implication or of consequence.

When she met his eyes he looked away.

A hand reached from behind her to fill her weqa glass. As the server continued around the table, the man on Adelaide's left turned to her. He had greying hair and a hooked, distinctive nose. It was the Councillor of Estates, a man Feodor was no doubt eager to court.

"Delighted to meet you, m'dear," he said. "Such a close family, you Rechnovs. I'm sure Feodor is delighted to have you back."

What had Feodor told people?

The man complimented Adelaide on her bone structure.

"Nice to see a Rechnov girl. Great men in your family, of course, quite a line, but few women. Which would you prefer, a boy or a girl?"

Adelaide took a demure sip of weqa.

"I hear the abortion rate is very high these days," she said.

The Councillor looked surprised, but nodded. "A valid fact. Pregnancy is a serious notion for any young woman."

She was not sure whether he was hinting at her as a potential breeder, or trying to gauge her attitude to the practice. She offered no response. The Councillor tried again.

"I'm told you have a fascinating little outlet of your own on the outskirts. Do you ever find it lonely living with such a view?"

"I like my own company," she said.

"If I might recall the popular saying, Miss Rechnov: a Rechnov dreamt the City, a Dumay built it, and an Ngozi lit it. I propose that you, Miss Rechnov, are a dreamer."

She felt the hooks digging in. It would start here, over a five course dinner. The tug would start with tonight.

On her other side was the Councillor of Netting, a man it would also be useful for the Rechnovs to forge an alliance with. Since the population control laws were introduced twenty years ago, choosing a mate had become a matter of vital importance. She noticed that Tyr had been seated between two influential women. On his left was Zakiyya Sobek, and on his right was Hildur Pek, Councillor of Assessment, who had lost her husband in a shark attack many years ago and had formed an almost pathological obsession with the ring-net ever since. Feodor must be incredibly sure of Tyr's loyalty to consider setting him up like that.

She turned her gaze to Linus. Did Feodor have anyone in mind for him? Linus was devoted to the Rechnov line, but he had independent political ideas which Feodor would prefer to curb, not least of all his anti-Nucleite stance. And Linus's support for Vikram and the west had no doubt been a contentious subject in the domestic core.

"Guava dressing, Miss Rechnov?" The Councillor of Netting indicated the platter hovering beside them as though he had produced it personally.

"Thank you."

She wanted to push her chair back and stretch out her legs, but not wishing to brush against either man, she kept her elbows in and her knees pressed together as she ate. The Councillor of Netting was discussing the state of the kelp forests with his neighbour—"It won't be a good year for weqa, my dear"—whilst across the room, Hildur Pek had cornered Tyr with horror stories. Elsewhere, Adelaide overheard snippets about the educational syllabus. A small group including Linus were debating the relevance of taught history.

"—essential to have a world understanding—"

"But in the current climate, practical and sociological issues are far more important. Osiris must remain strong—"

"But informed." That was her brother.

"What about the south? What about Tarctica… surely we should be considering…?"

"Still decades away."

"And it could act as a terrible temptation. I mean, technically, we're still under quarantine."

"Precisely. Any eventual excursion would have to be heavily supervised—not to mention kept under wraps."

"Personally, I believe quarantine is a technicality that should have been lifted years ago. The idea that it's actually illegal to leave the City is absurd in this day and age, and as for the map ban, it's quite simply ludicrous." Linus was in argumentative mode. Adelaide wondered, suddenly, what he would have made of the balloon room.

"That law keeps people safe. We don't have a seaworthy boat left in the City and everyone knows it. Start bandying Tarctica about and I tell you, people will be tempted to make rash decisions."

"Then again, we do have a population problem. Maybe these futurists shouldn't be disencouraged?"

"That's a rather cynical view—you don't really think?"

"Oh, of course not. Just a little gallows humour."

Low laughter.

"Well, we've already got an issue with psychological containment trauma." The voice was lowered but Adelaide just made out, "Everyone knows the—well, that *particular rate* is high enough already."

The debate rescinded. Suicide was not a dinner party topic. The woman who had spoken flushed, aware of her mistake. Adelaide, remembering Radir's last words to her, felt her own colour rising. Surely nobody else imagined Axel could have taken such a course?

The second course was brought out. Around the table, glasses chinked in private toasts and engraved cutlery scraped on plates. In Adelaide's ear, the Councillor of Estates was praising her family's architectural skill.

"I understand the Osiris Board never really considered anyone but Alexei Rechnov. And wisely so. Through his and your grandfather's great work, the city has endured. And this residence is—quite spectacular."

Grandfather calls it a house, Adelaide felt like saying, but she did not, because that was a personal piece of information. Tonight would be the only occasion that she had been in the Domain without her twin. He had always stood between her and them, fighting her fights, sharing the blame for her mistakes. There had been no mention of Axel. It was as if he had been whitewashed.

Adelaide's hand shook as she cut into a rainbow-fish fillet. She put down the knife to hide it.

"Delicious," said the Councillor of Estates. "Highly cunning of Feodor to slip this dinner in before the official ban goes through."

"What ban?" she asked.

"Oh, you don't know?" The Councillor looked pleased at this opportunity to repair Adelaide's ignorance. "Rainbow-fish is on the danger list until the stocks rebuild. Along with a few of the bigger staples. We'll all end up vegetarian by the end of it." He gave her a wink. "Of course, there are ways around these little rules, if you know the right people. In fact, I sometimes hold soirées of my own. Nothing on this scale—just a few, intimate acquaintances."

Adelaide turned to the Councillor of Netting on her other side. "When you said it is going to be a bad year for weqa, Councillor, did you mean, just the weqa? Or did you mean, the kelp harvest as a whole?"

Her voice, which carried clearly in the vault of the banquet room, was louder than she had intended. She saw Feodor glance in her direction. The Councillor of Netting looked uneasy, but rallied.

"There are always good years and not-so-good years, Miss Rechnov.

That is a perfectly normal and healthy state of fluctuation. It may be one of our not-so-good years, but the next shall improve."

"And with that and the new ban on certain fish stocks, do you anticipate food shortages this winter?"

"Not in my household," murmured the Councillor of Estates.

"Supplies will be adequate," said the Councillor of Netting firmly.

"Forgive me," said Adelaide. "I'm something of an amateur in these matters, but wasn't the last major crop shortage three years ago?"

"I believe it was, and, as you see Miss Rechnov, we survived to live another day." He gave a little laugh.

"Yes," she said. "It didn't stop the riots, though."

Now she saw the spots of colour in Feodor's cheeks. The look he gave her this time was pure warning, but the Councillor of Netting had misunderstood her tone.

"I assure you, my dear, you have no need to fear for your safety. The Minister of Security has everything in hand, is that not the case, Ailia? Any hint of violence from the west shall be swiftly crushed."

"But that's the point, isn't it? If the supplies were adequate, westerners wouldn't feel the need to riot, would they?"

"I don't think you quite understand, my dear," said the Minister of Security kindly.

"I understand that three years ago, food supplies were stockpiled unnecessarily in the City and withheld from the west. Is that what's going to happen this time?"

"You'll have to forgive my daughter's passion," Feodor interrupted. "The west is her latest whimsy."

"It's not a joke—"

"Of course, of course, very admirable—and you have been championing that young man with the schemes, have you not? It's an excellent cause."

"He won't fail."

"Yes. Yes, well, we all hope for that."

The words filled Adelaide with unexpected rage. *I was at that address too!* she wanted to shout. *You weren't all so complacent then.*

"Perhaps you should take the west more seriously," she said.

"I doubt anyone takes the west more seriously than the people in this room," said Feodor. "After all, we all witnessed the scenes at the execution."

Viviana, perhaps anticipating a showdown between father and daughter, clinked a spoon vigorously against her crystal glass.

"Goodness, aren't we all bored of talking shop? I thought you ladies and gentlemen had enough of this political claptrap in the Chambers!"

Laughter and a few claps echoed her regaling, and Feodor's brow relaxed as the servers stepped forward to clear away. He needs her, Adelaide thought. He needs my mother back on form and she appears to have gained it. Viviana was talking now to the Minister for Finance—a big coup at a dinner party—motioning to a server to refill their glasses, nodding with intense interest whilst half an eye skimmed the rest of the table.

The mourning period is done, she thought. Was that what she had come to find out?

Feodor stood, raising a glass of rich, golden weqa.

"Ladies and gentlemen, before we enjoy our next course, a few words, if I may. Tonight is a special night for myself and Viviana. We are delighted to have our daughter Adelaide back with us." Viviana inclined her head, the picture of modest support. Feodor's eyes rested upon Adelaide. She could read the duality, even if the rest of them could not: tension in the jaw, tolerance masking reprimand. Now mention Axel, she pleaded silently. Say just one thing.

"I had long hoped to lure her into the mysteries of politics and cannot overstate my joy that someone else has achieved this seemingly impossible conversion. Of course—" Feodor's gaze roamed the room, a wink of humour now present. "I had hoped we would have similar objectives. We teach our children the art of independent thought and what does it beget us?" Laughter from the guests. Adelaide's hands clenched under the table. "What can I say. We must give them their heads. Ladies and gentlemen, esteemed colleagues—a toast. To those that follow, and the great City that we bequeath them. May they too guard Osiris with a watchful eye and a strong heart."

"To those that follow," the table echoed.

"And to those who cannot," murmured a voice. It came from Hildur Pek, whose eyes, no doubt in memory of her own loss, were wet. Hildur's words accomplished what Feodor's had not. Adelaide's vision was no longer clear. As the servers re-entered the banquet hall, she stood up, muttered an excuse to the Councillor of Estates, and left the room.

Behind the closed door the noise of the diners faded. She held her wrist against her eyes and blinked quickly, catching the moisture before it could smudge her make-up. Closing her eyes, she drew long breaths.

"Are you alright?"

It was Tyr. She averted her face. She could not look at him.

"You shouldn't be here."

"Feodor sent me."

"That's ironic." Not quite as ironic as Feodor's speech, embracing one delinquent child as he erased another. In sudden anger she said, "How can you stand it?"

He cupped her face, turned it gently towards him. "I have to work, Adie. I'm not like you. I don't come from a great family."

"You're part of one now. One way or another. Aren't you glad?"

"In some ways," he said soberly.

She knew she should draw away but found herself pushing into his hand. When she spoke her lips moved against his palm.

"Cover for me? Ten minutes and I'll be gone."

"Is that wise? Your being here tonight is an olive branch to Feodor. It will be worse than reversed if you leave now." His grey eyes were concerned.

"Tyr," she pleaded.

"Alright," he said softly.

She kissed his palm and felt him tense. They stood there in the empty lamplit hallway, equally aware of the currents conflicting one another. Their situation was what it was; she had never thought of it as unjust, because she could not imagine permanence with anyone, not even with Tyr. The heat of her own breath came back to her lips, trapped by his palm. Why was tonight different? She felt close to giving up. She was ready to ask. *Let me come over later, let me stay. I don't care if they find out.*

Tyr dropped his hand.

"Better go," he said.

The words she might have said edged away. She took off her shoes and ran. She did not look back. Vikram had fastened the shoes earlier, when her hands were shaking. He had sat her on the bed and said *give* in a voice that brooked no argument. Watching his hands do up the buckles, one part of her mind had warned that this was not part of the bargain; it was not sex and it was not information. It was something else.

She ran to the end of the hallway. Heaved the doors open. The floor was slippery in her stockings. She passed the drapes, the alcoves, the Alaskan paintings. Old friends, old enemies. Here was a favourite hiding place, there a tunnel exit where the twins had been caught, Adelaide's sandal sticking out under the curtain. Goran found them. He always did. He grabbed her foot and hauled her shrieking into the corridor whilst Axel hung onto her arms, Adelaide screaming, Axel yelling, *no, don't, don't hurt her!*

Goran would be loitering nearby. She picked up speed down the galleries. She couldn't let him catch her. An archway neared on her right. A silk curtain sighed in its frame. Flouting all reason, her feet slowed. Behind that curtain was a passage to the twins' old bedrooms. The twins thought they had discovered all the secrets of the Domain, but what if they hadn't? What if the family had Axel right here, under her nose? What if he was straitjacketed, sedated, unable to call out?

Close to the ground, the silk wavered. Adelaide's heart beat faster. The swelling folds gave way to the triangular head of a large orange cat. Its nose wrinkled as it sniffed the air. She sighed.

"Oh, you."

Out of habit, she scooped the animal up, hugging it awkwardly with one arm, her shoes gripped in the other hand. The cat was warm and heavy; it had grown fat. The feel of its soft fur alleviated her panic. Now she felt silly to have been running, silly for her ideas. What could the family do to her, anyway? She wasn't mad.

They reached the second floor unscathed. There was a strip of light under the door of her grandfather's study. Quietly, Adelaide turned the handle. Leonid was in his favourite armchair. He wore a tartan dressing gown over his flannel trousers and his bare feet were propped up on a stool. A book lay open on his lap. His spectacles had slipped down the bridge of his nose.

She lowered the cat to the floor and gave it an encouraging nudge. It stalked inside. She pulled the door gently back. Soon, someone would come to look for her. Goran was patrolling. She could not stay.

"Who is it?"

She paused, the door ajar. "Feodor said you weren't well."

Her grandfather's eyelids lifted. "Adie?" A smile pulled his lips back from his teeth. "My back's been playing up a little, that's all. I have some injections for when it gets difficult."

"You mean morphine," she said accusingly. His face had lost weight; the papery skin stretched taut over the egg of his head. "It must be bad."

"I don't need them often." He patted the arm of the chair. "Why don't you come and sit a minute."

She curled her fingers around the door frame, reluctant to enter when she had been about to make her escape. Then she came in, shutting the door behind her. The room had not altered. It still smelt of tobacco and pine cones; it was still crowded with blueprints and piano scores.

Adelaide glanced to the piano in the corner, which her grandfather had played often when she was a child and less often as she grew older and his hands grew arthritic. The cat had slumped upon the stool. Its stomach began to rise and fall in contented waves of purrs.

"I'm amazed he's still alive," she said.

"I think he will outlive me," her grandfather replied.

She went to sit at the foot of the armchair.

"You should renounce the rest of the family, Grandfather." She tilted her head back, smiling. "Hiding out here, complaining of back pain… I think you're trying to escape."

He chuckled.

"It is the duty of the young to rebel. I am too old for all that, Adie. I need my pipe, and a good bottle of octopya." He gestured to the table. "Perhaps you will do the honours."

She prepared two measures of liqueur. Her grandfather inhaled deeply before taking a sip. Adelaide nestled her glass between her knees. She had always loved this room. It felt both old and ageless. A thing treated with attentive care. A thing from a time before Osiris. Now the room seemed smaller too, or herself too large for it.

"This house is my bequest to you all," said her grandfather softly. "But you, Adie. I know what the Domain means to you. You feel as though you have surrendered your agency. You prefer to live in a cage of your own making rather than one designed by somebody else. Tell me, what brings you here tonight?"

The heater was warm on her face and neck. "I don't know, Grandfather. It's a peace gesture, isn't it. And partly for information—Vikram thought it would be useful. And... Axel. I suppose I thought it might help, to come back."

"Did you?"

She fell silent.

"You don't believe Axel is dead," he said.

Careful, she thought. She realized then how far she had come. This was her grandfather who she loved and trusted.

"I don't feel that he is," she said. "In my heart."

"Sanjay Hanif will find out. He is a good man."

"So everyone says."

The marmalade cat woke, arched its back so that all of the hairs separated along its spine, and hopped off the stool. It regarded Adelaide with blank eyes. She stroked its head automatically.

"I find it hard to believe that the boy would go away without any communication to you, Adie. Even through his delirium, he was aware that there was someone he should remember."

"You saw him after Radir's last session, didn't you?"

"Yes. That was the last visit I made and he was very secretive. There was one room in the apartment which was locked. Axel did not respond when I asked him what was inside. Now, I think perhaps he was planning something."

Oh, he was. He was.

"I should have gone," she said. "I just—I couldn't."

"You took care of him in other ways." He paused. "The bond between you twins was so strong, a break was bound to be dramatic. If he had regained his mind, I suspect the reunification would have been as abrupt."

She imagined the scene: Axel's return, healthy, jubilant. But almost at once another image replaced it: Axel in a balloon, at the heart of a storm, flung this way and that. Her grandfather packed another layer of tobacco into his pipe and lit it.

"Bring me the photograph, Adelaide."

She knew at once which photograph he meant and went to get it from a drawer in the cabinet. The image was faded with age but the construct was still clear: a man, a woman and a small child standing in front of a huge stone building. The building was hewn out of a mountain, and the mountain rose upward in striates of grey and green.

Leonid held the photograph in both hands.

"Do you know where this was taken?"

"Yes, grandfather. That's the Osiris Facility, in Patagonia."

"I was born in that town. For a few years, the whole of our family lived there whilst the City was under construction. Imagine it Adie, to see the pyramids rising from the sea for the first time—what a sight that must have been!"

Adelaide leaned on the arm of Leonid's chair, resting her chin upon her hands.

"I wish I could have seen it."

"As do I. As do I... but much of the footage was lost. A great tragedy. I often wonder how they first found the site, those entrepreneurs of the Board. There were old sea maps, of course, but even then, navigation was almost impossible. The sea was ravenous. The winds were wild. Instruments ran haywire, driven mad by all the broken currents in the atmosphere—oh, it must have been an adventure, Adie. But they found it—the fabled Atum Shelf."

A wistful expression occupied his face and Adelaide knew that he was seeing those strange, wonderful visions from decades ago. The cat's purrs reverberated against her legs, a warm, steady rhythm that reminded her of time moving on. But she could not tear herself away. Not yet.

"Tell me more about Patagonia, Grandfather."

"Ah, Patagonia... it was a beautiful place. Yes, I remember land. I remember the rocks, especially. The sound of the waves crashing on the shore. Of course, even then the storms were terrible and pirates were forever raiding the local towns. My grandparents died there, they were too nervous to take to sea. So they never saw Osiris. But I believe they were happy, and proud."

He pushed the photograph abruptly towards Adelaide.

"All those people will be dead now," he muttered.

"But some of the refugees must have come from Patagonia?"

"They came from everywhere, Adie, everywhere. Every place was destroyed. You've been taught all of this."

"Yes, I know."

He passed a hand over his face. Adelaide put the photograph back, afraid that it was distressing him. She regretted now that she had kept him talking.

"You still miss Second Grandmother, don't you?" she asked quietly.

"Every day. I miss a lot of things, Adie."

"Land?"

"Land, yes. The things that were… the things that should have been."

She waited, aware that there was more, not wishing to rush him. The pipe clacked between his teeth.

"Osiris was an experiment," he said. "To herald a new era. Osiris was meant to reunite nations in a way that had long been lost. To bring the hemispheres together again. That was the intention." He was silent for a moment. "But the world changed too quickly to see if it worked. And the City has changed because of that."

She looked at him, not understanding. He said, "Your generation is the evidence of it."

The words were gentle, but without comfort. Adelaide felt as though he was trying to explain something to her, something important, but he wanted her to work out what it was for herself. She was ashamed to ask; to confirm her ignorance.

"I should leave before Feodor finds me here," she said.

"Come and visit again some time."

She crouched, and took her grandfather's mottled hand.

"You could always visit me."

He chuckled. "At your fancy apartment? I hope you are enjoying it, by the way. But no. I can keep an eye from afar. I follow your adventures rather avidly in the feed of—what is it, that rag—the *Daily Flotsam*."

"Magda Linn."

"That's the woman. She has a void where some of us have a semblance of moral integrity. One has to admire her for it."

"Admire, and destroy," said Adelaide, standing. She dropped a kiss on the top of his head. "I really must go."

Leonid's hand curled around hers, holding it fast. The joints were swollen. They looked painful.

"Before you go," he said. "I would like you to promise me one thing."

"What is it?"

"You're a smart girl. Young, impulsive. You must be wise as well. Don't be too quick to judge, when the time comes. Don't be too quick to judge me."

"Why would I judge you, Grandfather?"

He squeezed her hand with his trembling one.

"Adelaide." Her name alone seemed to cost him a great effort. She was startled to see the change in his expression—as though he were abruptly battling great pain.

"Grandfather, do you need the morphine? Where is it?"

The words rushed out of him.

"Adie, the truth is this family has done some terrible things. Terrible things."

"Do you mean the execution, is that it? You mean the west?" Her heart pounded. "Axel?"

Leonid shook his head, impatiently. Still clinging to Adelaide's hand, he pulled her very close. He lowered his voice to a whisper.

"I have to tell you something, Adie. I have to tell you. There was a boat. Years and years ago. Long before you were born. But after—after the Silence. There was a boat."

A tingling sensation spread from Adelaide's scalp, to her neck, one by one down her vertebrae. When she spoke, she struggled to keep her voice steady.

"I don't understand. There were no boats after the Silence. There was no contact."

There couldn't have been.

"That's what they all think. But there was one. It came many miles—an inconceivable feat of seafaring! They had been at sea for over two hundred days. And they got almost as far as the ring-net. And then—everyone on board—every one of them—killed! Shot in the dark. The boat was sunk, out beyond the Atum Shelf. We couldn't let them go. We couldn't bring them in. It was a great secret, d'you see, a secret. No-one can ever know about that boat. No-one. No-one can find out."

He's starting to ramble, she realized. He's old. He's old, and his imagination is bringing dark things into the room. That's what it is. It must be. And yet—

"Where was the boat from, Grandfather?"

There was an almost cunning look about the old man now.

"The Boreal States," he whispered. "From Siberia. They came to look—"

A cough seized his throat.

"Grandfather." Her own voice was trembling now. "What are you trying to tell me?"

"Nothing more to tell." He coughed. "Nothing but the white—"

His eyes bulged. Adelaide ran to get him a glass of water. She held it to his lips, but the coughs still hacked at his throat, and he could not swallow.

"I'll get someone—"

"No." He grabbed her wrist. "No—no." The fit subsided. He drank a little water. The gulps resounded in the room. The cat's purrs grew stronger. "Nothing but the white fly," Leonid muttered.

"You're talking in riddles, Grandfather. What is the white fly?"

He interrupted. "No, that's not important. Not what I meant to say at all. What I meant to say is, whatever our family has done, they would not hurt Axel. No one would ever hurt your brother. Believe that, if you believe nothing else." His face was open again; relaxed and smiling. She could not quite believe that the last couple of minutes had been real.

Leonid tapped her hand. "Goran is upstairs. I know his tread. Go now, Adie, if you don't want them to find you."

"But the boat—"

"What boat? What are you talking about?" He looked confused. "Remember, my girl, my darling girl. No decision is lightly undertaken. Reversal is—impossible."

"I'll remember." She was worried and frightened, and wanted to say more, but there seemed no conceivable response. She doubted her own sanity. She needed to get out. "I promise. Goodbye, Grandfather."

She checked there was nobody in the corridor outside before shutting the door behind her. She was no closer to finding out what had happened to Axel; if he had left or if he had been taken. And now, it appeared, there were other secrets that her grandfather wanted her to know—secrets, if he was to be believed, too terrible to speak. Secrets that had walked the deepest trenches of his mind for years, the way cantering horses had followed Axel across the waves.

There was no sign of Goran.

Barefoot, Adelaide ran down the staircase. The Domain was quiet, as though it awaited a long overdue arrival. Or a departure, she thought.

"Axel?" she whispered. Her voice echoed back at her: *Axel Axel Axel Axel.* She called again, louder.

"Axel!"

Nothing. She stepped out of the front door and was faintly surprised, as always, to find the lift before her. The cables clunked. The glass car began to rise. Adelaide slipped on her shoes, leaving the straps undone. She had a terrifying sense of things diminishing. A pan of events from before her time receding into the distance, like stills from an archive reel being blotted out: pixel by pixel, image by image. At the very end, last to disappear, was a tiny Siberian boat.

30 | VIKRAM

Winter had Osiris under siege. Daylight was fleeting. The entire city glittered, like an ice ship dredged up from a century's slumber in the deeps. At the shelter, people arrived with ice in their hair and beards. The doctors treated cases of frostbite. Sometimes they had to cut off fingers, toes, parts of limbs. The nights were loud and long with the sounds of hacking coughs. Vikram and Shadiyah did the bed rounds with extra blankets, tucking them tightly around the thin shivering bodies, feeding bowls of soup where hands were too shaky to hold a spoon. Not everyone who came in made it through to the morning.

Late one night he arrived at the Red Rooms. Adelaide opened the door and exclaimed.

"What happened to you?"

He looked down and saw that the blood had seeped through his jacket and there was dried blood all over his right hand.

"I'm okay. Marete patched me up."

She took his bloodied hand and led him inside, easing the jacket carefully from his shoulders and placing it on the back of the futon. A month ago she wouldn't have let it touch the floor. She lifted his bandaged arm.

"Do you remember the guy I told you about last week?" he said. "The one using the shelter, that we weren't sure was genuine?"

"I remember. He did this?"

"He was an ex-Juraj gang member. Shadiyah caught him trying to recruit some kids. When we challenged him, he pulled a knife."

"Stars, Vik. Does it hurt? Have they given you painkillers?"

"Marete gave me a local anaesthetic."

He didn't tell her of the terror that had blocked his throat when he saw the knife, not for himself but for the people he worked with, the people sleeping in their beds that he was meant to be protecting. It was terror that had delayed his responses for a full two seconds. That was the reason he had been injured; he'd been too slow.

"I don't like to think of you in this kind of danger," said Adelaide.

"Our security man caught him. The police have taken him away now."

"You're shivering."

"I'm cold."

But he could feel himself sweating; his head felt like it was on fire.

"Come on. Let's get you cleaned up."

After she had washed the dried blood from his hands, she coaxed him into the bath and they sat opposite one another, her ankles resting on his thighs. Adelaide turned on the jacuzzi and foam billowed on the surface of the bubbling water. She was trying to help but he could not relax.

"Being here—all this luxury—it makes me feel so guilty," he said.

"Hush. Think about what you do every day. You've earned it, far more than anyone else I know."

"It's difficult to think like that when you see people freezing to death."

"Not the ones who come to your shelters."

"Not all of them."

Now that he was back in Adelaide's world, Adelaide's life, something was bothering him.

"You know that guy we were talking to at the party last week? The one that works for your father?"

Adelaide drew circles in the bubbles.

"You mean Tyr? What about him?"

Vikram tried to recall the scene, the smooth expression of the man's face, the same man who had thrown him out of here all those weeks ago.

"This might sound weird but... I got the impression that he was spying on you. If he tries to get anything out of you about the aid schemes, you will tell me?"

"I don't think you've got anything to worry about, Vik."

"He works for your father. Your father hates me."

"Alright. I'll keep an eye on Tyr."

"Thank you."

He sank lower amidst the bubbles. He wanted nothing more than to let his mind unravel, drift, forget.

"You still look worried," said Adelaide.

"I am worried. I'm worried about the aid schemes. That they're not doing enough."

"Would more money help? We could canvas. Approach private funders. We could do other things."

"I don't think it would make a difference. I mean, yes, of course we can use more money, it's just—I think the problem's deeper than that."

"Is there anything I can do?"

"I don't know. This sounds crazy, but sometimes Adelaide, I honestly think people want me to fail."

"Then you'll prove them wrong."

"I feel overwhelmed. I feel like I was insane to think I could make a difference."

"Vik." She leaned forward and ran her hands up his good arm. "I understand. You know, it's like when Axel—when he vanished. I thought, Osiris is so huge. How on earth will I begin to look for him? But you have to start somewhere."

She smiled at him, encouraging, and he nodded tiredly. She was right.

"I had a letter from my mother today," she said. "Viviana is disowning me."

"Will you be able to tell the difference?"

He wondered after he'd spoken if the question sounded callous, but Adelaide did not look offended.

"Not really. But it's more of a statement, coming from her. She said she was disgusted with my behaviour at the dinner party."

"I was proud of what you said."

"It was unwise." Her wet fingers trailed his chest as she leaned back, mirroring him. "But you know, Vik—more and more I can't bring myself to care. About any of it. I missed Gudrun's party last week. She'll take it as a snub but I couldn't bear to stand there, seeing the same faces, hearing the same conversations... Jan's calling me every day about organising her twenty-second, I keep making promises and I haven't done a thing."

"Then don't. Let them fend for themselves."

She ran her toes down the inside of his thigh.

"That's not very altruistic, is it?"

Vikram captured her nudging foot in his hands. There were calluses on the tendon where one of her absurd shoes had rubbed. Adelaide wriggled her toes, trying to free herself.

"That tickles!"

"Do you hate being tickled?" he asked.

"Ye— no. No, I don't. Stop it!"

He moved his finger slowly along the inside of her foot. Adelaide solved her dilemma by sloshing water at him. He cupped a plume of foam and sent it back. Adelaide returned a larger plume. They sank back and she rested her ankles once again on his legs.

"Adelaide, there's something I need to—"

"Vikram, have you ever heard—"

The sound of popping bubbles filled the room. Steam was beginning to varnish the tinted window-wall.

"What is it?" Vikram asked.

"You say first."

"No, you go."

Adelaide pushed a damp strand of hair behind her ear. She was wearing her serious face.

"Vik, you won't fall in love with me, will you?"

He laughed. "No." He thought about turning the question on her, teasingly, but she had a habit of only getting her own jokes.

"It would be a shame if you did," she said. "Because I can't care about anybody."

"I can see how that would be inconvenient." He flicked foam at her. "I'll try and restrain my passion for you for as long as possible."

"Don't be a gull. I have a reason, you know."

He sensed that she was, in her convoluted way, trying to tell him something. He remembered knocking on her door in the middle of the night, a stranger who might have been anyone, an amusement for an insomniac girl. Here he was in the austere beauty of her bathroom, their skin brushing, almost fused by the distortions of water. There must have been a transition, a moment of impasse. He searched his memory; he could not find it.

"Well, what's the reason?"

"Osiris—Osiris demands some sacrifice on our part. It's not a lovers' city. That's the price we pay for our hospitality here."

"Is that your doctrine?"

"It has to be."

"I can't agree." Osiris takes so much from us, he thought. Surely what Adelaide was talking about—intimacy, companionship in the night—was one of the few things they could hope for.

"What's your doctrine?" she asked.

"I don't see things as clear-cut as you do."

"Things aren't always complicated. Sometimes they just are." Adelaide popped a bubble with one fingernail. "Anyway, I interrupted you, before. What were you going to say?"

Vikram thought of Axel's letter. He should tell Adelaide. Stars, he should really tell her. Now was as good a time as ever.

She smiled at him, waiting. He tugged her leg, pulling her towards him. Her body slid underwater until he could see only her hair, spreading out in a three dimensional fan through the bubbles. She resurfaced in front of him, took his face in her hands, and kissed him. He kissed her back. "Nothing important," he said.

"Tell me."

He shook his head. "It doesn't matter. Anyway, what were *you* going to say before? You changed your question."

"Oh. That. I was going to ask if you'd ever heard of something called white fly."

"What's white fly?"

"Just a phrase I heard and I didn't know what it was. I wondered if it was a western thing?"

"Not to my knowledge."

Adelaide twisted in the water so that she could lie against his chest. He poured a globule of shampoo into his hand and began to lather her hair.

"That feels nice. You know Vik, what you're doing—it's really, really important. You mustn't let anyone tell you otherwise."

"I'm glad you think so. Without your blessing, I probably would have quit the entire programme."

"Ha ha. No, I mean it."

His hands, massaging her scalp, slowed. Despite his efforts to keep it dry, the bandage on his arm was soaked and had turned pale pink. He could see tiny strands of red diffusing through the water.

"Adelaide, what are you doing with me? Honestly?"

She had her eyes closed, so as not to get soap in them.

"You can't ask me that."

"I just did."

"Well, I can't answer. I told you I wouldn't lie, didn't I?"

Vikram rinsed the soap from her hair, watching the water turn opaque.

"What are you doing with me?" she asked.

"I don't know," he answered honestly. "But you know what, Adie? You could do so many things, if you wanted to. Not what your family wants. Not like Linus, or Dmitri. But things that make a real difference. Think about that, will you?"

/ / /

Hours later when it was still dark he woke and Adelaide was sitting upright, her body pale in the twisted sheets, her eyes wide and staring.

"Adie, what is it?"

"I had a nightmare."

He put a hand gently on her shoulder. Her skin was covered with sweat.

"Tell me."

"There was this giant thing—crawling, crawling everywhere, up the towers and over the bridges, and I knew wherever I ran, however fast, it would find me. It had these twitching—feelers, and its wings made a noise—an awful scraping noise. It plucked people out of the towers and grabbed them in its mouth and then it flew them out past the ring-net and into the sea and it—drowned them."

He squeezed her shoulder.

"It's just a dream. It's over now."

"A dream?" Her voice was uncertain, barely audible.

"Monsters in the night, Adie."

He pulled her against him and they lay down, his body curled around hers. Her back was cool and damp. For minutes, hours, he held her like that while she trembled, unprotesting, and he wondered what it was that could make her so afraid when he'd never known her to be scared of anything.

31 ┆ ADELAIDE

As Lao sat down next to her on the bench, five or six butterflies rose in a small explosion of colour. Lao ignored them. He went through the usual routine of taking out his Surfboard. She knew that he was scanning the paths from behind his dark glasses, listening carefully for sounds of eavesdroppers.

"Lovely afternoon," he said pleasantly.

"You said you had information. Did you check Radir's client list?"

"I do, and I did. I managed to track down the woman who worked for your brother. Not either of the two that you employed, but another. I was right. She is an airlift."

"She worked for him? Was she one of Radir's patients?"

"She wasn't on his list, unless she used a pseudonym. Lots of them do. However there is a connection. At one stage she worked as a cleaner for the reef farm, which is, as you know, adjacent to Radir's offices. I would venture to hypothesise that this is how they met."

Adelaide felt a spark of triumph.

"I want to meet her."

"You can't. She was very reluctant to talk, very scared. She spoke to me only on the condition that this was the last contact she had with any of the Rechnovs. I gave her my word."

"You had no right to do that," she said furiously.

Lao removed his glasses, polished them, put them back on.

"I have recovered all the relevant information, Miss Mystik. This woman ran errands for your brother, odd things which sound, to be frank, the product of insanity. There was one particular incident, however, that I believe is of import. Axel came across some documents. Paper documents, I should add. He had them with him when she arrived one day at the penthouse—this was some months ago. Usually, she said, Axel was exceptionally secretive, and would have hidden the documents from her sight. But he was excited. Elated, she said. He told her straight away that he had found something for the horses."

A Red Pierrot landed on Adelaide's hand. She stared at its spots.

"That could have been anything."

"So one might think." Lao cleared his throat; a small, anticipatory noise. "But the woman had a glimpse of the papers before he put them into an envelope. She said they looked official. There was an unusual motif in the top right corner—an insect—and each paper was stamped with the same legend: Operation Whitefly. Does that mean anything to you?"

In the warm, sticky heat, Adelaide felt suddenly clammy. She shook her head, intensely grateful for her own dark glasses. Not by a flicker in her face could she let Lao see her recognition.

"Axel told her he had been instructed to take the papers to the Silk Vault, for safekeeping."

"He means that the horses told him."

"Either way, we must assume that he took them there."

Lao looked at her expectantly. She realized that an answer was necessary.

"Well? What do we do now?"

"I cannot make enquiries about a vault in Axel Rechnov's name—or under an alias, for that matter—without raising Hanif's awareness. This line of investigation, should you choose to pursue it, will take time. We will have to bribe someone on the inside of the vault. I will have to identify a suitable candidate, which will involve background research—among other things."

"And? If it does exist?"

"I will not be able to access it. I imagine, however, that you might."

She looked at him quickly. "Because there's always a secondary holder."

Lao flicked a Monarch from his knee. "That is correct. Presumably it will be yourself. I suspect, Ms Mystik, that whatever lies within that vault may offer us valuable clues as to why Axel disappeared—or why, we have to consider, he was removed."

"But the woman said he was acting for the horses. Axel probably had no idea what he had found. Anyway, 'Operation Whitefly'—it could be anything—or nothing at all."

"Precisely. Whether Axel realized or not, finding those documents could have placed him in danger." For the first time, Lao looked at her straight on. "Do you want to proceed?"

Adelaide met the blank discs of Lao's shades. She could not decide if there was a note of glee in his voice—the delight of discovery. *Whitefly* thudded in her head like a hammer.

Think, Adelaide.

If there was a vault, and if there was anything inside, Lao would expect to be party to it. And if what Axel had found had anything to do with what her grandfather had been talking about—she was potentially in a very dangerous position herself.

She could leave the vault be. That would be the safest option. She could pull Lao off the case altogether. But could she guarantee that his suspicions had not been raised? That he might not try to find the vault on his own?

"Find out if the vault exists. Do what you have to do. Let me know as soon as you have news."

"It will cost, of course. My fee and the insider's. You will trust me to negotiate the price?"

"Of course. Money is no object. I want you to do something else as well."

"Which is?"

"I want you to search the prisons."

"You think he may be underwater?"

"I don't know what I think." She struggled to keep her voice from rising. "Just search them. All of them."

"Very well." He tapped the Surfboard. "I'll—"

"You'll be in touch."

Lao left first. He walked off in his usual easy, inconspicuous manner. After he'd gone she wandered through the garden, hoping to lose her thoughts in the succulent lure of the greenery. She ducked under a low hanging branch and into a canopied grove. The rustle of wings filled the air. The husks of cocoons hung from branches, split down the middle where the insects had crawled out.

She noticed a scattering of dead butterflies on the ground. Some were entire, perfect but motionless. Others had lost a wing. One was flapping. She crouched and scooped it up, careful not to handle its wings because the membrane was so thin, the scales would fall away at a touch. It lay in her palms, barely moving. It could not fly. She did not know what to do with it and after a moment she laid it back upon the ground.

There was a boat, Adie… an inconceivable feat of seafaring!

As she walked on, more dead ones littered the edges of the path. The thoughts that she had struggled to suppress ever since visiting the Domain rushed back to the front of her mind. Why had her grandfather told her about the Siberian boat? Did he want to be found out, or did he want the family to be found out—who else was in on this secret? Her father? Her mother? Linus? And if the family had authorised the massacre of an entire crew of Siberians, what else were they capable of?

She thought of the vault, of Axel holding documents that he did not understand, or only understood when he was lucid. She imagined him sitting on the balcony, smiling that half smile, when assassins broke in. Or perhaps he'd been afraid, perhaps he'd tried to hide—alone and muddled, unable to escape, running from room to room. Perhaps they'd dragged him away screaming, thrown him into an underwater cell where no one would ever hear him scream again.

Perhaps they'd killed him after all.

No. She remembered her grandfather's words. *No one would ever hurt your brother.* She had to believe that.

Her twin was still alive; the connection was there, she felt it. Some part of him must have known the power of those documents. He'd left on purpose. He'd gone into hiding until she found him.

And then?

The answer was obvious. And then he planned to leave Osiris. With her. Because if there had been one boat, might not there have been others? Who else was out there, waiting to be found?

She kept walking. The path through the farm was circular; soon she was back to where she had started. Through the foliage she saw the external walls of the tower, their hexagonal pattern repeated over and over again. Endless repetition, the way a wheel turned, or a horse's hooves beat.

She could not get away from one inescapable fact. If her grandfather was telling the truth, if there really had been a boat—then everything Adelaide had ever been told was a lie.

32 | VIKRAM

A light mist trickled into the harbour as their speedboat approached. It blurred the hulls, red with rust, of gigantic ships whose load lines sat high above the water. It touched cool fingers to Vikram's face. Only the cries of circling gulls broke the silence, and there was nobody present to hear them, except for Vikram and Adelaide, and Adelaide's boatman.

The craft pulled up alongside a jetty which sloped down into the water. A maze of piers and walkways crisscrossed the harbour. Most were visible; some, more dangerously, were submerged. Vikram and Adelaide climbed out. They wore thermal wetsuits: Vikram's red, Adelaide's green. Adelaide's hair swirled in the wind as she crouched to say something to the boatman. Vikram stood motionless, struck by the stillness, and the quiet.

"Let's go!"

Adelaide started walking. Vikram gave chase and they ran, shrieking, to the jetty's edge. The sea before them had a brownish hue; their forms were murky shadows.

"You know smugglers used to come here," said Adelaide. "Before the border."

"Maybe they still do."

"No. It's deserted now. Sometimes this place gives me—a queer feeling."

They turned back and crossed a bridge into a floating cabin. Inside sat two identical waterbikes, sleek and silver. At the sight of those beautiful crafts, Vikram felt a surge in his head like the release of a pressure valve.

It had been building over the last few weeks. Subtly, so subtly that at first he barely recognized them, the responsibilities had been lining up: to the west and to the City. He needed this break.

Adelaide had mounted her bike. "What are you waiting for?"

He climbed onto the other bike and squeezed the handlebars, as she did. The motor hummed into life. They eased the bikes down a ramp and bobbed into the water, the aerodynamic bodies lying low. They emerged on the opposite side of the cabin, out into the mist.

Adelaide leaned over and grabbed Vikram's handlebars. She had tucked her hair under a green hood.

"You ready?" she said.

Vikram pulled a pair of goggles over his eyes. "Absolutely."

"Watch out for floating junk. This place is a scrap heap."

She squeezed the handlebars, increasing the power. He did the same and felt the engine reverberating. Ripples of froth welled around both crafts. They leapt forward.

Out of the fog loomed the vast shapes of forsaken ships. Vikram glanced up as they skirted the length of a tanker. Its parts creaked like old bones. The hull was bleached with salt and green with algae. Despite their physical deterioration, the ships seemed to him to be sleeping, still semi-conscious.

The bike veered close to the hull on a wave. He edged left, maintaining a wider corridor. Ahead he watched the streamlined shape of Adelaide and her bike weaving under the shadows of the abandoned vessels. Several times he had to angle around debris or nudge the bike over a hidden walkway. The air on his face was freezing but it was good to be out here, with the elements, on his own terms. Winter and work had been choking him.

They passed between the last two ships, prows angled together to form a gateway. Before them lay the open sea. The mist was clearing. Some way ahead, Adelaide stopped and wheeled around.

"I'll race you to the ring-net!"

She was already leaping forward in the water, streaking away so fast that the spray almost obscured her completely. He gave chase. The wind battled him, the waterbike bucked and rolled beneath him and at first he felt almost sick, but then he got used to it, and was aware only of speed.

Minutes passed but it felt like nothing. He was filled with exhilaration.

He opened his mouth and had to shout, not words, just joyful noise.

Suddenly there it was, a vast dark wall rising twenty metres out of the water. It loomed closer and closer. The sea soaked him. Salt was bright in his mouth. Adelaide wasn't far ahead now, swivelling left and right and left again, over the waves, down into the troughs. Glancing up he saw it for the first time in daylight, a series of interlocking chains: the ring-net. He was on Adelaide's tail, in her slipstream, close enough to hear her laugh above the sea and the wind and the metallic music. Then she cut sharply to the right and he was under it. Horror clenched him. He was going to crash. He wrenched the handlebars with all his strength, panic sucking the oxygen from his lungs. The Dolphin careered right until he was practically lying along the waves, and the engine cut.

He wrested the bike upright, sucking in air, scared and exhilarated in equal measure. Five metres away, Adelaide's waterbike was also at rest. She leaned over and touched the ring-net with one hand. He knew she was grinning.

"I won!" she shouted.

He looked up. The chains of the ring-net clinked and chimed, the whole construction rippling like a ponderous sheet of material. The metal was covered in algae. The net stretched from outpost to outpost in a giant fence, but wherever they were, the nearest one was too far away to see. So was the border, which ran up to the ring-net. He looked beyond Adelaide. The green lights he'd seen before illuminated the ring-net's path. It curved away as far as he could see, cutting through the ocean until it was lost in the distance.

"Quite colossal, isn't it?" Adelaide cried. "Keeps out the sharks."

"Not always," he yelled back. Adelaide nudged her Dolphin the short distance to him, and took hold of his handlebars once again. They rose and fell together on the waves.

"What?"

Beneath the goggles her face was pink and glowing.

"I said not always," he repeated. "I saw sharks when I was underwater." Her mouth opened dramatically.

"Big ones?"

"Big enough."

He felt a sense of menace, knowing what was on the other side of the net, and yet knowing nothing at the same time. The significance of the net overwhelmed him. Even here, in the middle of the ocean, with as much space around him as he could have desired, he was both locked in and locked out.

"If anything got through the net now we wouldn't know anyway. Not since the alarm system broke."

Vikram stared at the interlocking chains.

"It doesn't work?"

"Hasn't for years. My grandfather told me. Can't even zap a shark."

She pushed a button on his handlebars, then on hers. The Dolphins turned luminous. Against the brightness, the rest of the sea turned black. He realized it was already nearing dusk, and he was cold.

"You've not looked back," Adelaide said. "Axel never looked back. Always out there, beyond the net."

"You came out here together?"

"We did everything together."

She was looking past him, back the other way. He spun the Dolphin around. With the onset of dusk it was difficult to distinguish the outlines of the towers; he saw only a geometric construction of light. Osiris a blazing star in the crepuscular ocean. If anyone had been left to find us, he thought, it wouldn't have been hard.

"Have you ever gone past the ring-net?" he asked Adelaide. She did not respond, gazing at the City with an intensity that was uncanny. He repeated his question. He thought she hadn't heard, but as she gunned her Dolphin into life she yelled, "There's nothing out there."

They sped back across no-man's-land. He felt the gridlock of the City pulling him in. Adelaide poised rigidly on her bike, her head pushing forward. He saw huge waves breaking against her bike, and prepared himself for the same impact. It never came. It took him a few seconds to realize she must be deliberately colliding with the swells. At the same time he realized she had speeded up.

They were approaching the harbour. Vikram accelerated. His bike skimmed the sea like a petrel, almost flying now. Adelaide remained ahead. He could see the gateway from where they had ridden out before, the two ships pointed towards one another. The gap seemed narrower, and she was travelling far faster, hurtling at impossible speed, plunging her bike nose first, leaping up again, almost invisible behind a mask of spray.

"Adelaide!" he shouted.

She shot across the final stretch of water.

The bike and the hull smashed together. She was a bolt of green through the air—his own bike was charging forward, some part of his brain telling him to slow down and she was falling, almost gracefully. She was face down in the water. She didn't move.

The waves raised her and lowered her, and her body bumped once against the ship's side.

Vikram surged his bike forward. His heartbeat trebled in his chest. He leaned into the water and grabbed her arm, pulled her almost viciously towards him. Her body was cold and awkward. *Not again, not Adelaide too.* The suit, he told himself, it's just the suit, she's warm inside it. *Please, not Adelaide too.* The bike tipped as he hauled her up, both arms around her. Stars, if she was dead they would never believe he hadn't killed her. He pressed his hands beneath her ribs and jerked, once, twice. They'd drown him the way they'd drowned Eirik. *Please breathe.* Her chest heaved and her mouth opened and water poured out. She gasped, choked, spat. Spasms racked her body.

He pushed her goggles up. Her eyes wheeled crazily, then settled on his face. She tried to say something. It might have been "A."

"Adelaide," he said weakly.

"I'm okay," she rasped. "I'm fine." She glared up at him. "I'm fine!"

Relief gave way to anger in a blink.

"Your bike fucking isn't, though, is it?"

The Dolphin floated listlessly on its side, handles twisted. Its light had gone out.

"What the fuck were you doing?" he shouted.

Adelaide's head was shaking. He was clasping her so tightly she could barely move. Her body was shaking too and he felt each tremor hard against his ribs.

"Let me go." Her teeth chattered.

"You're going to have to ride back on my bike."

"It's not your bike," she said. "It's Axel's."

He wanted to hit her. He looked around him and saw the waves slapping against the ships. Seagulls rose from their perches to circle overhead.

Adelaide gasped as the birds came into her line of sight.

"We have to get back," he said. "Can you climb on behind me?"

She hauled herself up, wrapped her arms around his waist. One of the birds dove low and she screamed and lashed out at it.

"Leave it alone!"

"I hate them."

"It's not going to hurt you."

He nudged the bike across to the other Dolphin and tried to start it but they both knew that it was futile.

"The speedboat can pick it up," she said.

But a storm was coming in and they knew that as well. Vikram did not respond. If he opened his mouth he would say unforgivable things. He wove back through the harbour with grim determination. When they reached the pier the man in the speedboat gave a shout of mingled relief and alarm.

"What happened to the other bike?"

"It broke," said Adelaide shortly. They climbed into the speedboat stern, shivering. The boat took off at once. Incoming hail chased them all the way back, sweeping across the ocean and the harbour before it slammed into the walls of the pyramids. The deluge caught them moments before they banged to a halt against the first decking they found. Adelaide leapt out and darted inside. Storm sirens began a wailing crescendo. The boatman cursed as he secured the craft with fingers already deadened by the cold, Vikram straining to hold the boat steady. Hailstones whipped against them. The decking was treacherous with ice, and they almost slipped running inside. Vikram heaved the doors shut.

The sirens ceased. The door sealed with a soft hiss. Vikram listened to the barrage, gasping for breath, praying that none of his friends were outside.

They were on an empty floor. Lifts and stairs ran up the back of the tower, a couple of flat trolleys were parked by the lift. Faint sounds of machinery, the lifts and other workings, filtered down the building.

"We'll have to wait it out," said the boatman. His voice echoed in the open space. "Unless you two want to hop on a shuttle line?"

Vikram glanced down at the puddle forming around his feet. A watery trail crossed the concrete floor to the other side of the tower, where

Adelaide sat on the first steps of the stairwell, arms wrapped around her knees. Her eyes were cloudy.

"We'll wait," he said. "Where are we, anyway?"

"Probably some kind of storage place," said the boatman.

Vikram slumped against the wall. It was warm compared to outside, but Adelaide should get dry or she'd catch hypothermia. She didn't look like she wanted to move though, and he told himself it was her own stupid fault. Nils had been right about her.

He had seen his friend a couple of days ago. Vikram was holding a meeting of representatives from the west who would be heading up work parties in the spring. He'd asked Nils to come, but Nils was being oddly cagey, and had only shown up afterwards. He had brought fish from Market Circle. They drank coral tea and ate the fish with their fingers in Vikram's office.

"What's your new place like?" Nils asked.

"You know. Big. Clean. It's nice."

"I bet."

"When are you going to come and see it?"

Nils wiped his fingers on the already greasy paper.

"Whenever you have the time."

"I always have the time."

"I thought you were all taken up with the crazy girl these days."

"She can be demanding," Vikram acknowledged. Nils laughed.

"Fucking Citizens, huh. So what's she really like? You still think she's a bitch?"

A bone was stuck in Vikram's teeth. He worked his tongue, trying to free it. He wanted to explain that there was a connection between himself and Adelaide, but could not find the words to justify it.

"She has her moments."

He hesitated. Nils, taking a large bite of white fish and batter, raised an eyebrow.

"I think she has a secret. Something she's not telling."

"Are you kidding me? She's a Rechnov, they probably have more skeletons than they have closets, and that's saying something. What, you think she's going to bare her soul to you?"

"No, of course not. It's just—" He stopped. It was no good, he did not even know what he meant himself. "Anyway, that's not what I wanted to tell you. I found something. A letter. It's from Axel to Adelaide."

Saying it aloud, he felt the heat of it, transferred from pocket to drawer to pocket and back, burning a hole in every garment it touched. Nils shrugged.

"So give it to Adelaide."

"It's a goodbye note. You know what that means."

"Then you'd better burn it," said Nils.

"I can't burn it, it's probably the last thing he ever wrote."

"Exactly. You want to be caught with that on your hands?"

Vikram's hand went to his jacket.

"Actually, I have it here—"

"Are you crazy?" Nils hissed. "You're walking around with a dead guy's—you know, I don't even want to know what it says. Burn it. Here." Nils delved into his jeans and produced a lighter. He flicked it on. "Get rid of it now."

"I thought you could look after it. Until I decide what to do."

Nils wiped up a few last crumbs of batter and scrunched up the paper. He tossed it into the bin.

"Think again. I'm not touching it. You give it to me, I'll burn it for you. I want nothing to do with their pretentious society."

"What I am going to do with it then? I can't give it to Adelaide."

"Why not? It's her letter."

"You don't get it. If I give it to her, she'll stop working with me. The only reason she's helping me is because she needs to find out what happened to her brother."

"And what if it's a fake?" Nils demanded. "What if it's a plant? Where did you even find the bloody thing?"

"This woman turned up at the door. Said if Axel went away, she'd been instructed to deliver this. Adelaide wasn't there and I was."

Nils shook his head. "Fucking hell. You're meant to be the smart one."

"I can't tell Adelaide."

"Why not? So she stops seeing you, so what? They're not going to take away your flat."

"I still need her. I can still use her."

Nils gave him a shrewd look. "I think you've gone past that."

"She's not a bad person, Nils."

"Fine, I believe you. Does that make her any less dangerous? You can't trust these people, Vik. They're eels, they'd turn on you in a second. Take you in, and spit you right back out. You should be trying to set yourself up, not holding out for some celebrity pin-up."

Vikram was angry at that. After all, Nils had encouraged him to go to the Rose Night in the first place. He was the one who'd suggested meeting Adelaide.

"You're determined not to give her a chance."

"How can I when I've never even met her?" Nils protested.

"You don't want to meet her."

"Well, she don't want to meet me. You see her coming down here? Dazzling us all with her presence? I don't think so. This is a game for her. And you knew that, before." Nils paused. The rest of the sentence, unsaid, hung in the air. "Look, Vik, I don't mean any harm. Maybe you really like this woman for whatever reasons I don't get. But if you're asking me for advice—and it seems like you are—I say you've got two options. You give her the letter and take the consequences, or you destroy it right now and pretend you never saw it. Your call."

Vikram fell silent. Nils didn't understand that the choice was much more subtle, more complicated than that. Vikram couldn't just destroy the final words of a dead man. It would be wrong. But neither could he show them to Adelaide. She was the only thing guiding him through this nest of eels. He couldn't lose her. Not yet.

Nils clapped him on the arm.

"Look, I've got to go. Just—" He broke off. His voice when he spoke again was strained. "Just don't forget what these people have done. Not just Eirik and Mikkeli. Osuwa, even the greenhouse, they're not that long ago. For all we know, our families died in the reprisals. Maybe at the hands of people you've met," he said pointedly.

Vikram winced. "Osuwa is complicated."

"What happened afterwards isn't. Giving Citizens guns? Murdering children? You know what they say. When the executions took place you could hear the shots right the way to the edge of the city, it was that quiet. Sound of a guilty conscience, I say."

Nils gave him a hard, almost a challenging look. He was driving the conversation into territory Vikram wasn't sure he wanted to cover. Not today.

He thought of what Shadiyah had said. *They is an elusive term.* But she had also told him something else: home was in the west.

"We could torture ourselves forever wondering about our families," he said. "But what good will it do us? Or them. It doesn't help them. They're beyond our help."

Nils shrugged. "Maybe. Maybe not."

"Come over and see the new place," said Vikram. "We can talk properly then." He wrapped up the remains of his fish. Suddenly he wasn't hungry.

"Sure." Nils still sounded reluctant.

"You don't want to?"

"No, it's not that." Nils screwed up his face in admission. "I've been sort of seeing that girl."

"The one I met? Ilona?"

"Yeah. Her."

It was Vikram's turn to be worried. He had hoped that Ilona was a one-off occurrence.

"I know what you're thinking," said Nils.

"Do you?"

"The answer's yes. She works on the boats."

Vikram remembered the dyed wing of hair. The averted gaze. "You mean she's a prostitute."

"She's a nice girl."

"It's not that she isn't nice and you know it. It's that she could get in real trouble for seeing you. You know what the shanty town's like, you've seen the corpses, what happens to those girls, we both have."

Nils's shoulders quivered. He squared them.

"I like her. I want to get her out."

"Well, why didn't you say before? I'll help you, we'll sort something out—"

Nils shook his head then bent double in a sudden convulsion of phlegmy coughs. Vikram stared at him.

"Are you alright? That doesn't sound good."

"I'm fine—" Nils cleared his throat. It was a loud, tearing sound.

"Are you sure?"

"I'm fine. And I know you would help me. But I want to get her out. Myself." He glanced at Vikram, wiped the back of his hand across his mouth. "Anyway, I think you've got enough to deal with."

They parted, each looking a little wearier than when they had met an hour before.

/ / /

The squall passed over the northern quarter, leaving a clear icy night. The boatman dropped them at the waterbike centre, where Adelaide stalked into the changing rooms without saying a word. Vikram followed her. He wanted an explanation, any kind of response. She gave none. She went to her locker and began taking out her clothes. The ordinariness of the action was too much for Vikram.

"Well?" he exploded. "Are you going to tell me exactly what you thought you were doing out there? You could have been killed!"

Finally she spoke.

"Don't be so dramatic, Vikram. You think I haven't had accidents before? The sea's unpredictable. I know what I'm doing."

Vikram banged open his own locker and yanked out his jeans. He began to change as quickly as possible.

"If I hadn't been there you would have drowned!"

"Don't give yourself so much credit," she snapped. "I wasn't drowning. You didn't give me a chance to drown before you yanked me out the water. I practically dislocated my shoulder."

"So next time I should leave you there, should I?"

"Maybe you should," she said. "Maybe you should just keep out of my affairs."

"You're the one that wanted to go out there."

"And you wanted to come. So stop acting like you've done me some kind of favour."

He shook his head. "You're an ungrateful bitch."

Adelaide shrugged. "Told you that when I met you." She presented him with her back.

He wanted to take hold of her shoulders and rattle her until the truth came out with her teeth. She began to peel off her wetsuit, top to bottom, stripping as though he wasn't there. She hung up the suit and walked naked into the showers. A moment later he heard the patter of water on her skin.

The first night he stayed in her bedroom, she'd passed out on him. He'd smelt the fumes of alcohol on her breath, seen almost invisible particles of green powder on her upper lip. She slept the deep, dead sleep of a body that rarely let go consciousness, and when it did, surrendered completely.

They had each set out to use the other, but the ties had become more complex than that. Now they were tangled in each other's lives.

He could smell the perfume of her shampoo rising with the hot water. She stepped out of the shower, towelling her hair. Everything about her actions said unconcern, but he didn't believe it. He couldn't.

"I thought by now you trusted me," he said. Adelaide sighed, as though she was surprised to find him still there. She rooted through her bag for a hairbrush, and attacked her hair with fierce strokes.

"I don't trust anyone."

"It didn't look like an accident."

She whipped round to face him. He saw then what there was to see, the anger and the fear.

"You know nothing about biking, Vikram."

"I know what I saw," he shot back. "So were you showing off, is that it? Or have you got some kind of death wish?"

Adelaide's hands clenched. "You insult me now? You'd accuse me of that, would you, accuse me of that—monstrosity? Go on, spit it out, say what you want to say!"

He looked at her.

"You fucking bastard." She hurled the hairbrush at him. It slammed against the metal locker and clattered to the floor. He bent and picked it up. There were dozens of strands of her hair caught in its bristles. Her face challenged him to lob it back.

He took a step away from the locker. "Why don't you answer the question."

Adelaide turned away. When she spoke, her words ricocheted off the wall.

"I snagged on a current. The bike veered. That's all there is to it. And don't you ever suggest that again."

She began to dress, twisting her arms behind her to hook up her bra and then her suspender belt. He had thought of the garments as camouflage, but the nights he'd spent holding that body naked had given him no further insights.

He tried one more time.

"Just tell me what happened. I want to understand—I have to understand. Or I'm out. Done."

Adelaide slipped into her heels. From head to toe, she looked immaculate. When she spoke, her voice was as stripped as it had been when she had said goodbye to him that very first time.

"You must really hate my family, Vikram. I am aware of this. What I don't get is, why don't you hate me too? After all, we've done some pretty terrible things, haven't we? Even I don't know the half of it."

"I'm not talking about your fucking family, Adelaide, I'm talking about *you*."

Adelaide continued as if he hadn't spoken. "So you probably do hate me too. You've probably hated me all along. This isn't really anything to do with the biking, is it? This is about you and me. And the truth is, there is no you and me. Oh, you've been entertaining for a while, I'll grant you that. But sooner or later, it had to end. It might as well be now."

She paused only to draw breath. It was as though she had become a mouth; every other part of her diminished.

"You know what, Vikram? I've been so caught up in your miserable activities, I've almost forgotten about what's important to me. Well, enough. I've got my own mission. I'm going to find my brother, and I'm not going to let anything distract me. Especially not some righteous westie trying to tell me how to run my life."

She flung each word at him like a specially prepared, poison tipped dart. He ignored their impact. Like all wounds, the sting would come later. But he couldn't suppress his rage. He almost blurted out about the letter, the truth about her brother, but some reserve of caution held him back. There was an alternative, and if Adelaide wanted to play dirty, he'd send it straight back at her.

"Maybe you're right," he said slowly. "Maybe we should be talking about how I hate your family. While we're at it, maybe we should talk about how you're exactly like them. You can give yourself a new name, but you can't change yourself, can you Adelaide? However hard you try to get away from it, you're just another Rechnov liar."

He knew that would hit home. He saw her eyes narrow and he pushed his advantage.

"You told me once that lying was the one thing you couldn't stand. But if we're honest, it's the thing you do best, isn't it?"

Her mask remained intact, but he knew her better now. He could hear the tiniest crack in her voice when she spoke again.

"If we're really being honest here, I have to say that you're delusional. Do you imagine anyone takes you seriously? You think your schemes will make one jot of difference? The Council will never remove the border. You're up against my lying bastard family, Vik, and they will never, *never* let you win."

He felt that. He felt it now, and he would feel it more later.

He had to get out.

"I feel sorry for you, Adie."

"Don't you dare call me that!"

"I'm done. Goodbye."

He hiked his bag onto his shoulder. Axel's letter was crumpled in the inside pocket of his coat. As he walked out, his lungs burned as though he were breathing in acid. But he had made his decision, and Adelaide had clearly made up her own mind. If she wouldn't give him his answers, he wouldn't give her hers.

33 | ADELAIDE

She switched on the changing room's hose and ran the jet of water rhythmically over the red suit and the green, first up and down, then in horizontal passes. The drain guzzled gently. With their lolling hoods and missing hands and feet, the suits reminded her of gutted fish. She thought of the executed man. She turned them over to wash the other sides. When she reached up to put the red suit back on its hook, she found she could not take the step away. Her legs had become rubber too.

She squatted on the tiles and pressed her face against the suit. The hose still bubbled in her hand, drenching her clothes. Her shoes sat in the scummy water running towards the drain. Now the gargling was vociferous. No, it wasn't the drain. The noise was in her own throat. She pressed her face close to the damp material, closer, until it hurt.

The tears streamed faster, but tears would not repair the damage she was doing, to Axel, to Vikram. Tears would not make the vault disappear, or spare the repercussions if Lao had, somehow, already found a way in. Tears were useless.

The noise subsided. With the silence that followed came a raw clarity. She lifted her head. For a long time she stared at the wall. She knew, as clearly as if she had been told, where she had to go. In the kelp forest, a sliver of mercury paused. The fish was waiting.

She hung the suits side by side to dry. In the changing room mirrors she caught a glimpse of her face. It was blotched with red, ugly. It didn't matter. She knew where she was going now. There was only one place left.

34 | VIKRAM

Linus's secretary ushered Vikram into the office. Linus was at his Neptune, his eyes flicking back and forth as he scanned the body of text. Some report or other, Vikram supposed. As Vikram came in, Linus stroked the activation strip and the screen went black.

"Vikram, good to see you. Can I get you a drink?"

"I'm fine, thanks."

Linus dismissed the secretary with a nod of his head. He rolled over a chair.

"Please, have a seat. What can I do for you?"

There was a sense of the mechanical about Linus's office. It contained mathematical lines, faintly humming machines. The walls held graphs and charts. The only other colour was a yellow rosette stuck to the window-wall. Vikram recognized it: one of Adelaide's invitations.

"Are you going to that?"

Linus looked and laughed.

"Certainly not. Adelaide and I have a deal."

Surprise must have shown in Vikram's face, because Linus added, "She sends me invites and I ignore them. It's a very simple arrangement. A little odd to outsiders, perhaps." Linus clasped his hands. "But Adelaide is still a Rechnov, whether she wants to be or not. Oh, she can play at society. She may even have some social influence, through that set of hers, and I admit that she's popular with the press. Eventually, though, she'll come back to us. She won't be able to help it."

Vikram kept his face still. Linus's words did not make him feel any better about what he was about to do; on the contrary, he was inclined to delay the decision. But it had to done. He could not allow Adelaide to jeopardise everything that he had worked for.

"So what is it you actually do here?" he asked. "Apart from attending Council meetings, that is."

"You don't think that's enough?" Linus allowed himself an ironic smile. "I can see your point. Well, when I'm not haranguing old men who should have left the Chambers years ago, I liaise with the meteorological office." He waved his arm in an encompassing gesture. "These charts are weather maps."

"You're mapping the weather?" Vikram stared curiously at the nearest chart. Linus watched him.

"It didn't use to be a phenomenon."

"Will it work?"

"One day. It would be easier, of course, if we had access outside. But for that to happen, we have to change mindsets, and Osirisers are stubborn. They believe they are living in the last city on earth—it has quite a ring to it, of course." Linus looked thoughtfully at the Neptune. "Almost... glamorous. But not true."

Vikram had a sudden sense of the scale of Linus's ambition. He wondered what future role Linus had in mind for himself—revolutionary charter of weather? Discoverer of distant shores? At this moment, on the verge of giving away Axel's secret, Vikram felt less certain of Linus than he was of Adelaide. But he was angry, and he needed someone on his side.

"Don't you think we would have been found by now? If there were still people out there—people on land?"

Linus turned his head, focusing gradually upon Vikram. Vikram sensed him sifting possible responses. As always when talking to Linus, he had that sense of his own insignificance; that it did not matter what Linus said to him, because nobody would ever believe an airlift's word over a Rechnov's. Then Linus's lips quirked in a thin smile.

"I suppose that depends upon whether we want to be found." He paused. "There's certainly a multitude of reasons why it's desirable not to be. Anyway, I could talk to you about this all day, Vikram, but I sense that's not entirely why you're here."

Vikram gave the yellow rosette a last glance. He reached inside his coat pocket and pulled out the envelope. Wordlessly, he placed it on the desk. Linus glanced down.

"It's from Axel," said Vikram.

He heard the intake of breath, slight but sharp, that followed. Seconds passed whilst the two of them stared at the envelope.

"I take it you're aware of the contents," said Linus.

Vikram nodded. Linus picked up the envelope, took out the letter, and unfolded it. He read in silence. Vikram knew the letter by heart. He could only imagine what magic Axel's phrases might be working on his brother.

When he had finished, Linus put the letter back in the envelope. Vikram noticed that the other man did not fold it in the right way; some of the creases were doubled back and the shape was all wrong. He pressed his hands together to stop himself reaching out to show Linus how it worked.

"Has Adelaide seen it?" Linus made as if to put the envelope down, then kept it in his hand.

"Not yet." He saw Linus take note of the qualifier. Good.

"How did you get it?"

He listened to Vikram's story without interrupting. His face was expressionless. Vikram felt his own unease growing as he continued, but it was too late to back out now. Linus's face creased in much the same way that Adelaide's did when she was tending to her balcony plants.

"Why did you bring it to me?"

Vikram strove for the same level of impassivity.

"Adelaide's helping me because she wants to find out what happened to Axel. If she knows, she'll stop. I can't keep this letter but I can't give it to her." Vikram shrugged. "You're the next logical option."

"You want to watch out, Vikram, you're getting quite Rechnovian."

Vikram said nothing.

"I think your assessment of Adelaide is correct," said Linus. "And I'm inclined to agree with your actions. My sister is doing something useful for the first time in her life—and you, Vikram, you've been instrumental in that. She doesn't need any—distractions."

"Not even if it means finding out the truth?"

Linus tapped the envelope.

"What does this tell us, really, Vikram? All this talk of missions. Horses.

It's not an answer."

"But you believe the letter is genuine."

"Yes." Linus was decisive. "I do. And for that reason, I think it's best that I keep it in the family. As they say. This investigation—it's put us in a very difficult position, as I'm sure you can understand. Axel generated enough publicity in his lifetime. We don't need any more. This way, the investigation can just... peter out."

"She's sure he's alive," said Vikram. "You do know that."

Linus loosened his collar slightly, pulling its tight starch away from his neck.

"Adelaide is sure about a lot of things," he said. "Besides, as we said— what does a letter prove?" He looked at Vikram directly. "Thank you for trusting me with this. I trust I can show my appreciation in some way— lean on the Council for those extensions to the aid schemes? Perhaps have a look at the flooded buildings?"

"You can do both of those. Will you show her the letter?"

"Of course. In time." Linus glanced up at the clock. "Now don't think I'm trying to get rid of you, but I have a meeting to get to."

"It's fine. I've got places to be myself."

Linus shrugged on his jacket, tucking the envelope into his inside pocket. Vikram felt the weight of it then; his part in what must now be a conspiracy between himself and Linus. From this moment Vikram would carry that knowledge around with him like a microchip embedded in his brain. It would surface every time he saw an image of Adelaide's face, or heard her voice on the o'dio. The thought that he would probably never see her in person again hit him with a terrible wave of loneliness.

A low burring noise jolted him out of his thoughts. Linus hooked in an earpiece and slid his Sobek scarab into one pocket.

"Hello?" He picked up a slim briefcase and mouthed to Vikram, "I'll walk out with you."

Vikram opened the door and Linus stepped out with him, passing an electronic key over the lock.

"I'll be there in ten. Yes... I've got the whitefly notes." At the entrance to his offices, he pressed his wrist to Vikram's. Then he walked away, confident in his pinstriped suit, a man at ease in every way that Vikram was not; with himself, with his place and with his times. Vikram felt his own wrongness like a physical ailment. To the west, he had treated with the enemy, even if it was for their own good. To the City, he would always be an impostor. Only Adelaide had accepted him for what he was, and Adelaide was a liar, and now he had betrayed her and her twin.

35 | ADELAIDE

Boats with black hulls and crudely painted eyes slunk down the border, each vessel thick with Guards. Dark, bulky overcoats and furred hats hid their features, but the men bristled with guns.

Adelaide sat in the stern of the speedboat, hunched over, gloved hands at her chin. She stared determinedly westward through the checkpoint. She had been out here for thirty minutes, watching; she could no longer feel the exposed parts of her face or her feet. Gulls flapped overhead, pale and sharp beaked against the overcast sky. Their raucous calls pierced the cold air. Adelaide did not move.

The boatman gave her an exasperated look.

"Miss, haven't you seen enough?"

"No."

He folded his arms, sighing loud enough for her to hear.

Every waterbus that came out of the west was stopped. Each time, the officer in charge boarded the waterbus and forced its passengers to form a line. He walked the length of the line, pausing in front of some passengers, barely glancing at others. The officer carried a stick with which he rapped the decking in time to his footsteps, and she could tell by the dull contact sound that it was made of metal.

Beyond the checkpoint and the border net, western pyramids and scrapers rose grim and sallow. Faded graffiti covered the towers, layer upon layer, angry slogans and figures like manga cartoons, frozen in action—mid-leap, mid-punch. Their oversized eyes followed her across the border.

Further in, she could make out more boats, or things that had been coaxed to float, rafts and metal basins, clustered around the bases of the towers. There were shapes inside the boats and propped up on the deckings. Their movements were slow and laboured. At first she did not realize they were people. They moved like another race, one long lost and forgotten.

This was it. The last place.

For the first time since that day, she allowed the execution scene to crystallise in her memory, looking at it without flinching. Looking at it from Vikram's side.

"We're going across," she told the boatman. He stared at her as if she was crazy. Perhaps I am, she thought. Crazy like Axel. He'd have to be crazy to come here, and she knew suddenly that her instinct was right.

"I'm afraid I can't go any further, Miss."

"I'm ordering you to take the boat across."

"Miss, with all due respect, I'm not going to. Your father would have a fit."

"My father can go hang himself."

"Your father's orders come above your own, Miss Rechnov. There's no way in Osiris I'm taking you into the west. Do you want to be shot?"

She wanted to hit him for the way he was looking at her, defiantly, insolently, but more than that—as though she was something to be contained, even pitied. She clenched her teeth.

"I have to cross the border, Foma."

How long they might have argued for in the bitter cold, she would not find out, because another dispute, louder than theirs, carried over the water. A waterbus had stopped at the checkpoint. The shouting was between the officer and one of the passengers. Adelaide could see those not involved fidgeting, the other passengers anxiously, the Guards with a twitching impatience.

Uneasily now, she watched as the officer hauled the passenger out of the line and off the boat, onto the jetty. He jerked him along the decking and thrust him onto his knees.

"Miss, miss, we should really go now."

Foma shook her shoulder gently, but she felt it with the force applied to the passenger.

"Miss, you don't want to see this."

The officer lifted his stick, high above his head. It cracked through the air. A scream was quickly muffled. The officer leaned over to wipe the weapon against the man's coat. He stepped away, twisting his wrist.

At a sign, four of the Guards gathered around the man. Systematically, they delivered a series of kicks and blows until he shrivelled against the decking. At first there were no sounds other than that of impact. Then he began to shriek.

It took barely a minute, and his face was no longer recognizable as a face.

One of the women on the boat turned away with a moan of horror. A Guard marched her to the rail and pinched her chin, forcing her to watch. Adelaide saw the woman's body convulse as she retched.

"Miss, come on. Let's go."

The boatman reached for the ignition, but Adelaide put her hand over it.

"Wait."

The officer in charge raised a hand. The beating stopped. The man's howls grew shakier. The officer stepped forward, put the muzzle of his gun against the man's head, and pulled the trigger. Two Guards took the wrists and ankles, and slung the body into the sea.

The dead man floated, his ruined face to the clouds.

"Miss, can we go now?" Foma's voice had lost all its anger; now it was pleading. Adelaide nodded, numbly. She felt the boat gear into life, knew there must be something she should do, but was incapable of finding words or means. As the speedboat whirred away, three or four seagulls began spiralling downwards. Knowing their intent, she clamped her hands over her mouth, suppressing a noise of horror and disgust that one reborn soul could do that to another.

/ / /

Adelaide opened the balcony door and shut it quickly behind her before the rush of cold could change her mind. Clouds hung low in the darkening sky, their bellies distended with unfallen snow. She sensed the City holding its breath, and held hers with it.

It was unusual for Tyr to want a meeting this early in the evening—Jannike's birthday celebrations had barely begun—but she was glad of the opportunity. She had made a decision: she was going to tell Tyr everything. About Lao, about the airlift and the vault, about Operation Whitefly. It was a relief. She had to tell someone, and she had alienated Vikram. But she didn't want to think about that.

Once she had told Tyr, they could work out what to do next.

The balcony door opened and shut again behind Tyr. He did not have a coat either.

"We'll catch our death," she said with a smile.

Tyr walked slowly across the balcony and stopped a metre away from her. They were both shivering. Adelaide took a step toward him.

"You're sleeping with Vikram, aren't you?"

The question caught her off-guard. She had assumed he knew; she had not thought he would ask.

"Yes."

"How long have you been seeing him for?"

His grey eyes watched hers. She tried to mirror their blankness. He knew her face so well. They had learned one another like books by rote; a dip of the head, a blink, could act as code.

"Oh, I don't know—"

"How long?"

"Couple of weeks."

"You're lying."

She lowered her eyes strategically.

"It's just a diversion. It's over."

"He stays here. You stay with him."

She felt her way carefully around this iceberg.

"He's a westerner. It annoys Feodor more."

"I see."

"I don't think—"

"No. I get it."

A tiny snowflake whirled out of the sky. Another chased it, then another, and another, and all at once they were surrounded by a maze of swirling shapes. They landed cold darts on Adelaide's face. They blew onto Tyr's scarf and the sleeves of his jacket.

"I can't keep doing this, Adelaide."

She saw his lips moving, but they did not seem to match the words that came out. It was not really Tyr talking. The person who replied was not really Adelaide.

"What are you talking about?"

"I'm talking about you and me." He sounded almost gentle now, and that made him more distant because the Tyr that she knew had no need for softness.

"We have to stop," he said.

"But there's no need," she said. "Tyr, why—"

"Adelaide—" His voice broke her name. "The terms of our agreement—I can't stand by them any longer."

He looked away. Now the flakes were coming thick and fast, a sheet, then a quilt of snow, and there was nothing to see, only her and Tyr at the centre of a shaken paperweight. She reached out and touched his sleeve. It was thin and wet and reminded her of blood. She thought of the western man dumped off the jetty, felt herself caught in that same hopeless motion.

"Why not?"

He moved his arm away.

"Because—I love you, Adie."

She tried to read his face, to unearth some aggression there, anger or blame, something strong that she could grasp with both hands and fight. She found only sadness.

"But you can't," she said. "I'm not that person."

"Then I am. And I can stand the pretence, I can stand the lies—I've enjoyed that game, I don't deny it. But seeing you let someone else into your life—I won't do that."

"What, you think he means something to me? He doesn't. None of them do. Only maybe—he reminds me a little of Axel. That's it. That's all."

You mean something to me. The thought, dormant at the back of her mind, suddenly clarified. But she could not say it.

Tyr sighed. "Let's face it, Adie. We can't be together. Even if you wanted it, we couldn't."

"Don't say that. We can do what we like."

He gave a helpless smile.

"I'd lose my position. Feodor would disinherit you. I'm his spy Adie—you know that. You've always known. Every month I write him a report. What you're doing, who you're seeing. Lies, years and years of lies. He finds that out and what then?"

"I don't know."

"I do. Then nothing. You want to get a job, run away to the west? We're creatures of habit, you and I. We like our lifestyles. We're both too selfish to give them up, and anyway, what compensation would there be for you."

There was an ache in her teeth and in her ribs where her lungs constricted. It was the cold. It was the cold.

"I can't care about anyone," she whispered.

"That's right. You can't care about anyone."

He sounded infinitely weary. It made her see them both standing there, the snow settling on their hair and faces, resting on her eyelashes, in the corners of her eyes, where new snow was being made in hot, brittle flakes. He was going to walk away. He was going to abandon her.

"I need you," she managed. "There are things I have to tell you."

She felt flooded with the weight of it, almost frantic.

"Tyr, please—for stars' sake—"

"You've had years to tell me anything you wanted, Adie. What could there possibly be left to say? Listen, I'm sorry it's early. I knew I had to talk to you, I wanted to be lucid when I did."

On his right temple was a tiny scar; she knew it was from a childhood accident but she did not know what the accident was. She knew everything and nothing about him. She had run out of time.

"And what now? We both go back and—pretend?"

"Like we always have. You're a good enough actress, Adie."

"But you can't—you can't just walk away."

"I can," he said. "And I will. One of us always has."

He lifted her chin gently. For a long time he gazed at her face. Then he pressed his lips lightly to her forehead. She closed her eyes.

"Goodbye, Adelaide," he whispered.

She didn't hear him go inside. Her head was full of the sound of snow. The City had never seemed so cold and unyielding, and all at once she hated it.

"Adelaide! Where were you? We're about to leave!"

"I'm ready, Jan."

"Come on, everyone, we're moving out! Got a shuttle to catch and a pool to find!"

"Everyone follow the crazy woman."

"Out everyone, out, out, you too Adie, OUT!"

This wasn't meant to happen.

They went to the Strobe. The first liquid cascaded into her mouth like oxygen as the music bombed her skull. She kept it on her tongue. She wanted to burn. Then she swallowed and swallowed until the glass was empty. She lifted her glass and the server leaned over to refill it. She repeated the ritual twice. When she swam away from the bar, the world was the way it usually was—bright and shifting. A boy dressed as a puff-fish snorkelled past. The sight of the ruptured scales made her feel nauseous. She found Jannike on a pink plastic float. Jannike slid off the float and they water-danced. Two reeds. Her limbs weird in the water. The music was phenomenal. Someone gave them fin-shaped pills which they put on each other's wrists and licked off. Her vision fizzled. The music grew louder. Quieter when she slipped underwater.

"Fu-u-ck." Jannike's voice filtered down, strangely elongated. "Magda Linn's here."

Adelaide opened her eyes underwater. Her hair swirled around her head. A girl's legs scissored slowly in the neon blitzed water. Red lights. Green lights. White flashing lights that were not part of the club's rigging but somehow lost in it.

"How—she—get—?" Jannike burbled. Adelaide surfaced.

Where there had been people there was space. The large pool bare and strip-lit, littered with the debris of the night—plastic glasses, stolen bikinis, deflated floats. Overhead, the multicoloured spotlights had swivelled to a halt, but the tower still rotated and lights from outside swept in bars over the pool. Jannike's elbow hooked into Adelaide's. The tug of Jan's arm. Bouncers herded out the stragglers. Voices echoed in the open space.

"Where to, Jan?"

"The late lounge, Adie."

An ankle twisted. Not sure if it was hers or Jan's but they almost fell. She felt the pain for both of them. Flashing lights, right in their faces. *Look this way, girls! Lovely!*

The waterbeds engulfed them like a dream. A woman brought two pipes. The smoke made haloes of their heads. Jannike's lips struggled through the crusts of their lipstick.

"What's the matter, Adie? I know something's the matter."

Adelaide knew Jannike would forget this night. She would forget it too. Part of her already had.

"My family are murderers," she said. "A boat came and they killed everyone on it."

"Yeah?"

"And I biked into a ship. I don't know what I was doing—I had this idea that Axel might be hiding there, and if he saw—he'd have to come find me—but he didn't so he couldn't be there, he's got to be in the west, it's the only place left—"

"I'm old, Adie. I'm twenty-two. I'm ancient."

"That's half a life, in the west."

"Stars, Adie." Jannike drew deeply on the pipe and halfway through exhaling, yawned deeply. "I tell you *I'm old*, ancient old, and you come out with... you know what's weird, I can't work out... how Magda Linn managed to get in..."

Her eyes turned upwards in her head. Adelaide did not understand at first that her friend was unconscious. Then Jannike's pipe clattered to the floor and she knew she should pick it up, but she could only stare at it, the pipe lying useless on the crisscross matting, until the proprietress came to retrieve it and gave Jannike a glance, and then lay the pipe, extinguished, on a round wooden dish beside her. Adelaide inhaled and somewhere in that one breath time unfolded and dissolved.

Hours later she walked home. She climbed over the barrier and walked along the double snail trails of the Pharaoh shuttle line, from the south quarter to the east quarter, where she walked twenty flights upstairs to jump the barrier to the Sphinx line. Her sandals made blisters on her feet. She took the shoes off and walked barefoot. The silver tracks were cool.

Her fingers stretched out to touch the convex, translucent wall.

Once a night shuttle streaked past, blind and pilotless, and she pressed her spine to the bufferglass and cringed her stomach inward in the slipstream blast.

She passed a siding where a group of shuttle pods were lodged. Lights were on in the repair stations behind and she heard the sounds of machinery. A man in overalls carrying a tool kit came around a shuttle. He stared at her. Grease darkened patches of his face. She gazed back at him, clutching her shoes tightly. Neither of them spoke. He passed an arm over his face and then he got to the ground and slid under the shuttle and his hand shot out and grabbed a tool and disappeared again.

Dawn began to crack the night's rigid cocoon. The city was rousing. Maintenance men and cleaners collected behind the barriers of the stations, smoking a last cigarette before the day's work began.

"Hey! Hey, miss! What you doing down there?"

She looked around, then up. A man stood on a platform. She squinted.

"You're on the shuttle line," he said.

Adelaide did not reply. He reached out a hand. She let him help her up onto the platform where he peered closer at her face but she turned her head away.

"What scraper is this?"

"S-one-nineteen," came the reply, and Adelaide knew she was close, now, to her destination.

She padded out of the platform to where a vendor was setting up his stand, laying out energy bars and fruit. The newsreel ran across a screen attached to the stand. His eyes followed her as she climbed the stairs to the footpath that ran over the line. Stumbling now, her feet guided her along the last few stops.

The key was the wrong shape for the lock and it took her several tries to force it in. A shadow passed as the lift went up, past her floor to the meteorological facility. The door gave way at last. She fell forward into the hall of mirrors. Home.

/ / /

Dream fragments chased one another through her head; Jannike, aged thirteen, arguing with Feodor. Lightning struck both of them and burned their faces but neither died, they kept arguing, and she realized it wasn't Feodor but the man from the border with no face, the water parting to receive his body, and white horses were running on the sea, leaping one over the back of the other. Their hooves made a horrendous noise, drumming the ocean with a tattoo that called the world to arms.

Adelaide woke suddenly. She was in bed, face down. She had forgotten to darken the window-wall and the room was full of lancing sunbeams. She screwed up her eyes. The noise of galloping hooves resolved into a persistent banging. There was someone at the door. Someone insistent.

Turning her head, she saw how the night had ended. The decanter, empty, an arm's length away. The glass knocked onto its side. A bottle of pills she hoped she hadn't taken and the grey dune of the ashtray. The smell of stale ash was a physical assault.

Adelaide groaned. She sat up just before she thought of Tyr and then she reeled forward, head to knees, and thought she might be sick there and then. Her mouth tasted of sour milk. She caught a glance of herself in the mirror; make-up blackening her eyes, her hair latticed. She pulled on her kimono, scrubbed her teeth and splashed water into her face before going to the door. Every bang drove another nail into her skull.

Tyr? Vikram? Her heart squeezed.

She slid the bolt across and opened the door a crack. Disappointment barbed her.

"Linus?"

He barged through the gap. In one white knuckled hand he clutched his briefcase.

"Where the fuck have you been? I've been trying to get hold of you all day."

"I've been sleeping." She followed him back into the apartment, massaging her temples.

"Your beeper's off—"

"I never use that thing."

"I've been calling since eight o'clock, you don't answer, I only just managed to get out of the office. Father's been fielding questions all afternoon. Even Mother came up here and knocked, nobody could get hold of you—"

His voice was bringing on her headache in full force, and with it, everything that sleep had let her forget. She tried to concentrate. She had to get rid of him.

"I was out, Linus. Then I was sleeping. My scarab's probably run dry. What's going on?"

Linus glared at her. A wisp of morning shadow on his upper lip and jaw. Linus was always clean shaven.

He propped his briefcase on the table and yanked it open. The contents spilled onto the floor. Linus grabbed a Surfboard and dangled it in front of her.

"You haven't seen this, I take it?"

Adelaide peered at the screen. Her own face greeted her, eyes unfocused, mouth slurred. She looked a mess. Last night's events reassembled themselves slowly. She remembered the pool. The pills.

"What have I done now?" she asked wearily.

Linus shoved the Surfboard towards her as if he was too disgusted to speak. She bent to pick it up. The words seemed jumbled; they did not make sense. They could not, because how could anyone possibly know? Shakily, letter by letter, her finger followed the newreel headline.

Adelaide Rechnov breaks investigation decree.

"Oh shit," she whispered.

Below the initial hideous picture was a grainy but unmistakable image: herself and Vikram entering the penthouse.

"I think you'll find that's one of the better headlines," said Linus. His face was steady now, nastily so, a gull about to skewer a fish.

Her legs stopped working. She had to sit down. She knelt where she was. Her kimono divided over her knees; mindlessly she smoothed out the silk. She flicked from one newsfeed to another. *Adelaide and western lover Vikram flout committee... Adelaide uses criminal friend for break-in... Adelaide finds new vocation... Adelaide's new love-shack?*

It didn't end there. Selecting the *Daily Flotsam* feed, she found full-colour evidence of last night. There were photos of her and Jan, naked on a pink float, entwined with two girls that Adelaide did not remember. She had a dim memory of Jannike shouting that she had seen Magda Linn, although her friend had not known then that Adelaide had betrayed her.

"How..." Her voice faltered. Linus's shoes shifted angrily.

"You idiot, you bribed someone to cut the camera, didn't you? Apparently Hanif had a feeling you'd try it on. He promised to match any bribe you might offer. The camera was recording the whole time."

Words and pictures advanced and receded in front of her.

"But why now? It doesn't make sense… If they had this—why wait until now, why would Hanif…?"

"Hanif's in the middle of a Council-authorised investigation, it doesn't help him to throw this information to the press. But you can guarantee that some lowlife scum in his team has just made a fat payload leaking this. And believe me, we will find out who it is."

She went hot and cold. So Sanjay Hanif had been hoarding this information all along, waiting for the optimum moment to pounce. Only his thunder had been stolen before he had the chance. Sweat trickled between her breasts.

"Where's Vikram?" He must have seen it already. She swallowed. "He'd better come over."

"He's not coming."

"I have to speak to him." The sunlight, skittering off polished surfaces, was blinding. She imagined reporters in the adjacent towers, their cameras trained on her windows whilst they scanned the feeds, rereading, joking amongst themselves, relishing her humiliation.

"Vikram will be safest here," she said. She spotted her scarab in the bowl on the table. "Then we can work out what to do."

"Has it not occurred to you that this fiasco ran first thing this morning? It's fifteen o'clock. Vikram's on his way to jail, if he isn't there already. Father's pulling strings like a marionette to keep the police away from you. Congratulations, Adelaide! Not content with wrecking your own life, you have to drag everyone else down with you."

Linus touched a finger to his earpiece. His expression changed: settled and ironed out, before he spoke again. "Father, hello."

"Jail," she repeated. She remembered Vikram locking up the penthouse door. *We're in it together.* Vikram had not said that, but it was true now. They would take him back underwater, to the green cell and the eye of the porthole, unless she stopped them. The kimono stuck to her clammy skin. Her muscles felt weak, useless. *Ignore it.*

She needed a plan. She needed Linus gone so she could clear her head. *Think, Adelaide, think.*

Linus took a few steps towards the window. He was nodding to himself. "Right, yes. Did you get onto the *Flotsam*? Yes, I understand. Ten minutes? No problem, I'll hang on." The conversation ended abruptly.

"How's Daddy?" she asked.

Linus folded his arms. "This isn't the time for flippancy. Father's not happy. He's putting you under house arrest."

"How old does he think I am, six?"

"Judging by your actions, yes. He's sending Goran."

Her mouth dropped in horror.

"*Goran?* He can't send Goran here…" She thought of the eye tattoo on the back of the bodyguard's neck. His real eyes, dual toned, searching. Every nerve in her body twanged. "Linus, you cannot be serious!"

"Apparently Father is. You've overstepped the line, Adelaide. He's fed up with it. We all are. The more licence we give you the more you throw it back in our faces."

She lurched to her feet. Red and green dots speckled her vision.

"Licence for what?" she shouted. "Not to be like you? Well, sorry if I'm not interested in your political machinations. I have my own life. We both do. Me and Axel. We're nothing like you." She jabbed a finger an inch from his chest. Linus surveyed her, unconcernedly. When he spoke, every word was crisp with contempt.

"Spending our money getting high every night and flaunting yourself for the *Daily Flotsam*'s pornographic photographers? Fucking our father's employees? Frankly, Adelaide, it's boring. Father has tried just about everything with you. He's asked you to tone down the parties and cut back on the milaine. He's appealed to you as a Rechnov, but you have no sense of familial duty. I've even tried giving you an outlet to do something useful with the aid schemes. Nothing seems to make a difference. Nothing makes you *see*. There's a whole line-up of people out there who would love to see our family eating surf, Adelaide. You've jeopardized our position one too many times. Now you've forced Father to take drastic measures. Goran's coming to housesit."

"Like fuck he is! I won't let him over the threshold."

"You'll do what we decide is best for you. You're so selfish you can only think about yourself right now. But if you looked beyond this narcissistic paradise, you might realize that *this*—" the Surfboard in Linus's hand shook. His voice was rising opposite hers. "This has greater ramifications than you being grounded. This article questions the whole family's integrity. You had a chance to prove yourself. You've thrown that away. You've pissed, Adelaide, on my fucking career."

Adelaide was trembling with shock and fury.

"Selfish, Linus? Listen to yourself! You haven't even asked what I was doing in the penthouse. Aren't you curious? Don't you want to know what happened to your brother?"

Linus hurled the Surfboard at a plant. It hit the pot and landed beside it. The screen went blank.

"I don't give a shit what you were doing there," he spat. "This is a containment issue. Bribing a member of a *Council investigation*—how the hell does that make Father look?"

Adelaide could not remember ever seeing Linus lose control. It was like a rock cracking and gushing forth water.

"Our father cares more about his reputation than he does about his own son." She was shaking.

"Don't bring Axel into it!"

"Why not? He's what's important!"

"He's dead. Wake up, Adelaide! Stars above, it's hard enough trying to mourn him without you raking these insane theories over our heads day in, day out—"

"How do you know unless Feodor had him murdered? Did Goran do it? Did he? And now he's coming to sort me out?"

"Don't be fucking stupid."

"Then tell me the truth!"

Linus's hands went to his head, kneading and clenching. An animal noise came out of his throat. "You just—don't—get it."

"I never did," she said.

On the table, her scarab was flashing. An inbound call. Lao, she thought numbly. I know that's Lao. Her fingers itched.

There was a knock at the door. Neither of them moved. A second knock. Finally Linus went. Goran strolled into the room, a holdall and a brown paper bag in one hand, a mango in the other. He wore the usual dark blue suit, specially tailored to fit his heavy, muscular frame. His head had been recently shaved. It was pale and shiny.

"Hi AD," he said. "Long time no see."

His neat white teeth bit into the mango, skin and all.

"Don't you dare call me that," she hissed. "Get him out of here, Linus, I'm not even dressed."

"It never seems to bother you anywhere else." Linus extended his hand. Goran juggled mango and bags until he could press his wrist to Linus's.

Adelaide yanked the cord of her kimono taut. She could not miss anything they might say.

"Never was too polite, was she?" commented Goran. He did not seem to care whether he received an answer. He ambled around the room, sucking gently on the flesh of the mango, touching things with his tattooed fingers. Perspiration collected on Adelaide's scalp. Her own sweat felt unclean.

"Don't touch that," she said, as his fingers hovered over a photograph of the twins. Goran paused, as if he might obey, then picked it up.

"Interesting place." He pulled back the red and orange curtain that hung from the mezzanine and peered into the space beneath. "Nice den. Guess I'll be sleeping here." He nudged the sofa with his leg. Adelaide froze.

Goran let the curtain drop and wandered towards the kitchen.

"Linus—" she said.

Her brother closed his briefcase and patted the left breast of his jacket. "What, Adelaide?"

"You can't do this. That man—cannot stay in my apartment." Linus shrugged and made for the hallway. She ran in front of the door. "You can't leave him here! This is my home!"

"It's Rechnov property, Adelaide." Linus smiled. "And as you keep reminding us, you've got a different name now. Mystik, isn't it?"

"You bastard." Her voice shook. From the kitchen she heard the sounds of breaking glass and running water. "What the hell's he doing?"

"Getting rid of your alcohol, I think. Move away from the door. Or shall I get Goran to remove you?"

Keep calm, Adelaide. She put her hands up. "Okay, okay. Joke's over. Now let's sit down and talk about this rationally."

"Adelaide," Linus hissed. "I have to things to do. Our father and I are attempting to clear up the enormous pile of shit you have landed us in. Now get out of my way." He shouldered past her and wrenched open the door. She wrapped her fingers around the frame, only just removing them before he slammed it. A key turned in the lock. Her eyes darted to the bowl on the table. He had taken her scarab as well. The bowl was empty.

"Linus!" she screamed.

There was no answer. She pressed her ear to the door. Nothing.

"Linus!"

There was another smash. Her stomach lurched. For a second she thought she heard pots and pans clanging; it was not Goran in the kitchen, it was Axel.

It was Goran. He was emptying a crystal decanter of raqua down the sink. The warm amber fluid winked in the afternoon sunlight. Adelaide grabbed his arm. The smell of a dozen mingled alcohol fumes rose from the sink. Orange and blue liquids made rainbows with broken glass. Goran stopped pouring. With Adelaide clinging to his arm, he smashed the decanter quite deliberately against the sink. Crystal flew. The jagged edge glinted in his hand. She saw specks of his blood. Goran smiled at her.

"Don't be naughty, now, AD. You know I can break you and it would be a real pleasure."

He flung out his arm. She spun backwards and slammed against the wall. Her eyes watered with the impact.

"Did you kill my brother?"

"He didn't need me for that, AD."

"You're evil."

She staggered out of the kitchen. This was not happening, not to her. Her family were despots, but they were rational people.

Goran worked systematically through the apartment. He ripped the sheets off her bed and lifted the mattress. He rifled through her clothes, pulling dresses off hangers and trampling over them. He wrenched open the balcony door and chucked out the dragon teapot, a gift from Tyr. He emptied her sleeping pills down the sink.

Within half an hour, the apartment was strewn with her possessions. Satisfied, Goran reclined on the futon and put his feet up. He produced a bunch of grapes from the brown paper bag. One by one, the green ovals disappeared into the dark cavity of his mouth.

"Just you and me, AD," he said conversationally. "Anything good on the o'vis?"

The shakes began in the centre of her head and they rippled to her muscles. Her legs, her arms, even her eyes twitched uncontrollably. She could not stop it, she could not think of anything but it. She became a living pulse.

The ceiling had grown a strange shape. It had wings and a segmented body. It was an insect, a fly, the colour of falling snow. It crawled inside the vault. It crawled on the collar of the man in the lift. Operation White-fly lived upstairs; all along, it had lived in the facility upstairs.

They were not measuring the weather up there. They were watching for boats. Like the Siberian boat which had found the City, whose crew they had murdered, whose bones now rested on the ocean bed. And if a boat came, they would destroy it. This was her grandfather's dark secret.

But it was too late for realizations. The gulls were descending. Their wings rustled sheerly. Her body and mind were riddled and the birds found hooks for their beaks, delved hard and deep. Their button eyes bore no pity. They were pulling her apart. She knew, when they had dismantled her completely, they would bear each piece of her in their mouths to some far flung corner of the ocean. The birds would feed her to their fledglings.

36 | VIKRAM

He opened the door. They grabbed him roughly and threw him face-first against the wall. He heard the contact crack and thought for a moment they had broken his nose but the blood did not come, just quick splitting pain. Someone locked a pair of handcuffs on him. He heard the word arrest. He didn't listen to the rest because he already knew why they were there. There could only be one reason. They had found out about the break-in.

"Get me a lawyer," he said through gritted teeth pushed into the plaster, and a voice warmly close to his ear replied.

"Airlifts don't warrant lawyers, Mr Bai."

He kicked back at that, catching someone because there was a yelp of pain. They retaliated, knocking his legs out from underneath him. With his hands behind his back and nothing to stop his fall he smashed against the floor. This time his nose did break. The blood gushed from his nostrils and he floundered in it. A boot pushed into the small of his back.

"Especially those who resist arrest," he heard. Laughter followed. He could not see a single face but he knew it was the skadi, not the civilian police force. He knew it by their taunts and their glee. Every gut instinct ached to respond. These were the bastards who had killed Mikkeli. Who had killed Eirik. The boot had him pinioned. All he could do was twitch and splutter. He heard the spark of a lighter and smelt cigarette smoke through his blood. Hot ash stung the back of his neck. Half his instinct said gurgle, start to drown, then they'll have to take you to hospital. But it was only too easy to record an accidental death. Especially an airlift death.

The skadi were in no hurry. They joked over his head. After a minute the door opened and footsteps rapped the floorboards. A woman crouched at Vikram's head. Vikram could not see her face, only her shiny black boots, heels just lifted from the floor, beneath a black and white photograph on a Surfboard. The image was grainy but what it contained was unmistakable.

The woman tapped the Surfboard.

"This is a still from a section of footage taken from a security camera outside a private residence. Date, April twenty-four, hour, three-oh-five. The residence was and remains under Council jurisdiction. The couple in question use a stolen high-security swipe card to disable the police barrier, then pick the penthouse locks with crude metal before entering and leaving approximately fifty minutes later. This evidence serves as a warrant for arrest and detention. Is this you, Mr Bai?"

"No," he lied.

"I should also add that the evidence in question is sufficient to ensure jail without trial, should it be proven that you have a prior offence." Her hand came towards his head with a test tube. She held it under his nose. He tried to turn his head away but the blood dripped in. She passed the test tube up to someone standing. "Your DNA will ascertain whether you have a record. Do you have any prior convictions, Mr Bai?"

"No." He spat out blood. Not under that name. They would find it anyway. His skin began to crawl with fear. "Listen," he croaked. "I need to speak to a lawyer. Call Linus Rechnov. He'll vouch for me. I'm running the New Horizon Movement. I need to speak to people. I need a scarab, I need a lawyer—"

The officer stood up. "You can take him away."

"Listen to me!"

Two of them hauled him to his feet, nose still streaming. His face throbbed. He could feel where the bone had split.

The skadi shunted him to the lift, wrestling and kicking. Black space rushed to fill his vision. He was aware of shouting, a terrible screaming, did not realize at first that it was his own voice making that sound. His heels dug trenches in the floor. Pairs of eyes peered curiously from behind their doors as the lift began to bear him inexorably down.

He saw the porthole looming, the cold unearthly cell. He realized that his noise was words.

"Not underwater," he was screaming. The same words, over and over again. "Not underwater, not underwater, not underwater."

The fist came towards his temple. There was a pin burst of pain and then nothing.

/ / /

The teeth chattered in his head. He heard their clicking, one against the other, as if from miles away. His mouth was sore. He could not feel the rest of his face and he could not see. He panicked that he was blind and crawled his hands bit by bit up to his face, expecting to feel the open sightless orbs but it was the skin of his eyelids, clogged and somehow immovable. He thought he heard a voice, then there was an eruption of pain, something cold and wet in the centre of his face. The voice faded. He was deaf as well as blind.

His eyelids peeled open, pulling away from their crusts. He blinked, breathed in cold air, blinked again. He was lying on a bunk in a cell. The light was glaucous. It smelled of salt and damp and slow corrosion.

The space seemed no larger, no smaller than the last time. The walls were concrete. It was empty except for a bucket and the bunk he was lying on. Thin mattress. No pillow. They had patched up his nose, but he could still taste old blood. He touched it with fingertips that withdrew quickly when he felt the tender flesh. Whatever they had done, it was not set properly. His fingers explored upward, over the bump on his right temple. At least they had missed his eye.

He sensed, somehow, that he was further underwater than before. The porthole was obscured by algae. Fish swimming by were no more than shadows in a murky well.

His mind jumped between terror and rationale. He lay very still and ordered himself not to scream.

/ / /

"Adelaide Rechnov to see you." The guard's voice through the shutter was flat.

"I don't want to see her."

The guard opened the door. Adelaide came in. She was wearing a black trouser suit and tinted glasses and her hair was tied back in a tail. It gave her an androgynous look. Under the light of the cell, the pale peaks of her cheeks and the pointed chin took on a green tinge, watery and opaque. She reminded him of a mythical creature risen from the depths. A siren. An undine. He could smell scent on her, the sharp citrus one she wore sometimes. He had watched her apply that scent to hidden parts of her body.

"Thank you," said Adelaide to the guard, a gesture that was also a dismissal. The guard glanced from Vikram to Adelaide and then left. The door clanged shut.

"Hello, Vikram," she said.

He stayed as he was on the bunk, half sitting half crouched, arms balanced on knees and fingers interlocked. Adelaide's eyes flitted about. They did not pause for long; there wasn't much to see. The walls, the damp, the bunk. He saw her note the porthole and cursed himself for ever having mentioned it to her. With that weakness he had given her access to something deeply personal. He was a fool.

"Lovely place you've got here," she said. The joke was absorbed into the stifling air. Adelaide's handbag dangled at her side. The bag was awkward, out of place. She seemed to realize this, because her fingers clenched and unclenched on its strap. He let her squirm. Her eyes settled on his face and he saw them widen.

"You're hurt," she said.

He did not reply. A broken nose was obvious to anyone, and as they hadn't fixed it properly it would always be crooked now. Adelaide ploughed on.

"I'm so sorry about this, Vikram. I'm doing everything I can to get you out."

"Are you?"

"You can speak. For a minute there I thought they'd cut out your tongue."

"Not yet," he said.

There was a silence. Adelaide looked as though she might lean against the wall, but thought better of it. He did not suggest she could sit down.

"So," she said. "I've managed to get you a lawyer, a really good one. She's going to stop by this afternoon, go through all the technicalities with you, but I'd say you should only be in here a couple more days."

"I don't want your help."

"What?"

Behind the glasses, confusion rippled across her face, before she regained possession.

"Sorry, didn't catch that," she said. A flash of the real Adelaide at last. The smell of citrus was overwhelming; making him think of lemons and limes, the tang, the jolt of biting into a lemon slice after voqua. He had to think of her and what she had done.

He leaned forward.

"I. Don't. Want. Your. Help."

Adelaide folded her arms across her chest. Even her lips were pale green.

"Noble as that sentiment may be, Vikram, it's hardly in your interests, is it? Without me you're stuck down here for all foreseeable eternity." Her face softened. "Look. It's not like you're going to owe me anything, if that's what you're worried about. Think of it as me settling a debt."

Her arrogance really was astounding, Vikram told himself. His fingers untangled and locked again. He struggled not to clench them. She had taken enough of him already, he was not going to show her anything.

"I don't think you quite understand," he said. "You've got me in enough shit. I don't want you meddling in my affairs any more."

"You were happy enough for me to meddle up until now," she snapped. "What in hell's tide's got into you? I helped you get your schemes through, didn't I? I put your name on the map."

"And then you sent me right back where I belong, didn't you?"

He was standing, moving towards her. He slammed his palm against the wall inches from her head. She flinched. His hand stayed there, trapping her. With his other hand he ripped the glasses from her face. They clattered on the floor behind him. Pinned, Adelaide looked him right in the eye. There was redness, swelling, and for a moment he thought she had been crying, but that was impossible. Adelaide never cried.

"I didn't put you here, Vikram."

They were head to head now, close enough to see the tiniest contractions of the irises. Close enough to kiss. He looked at her mouth. Her lips were suffering from a lack of care, colourless and chapped. Still he remembered their feel and wanted to kick the wall and her too.

"How do I know you didn't set me up?"

She shook her head. She looked bewildered. He reminded himself that she had spent most of her life acting.

"Why would I set you up? I'd only be screwing myself as well."

"As opposed to screwing me?"

"Grow up."

He knew he deserved that, but he could not shake the belief that she had screwed him over, one way or another. Someone was to blame and it had better be her. His other hand flashed to her throat. He could see the vein pulsing there. Adelaide Mystik had given him nothing and taken what he had.

"Listen to me," she said, her voice restricted. "I know what I told you when we made that deal. I warned you. I told you not to trust me."

"And you were right," he snarled.

"I'm telling you the opposite now."

He placed his hand under her jaw and lifted it, appraising her in a cold, deliberate manner. There were dark shadows under her eyes; nightmares or nights without sleep. He imagined her tossing and turning in the empty width of that bed. The lilac silk sheets wrapping around her limbs. Her body sticky with sweat in the tropical heating.

"Not looking so hot, Adelaide," he said softly.

He felt the tension in her jaw, sensed she was gathering her resources for a crushing rejoinder. Her shoulders lifted a little.

"Well," she said. "It's fucking freezing in here."

He almost laughed. He had to hold his face under tight rein. He knew he had been successful because disappointment flickered in her eyes and they dropped. He had never known Adelaide to drop her eyes.

"I don't have much time," she said. She slumped against the wall.

"Got somewhere better to be? Don't let me keep you."

"You don't understand," she said.

The plea made him incandescent. He had to move away before he hit her.

"Oh, I understand you perfectly! You think I have a rat's ass chance of getting out of here in the next twelve months? You're fucking crazy. You asked me once what it's like down here. Well, look at it! Take a fucking good look, Adelaide! Getting claustrophobic yet?" He gave the metal bunk a vicious kick. Adelaide was frozen against the wall. He stepped towards her. "Not yet, perhaps. It takes all of a good hour to sink in. But after that, you'll stop feeling normal. That porthole drives you mad. You start thinking of ways you could get out, except there aren't any. Thinking you could somehow swim out, except you'd drown. And then you start to think you are drowning. You've played at that, haven't you Adelaide? You've played at drowning. Did you think it was fun? Think it was a game?"

The door opened. Out of defiance, Vikram did not move, waiting for them to order him away from her, wanting until the last second that pale face at the mercy of his accusing stare. But it wasn't who he thought. The big, muscular man in the doorway was not a guard; he wore a dark blue suit and his head was shaved to nothing. Vikram had never seen him before.

"I told you I didn't have much time." Adelaide turned to the newcomer, her face beseeching. "Just give me five more minutes—"

For answer the man took a rough hold of her wrist and yanked her towards him. She stumbled.

"Your brother said time's up, Miss Rechnov."

"It's *Mystik*."

"Rechnov since I've known you. She's under house arrest," he said casually to Vikram. "Daddy's orders, isn't it AD?"

Vikram stared at the man. Adelaide's elbow hit hard and fast. Her antagonist doubled over. Then he straightened, cleared his face of all expression, and hauled Adelaide out of the cell. The door slammed before Vikram could anticipate it. He heard a crack like someone being hit. If it was her she did not cry out.

Good girl, he thought automatically. The noise reverberated in his ears. Was it just prison playing tricks? He wanted to pull her back, examine her face anew for signs of proof. *Don't you understand*, he wanted to say. *Don't you understand, I have my pride too.* But she was gone. He felt stunned, incapable of rational thought. His anger was wasted. He had been waiting for her to show up, he realized, so he could say everything he wanted to say, but he had expected to get answers. Someone—he did not know who—had denied him that.

Adelaide was gone. She was really gone. The eerie light settled upon him like a shawl and in his solitary green cell he shivered.

/ / /

He watched the drop of water forming on the ceiling. Steadily, it grew. It bulged from the damp concrete, swelling, tugging at its life cord until finally it parted and fell—*plink*—into the puddle in the corner of the cell.

The puddle, when he arrived, had measured about four centimetres across. Over the last—how many?—days, it had stretched to seven. The puddle terrified him. From its meagre beginnings he saw the ocean grow and grow and surge through the porthole to flood the cell. He saw himself drown. He saw the water rising and himself swimming up with it as he cried out for help but none came. He swam from one side of the cell to another, pushing against the walls. Inch by inch his airspace receded. His mouth pressed against the ceiling which had turned to glass, he sucked in his last gasp of oxygen and then he was in a tank full of ocean and there was no more breathing.

It happened when he had been staring at the porthole. The glass broke and the water rushed in. The visions were short and abrupt. The longer versions waited until he slept. When the cell was full of water, his lungs burning and his consciousness prepared to switch off, he woke, hyperventilating. He lived his dying again and again.

Sometimes, when the water crashed in, he saw Adelaide's body inside it, turning over and over like a fish.

Time fluxed. The outside world, with its catalogues of sunrise, sunset, hail and snow, was estranged from him. The lighting was the same dim green twenty-four hours a day. When he was let out to eat the light in the hallway flickered, but in his cell it never changed.

He knew, from his last stint underwater, that his skin was draining of colour and his arteries were growing sluggish. He did sets of exercises twice a day, with the damp floor against his palms and his back. He ran on the spot but the buildup of trapped momentum made him want to slam himself against the wall. Sometimes he did so, screaming with the impact. His shoulders and hips swelled in purple bruises. From the condensation and the cold he developed a shiver and a hacking cough. He watched carefully for specks of blood: the first signs of tuberculosis.

Every twelve hours he scratched half a cross into the wall. He hung his watch on the stub of a nail. If they were worried about suicide they would have filed the nail down; it was, he speculated, just substantial enough to kill yourself. He pondered how it might be done, the best angle, the most likely site. The base of the skull, probably. They had left it for the same reason the cell was concrete and he had been allowed to keep his watch, which he could choke on. A person who committed suicide was not worth preserving until the end of their prison sentence.

A man five cells around from Vikram managed to hang himself. When he heard the news Vikram tried to imagine how the man might have done it. What had he hung from? What had he used? A shoelace? A belt? He took off his own belt and examined it, felt the metal studs and the taut length of it.

As he lay in the green, faces edged into his mind, old friends, members of Horizon, Nils, Shadiyah, Jannike, Linus, the brother and sister in the shelter, Hella. He had lost not one but two lives. Bad enough to be an airlift, but what happened when you had to cross back? He saw himself leaving prison, staggering into daylight like a manta addict. He could not go to any of those people. He would be as rootless as he had been in the orphanage before Mikkeli found him, a buoy cut loose from its moorings and cast out on the open sea.

It's not a lovers' city, said Adelaide, and she was right, in the end. Osiris mocked such fragility. I don't love Adelaide, he wanted to say. Don't punish me for what I have not done. He heard repeated the cell door shut and the crack that followed it and imagined the action that must have made it. Her theories of Axel's murder took up residence in the cell with him. He spoke to Rechnov murderers. Asked them how they had done it. He whispered lines of the letter to himself. *The white horse will talk first.*

He started from fits of dozing to find himself battering the concrete with his fists. The cell was growing smaller. *This has happened before, you know how prison messes with your head.* But this time it was happening faster. As the cell grew closer and the puddle grew larger, he recognized the seeds: fear that he would never get out, and worse, fear that he would not want to. He knew how it ended. Osiris became too terrible to envisage. The city's hand clenched cold around your heart and you preferred to stay submerged, away from sunlight and eyes that might stare.

Finally, like the man five cells around, you no longer cared for your own convictions and you found a way to hang yourself.

Her undine spirit haunted him. He replayed her, opening the door in black lace, telling tales of the rainbow-fish with her viridescent eyes wide, the slope of her back rising and falling, slumped in sleep against the lilac sheets. He watched the waterbike leap over the waves and her hair stream in a banner behind her. He felt the warm unconscious weight of her pushing on his chest. The smell of lemons and limes permeated the cell, for a day or so. Then he had to hunt for it on the air. Then it was just an idea.

Sometimes he heard his breathing and thought that it was hers. He saw her floating, face down in the water and she was both herself and Mikkeli, water and ice, the two fused in some halfway state between liquid and frozen. A bird rested on each of their backs. Its beak plunged. Their lungs had forgotten how to breathe.

The puddle grew. He had heard you could drown in an inch of water.

The woman in the cell next door wailed. At least, he thought it was her, but it might be Mikkeli howling with a chorus of ghosts out by the ring-net, or it could be Adelaide. If Adelaide existed.

Perhaps he had never left jail. He had been here all the time; everything had been a protracted dream, the produce of his brain, a diversion, a defence mechanism. He marvelled at the power of his own invention. He had conjured Adelaide out of adverts and headlines from years before the riots. Here she was walking along a red carpet. Clear voqua poured onto a mountain of ice which imprisoned her in a great column and melted from the inside out. He watched her drown. She turned blue.

His lungs were thick; he lay on the bed, too weak to move. Black lace curled around the door frame and produced twine that grew into her mouth and pierced the back of her head. Her hair writhed and bound her to the waterbike. She was pulled beneath the surface with it. On the seabed he watched fish turn her to mud. She stretched out a dissolving finger and he knew that when she touched him he would turn to mud too.

Her touch was liquid. The mud took his hands first, and last his eyes.

His ground-dreams wrapped around his nightmares. He began to think of land. A boat would come, a lost boat, a found boat. It would take him away from Osiris. Away from staring eyes. Better to die on the open ocean, with clean air on his skin and the sun on his face.

Adelaide whispered to him.

And when I come back we can find the sand. You'll like that.

I will, he said. I will.

No more mazes, no more clouds.

Another drip landed in the puddle. Everything returned to the sea.

PART FOUR

37 | ADELAIDE

t took until two o'clock for Goran's breathing to regulate and his pulse to slow. Adelaide stood under the mezzanine, watching his slack face. The eyelids slumped on their dual-coloured irises, heavy and creased, thin-lashed. The nostrils quivered. It had taken her a full week to remember the drugs she kept stashed in a hidden compartment of her bathroom; another week to summon the courage to use them. Goran woke at the tiniest disturbance. She was surprised he didn't sleep with his eyes open, like a snake.

She crept forward and placed the soaked cloth delicately over his nose and mouth. He inhaled normally, then with a sudden, violent breath. She shrank back. His lungs sucked in the opiate fumes. She waited. This was where Vikram had first slept. Vikram, who thought she had betrayed him. She made herself entertain the thought, holding it hostage for her heart, testing. She willed herself to care.

Nothing. She had spent the two weeks well. She had been in limbo, floating, in all the gaps between time. She had been lighter than vapour and thinner than air, but she was frozen now.

She was ready.

After a minute she took Goran's wrist. It was thick, muscle bound, and she had to push her finger deep to feel the pulse. As she expected, it had slowed.

For a further ten minutes she waited, allowing herself to hate him but coldly. Then she unbuttoned his jacket and felt inside the pocket and retrieved her keys and his scarab. She went to her room, put on her out-door gear and picked up her waterproof haversack. Her boots were rubber soled and noiseless as she walked through the apartment, checking once more under the mezzanine. This time she trussed him, tying his hands together and then his feet, her heart jumping every time he shifted. The apartment was filled with the sounds of his laboured breathing and the oscillating machinery from the floors above. Goran would be in trouble for her escape. She was neither happy nor sorry. She was steel.

She slipped the key into the lock. A bubble of pleasure rose as she heard it turn—but she pushed it down, no time for that. She locked the door from the other side.

"Goodbye, Goran. I hope they give you hell."

The corridor seemed overlarge after her incarceration. She glanced at the ceiling. As she lay night after night, thinking, plotting, she had wondered who knew about the facility, about the Siberian boat. Did Linus know? Had he lied to her all along? She had considered trying to break into the facility. But it would do no good; the scientists would hand her back to the Rechnovs the moment she was caught. The white fly had to wait.

She ran silently down the stairs, nervous of being trapped in the lift. Her lungs and calf muscles, inactive for too long, protested fiercely at the exertion. Once an apartment door opened and she froze in fear, but it was only a man staggering home drunk.

Surface level. This was the wager: her boat would still be here. There was no reason for them to move it, not with Goran guarding the door. She stepped out into open air. It smelled clearer and crisper than ever before. She walked around the decking, her heart thudding with anticipation.

And yes. There it was. Release gurgled in her chest. This time she let it, but kept her head focused as she stepped into the craft, reached under the seat where the spare key was taped, felt it drop into her palm. The electronic hum of the motor was one of the sweetest sounds she had ever known.

The dashboard flashed up with symbols. The battery was fully charged; she had at least twenty-four hours of driving before she'd need to stop at a charge point. Would charge points be easy to find where she was going? Someone would tell her.

As the boat pulled away from the decking, she allowed herself one glance up. She could make out a glimmer at the top of the scraper which might be from her apartment, or from the facility above. Steering with one hand, she tapped the familiar code into Goran's scarab. Somewhere in Osiris, Lao's o'comm rang and rang, but he didn't answer. He was no use to her anymore. She disconnected from the Reef and hurled Goran's scarab into the sea.

The water was choppy, crusted with foam. The towers slipped by with maddening slowness. Every impulse told her to increase speed—but it was a quiet night, and she could not attract attention. She avoided the main waterways lit with floating night lamps, and took a winding route through the outskirts. She aimed to reach the border at one of the sub-checkpoints. A transport barge passed her, carrying the stench of a fresh fish haul into the City. A late night waterbus followed it. The windows spilled orange rectangles onto the sea. Adelaide averted her face.

The wind picked up and she took the boat up a speed. Scores of towers lay between her and Goran; she was well away. She tipped back her head and relished the feel of the cold on her face, brittle and clean. Axel, if the delivery girl was to be believed, had spent entire days out on the balcony. Maybe her brother had not been so mad after all. Maybe he had realized what she had come to see: the City was a prison, which must be escaped.

He had to be there. She had scoured the City; there was nowhere left but the west. She could imagine it now: Axel packing his bags. The Whitefly documents—some part of his mind would have known they were important, had made him lock them up safe. And then he had run. *Go west.* The horses would have told him.

She was always destined to go there. The blind Teller had known it. She had told Adelaide months ago, but Adelaide hadn't listened.

It has been spoken, sister. Spoken in the salt.

She glanced up at the stars, half hidden by cloud, and imagined Axel watching the same patterns. Waiting for the arrival of his twin.

What took you so long?

That was what he would say.

Twin searchlights beamed across the gap in the border netting, one from either side. There was a gap of seconds before they crossed. On the jetty, about fifty metres away, Adelaide saw the shadow of a guard.

Her heart began to thud. The full realization of what she was doing—what she had done—hit her forcefully. For a moment she was paralysed with doubt. Axel, she thought. Think of Axel. She waited, watching the circular arcs, counting the seconds between their passage. The searchlights crossed and separated, crossed and separated. The guard walked slowly across the jetty. At the edge he stopped, looking about. Adelaide cringed back inside her hood. Then his hands moved away from his gun, and as the searchlight swept over she saw that he was unbuckling his trousers to relieve himself.

Now was her chance. Keeping the motor to an almost inaudible hum, she urged the boat forward into the hundred metre stretch of water.

Manoeuvring between the beams of the searchlight, she used all of her strength to haul the boat this way and that. It seemed to take forever. The searchlight drew near. With a final wrench, the boat slipped past the narrow gap in the netting, only metres from the jetty and, she saw with a shock, a hulking barge.

She bent low to the boat and, not daring to look back, shot into the maze of the west.

On the other side there were no lights. Her thrill of exhilaration dissipated in the odd stillness. She looked about: up at the tower window-walls, ahead at the waterways. Not a glimmer. Vikram had told her about the west's eternal problems with electricity, but this total darkness could not be right. Could it? She brought the boat's engine down to a bare minimum and kept her lights off. Now she was crawling forward in near blackness, with only the glow from the retreating City to guide her on her way. It was fading all the time.

Fear gripped her. She was tempted to retreat, to get back into the City and find a friend's apartment or a Boatel to hole up for the night. She turned the boat around, but the shadow of a bigger craft, crawling along the border, its searchlights seeking out the deepest troughs, made her steer towards the nearest tower.

You're a Rechnov, she reminded herself. You've got no reason to be afraid.

But there was no reason for a Rechnov to be this side of the border, and if Vikram had taught her anything, it was that the Home Guards shot first and investigated afterwards.

A pale lambency drew her south, only to find that the light came not from any artificial source but from the sky itself. Her lips whispered silently as the spectacle became clear: *aura australis*. The aura dappled the night, shifting from green to yellow and back like a living, chameleon thing. She gazed skyward. *Can you see this, Axel?*

But as soon as they had appeared, the southern lights retreated. The boat rocked as she shifted her weight. What was down there, far below the surface? For the first time, she felt alien to her terrain.

She carried on, further into the west. The darkness was complete. She had planned to head for Vikram's old tower, and from there to gain directions to the shelter, but without lights to guide her she had little chance of finding the right way. The lack of noise was beginning to spook her. It was as though the entire community had died.

She decided to navigate towards Vikram's tower anyway. She had to judge the route based on her knowledge of the city's contours, and an instinctive awareness of the west's structural layout. The boat responded dutifully to her steering, although the sea was growing more aggressive and her hands inside their gloves were numb. She flexed her fingers. She could barely feel them. She wondered if her hearing had been similarly impaired by the cold.

A light winked over the waves, flashed against Adelaide's boat and cut out.

"Psst! Get over here!"

After such a stretch of nothingness, she could hardly believe that the sound was real. But it had been human, that voice. She nosed the boat in its direction. The light winked on and off again, as she grew nearer. Her boat bumped against a decking.

"Hello?" she whispered.

"Stars! Are you crazy? Get inside!"

A hand latched onto Adelaide's shoulder and tugged. She followed its pull, helpless in the darkness to do anything else, and climbed out of the boat.

"I need to tie up—"

"Pass me the chain, I'll tie her."

Adelaide hesitated, loathe to obey the anonymous voice. But neither did she want to return to the inky silence. She pocketed the keys and handed over the chain. Their gloves brushed. If the boat was secured, it was done noiselessly. The stranger's hand found her arm once more and she was guided across the decking. There was a swish as the doors parted. They went into the tower.

The reek caught her by surprise. She coughed and swallowed the noise.

The voice switched on a penlight. Its tiny glow illuminated a blue hat pulled low over straggly hair, bright eyes in a dirty face. The girl was young; she could not be more than about fourteen. She cupped a hand around the penlight, shielding it between their two bodies.

"What are you doing out there?"

"I got lost," Adelaide said.

"Lost? You lose track of time, or something?"

"I made a few bad turns, before I knew it…"

"Before you knew it, you were past curfew. You got to be careful, lady! Them boats out there, they don't listen to excuses!"

"Yeah, I—I know."

"Lucky I spotted you. I'm on watch here. They say I have seagull eyes. You want to sit with me for a bit? Gets boring on my own."

"Sure."

The girl switched off the penlight. Adelaide heard her fumbling with a lever. The tower doors opened with a soft whoosh and the girl settled down in the entrance. Adelaide sat beside her. Stationary, she felt the bitter cold. She wrapped her arms around her, wondering how many hours until daylight.

"You see a light—the slightest light—you tell me," said the western girl, keeping her voice low. "And if you hear talking and all. That's the one thing about them skadi." She spat the word with venom. "They make one hell of a racket—always know when they're coming." She added, more bitterly, "Guess you don't need stealth when you got guns."

"I'll keep my ears open," Adelaide promised. The stars knew she had her own reasons to keep her distance from the Guard. *Skadi.* She practised the word in her head. In the darkness the watch-girl would not see her lips moving.

It gave her an idea. She rubbed her gloved palms silently over the floor, and then over her face. She didn't want to think about what was on the decking floor, but she was sure it had dirtied her face.

"They haven't done this tower yet," said the girl. "They might tonight. If they come we've got to shut this door quick. Ain't no locking from inside but we got a good warning system. Kind of relay thing."

"Do the boats come past here often?" Adelaide asked. She could not remember Vikram ever telling her about an alarm system, nor, now she thought about it, of patrol boats going through the western waterways so regularly.

"This neighbourhood there's one every hour or so," said the girl. "But they're getting more often since the greenhouse. You must have been lucky not to meet one. Horrible things. I hate the way they sort of glide by, you know, as if they wasn't really there."

"*Skadi*," said Adelaide, putting enough contempt into the word to cover, she hoped, any mistake in pronunciation.

"Yeah."

Waves lifted the decking. Spray landed on Adelaide's nose and cheeks.

"Have you been on watch long?" she asked.

"Three hours. I'm relieved soon. Gets a bit lonely, you know, but some-one's got to do it. I volunteered." The girl spoke proudly. "They wanted people who were involved, y'know, last time, but I said I wasn't old enough last time and you got to start somewhere. Fifteen, ent I? Got a good pair of ears. Heard you, didn't I? And you got a good quiet boat there. Why were you out so late anyways?"

"I'm looking for my brother. He's disappeared."

The girl gave her arm a sympathetic squeeze. "Everyone's gone disap-peared round here. Gone off to take a crack at the skadi, has he?"

"I think so."

"My little bro's talkin' about joining Maak's people—y'know, Maak. Ma's got a hell of a time keeping him in. I know how he feels. Sometimes I want to go and join up myself but a knife ent much use against one of them. Not if you only use it once. Reckon I'd be good at stealth work, though."

Something had happened since Adelaide had been locked up, something nobody had told her about. Home Guard boats belonged on the border, not in the western quarter, not unless there had been violence. What was the greenhouse? Who was Maak? Further questions would betray her ignorance, and her background, but the watch-girl seemed friendly, eager to talk, if Adelaide could find the right angle.

She was about to ask the girl if she knew about Vikram's aid schemes when they were interrupted.

"Who are you yakking away to down there?"

Adelaide sensed the girl swivel around.

"Oh Drake, hey, this is—y'know I never got your name."

"It's Ata."

"Ata. I'm Liis. She got caught out after curfew."

"You better hole up here till morning," said the newcomer. "I wouldn't risk the bridges now, wind's getting up."

"Is, isn't it?" Liis exclaimed. "I heard people saying a Tarctic's on the way."

"A Tarctic?" Adelaide was shocked into speech. She hadn't bargained on being in the west when a Tarctic struck.

"—'s what they say."

Liis got to her feet and Adelaide mirrored her. Her hearing was becoming more acute. They went inside. The woman called Drake flicked on a penlight. It seemed brighter this time. Drake smiled. One of her front teeth was completely black.

"She can crash with your folks, Liis?"

"Sure, she can!"

"Great. Good job, girl. You get some sleep now. Night, Ata."

A creaking lower lift carried them the first twenty-five flights, juddering all the way up. Adelaide was relieved when they got out and groped their way up the lightless stairwell for the next three floors.

"Mind if we sit out here a minute?" Liis asked when they reached her door. "I need a smoke."

"Sure." Adelaide perched next to Liis. She heard the rustling of paper as Liis rolled herself a cigarette.

"Do you want one?" Liis asked.

"Please." Goran had taken all of her cigarillos, which might have been useful here, if only to make contacts. In the flare of the lighter, Adelaide saw Liis's pale face, the outline of a scratched and chipped door, the stairs pouring away into the blackness. She lit her cigarette. It tasted cheap and dirty but there was a rough sweetness to it, an end of day sweetness. Her lips tingled. She could imagine Axel sitting here, in the nameless dark, only his horses still bright enough to see.

"You know, sometimes I get dead scared out there." Liis's voice was a tiny whisper. "Sometimes I get thinking, if I died out there, no one would ever know how, or what happened to me or anything."

Adelaide put an awkward arm around the girl's shoulders. Through the layers of clothing, she could feel how thin the girl was.

"I know," she said. "I know."

Adelaide slept deeply and woke with a jolt. She did not comprehend, at first, where she was—strange faces, people jumping to their feet—a lot of people, more than she had thought a room this size could contain when her head hit the floor last night. Shouts volleyed between them.

"What the hell!"

"What was that—"

"Was that an explosion?"

"—'s the fucking skadi."

The room vaulted into action. Adelaide scrambled out of the folds of her blanket, heart racing. A man lifted his shirt and checked a knife was at his belt. A woman—Liis's mother?—gathered together all the bedding. A boy held them in place whilst she yanked them together with her belt. Two smaller children poised by the doorway, wide awake and alert. Liis stuffed things into a rucksack; newspapers, clothes, a pair of boots. Nobody asked who Adelaide was. Nobody cared.

"Ata—grab the other bag," Liis said breathlessly.

Adelaide picked up the drawstring bag. It was lighter than she expected. In a matter of seconds, the room had been stripped to its peeling walls.

The boy opened the door and peeked out. From further down the tower came the sounds of invasion: people running up and down stairs, heavy boots, doors slamming, crashes and yells as doors were kicked in.

"Shit, they're early," said the boy. The woman shook his shoulder.

"Come on, move up."

Adelaide followed Liis's family, or friends, or room-mates, through the corridor and into the stairwell. This morning it was patchily lit. As they progressed upwards people were opening doors, peering blearily out. Some, like Liis's group, had already got their belongings together and were also moving up the tower.

Congestion built up, noisy and incoherent. Adelaide had never seen so many people in one space. Their faces were hard and dirty, frightened. Within a couple of flights, she was separated from Liis's friends and could only see the girl herself, blue hat bobbing in the crowd a little way ahead. She lost Liis momentarily, panicked and shoved forward. Where were they all going? No-one had said, because everyone knew—everyone but Adelaide.

A female voice shouted above the rest. "Liis! Over here!"

Leaning over the handrail from the floor above was the girl with the black tooth. Drake. Liis yelled back and Adelaide located her guide again. She wasn't far ahead. Adelaide pushed through to her, relief welling, and together they joined Drake. People streamed from above and below, funnelling into a corridor.

"Early raid," Drake panted. "We better get over the bridge. They're already at level thirteen."

"I've got me ma and all," said Liis, gesturing below. In the moving crowd Adelaide saw the gaggle of mother, the boy and the two children. Liis's mother had the bundle of bedding strapped to her back.

Drake gripped Liis's arm.

"I know, I know, it'll be alright, just make sure you get over, they mustn't find anyone in the network."

Liis waved at her family. "This way!"

Drake dove into the corridor. Liis followed Drake and Adelaide followed Liis. It was the lightest part of the tower that Adelaide had seen so far. Then she saw that the people in front were framed against a doorway. The light was coming from outside. They were going out of the tower, and there was no glass, no shuttle lines or enclosed bridges.

The queue in front of her dwindled in short bursts. There were twenty people between Adelaide and the exit. There were five. Then two. Liis was no longer in front. She gasped, tried to turn around, and was knocked forward. She was in the doorway.

Before she knew what was happening, her feet had stepped out onto an impossibly narrow metal catwalk. The wind whipped her hair out of its hood. She clutched at the rails and found two slack plastic ropes. She was wobbling on a rail in open air fifty floors above surface.

The bridge fed into the tower opposite. People in front of her were walking sure-footed along the metal. It was a good hundred metres away. The crowd pressed at her back. She almost lost her balance.

"Hey, watch your step!" The yell from behind was impatient. If she didn't move she'd be pushed.

Adelaide took one diving breath and sprinted. Halfway across she looked down and saw the sea churning below. She saw the metal catwalk, riveted, orange with rust and glued together with stars knew what. She staggered, grabbed the rope, righted herself, ran on. At the other end she fell into a pair of outstretched arms.

The man's mass was solid, safe. She stayed there, panting as though she had run the length of a shuttle line. She was aware of her rescuer shaking his head.

"Crazy!" he was saying.

Adelaide looked back, expecting Liis to be right behind her, but she could not see the other girl, only the impossible fragility of the bridge. She was not the only one frightened; others were refusing to cross, fighting to get back inside, but still more pushed forward. A man dashed across and Adelaide saw what she had not realized when making her own run—the bridge buckled under his weight. People pointed and cried out. Adelaide spotted Liis at last.

"Liis!"

She waved frantically.

The other girl raised her arm in response and yelled. Adelaide could not hear above the well of noise.

The man who'd caught her was shouting out.

"One at a time! Don't put too much weight on it! There's bridges on levels sixty-five and seventy!"

A woman stepped out. Adelaide recognized Drake. She had lost her hat. Drake put one foot on the bridge, paused for a second, and ran. Her boots struck the metal like gunfire. It was gunfire; the skadi were shooting.

Drake was over. Their eyes met in a glimmer of shared experience and then Drake too turned to look back.

"Okay, and another! One more!"

The crowd were no longer listening. Something had made them panic, something that Adelaide could not see. There was a surge and a line of people spilled onto the narrow bridge. Then a second surge and Adelaide's hands went to her face. They toppled, from the bridge, from the fiftieth-floor doorway, one after another. They went as dominoes did. Over and over. Cries echoed into the gulf.

The bridge groaned. It sagged under the weight of clinging bodies. Some dangled from the underside, holding on by two hands or by one. More were falling. They fell like dolls. The bodies were all sizes, some large, some incredibly small. She could hardly believe that they were real except for the screams.

She saw Liis. The girl was on the bridge, gripping the rope, urging on the woman in front of her. Someone pushed Liis from behind and Liis turned, gesticulated with her free hand, yelled.

The entire construction swayed.

"Liis!"

Adelaide was not sure if she or Drake had shouted. Both of them were staring, side by side, powerless.

"Help! Help us!"

"It's going, it's going to break—"

"This way, keep moving, come on, run, get off, run!"

Adelaide's rescuer was hauling those who had made it bodily inside. Adelaide and Drake were pressed against the interior wall.

There was a crack. At the far end, the rivets holding the bridge gave. The metal construction plunged downwards out of Adelaide's sight. People scrabbled on the ledge opposite. She saw three, four, five more fall. They grabbed at the feet of those above, who were in turn pushed out by the weight of the blind crowd.

Adelaide's hands shook against her cheeks. She stopped counting.

Her rescuer threw down a rope. A pair of hands, Drake's hands, reached for it and Adelaide took hold too, understanding that they must all pull to save anyone left to save. The bridge was still attached to their tower, hanging down out of sight. She heard the metal strain. The man was on his stomach at the ledge. He fed out the rope.

"Grab on!"

They were too late. The metal separated with a hideous, scraping tear. The screams of the falling seemed to reverberate on and on. She heard a burst of gunfire.

"Liis," she said.

Drake shook her head. The man on his stomach did not move. The message, finally, must have been passed forward in the tower opposite, because the crowd began to retreat, until only a handful of the marooned remained looking out.

"What you got there?" Drake asked. She was looking at the drawstring bag across Adelaide's body.

"I don't know—Liis gave—"

Adelaide opened the bag. There were only a couple of items inside, a tobacco pouch and a heart-shaped salt tin. She wanted to cry. The emotion came without warning and she had to blink it away.

"C'mon," said Drake.

Adelaide followed mindlessly. They were going downstairs now. A musty, sickly sweetish smell. She could see by the faint glimmer from cracks under doors. She kept her eyes on Drake's boots, solid chunky things, with caterpillar soles, the fraying ends of her jeans tucked into them. The boots moved regularly, though the stairs were uneven. Once Adelaide's shoes sent a scree of rubble tumbling away and she put out a hand to stop herself slipping. The wall was damp and spongy.

Twenty or so floors down, they turned into a corridor. Drake stopped outside a door that bulged in its frame. She knocked once and opened it without waiting for a reply. She gave Adelaide a nudge inside.

There were two people in the tiny room; one male, bearded, with blue eyes, the other female, with a wing of sheer peroxide hair. The man stared at her, a strange expression on his face. Adelaide stared back, confused.

"Look what I've found." Drake spoke from behind her.

An inkling formed in Adelaide's head but there was no time for her body to anticipate the blow. Drake's strike was efficient. In the seconds before losing consciousness, as pain gathered at her temples, Adelaide heard the beginnings of the peculiar conversation that must follow.

"Face like that, can't mistake it," said Drake. "Shame really—she seemed..."

38 | VIKRAM

His breath rattled in and out. The blanket was scrunched at his mouth, a futile attempt to keep what little moisture his breath produced as a barrier. All his energy was concentrated on quashing the tickle in his throat. If he gave in to it, his body would implode.

When he moved his wrist, the throat-tickle intensified. His eyes blurred, making tears with the effort of stilling it. He waited for his vision to clear. His watch face loomed large and indistinct. The hour hand pointed to the three, or the four. He lost sight of it; when he next focused it had moved to the other side of the watch face. A figure stood at the end of his bed. He was hallucinating again.

"Hello, Vikram." The voice stirred a memory. A calm voice, measured and assured. "You're looking in bad shape. I'm sorry to see that."

Vikram gazed wonderingly at the man in the elegant suit. He was grey, with slender stripes, like the hide of a tiger shark. The stripes refused to stay put; they swam over the man. What was Linus Rechnov doing in Vikram's head?

"Can you sit up?"

His own imagination was goading him now. Something strange happened. The figure moved towards him very quickly and took him in a steel grasp. The world lurched. The walls moved. The cell door became vertical.

Vikram gagged. He clamped his teeth, bit down, but it was too late. His chest began to heave. The coughs tore out of him. He spat blood onto the sheets and the filthy material of his trousers.

"Hello! You there!" Linus was shouting. "What's wrong with him?"

Other people entered the cell, crowding it. He cringed away. A hand came towards him. He tried to get back but it grew, round and pale, ready to engulf him. It clamped his forehead and squeezed.

"High fever."

"Dunno, looks like TB to me."

"Don't you inoculate these people?"

Vikram's insides churned. Something was chewing on his organs. Fish, probably. Perhaps he was already dead. When he closed his eyes, the idea did not seem so bad—then hands grabbed his shoulders once more. A bilious wave made him faint.

Linus Rechnov was here. There was something important that Vikram had to say to Linus.

"The boats." He tried to lift his arms, take hold of the other man's face. It was imperative that Linus understood. "The boats, they don't come back. Tell me why the boats don't come back."

He fumbled at air.

"What's he saying?"

"He's raving. Get a sedative."

Linus flickered, a creeping red darkness around him. His face became smaller and his voice got thinner and thinner.

"Listen to me, Vikram. I am going to get you out of here. I'm going to get you treatment. And then you are going to do something for me. Do you understand? Nod if you understand."

Vikram's head fell forward, but it was an involuntary action. His mind had already abandoned the visitation. He was sinking into unconsciousness.

/ / /

His arms lay immobile on crisp white bed sheets. A needle attached to a plastic bag was stuck in the crook of Vikram's left elbow, and a clear substance dripped steadily into his blood.

Linus Rechnov sat on a visitor's chair. Vikram was in hospital, and he had a visitor. He entertained this notion silently, knowing it must lead somewhere, wondering where.

"How long have I been here?"

"Three days."

Vikram blinked. Three days. The quiet of this place, the calm efficiency of the nurse who had entered earlier, changed the drip, taken his pulse and smiled at him, seemed unearthly. It had taken Vikram a while to realize that these were no longer the phantoms of his mind.

"You're not well," Linus said. "I can see that. But we don't have much time so I have to brief you now. Adelaide has been captured by renegades in the west. They have direct contact with the press and they are using her as leverage. They say her life is on the line if we don't cooperate."

His mind reeled.

"Captured? How?"

"They've asked for a negotiator."

Linus let the silence drag out, forcing Vikram to complete the implicated conclusion.

"You want me to negotiate?" His voice did not sound the way he remembered it. It was thicker. Hoarser. It sounded old.

"The rebels have specifically asked that we hand you over. They refuse to allow anyone else to negotiate. No doubt they see your release as another coup for their cause."

Vikram turned this over. His own instinct was less certain. The aid schemes might have been seen as a terrible failure: this request could be as much about revenge as it seemed to be about rescue. He tried to pull his mind into focus. He needed facts.

"There's been more riots?"

"Riots, yes, that's where it started." Linus was impatient.

"And what do the—the rebels want?" The gauze covering the needle in his arm irritated his skin. He scratched at it.

"With the current shortages, reserve supplies of fish and kelp are being held back. The renegades have demanded the release of these stores."

"Seems fair to me."

"You realize that this places me in a highly awkward situation. I have been seen to pledge my support of the west. Of your schemes, in fact. Now those same people have my sister as a hostage."

"What are you trying to say—I owe you something? I think your sister's intervention has secured me enough problems for one lifetime, don't you?"

Linus leaned forward.

"It doesn't look so good for your people, Vikram."

Their eyes met and locked. Anger took Vikram by surprise. He could feel the strain the emotion was putting on his body, only beginning to recover. He strove for calm. The facts. Just the facts.

"How did Adelaide get taken hostage?"

"I have no idea. It appears the little fool was in the west."

"In the west?" He was temporarily stupefied. He had assumed, hazily, some sort of covert raid. What did Adelaide think she was doing in the west? He thought of the last time he had seen her, the reddened eyes, the bald stranger's words: *She's under house arrest.* Adelaide had run away then. From one imprisonment directly into the arms of another. Vikram's lip curled. It was absolutely typical.

Linus looked away. "I was also… surprised, as you can imagine. It's not like Adelaide to go slumming it."

Vikram felt an intense wave of dislike for the man.

"Did you ever show her that letter?"

"The letter has no bearing on the matter," Linus said testily.

"It might if it made her go off on some insane mission."

"She hasn't seen the letter. And why she is in the west is no longer relevant. The fact is, she's there, she's been caught, and she's a bargaining chip. We need her back. The press are all over this."

Linus had the expression of a man who needed something, needed it badly, but did not want to admit it.

"So what do I get for negotiating for you?"

"You're out of prison, aren't you?"

"For good?"

"You'll get a full pardon and amnesty in the City if you cooperate fully with us."

"Us?"

"Myself and my father."

There had to be more to it.

"By amnesty, do you mean Citizenship?"

"Citizenship, amnesty, yes." Linus's lips compressed.

"They're not the same thing."

"Fine. Citizenship. As long as you cooperate."

"And by as long as you mean…"

"You understand what I mean, Vikram."

Linus sat back in the chair and folded his arms. Vikram understood the message, which Linus was so reluctant to spell out. Freedom he had got. That was the bait. Release, and medical care. It put him in debt, too. The drip, the expensive chemicals, the nurse's smile—all paid for by the Rechnovs. Citizenship he would get, but at a further cost; the cost of being in someone else's pocket.

"What do you want me to do?"

"We've been given a location. You're to go there alone. When you get there, one of their people will take you to Adelaide."

"Who am I dealing with? Is it the NWO?"

"No, we believe this is a new network. They're calling themselves Surface. The leader, or leaders, refuse to give any names, but the ringleader is referred to as the Coordinator. So far, that is all we have managed to ascertain."

"You're making deals with people and you don't even know who they are."

"It's a trait with the west," Linus said smoothly. "You seem to prefer anonymity—a mistake, but there you have it. You'll be tracked, of course."

"Tracked?"

"You don't think I'm actually sending you to negotiate, do you? You're a bargaining chip yourself. We already tried to arrange a prisoner exchange, but the rebels have refused point blank. They've refused all deals. Besides, you might defect."

"So what you're really asking is that I betray my own people."

Linus ignored this.

"Once you're in, proceed as the rebels expect. They'll think you're on their side. Keep your ears open for information. I imagine it will be a simple procedure—they'll give you a way of contacting us."

"If they think I'm on their side, why would they use me to negotiate at all?" Vikram interrupted.

"Because they have to negotiate," Linus said sharply. "I'm not going to play games with you, Vikram. You know as well as I do that the Home Guard could go into the west and crush these riots, and the City would turn a blind eye—more, Citizens would condone such a move. But this time, we can't, because the rebels have Adelaide and they've informed the press. Besides, the Council is anxious to avoid excessive bloodshed. So yes, I think the rebels will be aiming to negotiate, and you, as an airlift, are the obvious choice."

The word airlift sounded like a vulgarity on Linus's lips. Vikram did not reply. He noticed a red stain blossoming through the drip gauze.

Linus continued. "You'll have to make sure that it's you who brings Adelaide out."

"Whilst you're tracking me," Vikram said dully. He glanced up at the drip. The plastic crinkled inwards as the fluid ran dry. The nurse would be in to replace it soon.

"Precisely. Once you and Adelaide are out, you can leave the rest to the Guard."

"Skadi."

"What?"

"Nothing." He smoothed the gauze, trying to stem the blood. "I get it."

"You're in agreement, then?"

Vikram paused.

"What about the aid schemes?"

Linus shrugged. "They could be reinstated. Maybe next year. If the rescue operation goes successfully."

"And if I don't comply…"

"I only have jurisdiction to remove your sentence under the conditions that you are aiding the Osiris Council."

It was as he had expected; as he had known, from the start of the conversation. "I don't have much choice, do I?"

"Not really, Vikram. No. I'm sorry."

"When do I leave?"

Linus sat forward. Brisk and matter-of-fact now. "I'm told you need twenty-four hours before you will be fit to travel. A meeting place is being arranged with the rebels for early tomorrow evening. Your boat is already here. It will contain a decoy tracker. You can tell the rebels about that one. Someone is coming to fit you with a secondary device."

"I want some things from my apartment. My outdoor clothes."

"We can bring anything you need here."

"I want to go myself."

"Fine. You'll have to leave earlier."

Linus straightened his necktie. It had a subtle pattern, almost like wings. Something stirred in Vikram's memory; slowly, he dredged it out. Adelaide. The jacuzzi. The last time he had seen Linus. A phrase that had been spoken by both siblings.

"What's Whitefly?" Vikram asked.

"Whitefly?" Linus's polite smile hovered, but instinct told Vikram that he had hit a nerve. "What are you talking about?"

"Don't pretend it doesn't mean something. You and Adelaide both mentioned Whitefly—"

"Adelaide—" Linus spoke too quickly, broke off just as fast. Adelaide isn't supposed to know, Vikram thought. He watched Linus gather his composure. "You're right, it does mean something. Something I wish I'd never been told, frankly. My advice, Vikram—and as you know, I don't offer my advice arbitrarily—best forget you ever heard the word. You can consider that part of the terms of our agreement."

Vikram looked at him squarely.

"One other thing, Linus, before you go. Tell me, how does a man so interested in promoting equality end up sending in guns on innocent people? Or was it all a big sham from the start, helping me?"

A shadow crossed Linus's face. Vikram could not tell if it was anger, shame or simple contempt. He did not expect an answer from the other man, but there was some small satisfaction gained from posing the question.

"You once asked me something very similar, the first time we met," Linus said at last. "I don't suppose you remember now. Why would you? You're not a politician, Vikram. And you're not a Rechnov either. Take comfort in the fact that you have no knowledge of either." He checked his watch. "I have to go. I won't see you until your return. Good luck." Linus stood, brushing down his suit.

"Any messages?"

"I'm sorry?"

"For your sister."

For the first time, Linus hesitated. Then he said, "I'll see her soon enough."

/ / /

The nurse prepared a bag of medication. "Take one of these every few hours," she instructed, holding up a small plastic bottle. "They'll keep your energy levels up."

"Thanks."

He sat on the edge of the bed, shaved and dressed for outdoors. His face felt light. The back of his neck tingled where they had placed the invisible tracker. He did not tell the nurse that taking medication would probably be the last of his concerns.

"If you feel very weak or faint, give yourself a shot of adrenalin. I've given you antibiotics too. All the dosages are on the bottles. Read them properly. Your body is still fighting off the infection. Don't overexert your-self." She was speaking very fast. He had a sudden sense of the pace at which his life was about to run, and was bewildered by it.

"Okay," he said. "I'll read them."

He held out his hand for the bag. The nurse stared at it. Then she blurted, "I think it's outrageous the way they've treated you. Stitched you up. The Rechnovs. After all you've done."

It had not occurred to Vikram that he might meet with sympathy. He was touched. The nurse pushed the bag into his hand.

"Thanks," he said gruffly. He read her name tag. "Thanks, Yilla."

"It's not fair," she said.

It was paradoxical, he thought, that the first person this side of the border whose empathy he had recognized outright might also be the last.

Yilla escorted him to the lift. At reception he paused for a moment, observing the order of the place. Doctors in white coats held Surfboards with details ready to be checked. Patients waited to be called. He tried to imagine the resources it would take to set up three surgeries like this in the west. It occurred to him for the first time that such order might really be unattainable; he'd been shouting at the Moon.

"Vikram Bai?"

It was one of Linus's people. Not in uniform but with a face that said skadi to Vikram as clearly as text. Hoisting the backpack, he followed the man outside. It was late afternoon and the sun hung low in the sky.

The skad directed him to his boat. He showed Vikram where the decoy tracker was. He gave him a map with the location where he was to meet the rebels in three hours time. Vikram stuffed it into a pocket. The man said good luck, but did not sound as if he meant it, and left him.

The world in his absence had become colossal. Vikram hunkered down in the boat, feeling small and scared. His stomach surged with the movement of the waves.

Boats raced by. There were so many of them and the passengers' eyes were sharp like birds. He did not remember outside being this loud. The noise made him dizzy. He clamped his palms over his ears and bent over, putting his head between his knees. The gleaming towers bore down on him.

When he looked up, the world had not shrunk, and he still had to find his way through the waterways. Home. First he had to go home. The notion confused him: should he go east, or west?

Get a grip, Vik. Switch on the ignition. He leaned forward and turned the key.

A part of his consciousness observed the journey dispassionately. He understood that this time, prison would be with him forever. It would haunt him in every glimpse of green, in every wind-bitten cough. It would linger in his fear of small places, and his confusion at the very large. The three week spell had marked him in a way he would never again be able to ignore.

Whatever happens now, I can't go back.

I'd rather die.

He breathed deeply, watched the water. He was, as Linus Rechnov had informed him, on a tight schedule.

39 ｜ ADELAIDE

The storm raged overhead. Purple clouds lurched across the night sky, disgorging sheets of rain. Adelaide stood in an open doorway thirty-six floors above the surface looking at a nylon and fibreglass bridge sheened with water. A bolt of lightning lanced through the rain. She saw gaps yawn between the planks. Clinging to the ropes, halfway across, the figures of Pekko and Rikard tottered forward. The bridge blew back and forth. Adelaide dug her nails into the walls.

You've done this before.

They had crossed nine bridges tonight. Bridges made of anything and everything, obstacles lashed together, pitted with holes and rockpools, each less solid than the last.

You just have to take the first step. You can't let them see you're scared.

But she could not stop talking. The sounds made little sense, then barely any, then none at all.

"I can't do it, can't do it, not that not that not that…"

Behind her, Nils and Drake were growing impatient.

"There's no other way," shouted Nils.

"We could blindfold her," Drake shouted back. "She might go over that way."

"She'll panic more if she can't see."

"She won't if she trusts us."

"She won't trust either of us."

"She will if she wants to live."

The rain splattered the fibreglass boards, making them slippery as ice underfoot.

Don't look down—don't—

Too late. There was the sea, showing the whites of its eyes. Those waves would smash her body against concrete towers. The currents would suck her underwater and rip the air from her lungs.

The wind shrieked through the doorway. Nils was tying a blindfold around her eyes. She did not even try to stop him.

"Listen to me!" Drake's voice brushed her ear. "Do exactly as I say. If you don't move when I tell you, you're going to fall. Do you understand?"

"Yes."

"Put your left foot forward."

They stepped onto the bridge. Her foot slid and her heart leapt before the boot sole gripped. She clung to the ropes. The wind lacerated them. Like a baby, Drake nursed her every step of the way.

At the other end they took off her blindfold. She held out her hands automatically for them to retie her wrists. She looked at nobody and nobody said anything.

They took her through another wet, dripping, crumbling stairwell. Upstairs this time. She had overheard them saying that they might be followed by boat; this, it appeared, was the reason they were moving westwards via bridges. The bridges were never on the same level. They had been moving up and across and down and across in a never-ending game of squid and kelp. Each tower was less inhabitable than the last. None of the towers had electricity, and if anyone was living there she did not see them.

When they went into an empty room and stopped she sat on the spot, dead with exhaustion, too tired to look around her or even imagine trying to escape. The floor was wet, as it always was. Icy trickles dripped from the sodden fur of her hood and down her neck.

"Someone check her wrists," Pekko said curtly. He disappeared. The other three seemed to relax a little, although Nils sat in front of Adelaide and told her to hold out her hands. Pekko had tied the ropes against her skin, so that they could not slip over the material of her gloves, and in spite of the cold she could feel where it rubbed. Nils's fingers brushed against her wrists as he checked each of the knots.

"Vikram told me you're a good man," she muttered.

"And he told me you're a stupid bitch," said Nils, but amiably, she thought. "Which of us d'you figure he's lying to?"

She felt her bonds loosen, then tighten again as he secured them differently. The ropes lay flatter against her skin, and she realized that they would chafe less like that.

"Did he really say that?"

"He did." Nils paused. "It was a long time ago."

Adelaide wondered whether he felt sorry for her, and found the prospect more frightening than simple contempt. Nils probably knew what Pekko was planning to do with her.

She gave him a low lashed look, and as he tightened the knots, let her fingers curl up to his wrists.

"That's not going to work," Nils said.

"What's not?"

"Any of your tricks. Listen to me, and I'll tell you why, and then you can stop trying. I have nothing personal against you. Thousands might, but I don't. But that girl who was with us before—Ilona—I happen to love her. She sells her body to make a living and in these parts that means one thing—she's bonded to someone. Because we found you, and on condition that we keep you safe, her cunt of a pimp is going to let her go. So d'you see why you might as well give up now?"

Nils drew the knots taut and let her hands go.

"I guess Vikram was right," she said.

"Vikram's underwater because of you," he said roughly. "The way I see it, you don't have the right to speak his name."

"I never meant for him to get hurt. I tried to get him out."

"Makes no difference to me."

"Where's Ilona now?"

"Somewhere else."

"Why are these towers such a dump, anyway?"

"Because the City screwed us," said Nils. "Over and over again. You never kept a single promise you made in the last fifty years."

"Are you going to bargain for me?" she asked.

Whatever Nils might have replied was lost in a fit of hoarse coughing. His eyes streamed, he gasped for breath. Adelaide peered at him more closely.

"You're sick."

"Fuck off."

He went to sit with Drake and Rikard and the three of them conversed in low voices. Adelaide's hearing had grown sharper, but she could not make out what they were saying above the shrill of the storm.

Her captors were coordinating with other groups, but whenever Pekko took a call on his scarab he talked in secret. She had caught muttered references to the greenhouse and the desalination plant. They let slip no other information. She knew only that an insurrection was under way, and that she had become a part of it. She was the pawn.

The journey seemed to have taken aeons, but it was still dark. She could only have been awake for a matter of hours.

She had regained consciousness in the bottom of a boat, lying on her side, a tarpaulin covering her body to the nose. Her wrists and ankles were tied. When she tried to move she found that they were roped together. Her temples throbbed.

The splash of waves was strange from her position below the waterline, broken with knocks. The clacks were rhythmical. She realized they came from oars.

Her captors talked over her. Their heads were swollen lollipops against the fading sky. It swayed above her, the colour of a turning bruise, purple bleeding into sludgy green. The clouds looked ready to burst.

"—heard anything from Ilona?"

"Still waiting on Maak for a location."

"She'll be alright, Nils."

"I know, but I could've—"

"You know why."

"Yeah."

"Is that a…?"

"No. Waterbus."

The last voice was Drake. She was sitting in the stern. Her boots were close to Adelaide's head, close enough to see, in the disappearing light, the beaten quality of the leather under its waterproof waxing. A few wiry curls escaped the outline of her hood, nodding in the wind. Adelaide was concealed from the worst of the wind's blast which bagged and billowed the others' clothes.

The man with the beard was one of the two rowers. The other was a burly man whose hood was pulled forward over his face. Their arms worked in strong, regular motion. The fourth occupant, seated at the prow, wore no hood. His hair was shaved down to stubble and she wondered how he could stand the cold.

She noticed the bulge of guns in their clothes. They held them close, but not in the easy, caressing manner of the skadi. They held them as though they were scared to let the weapons go. That worried her more.

They passed beneath a bridge. Footsteps sprinted over with a hollow boom. A pair of dangling feet, a jeer and a missile splashing the water, not far from the boat. Then they were past. Peering back, Adelaide saw teeth ridged the underside of the bridge. Icicles. She could just make out other bridges higher up, like faint webbing in the dusk.

She tried to lift her head. The effort caused an explosion of pain behind her eyes, and drew the attention of the man with the shaved head. He observed her coldly, unblinkingly.

"Where are you taking me?"

"Shut up."

Those two quiet syllables held a world of hatred.

"Will you just tell me where we're going?"

"I said shut up. If you don't shut up, I will hurt you. Do you understand? Don't speak, nod."

Mute, terrified, she dipped her head.

"Blindfold her."

Drake's hands reached down. Adelaide saw the other girl's eyes intent on the task, before the material enfolded her vision. With the loss of sight, her internal compass clicked off. The boat's uneven motion nauseated her. *Open your ears*, she reminded herself. They were her most useful tool now.

Night would be setting in. She remembered the girl Liis saying something about a curfew, but she did not want to think about Liis, Liis who had fallen, lost Liis. Adelaide did not know what had happened to her family. She knew nothing about the girl at all, except that she had been fighting for something she believed in, and now she was dead.

On the backs of her eyelids she watched them fall again, slowly this time. Apart from Goran, Adelaide had little experience with the Home Guard, but if all of them were like Goran, then she knew what had happened after.

Goran was a man who enjoyed cruelty. He understood it as a science. Those falling bodies were not people to the Guard. They were target practice.

As the oars dipped and rose she had caught her captor's names. Rikard, the burly man, Nils, the one Drake had led her too. And Pekko.

From her journey in the boat to where they rested now, she had gained an idea of the group's dynamic. Pekko was in charge. She sensed his surveillance, a brooding pulse in the darkness. Instinctively, she understood that all of his resentment and rage towards the City was now conditioned into a sole desire: to spill her blood. She heard it in his voice, a rigidly controlled hunger when he spoke about her. She saw it in the way he took out his knife, and scraped it back and forth over a loose bit of metal.

She tried to speak to him.

"What do you want? My family can pay."

She knew immediately that it was the wrong thing to say. Pekko looked at her speculatively, as though she was an insect, one that he would like to flatten and lick the blood that came out.

"You Rechnovs..." he said slowly. "All you do is take, and glory in the taking." He stripped off his glove, held up his left hand, and she saw that the last two fingers had been crudely amputated. "You know how I lost these? No, it wasn't in the riots. It was the cold, a long time before. Stars, I despise your family. I think I despise you even more. You know, in the west you're a laughingstock. But you're dangerous too, dangerous like the senile are dangerous, because they're so stupid they can't see what they're doing. Money? What use is money to me? But I'll watch them crawl, your Rechnov clan. I'll watch their attempts to get you back."

He drew the knots tight and smiled.

"I wonder how hard they'll try?"

She had hoped that Vikram's name might act as a kind of talisman for her safety, or even a potential exchange which would release them both. It had met with anger, resentment and suspicion. Pekko grew sullen at any reference to Vikram's ties with Citizens. For him, her relationship with Vikram was akin to debasement for the west. Nils merely sneered.

Whilst they waited for Pekko to come back, Rikard opened his pack and distributed kelp squares. He came over and gave her one, then offered her the water flask. He went back to the others without a word. He had never spoken to her. The kelp was stale and hard but compact. She chewed steadily. Her tongue drained the salt from it and left her sucking thirstily.

She gazed out of the window-wall. Panes of bufferglass had broken away and were boarded up. What remained was filthy. Lightning flashed and she glimpsed the tower opposite. Confused, inexplicably afraid, she forgot her hunger and stopped, the kelp square half eaten in her hand. Her teeth chattered, but she did not notice. Another flash lit up outside. Thunder rumbled close by.

"It's leaning," she said. Nils shot her a glance. "The tower. It's leaning."

"Something's eating the foundations," he said shortly.

"Something?"

"Unhappy spirits. It burned once, that tower. An electrical fault, so they said. It was when the first refugees came. People were inside it. They burned too. Stands to reason their spirits haunt the place." Nils glanced towards the window-wall. "Other people say it's a monster."

Adelaide stared where the slanted tower had been. "That's ridiculous."

"Good," Nils said blankly. "Because that's where we're going next."

She could not suppress a shiver. Something about the tower chilled her. She had an unshakeable sense of premonition.

Pekko returned. He flashed his torch in her face and then onto her hands, as he always did when he had been gone for more than a minute. There was someone with him; a stooped figure in shapeless rags, who could have been male or female. The voice, when it spoke, was a hoarse rasp.

"No more bridges. Only seventieth."

"What's the seventieth?" Nils asked.

The figure shuffled back reluctantly. Pekko caught its arm.

"You agreed to show us."

"Not good to go there, cursed place, why you cross?"

"We have to get across. Where's the bridge?"

"Don't show. I tell. You listen, go if you must."

Adelaide lifted her eyes to this weird specimen, trying to see its face. She sensed her gaze reciprocated.

Nils went over.

The two men and the stranger conversed in low voices. Pekko muttered something under his breath. Nils responded sharply. Pekko nodded. They both glanced at Adelaide.

"What?" she said.

"We're going up," Nils said curtly.

The would-have-been guide disappeared as abruptly as he had come.

The five of them climbed to the seventieth floor and reached a door that careened on one hinge. Pekko flashed about a torch. The room was empty, completely empty, even without litter. There was a two metre gash where part of the window-wall had been ripped away. Icy sleet blew inside. It was freezing.

"Stars," muttered Nils. He was wheezing.

"Great bridge," Adelaide ventured. She had to get Nils on side.

"Oh, you'll like the bridge," said Pekko, a nasty grin curling his lips. He reached overhead and tugged on a length of rope which was attached to a metal ring in the wall.

"What's that?"

"That's the bridge," Pekko said.

Adelaide stared, uncomprehending. She looked at the metal ring, the thick tarred knots, the rope which ran close to the ceiling and out.

"You've got to be joking."

The others looked equally unhappy. Drake and Nils exchanged glances. Rikard pulled on the rope, testing its strength.

"Pekko, you'd better go first," said Nils at last. "We don't want her running off on the other side."

Pekko nodded. From his rucksack he took a tangle of rope and began fashioning it into some kind of harness. Adelaide watched his hands at work under the torchlight with a sick fascination. She glanced through the gaping wall. Now the leaning tower was invisible. Thunder rumbled again.

"I'm not going over a rope," she said. "We're seventy floors above sea level, are you all crazy? Did you hear what that—that man said downstairs, he said this place is cursed. I'm not going there and I'm definitely not going on that bit of string. It looks ready to snap."

"Leave it," muttered Nils.

"None of you want to use it either, this is fucking insane!"

She stared at Drake but Drake looked away.

"Would you gag her, please," said Pekko, continuing to work with the ropes. "She's doing my head in."

"With pleasure," Nils retorted. "Don't struggle," he said, as the material pulled once again at the corners of her mouth. "Or I'll use tape instead, and that's more unpleasant to get off."

Her nose sucked in air frantically. Pekko had slipped on his harness; a rudimentary construction which tightened under his arms and around his chest. He reached up and hooked it onto the rope. His face betrayed no fear; only the single-minded, merciless determination that was as much a part of him as his shaven skull. Nils checked all of the knots. He reached up and gave the rope a tug.

"You're good."

Pekko stepped up to the gap. He stood on the ledge, sleet lashing his face. Adelaide felt her heart treble. Pekko leapt and vanished.

She gave a moan of horror. Pekko had drowned, and Nils was about to send her after him.

Nils peered across the chasm. He gave a shout, and flashed a torch twice. An answering light blinked. Pekko had made it across. A minute later the harness came spinning back across the rope. Nils reeled it in.

"You're next."

She tried to make a bolt for it but they anticipated the move. She didn't even make it to the door. Nils pulled the harness over her head. She fought him, struggling with every weapon she had left. Her forehead contacted with his collar bone. She heard him grunt. Then Drake put a knee into the small of her back and she went down. She felt the harness tightening around her chest.

"Come on," said Nils. "Just get it over with."

She didn't move so he wrenched her to her feet. The harness fastened to the slimy rope. She tried to speak but even if the gag hadn't been there, only gibberish would have come out. Her body was dysfunctional with fear. Nils dragged her towards the window-wall. Her shoes scraped on the buckling floor. Thunder and lightning split the sky and illuminated the leaning tower. She was a foot away from the edge—her toes were at the brink—over it—blackness above and below—

Nils untied her hands.

"I'd hold on if I were you," said Drake from behind.

She gripped the rope. It was the only thing between her and death.

I don't want to drown. Oh stars, I don't want to drown. Give me any end other than that…

Hail fell in a gulf of oblivion.

Another rumble, another sheet of lightning flared. Nils's shove sent her spinning out. She closed her eyes against the onslaught of sleet and wind. Thunder growled and her scream was muffled by the gag and the elements. She saw the lightning that followed on the backs of her eyelids. She thought she'd been hit.

Arms were around her. She collapsed into the ungiving mass. She could not understand that her feet were on a solid structure; she couldn't support herself.

"Get up," said Pekko.

She opened her eyes. She was on the other side. Pekko, taking no risks, was retying her wrists before he untied the harness. He flashed the torch back across the brink. She saw tiny dots, Nils responding. Pekko sent the harness back.

Adelaide cringed away from the gap and from Pekko. The wall here had disintegrated even more than in the other tower.

"I wouldn't run anywhere," Pekko said. "The whole tower is structurally unsound. Listen. You can hear it eroding."

His voice echoed in the empty room. There were no lights. The floor was uneven underfoot, littered with unnameable, crunching debris. When she listened, she heard a deep, unearthly moaning. *There's something eating the foundations.*

Nils landed walking. He must have done this before, she thought numbly. Nils stripped off the harness and passed it to Pekko, who sent it back for the others.

Nils switched on a torch. It lit the planes of his face weirdly.

"Welcome to the unremembered quarters."

40 ¦ VIKRAM

The snow came down from the sky in dizzy swirls and collected in the well of the boat. It stuck to the hood and the shoulders of Vikram's coat. He hunched over, shivering. At the prow a red lantern produced a dim glow. Every few minutes Vikram leaned forward and brushed the flakes away from its casing. The lantern was his signal.

The westerners, Surface Level or whoever they were, were late. He could not think of them as enemies, but neither could he think of them as friends. He had no idea who he was about to meet.

He should have a plan. He should have a decision, at least. But he had nothing. The invisible circle on the back of his neck seemed to pulse gently. He knew it was only his own circulation. He was the only person who could feel that mark. No-one else could translate its soft message: *traitor, traitor, traitor, traitor.*

If that was the decision.

Something bumped against his boat. He glanced down and made out a broken square from a raft rack, covered with two inches of snow. He reached over the side to push it away.

Two hands grabbed his shoulders, toppling him backwards. He lashed out. His elbow contacted—something—someone. A cry was stifled. The return blow, hard and fast, caught him in the ribs. He wheezed. A hand clamped over his mouth, halving his air. He struggled and wrenched the wrist away—a surprisingly thin wrist—but his assailant already had an arm against his throat and was dragging him backwards. Vikram reached around and punched behind him. The blow returned a muffled grunt. They were at the edge of the boat. Vikram tilted backwards and he realized his assailant was using Vikram's own body weight as an anchor.

They tumbled overboard together, hitting the water with a compact splash. Vikram went under. The cold immersed him. His lungs seared with salt. He broke surface, gasping. Snowflakes poured onto his face. Arms wrapped once more around his chest and a voice whispered in his ear, "Quiet now. We're getting you out."

The cold was paralysing. He could not find the energy to speak, let alone fight. The assailant's legs kicked under him with strong movements. He was towed steadily away from the boat.

One moment he was looking at the boat, the next a billowing sphere of flames. A fiery cloud blossomed—it seemed to hang, for a few, infinite seconds—and then a shower of sparks rained over the surface. Hot ash sprayed Vikram's face. He did not think to wipe it away. He barely noticed his assailant hauling him into another vehicle. He was staring, mute, at the spot where his boat had been. The backs of his eyes prickled, and he felt a rush of sadness.

"Lie low," whispered the voice again. "You were being followed. They will come to see what has happened."

It was just a boat. He knew that. Vikram turned his head away from the destruction and saw his opponent's face in the last of the firelight.

"Ilona?"

Incredulity wiped out anything else. The girl, Nils's girl, was crouched low inside the boat. It was a tiny boat, and Ilona was inches from Vikram. She spoke urgently.

"Tell me Vikram, this is very important. They will be using you to find us. There was probably a tracker on board your boat. Is there one on you?"

"Ilona, what the hell are you—"

"Are they tracking you, Vikram?"

"Yes. Yes of course they are. Back of the neck. You can only feel it if you know it's there. It's like a disc…"

He pulled down his scarves and felt the cold thrill against the patch of bare skin. Ilona took something out of a pocket. He felt her gloved fingers push against his neck before the air numbed his skin to all sensation.

"What are you doing?"

"Dampening it. Done." She pulled the scarves back up. "Keep low."

"Where are we going?"

"The unremembered quarters."

"Why are we going there?"

"That's where Adelaide is. Don't worry. Nils is there."

"Nils? What's he got to do—"

"No more questions, Vikram."

Ilona began to row. His journey continued in silence. The shock was impacting on him now, physical and mental. Fate was playing havoc with his soul tonight. He felt sick.

Every few towers, Ilona eased into an offshoot waterway and stopped.

"Look." She pointed. Vikram saw the dull shadow of a patrol boat crawling past. Searchlights arced from their prows.

"If a searchlight comes over, get in the water," Ilona muttered. "These days they shoot dead bodies for fun."

The night had come alive at last. The blizzard was pierced by intermittent gunfire. Muffled by the snowfall, it was difficult to pinpoint from where the sounds came. Vikram was full of questions, but all of Ilona's concentration was on the boat. The air felt choked with halted conflict.

He saw Mikkeli, perched on the end of the coracle, her feet trailing in the water. She was made entirely of snowflakes and foam.

Keli? Is that you?

Oh, I'm here Vik. I'm with you every step of the way. Always have been.

Stay with me, Keli.

But she didn't speak again. Soon she too drifted away from the raft, and the faint plash of Ilona's oars in the snow-filled night was the only proof that they were both alive.

"Ilona? Is Drake safe?"

"Yes."

"What about—"

But she wouldn't know Shadiyah, or Marete and Hal, or Hella, or old Mr Argele.

They were approaching the unremembered quarters. Not even the shanty-boats or the dealers came here, only the dregs of destitution. These quarters were cursed.

"We're here," said Ilona.

The crooked tower loomed overhead, an absence where the snow did not fall. This was the one they said was inhabited, not by people, but by something else. The one that had burned. He imagined the ghosts clinging to the walls, their hands like suckered amphibians. He thought he heard them whisper. About him? To him?

There was no decking. Part of the wall was broken and the sea surged inside. Ilona steered the boat through the gap. Inside, the sound of her oars echoed back at them and water ran off the walls in small streams.

How could he possibly get Adelaide out without a boat? And shouldn't Linus have known that the rebels would find the tracker?

Ilona rowed through the flooded rooms until they reached the stairwell. She switched on a torch and secured the craft to the rusting rail.

"This way. We've blocked the other stairwells, this is the only way up."

Vikram followed her up the crumbling steps. The water logged in his upper clothing was beginning to freeze and he crackled when he moved. Every step was an effort. Ilona held the torch in front of them. They progressed slowly. Everywhere Vikram looked the building was falling to bits. Black powder fell away when he brushed the walls. Despite the freezing temperature, the smell of stale dead things reached his nose. Preserved carcasses of half-eaten animals lined the steps. Ten flights up Ilona's torch flared on a man sitting bolt upright, his eyes wide and accusing but no life left in their gaze.

They kept going past the corpse. Vikram's muscles were trembling with fatigue. He lost track of the floors and was disorientated by the time Ilona said, "This is us."

She knocked on the door. There was a pause, then an answering knock from the other side. Ilona replied with a more complicated pattern. Vikram heard the sounds of furniture shifting and then the door scraped open.

"Vik!"

Something hard and furry flung itself at him. He disentangled himself from the pair of arms and found himself looking at the dark eyes and slightly squashed nose of Drake. She was grinning from ear to ear. His answering smile was wobbly with relief.

"I told you he'd make it," Drake flung back over her shoulder. "Get inside, Vik, you're freezing."

The room was dark except for the torchlight and the glow of a heater, around which the others were gathered, bulked up in shapeless layers of wool and hide. Ilona went straight over to Nils. He lifted his hand to his shoulder and she squeezed it and Nils said something to her Vikram didn't hear. He recognized Rikard, the guy Drake had said hello to that night in the bar. So there'd been something to it after all, or there was now. There was a third man that he did not know.

Rikard and the stranger were staring at Vikram openly, but Nils did not look at him.

"Hi, Nils."

"Vik."

For a moment, the tension between the two men was like salt on a wound. Slowly, Nils stood up and crossed the room. Nils hesitated. Then he lifted his arms and engulfed Vikram in a hug.

"You got out," said Nils. His voice was gruff.

"You got me out, it seems."

Nils glanced around.

"Yeah, well, long story."

Vikram had the same sinking sensation he had felt talking to Linus. There was something else going on here, something he did not yet understand. Drake's grin began to falter.

"Long time no see, Vik," said Rikard. Hostility there, Vikram thought. He met the other man's eyes squarely.

"Yeah, it's been a while."

"You dealt with the boat?" The third man spoke to Ilona, curtly, but his eyes flicked to Vikram. He wore no hood or a hat and his head was shorn; he was either immune to the cold, or it was a statement.

"It's gone," Ilona said.

"You've checked him for trackers?"

"One on the neck. Dampened. I can't get it off, those things stick."

"That's Pekko," Drake murmured.

"What do you mean stick?" Vikram said uneasily.

Pekko gazed at him. "The Citizens use semi-implants as trackers. Don't worry. You'll get it off once we're done here."

An icy pool was forming around Vikram's feet. The heater was beginning to melt the ice in his clothes. Its warmth, coming out of the cold, was almost an assault. He was starting to feel giddy.

"So what's going on?" he asked. "You've got Adelaide here?"

Drake's smile dropped away. Nils frowned. Suddenly Vikram wondered if even his best friends did not trust him. He was acutely aware of his appearance. His clothes, even wrecked by water, had a different cut. His hair felt clipped and wrong. He had a stamp on the back of his neck.

Pekko broke the silence.

"Nils, check him again, get him new clothes." He gave the orders in this cell, then. Was Pekko the coordinator that Linus had described?

"Oh—" as they turned to move. "And don't touch this wall—it's live."

Vikram glanced back. Pekko was standing, his hands thrust into his pockets, a smile curving his lips but not parting them. Vikram looked at the wall. It was damp. He thought he saw a spark, but in the murky light and his current state of disorientation, he could not be certain of what he was seeing.

"Sure," he said.

Nils took a torch and led Vikram into the adjacent room. The torch flickered over rows and rows of metre-high counters. The strip lighting over each unit was broken, the glass long stolen and wires dangling down, frozen into twisting spirals. Vikram recognised the layout of the space. He had seen it in working greenhouses.

"We're using this for storage," said Nils, indicating a unit where a few blankets were folded and stacked. There were sealed containers of food, a toolbox, a couple of pans, a disconnected Neptune.

The door swung closed behind them. Vikram grabbed Nils's arm.

"What's going on in there?"

"It's a fucking awkward situation," Nils hissed.

"Then tell me about it!"

"They don't trust you. Pekko. Rikard. The people running this show. Here, change into these."

Nils handed him a bundle. Vikram stripped off his dripping clothes, retrieving the medicine given him by the nurse, and changed quickly. The new clothes were shabby and didn't fit well, but they were warm. Someone must have placed them near the heater before he arrived. Drake, probably.

"Why did they get me out if they don't trust me?"

"Because you're one of ours."

"Precisely!"

Nils hesitated. "The Citizens must have offered you a deal."

"Yeah, so?"

"Pekko thought you might have—accepted."

"Who the hell's Pekko, anyway? I thought there was some kind of rebellion group—is it just you guys?"

Nils leant against the door and folded his arms.

"Vik, this is more complicated than you realize. Pekko's in charge here. And it's not just us, he's working for Maak. Remember Maak? The guy Mikkeli used to take deliveries for? He's way up the ladder now. They call the group Surface, as though it's a movement, like Horizon, but it's not. It's Maak—or his people—that own Ilona. He probably brought down Juraj. And he's orchestrating this uprising. They're playing a game, Vik. It's about more than territory now, it's about people. Getting Adelaide—and now you back—it's a statement, you see. I mean, there's never been a hostage situation before. Why d'you think we're holed up like lice in this cursed place?" Nils spat on the ground to ward off any spirits that might be listening. "You should also know that Pekko hates Citizens," he said. "Pathologically."

"So I'm a Citizen now, am I?"

"I didn't say that."

"Do you trust me?" Nils did not reply. "Nils, do you trust me?"

"Yeah. Yeah, 'course I do." Nils scooped up the pile of Vikram's old clothes and began to wring them out. "I suppose we'll have to burn these."

"Great, we can have a fire."

"Look, just be careful, okay? You've been away for a while. Things have been happening. Riots have been on the cards for a good while now."

"Yeah, well, I wish you'd said something before."

Nils shrugged.

I wasn't here, thought Vikram.

"You look terrible," Nils said. "I guess it was hell in there."

Silence fell between them; Vikram trying to find a way to communicate what could not be explained, Nils no doubt trying to imagine a place which could not be imagined.

"Thanks for getting me out," Vikram said. "I was going mad."

"Yeah." Nils's eyes dropped. "You can guarantee Pekko wants something from you. He likes making people do things. That's why he sent Ilona to get you, not me or Drake—as if she has to prove herself before they'll let her go."

"Right."

It came as no real surprise. He felt only resignation, and a dull ache, where another hook had been planted in his body for someone else to pull upon, in yet another direction. Linus Rechnov, Maak and Pekko—between them they would tear him apart.

They were about to go back when Vikram said, "Where is Adelaide, anyway?"

Nils scowled. "In another room. She's a pain in the ass."

Vikram forced a laugh. "You think so, huh?"

"Never stops talking," Nils mumbled. He stopped. "Vikram, tell me honestly. Have you got a thing for that girl?"

"Honestly? No."

Nils looked at him and Vikram wasn't sure his friend believed the lie.

"Why?"

Nils did not answer.

They gathered around the heater, Nils and Ilona huddled together, Drake next to Vikram. Scraps of material and a scissored tarpaulin had been wedged into every crack around the window-wall board, but there was still a draught at Vikram's back. Damp char was everywhere. The others had tried to sweep the floor but the stuff came off on his clothes and all of them were sooted with it.

"Can someone explain the situation?" he asked. "I didn't get much out of the Citizens."

"It's fragile," said Pekko tersely. Vikram kept his gaze neutral. Clearly he was gaining no votes of confidence from Pekko. "The city is withholding kelp and fish supplies. We're already on rations and rumour has it supplies are running out, so as you can imagine, panic's set in. I hear Market Circle yesterday was a bomb site."

Rikard was warming a flask by the heater. He sipped from it, testing the temperature, then put it back.

"What about our fishing boats?"

"Skadi curfew," said Nils. "One or two boats are getting out but it's a risky business. We've already lost one."

"And the uprising? Coordinated or independent?"

"There're three cells," Nils explained. "All answering to Maak. An inside team are guarding our lines to the desalination plant, so we won't have a repeat of last time." Drake's eyes lifted to Vikram's, and he knew that all three of them were thinking of Mikkeli's last insane action. "A second group have taken S-801-W, the greenhouse. And we've got the Rechnov girl."

"The bargaining chip."

"Exactly."

Logistically, it was not a bad plan. Maak, or whoever was orchestrating the cells, had obviously taken previous mistakes into account. It sounded like they were serious. Rikard tested the contents of the flask again, and passed around a thin, salty broth.

"So what are we asking for?"

"Release of the fish and kelp boats, and the skadi to withdraw. For now."

"D'you think they'll accept?"

"They've let you out," drawled Pekko.

"If they think you are dead, that's an advantage," said Ilona. "It shows we have the edge."

"We'll offer them a deal," said Pekko. "The girl in exchange for our demands. Which will be incremental. Really, she's very useful. But I suppose you've discovered that already."

"We're rigging an exchange site," said Drake, too quickly. "Coordinating with Sorren, at the greenhouse."

"Sounds like everything's under control," said Vikram.

"Oh, it is." Pekko smiled. "As you see, whilst you've been fraternizing with Citizens, we've been busy with the real business of revolution. So why don't you just sit back and enjoy the show."

He kept his mouth shut and his ears open. The smaller room of the tower was the hub: this was where they ate, slept, and contacted the other cells. Pekko had a scarab and Vikram guessed that Maak's black market contacts had been at work. The heater was wired to a damp hole in the wall, hooked onto a rogue current. The electricity must run up an insulated vein in the tower from deep underground, or perhaps there was still some life in the burnt solar skin. Every few minutes a drop of water ran down the wall and Vikram saw blue sparks leap from the hole. He got used to it after a while. The sparks and the mistrust.

They huddled around the heater, playing cards. Every hour, someone went to check on Adelaide, and everyone else got up and stretched. Wary of Nils's words, Vikram was careful not to ask about Adelaide in front of Pekko. Once he caught Drake aside and managed to say, "Is she okay?" Drake shrugged and said, "What do you think?" and then Pekko was looking at them and he couldn't say anything more.

A couple of hours after he arrived, Rikard organized food, warming a few of the cans on the heater. It was a processed stew, the contents unidentifiable, and not enough of it. Vikram ate slowly. The stew lodged in his stomach, an indigestible lump.

Pekko's scarab buzzed whilst they were eating. The noise sounded odd, its robotic repeat echoing around the room. Pekko went into the storeroom to answer the o'comm. Drake rolled her eyes at Vikram, but he noticed that she checked straight after to see if Rikard had seen the look. Rikard was the unknown quantity. Vikram remembered nothing about the man except for his face; he'd known a lot of people involved in the last riots.

He had also noticed that Nils was coughing a lot, and trying to hide it.

When they had finished eating, Rikard collected up the empty cans and set to work cleaning them in a bowl of drip-water. The set of his back said quite clearly that he wished for no assistance.

Pekko came back. Vikram waited for him to explain, but the man said nothing, just picked up his can and spooned up the remainder of his food. Finally Nils asked, with a hint of irritation, "Was that Sorren's cell?"

"Tomorrow," said Pekko.

"Tomorrow?"

"I'll be talking to the Citizens—" he spat the word, his immobile face revealing a brief flicker of disgust. "Tomorrow."

/ / /

Vikram slept badly. The torches were off and shadows materialized from under the heater's glow. The night was filled with the sounds of breathing, of small creatures. He thought of his first night indoors, he and Nils, Keli and Drake. He remembered sharing plans, ambitions, talking other nonsense, a story of Drake's—something to do with a raft rack dare and a man with velvet eyes, Drake and Keli giggling. He woke in fits and starts, thinking he was there, with them. When he remembered that one of them was dead, the glass in his chest was as sharp as it had been three years ago. He woke later thinking he was in a bed, that the rough sacking was cotton sheets, and that if he rolled over he would touch the drowsy limbs of a red-haired girl. He threw out an arm and found damp floor. The sacking smelled of mould. She was not far, that girl, a matter of metres away, lying against the same hard floor.

Silently his lips formed her name: *Adelaide*.

When he woke again, a trickle of grey light was seeping through a crack in the boarded window-wall. He watched the wall turn from grey to brownish green to sickly yellow. It was a new day, and he already wished it were over.

41 | ADELAIDE

The man who wanted to kill her had taken away the light. Adelaide's wrists hurt. They were fastened to the piping with steel rings, but she could not see the steel or the piping. The room was black. Water dripped in a corner. She curled in the same position she'd been in for the past hours, or days, or however long, face buried in her knees, her arms raised overhead to where they were fastened. She knew that it would hurt too much to move, so she didn't.

In the dark, she wandered through childhood haunts: through the hidden dens in the Domain, the space under her bunk bed, her grandfather's room with the marmalade cat. She went to the Roof and drank Kelpiqua, giggled and gulped and watched Axel standing on his hands, grinning at her upside-down.

The Roof receded, flying away from them at impossible speed. Axel bowed to thunderous applause and went behind a curtain, so she followed him but he wasn't there, Tyr was, and after that she found Tyr in every place but home.

And then Tyr, too, went behind the curtain and there was only Vikram, the man from the ice, who would always be alone, as she would, as they were both destined to be. The crater in the ocean gaped, and there was the chromium mermaid, but this time the mermaid was Adelaide. Adelaide's tail swished. Here, in the molten sea mud, the truth awaited her with a silver smile.

She had always been chasing her own tail. Even if Axel were alive, even if she did find him, she was not recovering her brother. She was recovering what he had become.

Everyone she cared about had disappeared. Axel, Tyr, even Vikram. She was a curse. She was bad luck. She ran on.

On, along the gleaming shuttle lines, over the glass funnel bridges, from the lowest underwater boutiques to the roof garden parties at the top of the world, up and down, in lifts and through stairwells, until she reached the butterfly farm. The path twisted before her feet. The farm had become colossal, and its glass walls were made of diamonds. What was she doing? She was searching for Axel. She ran on. She called his name. *Axel! Axel, where in Osiris are you?* He was playing hide and seek again. He had been playing for too long now, and it wasn't funny.

She sat on a bench and sobbed because she could not find him. The butterfly farm moved away; it was attached to a boat, a boat that had travelled for months and for miles, a boat whose murdered crew lay in a graveyard at the bed of the ocean, where their bones rattled as they sang of their own slow decomposition. Adelaide held onto the dream. She held it tight because she was cold, colder than she had ever been, and she did not want to wake and find out what the cold had done.

Something crawled along her cheek, towards her nose. She thought it was a butterfly. But it was an insect, an invader from the real world. A white fly. She hunched her shoulder to knock it aside.

Now sounds raked at the dream, threatening to pull her into consciousness. She clung tighter to the spirit world. A door, opening onto the butterfly farm with an ungentle scrape, and there were people framed within it, and voices. The man who wanted to kill her was there. The girl with the black tooth was there.

She saw Vikram last. He had been walking the vaults of her dreams with the others; it made sense that he was here, allied with the cold. He had a green tinge. The cell had stuck to his skin, as it had stuck to hers when she left him last.

One of them spoke. She ran further into the butterfly farm. She saw the Red Pierrot balanced on a leaf, saw its wings opening and closing. It fluttered into the air and she followed it. Even when the man with the shaven head took her chin and she shivered and he lifted her face to stare into her dream-drugged eyes with his own, she saw only the red and black and white spots, the symmetry.

Vikram was in front of her. She kept very still. If she did not move he would not see her, and he mustn't see her, not yet. She hid behind the flowers. Vikram spoke her name. His lips moved. There was a look in his eyes, an unfamiliar, broken look that she knew she must remember, but even as she frowned he dissolved into the foliage.

/ / /

She found herself fully conscious, and she knew that the dream world had gone for good; she had woken up.

"Vik?" she whispered.

Her eyes were wide open but saw nothing. She was cold, so cold. Colder than she'd ever been.

"Vik!"

There was no light, because she had missed him. The room was empty. Vikram had gone.

42 ¦ VIKRAM

Pekko stood behind him, his disdain like a burn between Vikram's shoulder blades.

"Talk to her."

Adelaide seemed half-dead. Vikram crouched in front of her, looked right into her eyes as he said her name. There was no response but the drowsy flicker of her eyelashes, as though she was drugged.

As they closed the door on the tiny room, Adelaide's presence stayed with him, as if she had become a part of his own pulse. He could not set aside the image of her face under Pekko's torchlight. Somehow, he had to protect her.

One of them was always on watch. They patrolled the circumference of the tower, walking through the empty laboratories, past the torched counters, around metal twisted into weird sculptures and the traces of clumsily adapted sleeping spaces. Ilona and Rikard went to check that their blockades were still in place in the other stairwells. Peering out of the dirt filmed window-walls, they watched for any sign of skadi vehicles. The only boats they saw were fish barges heading out to sea.

Pekko contacted the other cells. He reported that they were holding out. The second cell had arranged a call to the Citizens which they would link to Pekko later in the day. The others played cards. They made up a game with a motley collection of chess, Shells and Sharkbait rules. Buried in the dirt, Vikram found a necklace carved out of bone. The string had rotted. When he lifted it the beads scuttled away. He collected them up and they used the pieces for counters.

Nils called Rikard on a point.

"That was five."

"It was a six."

"It was a five, I saw it tip."

"It was a fucking six."

"Guys, come on!" Drake grabbed the die. "Just throw it again."

Around lunch time, Rikard handed out kelp squares. Vikram knew that he should be hungry but his stomach felt like air. He had to force himself to eat. Afterwards, he swallowed a few of the pills surreptitiously.

Vikram's memories of the last riots were all vivid, fast-paced scenes—images of action, of violence, of cold clear mornings and wet nightfalls peppered with the clash of Home Guard guns. Perhaps there had been waiting too. Perhaps he had forgotten. He itched for information, for any news. He would have slid easily into the group's routines.

He spoke to Pekko.

"Why don't you let me take a patrol? Split the shifts between us?"

Pekko looked at him and said, "I don't think so."

"I want to help."

"It's not negotiable."

As they threw down hand after hand of Pirahna and Sharkbait, he went through every possible and impossible solution in his head. Vikram would not—he could not betray his friends. The act was unthinkable. That did not mean he wasn't searching for a way to get Adelaide out. Could one of fishing boats help him—could he get out a message? What if he let Adelaide escape, told her to hide in the tower until it was all over? Could he make it look like she'd got out by herself?

By mid-afternoon, he was exhausted. He curled up for a rest. He was only going to doze for thirty minutes but slept for several hours. The lost time worried him. His body never used to crash out with such dangerous oblivion.

When he woke, Pekko was out of the room. Vikram stretched his stiff, groggy limbs, easing cracks out of his knee and elbow joints. He winced as he kneaded the circulation into his muscles. He smelled tobacco. Nils lay on his side, dragging on a cigarette, hacking after every inhalation. Vikram had an instant craving for one of Adelaide's cigarillos, their warm, woody, complex taste, even their acrid afterbite. Next to Nils, Ilona was filing down her nails with a bit of metal. On the other side of the heater, Rikard and Drake sat talking quietly.

"My brother's over with Maak's people," Rikard was saying.

"Is he your real brother?"

"No. Good as, though."

"Course. What does he think?"

"Same as us. That it's changed. Used to be about equality, but everyone knows that isn't coming. Says there's been a lot of talk in the last year. About changing policy."

"In Surface?"

"Everywhere."

"I suppose your brother sees a lot of Maak, working with them."

Rikard had clearly seen that Vikram was awake, but he answered Drake nonetheless. "I don't think anyone sees too much of the man."

"Who is Maak?" Vikram asked. His voice came out hoarse and crackly, and he cleared his throat.

"Who is he, or who was he?" said Rikard.

"Both."

Rikard stretched out his legs. "He used to be a petty dealer. Greenhouse drugs, bit of manta on the side. Rose up to second in the Juraj gang. According to legend, he killed Juraj, then hacked him up and used the body parts for fish bait."

"But Juraj burned. On a pyre. We saw it."

"Not his limbs. Maak kept the limbs. But the fire fight—that was him, yeah. Crazed. A lot of Juraj's supporters died that night, shot to bits by the skadi. Conveniently for Maak."

"It's true," said Ilona. "When we heard about it, us girls on the boats, we were pleased at first. Juraj did terrible things to the girls."

Nils squeezed her hand.

"But Maak is no better than Juraj," Ilona added. "He burns people alive. He loves to burn things. He made a girl unconscious, then put her on a pyre all soaked in oil. When she woke up she was on fire. We all heard the screams."

Drake scoffed. "I never heard that. They're making things up to scare you."

"I heard the screams," Ilona insisted.

Rikard gave a lopsided smile. "Anyway, however Maak killed the old man, he's merged the Juraj and the Roch gangs. Now he's just known as the Coordinator."

"Except that he's never seen. The man's like a ghost," Nils put in.

"The Coordinator." So Linus Rechnov had been right about one thing. "But what does he coordinate?"

"Violence," said Rikard. "Assassinations. Hostages. That's the way it's going."

"It's not about justice any more," said Drake. "It's about war. That's the choice people have made."

"We never had a choice," said Nils abruptly. "They made it for us. They make the same choice every time they slaughter one of us."

"But we don't have the resources to fight them, never mind attack them," Drake said. "We never have."

"That's why Maak wants insiders," said Rikard. "He's taking on old principles. The man thinks like an Osuwite—the NWO radicals didn't go far enough for him."

Nils exhaled a trickle of smoke through his nostrils. "D'you reckon it was the NWO who killed the Dumays, Rikard?"

"I don't know. Maybe."

"Could have been anyone," said Drake. "You know what I think? I think the Rechnovs did it. Them or the Ngozis." She held her hands over the heater, rubbing them together. "Makes perfect sense. They wanted everyone to hate the west, so they killed off two of their own."

"Could well be," Rikard nodded. "Why don't you ask the girl?"

Drake laughed. "Adelaide? She don't know anything."

Rikard looked at Vikram, as if for confirmation. Vikram thought of his last conversation with Linus. He thought of the man's reaction when he said *Whitefly*. But Adelaide hadn't known about that either; she'd been fishing for information. Once again, he thought of her drugged, ice-bound eyes. There had to be a way to get her out without compromising the others. Adelaide would listen to him. If he told her to hide, she'd hide.

"Honestly," he said. "I don't think she does."

When Pekko returned, his face was agitated. He stood in the doorway, surveying them all, until one by one their conversations dropped away. His hands, buried in his pockets, clenched and unclenched. At first it was not clear whether the news was good or bad. Then a smile twisted Pekko's mouth.

"We have a location for the exchange," he said.

Everyone spoke at once.

"When, Pekko?"

"Who did you speak to?"

"What did they say?"

Pekko came to sit by the heater, not next to anyone but in a space of his own. He was clearly relishing his moment of triumph.

"Tomorrow, two hours after sun-up. S-294-W. They've promised to withdraw the patrol force. They're sending the food supplies."

Rikard rattled two die between his hands.

"Will they expect to see the girl before they release the boats?"

Pekko barked with laughter.

"The girl's going nowhere near the place. All we have to do is sit tight and let Sorren's cell take care of it. They'll seize the supplies. If the Citizens complain we can always send them a bit of the girl. A finger, for example."

Excitedly, the group discussed the logistics. Vikram said nothing. The back of his neck tingled where the dampened tracker was lodged. Implanted, Pekko had said. What in hell's tide had Linus put on him? Had he really imagined Vikram would trust Linus to keep his side of the bargain?

"I'll go check on Adelaide," said Ilona, as if she could read his thoughts.

"Already done," Pekko shot over his shoulder. He grinned. "Not in the best state, our little princess. Learning how the real folk live."

His eyes slid to Vikram: a slow, thoughtful look.

Sunset fell. Vikram accompanied Nils on his watch. They felt their way around the circumference of the window-wall, peering through the opaque glass for the telltale lights of skadi boats. The wind had dropped. On the other side of the tower, they stood watching the sea. The moon glimmered faintly on the waves.

Vikram spoke softly to Nils. "Do you blame me for going to the City?"

"You did what any of us would have done."

"That's not a no."

"You're still pedantic. Anyway, it's what Mikkeli would have wanted."

"She did?"

"Of course. It was her great plan. You were always the clever one. She had ambitions, that girl."

"But that's what Keli wanted. And she's gone. It's us that's still here."

Nils's sigh was heavy. "Of course I can't blame you, Vik. You were doing good stuff with those schemes."

"Didn't work."

"Not your fault. Things were already in motion." Nils paused. "Drake and I agreed we'd try and keep you out of it."

"What? Why?"

"C'mon, Vik. After last time…"

"You were trying to protect me." Of course they were, he thought. He'd have done the same, had their situations been reversed.

"Well I guess that didn't work either," said Nils. "I don't know what to think any more. Seems like people just keep vanishing. Keli. You. And it eats away at you. Makes you start to wonder about things."

"What kind of things?"

"What's ahead. I mean really ahead. I do think of those days, Vik—Horizon, Eirik, all the things he used to talk about—and he really, properly believed them. But it seems like madness. I don't know what we thought would happen. Maybe back then, everything seemed—well, further away. Like we could beat it. But it's here, isn't it. I realized that when they drowned Eirik. I mean, this is it. I'm standing here with a gun and we've taken a Rechov hostage. A Rechnov, for stars' sake."

Vikram had no answer. He understood what Nils meant. He had seen Adelaide, and he had a choice to make. He could not delay much longer.

Outside, there was nothing but a vacuum.

He said, "Don't think I haven't noticed the coughing."

"Stars, it's nothing."

"I've got City medicine. I'll give you some."

"It's not serious."

The lie hung between them, Vikram not knowing what to say, Nils clearly wishing the issue closed. Instead, Vikram asked, "What are they going to do with Adelaide?"

"It's up to Maak. He's in charge."

Vikram could not see Nils's face, but he heard the tension in his voice.

"Pekko wants her dead, doesn't he?"

"It's not Pekko's decision. If Maak has any sense, he'll strike a real bargain. We could get a lot out of that girl. We got you out of jail because of her, didn't we?"

"And what if Pekko doesn't listen to Maak?"

Nils's silence was all the answer Vikram needed.

/ / /

He lay awake through the hours of Pekko's watch and then through Drake's. Pekko fell asleep, his breathing quick and even. Drake got up and went on patrol. Vikram's mind wandered. He found himself revisiting the ships rusting away in the harbour, all the expedition boats that had left Osiris, years before he was born. For the first time it struck him as peculiar that none of them had ever come back. Not a single one.

The Rechnovs had a secret. What if no-one was meant to leave? What if "Whitefly" was the key to enforcing that?

The wind moaned and rattled the boards in the window-wall. He shook aside the thought. It was only ghosts whispering in his ear. Their malice was childish.

Drake returned. He watched her face, tinged red with the glow of the heater. She huddled over it, her hands resting on her knees and her chin upon her hands.

"What time is it?" he muttered.

"About half four. Get some sleep, Vik."

"I can't. My mind's too awake. D'you remember the story of the last balloon flight, Drake?"

She gave him a tired smile. He sensed she had been lost in her own thoughts. Perhaps now was not the time for his. "The one Keli talks about. Yeah, I remember. It's not a good story though, really, is it."

"No. I guess not."

He lay back once more, watching a drop of moisture form on the ceiling until it fell onto the heater with a hiss. Even though the plaster was crumbling and the tower was falling apart, the sight of the water did not fill him with horror as it had done in the cell. For the first time, he felt the full relief of his escape.

I'd rather die than go back.

"Keli said the balloon would appear one day," said Drake softly. "A huge, bright, striped balloon, floating through the sky."

She fell silent again. He noticed the lapse into the past tense, as though Drake was too tired to pretend any longer, to offer respect because respect could not restore the dead.

He glanced across at Nils and Ilona. They slept side by side, Nils's arm hugging Ilona's tiny body tightly against him.

But if I can't go back, then there's something I have to do.

Vikram got up and stepped stealthily around the sleeping bodies of the others.

"Drake. I need to see Adelaide."

Drake's eyes darted towards the door, towards the room where Adelaide was being held. She looked back at him and her forehead was creased.

"Vik—"

"It's alright," he said quietly. "I know."

He slipped away before she could protest.

/ / /

He turned the handle and pushed it open. The sour smell of confinement wafted out.

"Close your eyes," he said. "I'm going to switch on the torch."

There was no reply. He could not tell if she was awake or asleep. He flicked on the torch. She was in a foetal position, her face hidden as it had been before. Her wrists were tiny in the ring of the handcuffs and the joints of her hands were swollen. He felt a surge of pity.

"Adelaide. I've brought you a light. And something to eat."

No response. He moved the beam of the torch directly upon her.

"It's Vikram," he tried.

He shut the door and put the torch on the ground. He knelt in front of Adelaide to set down the two flasks he had brought. She looked to be carved out of stone.

He touched her arm lightly and she shuddered. A sigh of relief escaped him. She was still alive. Now he needed her conscious.

"Adelaide. Look at me, if you can."

Still she gave no answer, so he took her shoulders and turned her towards him. Her head drooped. He pushed aside the tangled hair. Her eyes were slits. Vikram brought the flask of water to her lips and dribbled a little into her mouth. She gasped and began to shake.

"Woke me," she mumbled. "Woke... me..."

"You need to drink," he ordered. "Water first. Open your mouth." He tilted the flask once more. "Swallow. Good."

He saw the effect of the liquid with every drop. She had been lapsing into hypothermia. It was lucky she had City clothes, ripped and filthy but locking in some crucial insulation. Next, he took the flask of broth. She choked on the first mouthful. Her eyes sprang open, suddenly bright. She glared at him. He knew that glare. He had seen it in other people, in westerners, in visitors to the shelter; the helpless defiance of the already defeated. He pushed the flask mercilessly against her mouth.

"Drink. If you don't drink this your body is going to shut down and you'll collapse. You mustn't go to sleep. You have to stay alert."

"Nothing... keep me awake."

"I won't leave you on your own again. You're getting sick."

He examined her properly, with a curious sense of reversal. Had Adelaide's brother looked at Vikram with this same, scientific scrutiny? Assessing his body's deterioration, its potential for one final surge of activity? The skin around her eyes was shiny and tender, but her face had lost weight. With her bone structure newly close to the surface, she had the freakish beauty of the otherworldly.

He took a bit of wire he'd found on the floor from his pocket and inserted it into the handcuff lock. It took only a minute to release them. He massaged her wrists to revive the circulation. She winced. He took an adrenalin syringe out of its plastic packaging and rolled up her sleeve. He found a vein in the crook of her elbow, inserted the needle, squeezed the fluid out.

"My leg got hurt."

He looked down. Her trousers had ripped and there was a six inch gash down her calf. The surrounding flesh was swollen with infection.

"Went through... a bridge..."

Shit, he thought. That would slow her, if she got the chance to run. But he said nothing, dug out a couple of the antibiotic pills from the nurse's bag and pushed them between her lips. He put the water flask into her hands and to her mouth again. Water trickled down her chin. She wiped it away. The gesture took a long time.

"Why did you come here?" he said. It sounded harsher than he had meant.

She blinked.

"What—what is—this place?"

"It's the unremembered quarters."

She put down the flask. The adrenalin would take effect soon. Her pulse would quicken. Darts of pain would spark in her limbs as sensation returned alongside full consciousness. He had experienced it many times; it would be new to her.

"Why did you come?" he repeated.

She wrapped her arms once more around her body. "Cold."

"I know. Adelaide—"

"Why did I come. To the west, you mean. To your city."

"It was madness," he said roughly.

"Then I came because I'm mad." She attempted a smile. He saw a bead of blood forming on her lips where the skin had flaked and cracked. He took her right hand and began to knead her muscles through the fabric of the glove. He worked steadily up the arm, towards her shoulder.

"There's no point in playing games now." He kept his voice even.

"Then let me out of here, and stop… talking to me."

"I can't let you out. You're the only leverage they have."

"They?"

His eyes flicked to hers. "We."

"I'm not sure you're so sure."

Vikram's thumbs paused. "Those people out there have been my life. Whatever's happened, I owe them mine and everything that's part of it."

"I suppose my father made you a good offer."

"I didn't see Feodor. I saw Linus."

"Even better. Don't tell me it hasn't played on your mind. Especially here. There's only death here. And cold. So cold. You don't like the cold, Vik."

The abbreviation dropped from her mouth, easily, a little sadly. How hard it is, he thought, to let go the trappings of intimacy. He knew this girl; he knew the patterns of her skin beneath the dirt, the conundrum of freckles. He knew the hiccups in her breathing cycle. He knew the smell of her, as though she was made from sea-stuff, as she would one day return to it. He knew that in the aftermath of a nightmare, her eyelids flew open and she would stare at the ceiling, oxygen stopped in her lungs, before she let go the breath.

They knew each other's loss. That was what had drawn them together; two spirits reaching into the past, whose fingertips had touched in searching.

Adelaide was shivering. Vikram's hands had stopped moving, circling her upper arm. He let her go.

"I'm used to the cold," he said.

"You told me you like fire. Love fire, you said."

"I told you a lot of things I shouldn't have."

Adelaide lifted her eyes to his. They were bright with moisture, like oysters glistening in their shells.

"Shame," she said softly. "I thought perhaps you were going to bust me out after all."

"We need you," he said. "You're too valuable."

Again she smiled, and the bead of blood spread. He suppressed the impulse to wipe it away.

"Don't overestimate me. I'm as much use to them dead as I am alive. Not the best ending for the Rechnovs, two children down, but I'd become a martyr. They're very marketable. And then other people would do other things, and gradually, they'd forget me. There's always someone to come after."

There was no doubt as she spoke; her tone was absolute certainty. She tilted her head to one side, looking at him as though curious to know if there could be any opposition. Single-minded, but always sure. If he loved one thing about her, it must be that. He inhabited a world of greys and doubts, a world that constantly shrank and receded. Adelaide held it still. She had made herself blinkered because she refused to look at alternatives.

Except in coming here.

"Why did you come, Adelaide?"

"I don't think, Vikram, that you truly wish to know. Things weren't so... agreeable... between us, when we parted last."

"What did you expect?" he flashed. "I was sent underwater because of you. You can't understand what it does to you, that place."

"I tried to get you out," she insisted.

"You had no chance. Your own family locked you up, you were fooling us both. You're an idiot."

A slow dripping in the corner reminded him of time ticking down.

"I'm cold," said Adelaide.

He pulled her against him, wrapping his arms around her, resting his chin on her head. One of her hands curled around his wrist. She was too weak for tricks. He was holding what was left of Adelaide Mystik. Or Adelaide Rechnov, or whoever she was. She felt fragile, strangely malleable, and tense all at once. She felt like the scent of dried roses.

Instinctively, he tightened his arms.

"That better?"

"I was never this cold before. You were, weren't you."

"Yes. Yes, I've been this cold. Lots of times."

He had told himself there was a way out, a way to save her and to save them. He could ask himself what Keli would have done, what Eirik would have done, even what his old self would have done. But all of those people, one way or another, were already a part of him. The decision was his own to live with—or not.

If he got her out—if he took her back east, and Linus kept his word—the guilt would corrode him from the inside out. Sooner or later he would blame Adelaide, and eventually, he would hate her.

He pressed his lips against her dirty hair. Between the roots, her scalp was chalk white.

"It was my destiny to come here," Adelaide whispered.

Vikram's throat was tight. He swallowed, quietly, so she would not hear. "You, of all people, make your own destiny."

"It's written in the stars. It's written in the salt."

"What are you talking about?"

"The Teller told me. And Second Grandmother, a long time ago."

"That's why you came to the west? Because of some stupid prediction?"

"I had to come. I had to follow Axel."

"You think he's here."

She didn't answer. His eyes were wet and he blinked the moisture away. He owed her the truth, at least.

"He's not, Adelaide. I know that because… he wrote to you. He wrote you a letter."

The silence stretched out.

"It was before we went to Council. A woman came to your apartment with a letter for you. I don't know who she was—a westerner, I think. An airlift. She gave me the letter. I read it."

"And what did this letter say?" Adelaide's voice was a tumble of hard little stones.

He told it to her, word by word, sentence by sentence. The image it of was glued to his mind. He saw Axel's handwriting, the green loops of the *y*s and the *g*s, the paper folded into a horse's head. Adelaide was shaking.

"Where is it?"

"I gave it to Linus."

"Oh."

"Adie—"

"Don't."

"He was saying goodbye. Adelaide, it was a suicide note."

"Don't you dare judge him."

"I'm not judging him. I'm not saying that what he did was wrong."

"He would never do that. He couldn't—"

"I'm sorry. But I think the letter makes it clear. There was no conspiracy. Axel was ill, you told me that yourself."

She wrenched away from him. Her face crumpled.

"Don't you say his name. Axel would never do that. He would never leave me. Don't you understand, Vik? Axel would never leave me."

"I'm so sorry, Adie."

"Get out!" Her voice broke. "Did you come in here to torment me? Is this another of your people's games? Get out!"

Vikram felt numb. Seeing her face, he wished now that he had not said anything. What had been the point? If Pekko had his way, Adelaide Mystik would be dead by daylight.

43 | ADELAIDE

Vikram backed away but he did not leave.

"Stop looking at me," she said, but no sound came out. The words stuck in a pump that refused to work. A dam built there. The ache swelled, spread through her lungs and throat until it packed against the backs of her eyes.

She tried to shut out the images; the penthouse, the balcony, her brother sitting on the rails, standing, believing that he could fly. She would not believe it. But more images came. The room full of balloons. Radir's reports. The horses, always the horses. Axel, on the balcony, his red hair bright on a dull day. Axel, aged sixteen, leaping from a boat, his arms wide to embrace the unknown shock of the sea.

Vikram was speaking.

"If you ever get out of here, go to Branch 18 of the Silk Vault. There's a deposit box under the name of Mikkeli, only you and I have access to it. I put a copy of the letter there. There was something with it. A necklace, with a shark tooth. It's in the deposit box."

"Axel," she whispered.

Her dream came back to her, looking for him, not finding him. She was bad luck. She knew the truth about Axel in the same moment as she knew the truth about herself. Even the sting of humiliation attached to his suicide gave way to incredulity—not at Axel's actions, but at her own blindness. Axel had skipped out of life. That had been her twin's final stunt.

She thought of the argument in Feodor's office months ago, demanding the keys, convinced that her father's refusal was proof of complicity. He had known something after all: he had known the truth, and if there had been any evidence of suicide in Axel's penthouse, she could be sure he would have erased it before anyone else got there. The Rechnov name always came first.

She felt hollow.

"I should have told you before," said Vikram. "I tried to, so many times. I meant to. I just…"

The tears that had fallen dried on her cheeks. She did not know who they were for. She thought of her brother's body sinking to the ocean floor and she knew the fish had stripped it to the bone.

"I wouldn't have believed you," she said.

A dull thud, as though something had struck the tower deep underwater, resonated through the walls. The floor shook beneath them.

She froze.

"What…?"

They stood, motionless. The second shake knocked them sideways. The torch went out. Plaster tumbled down the walls, clouds of dust rising in the aftermath. She heard Vikram scrabbling for the torch. The light flicked on, illuminating their dust-coated faces.

"A quake…?" Her uncertain response failed to convince even herself. Vikram shook his head. His face was grim.

"Skadi," he said. "They've found us."

She stared at him. Her brain, as numb as ice, gave way to a dawning comprehension.

"They're tracking you," she said.

Vikram's hand went to the back of his neck.

"No, Ilona found it, she dampened it…"

"That doesn't do anything, Vik, the tracker's in your blood. It's a classic security bluff—I'm so sorry."

He turned very pale. They stared at each other. She did not question what his original intent had been. In this moment, everything was changing. She wiped the moisture from her cheeks.

The door blasted open.

"Vik, get back to the other room, they've found us." It was Nils. He grabbed her arm. She saw a look pass between him and Vikram, but neither of them had time for words. "She's coming too."

With Nils's hand gripping her upper arm she hobbled through the corridor. Pain shot up her legs, her bad leg throbbed. She held onto the sensation. For now, at least, she was alive. Vikram grabbed her elbow, supporting her. Nils pulled her into the room where they had first arrived. Breaking daylight filtered inside, illuminating the dishevelled bedding, the broken benches and grow-boxes, the guns. Drake had torn away part of the boarding and was stationed at a gap in the window-wall. The large-barrelled gun in her arms angled downwards. Rikard was on the other side in an identical pose. Ilona was checking her weapon. Pekko barked into a scarab. When he saw them, he dropped the scarab and launched himself at Vikram, grabbing his shoulders and shaking him violently.

"This is your fault! You brought them here!"

Vikram landed a fist into Pekko's stomach. Adelaide jerked forward but Nils held her fast. Pekko let go of Vikram. A cold rage locked in his eyes. The next second his gun was pointing at Vikram's head.

"Traitor," he spat.

"Don't you dare!" yelled Drake. Ilona's head jerked up and her hands stilled. Rikard's eyes glanced away from the window-wall only for a second.

"I had no idea they would find us," Vikram snarled. His face was contorted with equal rage. His hands dropped at his sides, fists clenched but helpless. The gun pushed into Vikram's temple. The two men were inches apart. Blood rushed to Adelaide's face.

"Pekko he's telling the truth! He didn't know. The tracker's not on his neck, it's in his blood. That's how they always find people."

"And why didn't you say something before, Citizen?" The gun did not move. Pekko's voice was quiet now, quiet and cold. "Instead of playing mad and half-dead."

"I'd hardly tell you anything if I thought I was going to be rescued, would I?"

Pekko's grip on the gun tightened.

"Would I?" she shouted.

Nils spoke with forced calmness. "Pekko, there's no time for this now. They're sending skadi into the building. We're going to have to defend the floor. We need posts. Vikram's with us. If he's not, the skadi will kill him anyway."

The tension between Pekko and Vikram was electric. Adelaide's heart thumped in her chest. She did not dare to say anything further.

It was none of them, but a voice from outside that made Pekko lower the gun. The skadi spoke through a tannoy. Travelling up from the surface, the words sounded distorted.

"You are surrounded. You have ten minutes to release the hostage, or we will send enforcements in. No prisoners will be taken. I repeat, you are surrounded..."

Releasing Vikram, Pekko moved with sudden speed. She saw his intent and ducked a fraction too late to avoid him altogether; the barrel of the gun struck her shoulder. She fell against the wall, winded by the strength of the blow.

"Tie her up!" yelled Pekko.

Nils secured her wrists, but loosely.

"Keep your head down or you'll get killed," he muttered. "The tower's surrounded by skadi. I don't think they're here to negotiate."

Over Nils's shoulder she met Vikram's eyes, bright with anguish and fury.

Pekko scooped up the scarab and pressed it hard to his ear. His face was taut with tension.

"Sorren, what's going on? How long until you get here?"

All eyes were on Pekko now.

"We've got at least a dozen skadi vehicles down there, I've got zero contact with the plant. What the fuck d'you mean you can't—Sorren?"

Pekko paused, took the scarab from his ear, shook it.

"Sorren? Sorren. I can't hear you. Get Maak on for me. You got that? Get Maak. Sorren—"

He lowered the scarab. Tinny pops came out of its speaker. Static mingled with raised voices, with shouts. Nobody said anything. Pekko, facing away from them all, seemed to have frozen. Then he switched off the scarab and slid it into a pocket. He did not spare Adelaide another glance.

The ten minutes passed slowly. Adelaide knew that there was no point in asking if the skadi would negotiate. There were no further announcements. Finally Drake said that the skadi were moving in. Rikard was allocated to guard Adelaide. None of it felt real. She watched the others leave the room, and was conscious only of a quiet disbelief.

44 | VIKRAM

They ran down the treacherous stairs as the skadi ran up. There was no caution from the skadi; they had no need for subtlety now.

The weapon in Vikram's hands was heavier than the one he'd held last time. One part of his mind looked at its specification and noted the weight, the heft, the resistance of the trigger whilst the other listened to the mounting skadi steps and wondered where Pekko had got their guns from, if he had bribed a skad, or if the Rochs had supplied them.

They had one advantage, being upstairs and the skadi being down, and knowing the place as the skadi did not, but it would only be an advantage whilst the enemy kept the attack inside.

"Everyone take one of these." Pekko passed gas masks to the others and threw one at Vikram. He pulled it over his head and wiped a sleeve over the smeary visor.

They waited, halfway between their base and the surface. They took up positions overlooking a landing where the corridor spilled into a narrow funnel. They would see the skadi approach before the skadi could see them. They waited.

He could hear the shallowness of the others' breathing. A tiny cough from Drake, suppressed. Pekko fidgeting with the safety catch of his gun.

He heard pounding boots. The sound drummed like Vikram's own heartbeat. Like Juraj's crazed escort of rafters on the night of the firefight.

They were coming.

The first man appeared. Black gear, mask, rifle. He hurled a canister and retreated. A swirl of gas rose up, the canister hissing as it expelled its contents. Drake touched her mask nervously. Vikram felt his chest constrict and forced himself to breathe.

Without warning Pekko opened fire, screaming as he did so. Skadi emerged through the dispelling gas. When Vikram started shooting he felt nothing but inevitability, as though he'd walked a full circle and found himself exactly where he had started: home. He squeezed the trigger and the gun flashed and the bolts slapped into the heads of oncoming men.

You don't make your own luck, he thought. That's all a lie.

The confined space exploded with ricocheting gunfire. The sound was phenomenal. There was no light, no true darkness. A whirl of grey shadows, moving, running, flying to the ground where they stopped, dead or injured. He heard Nils hiss and knew his friend was hit but Nils kept shooting. Vikram did not see the eyes of any of the men he killed, except one who looked straight in his direction as though he could see Vikram, really see him, not just the mouth of his gun from his concealed hole.

He did not count the men as they funnelled into the death-trap. He reminded himself that each man was a skad, without any comprehension of the worth of a life. He reminded himself he was fighting for his own life and that of his friends. Then his mind went blank and his muscles took over.

They heard the sounds of the skadi running up other stairwells, only to discover that the way was blocked with rubble and there was no route up except via the five of them.

A point came when they realized all the shots were coming from their side and ceased. They waited and listened for a second wave. It didn't come.

Nils's breathing came heavily through the quiet. Vikram heard mutterings between Nils and Ilona as they examined the damage. None of them yet dared to move from their stations, fearful of a skadi trick.

"What's happening?" whispered Drake. "Why are they withdrawing?"

Vikram could only think of one reason. He looked at Drake and she looked back at him, scared.

"Why would they go?" she said, not bothering to keep her voice down now.

Nils and Ilona came out into the open.

"They're not going to get any more of their people killed," Nils said. His arm hung useless at his side, bloody and clumsily bandaged, but he appeared otherwise unhurt. "They don't need to."

"Where's Pekko?" asked Drake.

Vikram was alerted by the sound of footsteps. Turning, he saw the other man was already running back up the stairs. He swore and pelted after him.

45 ┊ ADELAIDE

She would have screamed if the flat side of the knife hadn't crushed her throat. Rikard stood in the gloom of the shadows, a metre away, expressionless. The others ran in moments after Pekko.

"I have no qualms about this," said Pekko. He gripped the knife tighter in his three fingers. A spasm coursed through her body. His other arm was locked tight around her chest, pinning her arms, holding a gun.

"Pekko, we've got bigger problems, you can't—" Drake went straight to the window. She crouched, her gun angled down but her eyes flicking back to the interlocked figures.

"She's the only leverage we have," said Pekko. "Move away from the window, Drake."

"Adelaide, keep still." Vikram took a step towards them.

"Move away from the window, Drake!"

"Not whilst they're down there," she said grimly.

She began to fire, in ordered bursts.

"Fuck."

Nils joined her. Rikard and Ilona took the other gap. Each shot exploded in Adelaide's skull.

"Pekko, let her go," Vikram said. Pekko raised his gun to point at Vikram.

"We're dead anyway," said Pekko. "I just want you to watch her go first."

"Let her go. She can help us. We can still negotiate—"

Pekko laughed. His ribcage shook with laughter.

"They're about to blow this place up, and you're talking about negotiation?"

She could picture the black-hulled boats in formation on the sea. Through the ripped boards, strips of cold grey light filtered into the room. The sun was rising.

Pekko held the knife to her throat. Vikram faced them. The others fired repeatedly. Her eyes were on the floor and she saw amongst the blankets they'd discarded when they ran downstairs a pile of yellowish globes. Drake ducked back from the window-wall. The globes dislodged and rolled across the floor.

It was not the end that she had imagined. There would be no burial rites, no flaming pyre. There would be no sea journey. Just a flash of silver, and shortly after, an incineration.

I won't join the ghosts, she thought. And then, *You didn't want to anyway. A trapped thing? That's not for you.* And then. *What then? Nothing.*

I know you now, Axel. I'm you and you're me. Who asked you to jump off the boat that day? I did. The madness is in us both. I've got horses of my own, they just don't look like horses. That's what Osiris is. It makes madmen of us.

Pekko twisted the knife. Her blood pulsed where it pushed.

Vikram was still talking, but she no longer heard what he said. She only heard the tone of his voice, familiar, like worn-down sandpaper.

A flare of light from outside lit up his outline and she saw his expression, the horror, regret and sorrow. I could have loved you, she thought. Maybe I do. In that second, the lance of orange signalling what would come, she saw connections converging like lines of chalk: Second Grandmother's diary; Axel's suicide and the drowning of Eirik 9968; the border and the horses; the white fly and the Siberian boat—

"Adelaide—" he said.

46 | VIKRAM

The explosion knocked the world from under him and the air from his lungs. He was thrown to the floor, choking. He smelled fresh fire and knew the hit had been close. Rubble rained from the ceiling. Part of it had caved in.

Shapes moved. He heard Pekko groan. He sensed movement, Adelaide, raising her head, lifting her body slowly from the ground. There was a familiar sound and Pekko grunted and he knew what she had done. He felt her eyes searching for him but she would see nothing in the dust. He had one insane impulse to crawl forward, take her face in his and kiss her, whisper a goodbye. There was no time.

"Adelaide, run!" he shouted hoarsely.

47 ¦ ADELAIDE

She found herself on the floor, coughing, a ringing in her ears. The air was thick with dust. She felt slick blood at her throat where Pekko's knife had grazed. Her eyes burned. She could hardly see.

She wriggled forward. Her hand closed over metal: the knife. Pekko grabbed her ankle. She kicked but he hung on. She jabbed the knife behind her, felt it sink, stick, could not see where. Pekko made a noise. The grip on her ankle loosened. Blood dripped on her hand.

"Adelaide, run!"

Vikram's voice propelled her onward. She found her feet. The door was before her. She wrenched it open and ran.

48 | VIKRAM

Scrabbling on the floor. Pekko, a knife sticking out of his shoulder, lurched to his feet. He raised his gun, but it never fired. Nils was too quick. He swung his own weapon and hit the other man squarely on the temple. Pekko collapsed once more and was still.

"I never liked him anyway," said Nils, as though Pekko was the problem they now faced, but Vikram understood that the gesture was more than that. Nils no longer cared about what Pekko could do. Very soon it wouldn't matter.

"Rikard's dead." Drake's voice came through the gloom. As the dust settled, Vikram saw Pekko's body, inert, and Rikard's slumped by the window-wall. There was a two metre hole in the ceiling. The others were standing, bruised but alive. Their faces were dirty and scared.

"We can still run," Ilona said. Nobody moved.

"They'll kill anyone who comes out of this tower," said Vikram. "Adelaide—"

"She's got a chance," Nils said. "If they recognize her." Nils turned to Ilona. "Lona, we've only got a few minutes before they strike again. You go. Catch up with Adelaide, take your chances together."

The girl shook her head. "Not without you."

He remembered a conversation with Adelaide, lazing in her jacuzzi, surrounded by soft white bubbles. It seemed impossible that it could have happened mere months ago.

"You don't have any family, do you?" she'd asked, with that abrupt intimacy she sometimes offered, or demanded.

"How would you know?"

"Because it's written here." She touched, with a wet fingertip, the violet skin beneath his eyes. He realized she'd said it because she felt the same way.

If he could save one person, it had to be her. There was no-one else he could stand in front of now. He could not help Nils, or Drake, and they could not help him. All of them knew it; sensed their fates, Mikkeli's fate, in the way they tensed, reforming. Ever since that day they had been marked. Mikkeli had shown them all that was possible. A gesture, a story to pass on. He had told Adelaide that she controlled her own life, believed the same of himself—but here he was, caught in a crumbling tower in the smoke and the flames.

You didn't make your own luck. Things happened; they had no rules, no order. Would it hurt to burn? He'd never thought of burning. No, the smoke would take him first. He'd asphyxiate, or suffocate under the rubble.

Drake hiked her gun.

"Right then," she said. "Let's take out a few of these bastards."

He picked up his own weapon. Barrel still warm. He snapped in a new cell.

They gathered at the broken window-wall. Nils and Ilona on one side, Vikram and Drake on the other. Dawn had fully broken. A flotilla of skadi boats encircled the tower below, dark blights on the sunrise sparkled water.

He remembered their faces under the light of a single electric bulb, in his memory now so young. He remembered the fierceness with which they had argued their beliefs. Horizon, Keli's dream, their ideals. He felt a moment of gladness for those times shared. The smile in his mind lingered even as the sharpness of loss overcame him, for the stymied future, for the lives that might have been.

Mikkeli was crouched in the heater, her skin crackling as she burned. "Come on Vik," she said. "Being dead's not so bad. You get to haunt the living, don't you?"

Nils took the first shot. They took it in rounds, firing without speaking, each bolt a hotness against their faces, none of them acknowledging that most of their attempts would find no mark.

In the last seconds, Vikram thought that he heard footsteps, running footsteps. Perhaps it was Adelaide, making her escape through the tortuous stairs of the unremembered quarters. Perhaps it was another Mikkeli, grown and old, her bare feet slip-slapping the road she walked in her dreams, the road lined with a wall, the fields verdant beyond. Or perhaps it was his own ground-dream. This was the noise of his feet on the beach, sinking into golden grains, dampened by the sea's light rush. Onto the pebbles and into the grasses. The grasses brushing against his sun-drenched skin. A glimpse of what lay beyond—

He squeezed Drake's hand; met Nils's eyes. The contact felt impersonal, as though they'd all sunk into their own worlds, already let go of this life.

Don't give up, he thought. You can't give up yet.

But that wasn't the way Osiris went.

49 | ADELAIDE

S he skidded down the impossible stairways. Twice the ice stole her footing. She toppled, hit the wall, barely kept her balance.

The tower she had thought dead and dormant was waking up. Shapeless piles turned into figures. As flames began to lick at the tower's exterior, comatose creatures found a scrap of life to haul them to their feet. They moved as one, towards the stairwells, a current of sluggish limbs.

Her breath was torn. Blood rushed in her ears. Vikram was calling. Was he calling? Was he following? He must be.

New voices. *What's going on? It's burning, the tower's burning!* Panicked screams. The stairwells filled. Cats and rats emerging from crannies, streaming ahead. The acrid smell of smoke beginning to filter down through the building.

Fire! The tower's on fire—it's the skadi, the skadi are here—

Not running now, she was fighting, using elbows and fists to barge her way down another flight and another. Hot with sweat and the crush and then she realized it wasn't that. It wasn't people. It was the heat of flames.

It's happening again, it's burning!

A woman in front of her held a baby. The child wailed, the two of them rocking and keening whilst the human tide pushed downwards.

Doors banging.

Not doors, gunshots.

She didn't know what floor she was on. She shouldn't have run. The keening woman stopped and sat in the middle of the crush. She couldn't go back. Someone tried to take the child from the woman but she resisted and the child's small body was tugged between them. Adelaide tried to help the woman move. The woman lashed out and Adelaide tumbled half a flight.

A kick to her bad leg. The pain almost paralysed her. She clawed herself upright.

A colossal rumble from above. Cries, one person to the next—

It's coming down! The tower's coming down!

Adelaide fought her way out of the stairwell, back into the deserted maze. She ran from room to room. Light streamed inside, half-blinding her. Now, when she needed a broken window-wall, there were none. She ran back and forth. Surely this was the same room, hadn't she been here before?

Finally she found a gap, sharded with glass and dripping ice, barely large enough for her head to fit through. In one corner was a heater, still hot. She swung it at the grimy window-wall. The bufferglass cracked, but did not give. Her palms burned. Again and again she pounded.

The window-wall gave in a rain of bufferglass. Particles showered her hair and clothes. She leaned out and gasped.

She was fifteen floors above the sea, facing the volcanic city. Below, she saw the skadi boats, black dots circling the tower's base. Above her, the fire. Plumes of smoke rose in other areas of the city. The sky was red and utterly cloudless.

The remaining lights in the city flickered and went out. She knew what that meant. The Guard were rerouting energy. She saw a hive of activity at the base of the adjacent tower, the mouth of a huge cannon, angled upwards. She had heard of these monsters but never seen one until now. The cannon jerked as it began to spit out liquid fire. She, like Vikram, had been deemed dispensable. Who had given the order? Had the skadi overridden her family, or had the Rechnovs consigned her to Axel's fate?

Flames licked at the tower wall, billowing from broken portals. A piece of burning junk rushed past, narrowly avoiding her head. She ducked back. Beneath her, the foundations growled. Stars, the tower was coming down.

She inched towards the edge. Fear paralysed her.

Somewhere up there was Vikram. No, he couldn't be, they must have deserted their stations by now—they must see it was futile?

But what if he hadn't—

She took a step back, prepared to turn and run back up—she'd deserted him once, she couldn't do it again—but he'd told her to go—

The floor shook beneath her. Her feet slid apart.

She leapt, and was surprised for an instant to find herself falling, as though she might have flown after all. The wind flung her limbs wide. The world somersaulted. She strained to point her feet towards the waves—the waves, the sea, so close now—take a breath! she thought, take a deep breath now—

She smashed into the water. Icy shock, a burn like lye. It coursed up her spine and then she was under.

Water filled her mouth. Her legs flailed. She pushed one toe against the other heel, trying to get rid of her boots. It was stuck, it wouldn't budge, she needed air—

Her head broke surface. She dragged in oxygen but another wave pushed her back under. She tugged at the boot, got it free. Her coat weighed her down. She grappled with it before her shoulders shrugged free, then her hands, and she hauled herself once more to the surface—

Oxygen and noise and light—

Currents tugged her below. Her arms were no match for the ocean. Bubbles streamed from her mouth. Her lungs burned. She couldn't fight it for long. She got the next lungful of air and screamed for help. She saw a boat, close enough to reach her. The hull gained and they hadn't seen her. She floundered to the left to avoid being hit, heard shouts on board, the air full of cries and the smell of fire. Other boats, not far away. Their occupants standing transfixed, the searchlights redundant echoes on the tower—

Get away, swim, get away—

Under. Arms and legs barely moving, her body numb everywhere but her heart and lungs. She opened her eyes. Flares of light through the water. Was this how Axel died? Drowning, like Eirik 9968 had drowned, like Adelaide was going to. Had he thought of her at all, falling, dying? Did he have time to think? Did the sea take him quickly? Did he open his mouth to welcome the water?

She drifted.

They were drowning, she and Axel. They did everything together. It made sense that they would die together.

But Axel's not here.

She kicked. She broke surface, heaved. Water streamed from her mouth. She spat, gulped in air. She would live. She would.

Fighting to stay afloat, she saw a terrible and unreal sight. The leaning tower began to shudder. Ablaze, it collapsed in on itself like a castle made of sand. One moment it was there, black and burning. The next there was only a strip of lightening sky.

The sea boiled. She screamed.

Vikram!

Hands hauled her out of the water. She fell back into the stern of a boat. She lay prostrate, unable to speak, staring at the space where the tower had been.

"It's alright, we've got you."

"Breathe easy now, cough up that water."

Two westerners leaned over her, a man and a woman. Their faces were thin and anxious.

The sound came then, a high, eerie, keening sound. She did not realize at first that the noise came from her. Even when she knew, she found that she could not stop, even when the woman crouched close to her, patted her shoulder gently, and the boat sped away from that absence on the horizon, from the fire on the surface, everything growing smaller, everything fading.

"It's alright," they said. "You're safe now. You're out."

50 | ADELAIDE

In the night, the bodies that they found were piled onto rafts. They stiffened and frosted. The flames would unglue them. The mourners gathered in boats and wept, but no words, no tears passed Adelaide's lips or eyes. She watched as a woman with long grey hair was ferried from raft to raft. The woman drew a line of salt on their foreheads and then she poured oil onto the human pyres.

The mourners threw burning torches through the air. Flames leapt from the oil; embraced the hands and feet and faces of the dead. They wore no shoes. Their shoes had been taken for others to use. Her rescuers said they would not mind.

The fires crackled and spat. She watched the flames unravelling vessels that had held running blood, flickering consciousness; returning matter to the ashes and salt it had once been. The bodies, none of which she had recognized as his, were swarmed by smoke.

Austral lights glimmered overhead. In another week it would be mid-winter night. Four boats towed the pyres away. They glided on their final journeys, the cradles of fire dimmer and dimmer, out to the ring-net. She wanted to call out—stop! Don't take them! Don't exile them. Just in case he was there. In case he could not get back in.

Now a soft keening filled the air. It was a sound like none Adelaide had heard before, neither crying nor song. The wind was in it, the waves. The ghosts, too.

She imagined Vikram's ghost was standing beside her, seeing what she saw, hearing what she heard. He asked, "What do you want to do?"

She looked at the tiny lights on the ocean surface.

"I have to get into the Silk Vault. There's something there that I need to see."

"And then?"

"I want to disappear."

EPILOGUE

A flock of birds rose, circling. The ships creaked in the derelict harbour. Beyond them, a salmagundi of floating crafts lined the ocean, crammed with spectators. Boats nudged against rafts; coracles skidded between barges. Early spring was still cold, but the sun turned the water silvery gold and the illusion of warmth almost convinced the crowds that a fabled summer was here. On the sixth clear morning of that month, the first expedition boat in fifty years prepared for departure.

Dignitaries stood upon the pier, Councillors in purple surcoats, founding families; the Rechnov family, amongst others. They were still in mourning. Earlier that week, Sanjay Hanif had formally closed the investigations into the twins' disappearances. Adelaide and Axel Rechnov had been pronounced missing, believed dead.

Feodor gave no speech today. The Rechnovs were quiet, and others did the talking. Eyes watching closely might have observed that the Architect stood a little way apart from the rest. It was said that the loss of his grandchildren, the boy to a terrible accident and the girl to the hands of western extremists, had broken the old man's heart.

The expedition boat rested by the end of the pier, at the mouth of a corridor leading out to sea. The corridor was lined with bunting. On either side, well-wishers waved bright squares of cloth. The expedition crew could be seen making last minute adjustments, checking equipment and saying farewells to family, or simply standing on deck, looking back at the city. On the far side, a man emerged from the hatch and climbed up onto deck. He raised his hand to his brow, scanning the crowds.

Vikram did not expect to see anyone he knew; nor did he intend to be seen. He glanced up at the burnished skyscrapers that rose beyond the rusting ships, the waving banners, the cheering crowd. There was nothing left for him here. He owned nothing but the unknown future, or perhaps it already owned him.

As people strained to see, there was a small commotion to the left of the corridor, and the boats surged forward in a tidal wave.

In one of the jostling crafts of the western section, Adelaide steadied herself as the boat rocked. She pulled her hood back up over her shorn hair. She was no one now, just a girl called Ata, her drab clothes inconspicuous in the crowd. Rows of boats ahead, the crew of the expedition boat moved over the deck like ants, making their goodbyes. Her heart ached. For the crew, about to discover that distance. For all of her own denied farewells.

From somewhere deep in the crowd, a drum roll began. The crowd took up the beat with feet and hands. Adelaide stamped with the rest.

The ceremonies were done. The boat edged away from the pier. Cheers followed it all the way down the water corridor. It glided past Adelaide. People threw things on the deck, flowers, messages. A single rose. When it reached the gateway to the open water the boat seemed to hover. It was beyond the reach of an outstretched arm. Then it was beyond the thrown flight of a flower.

The sky, blank and blue. The sea, infinite.

Don't look back, he thought. *Never look back.*

Even if he had, he would not have seen the girl far back in the crowd, her arm stretched overhead as she waved frantically, and she would not have seen him.

Osiris fell silent.

Adelaide pressed her hands tightly to her chest. She watched the boat diminish. It carried ambassadors, wishes and dreams, the memories of the dead.

Vik—

The craft became the size of a balloon, then the size of a human eye. It grew smaller and smaller on the bed of the waves until finally, it bled into the wash of the horizon and vanished.

ACKNOWLEDGMENTS

Osiris has been a part of my life for a long time, and inevitably those around me have shared in both the joys and struggles of its creation. There are many friends without whose wisdom and support it would have been so much harder. It is impossible to thank everyone here, but in particular I would like to mention the following:

Kim, my sister, who reads everything first. My fabulous housemate M-P, for among many other things sitting up with me late into the nights to help work through seemingly impossible manuscript problems. The lovely and talented Clare, for taking the time to read and offer advice on early drafts of this and other works, and surely more to come. The inestimable Millcat, without whom there would be no Emcat. Björn Wärmedal, for being a joy to write with upon my first forays into science fiction. Fellow writers and friends David Bausor, Christabel Cooper, Jacqui Hazell, Dominique Jackson, Kyo Louis, Suzanne Ramadan, and Colin Tucker, for their invaluable criticism, support, and much consumption of red wine over the past five years. Bobby Williams, for always listening, and for making me the most beautiful piece of film any novelist could wish for. Alexa Brown and James Harris for giving their time and talent to film it. Mau to you all!

I want to thank my wonderful agent John Berlyne, who has believed in the book from the start and refused to give up on it even when I almost had myself. I want to thank Jeremy Lassen and Night Shade Books, and Michael Rowley and Del Rey UK, for giving *Osiris* a home, and welcoming me so warmly into the fold.

Last but most importantly: thank you to my family, the often madhouse of Swifts, for encouraging me to follow my dreams; for being there all the way and always.

ABOUT THE AUTHOR

E. J. Swift has been making up stories for as long as she can remember, from the ridiculous to the epic. Although her work has always contained elements of the fantastical, she came to writing science fiction almost by accident, and it's given her an entire new world to explore. She loves reading and writing fiction which creates new worlds and is inspired by writers who bring the extraordinary to the ordinary.

Her first published story, 'The Complex', appears in the collection *Best British Fantasy 2013*, as well as the January/February 2012 edition of *Interzone Magazine*.

Turn the page for an exclusive interview with

E. J. Swift

the author of Osiris

IN CONVERSATION WITH E.J. SWIFT

1. What made you first want to be a writer, and who are your major influences?

I've always written stories, so I can't really remember what made me want to be a writer – just that it was an ambition from an early age. As for influences, there are so many authors and works I could list. David Mitchell, Margaret Atwood, Cormac McCarthy, Jeanette Winterson, and Haruki Murakami are some of my favourite writers; I love the way they use language.

2. How does it feel to achieve the goal of being a published author, and what advice can you give to other aspiring writers?

It's a deeply wonderful thing and at the same time a not-quite-real feeling... the best advice I could give to anyone is to persevere. You can always write for yourself, but if you want to see your work out there, be prepared for the long haul.

3. You were published last year in *Interzone magazine*, can you tell us more about that, and the story they printed?

The story was called 'The Complex', and it was the first thing I ever published, although I actually wrote it after *Osiris*. It's about a prisoner on an off-world penal colony who is about to be rehabilitated to Earth. I was interested in the 'twin paradox' caused by time dilation, and what it might mean to return to a world where everyone you had known was already dead. (As you can probably tell, I love a good upbeat tale.) Yun's story evolved out of that.

4. *Osiris* **is an ambitious, socially aware and complex book. What led you to write a futuristic dystopia, and what issues were you keen to address?**

One of the things that interested me in writing *Osiris* was the idea of a failed utopia – a city that was meant to be something inspirational, a technological wonder, but also a place where anyone could reinvent themselves; but when it came to the pinch (or in this case the Great Storm), that ethos inevitably collapsed into inequality. I think that's a very human pattern.

5. Adelaide and Vikram are very interesting and different characters. How did you go about developing them, and what are your thoughts about them?

Adelaide and Vikram are both products of their environment, and in their cases, the two extremes of that world. Osiris is a harsh place, to put it mildly. They are both survivors in their way. But as well as the stresses of the physical landscape, I wanted to explore the impact of a city that believed itself the last on earth on the psyche of its citizens – partially through what happened to Axel, and of course his fate affects the actions of Adelaide and eventually Vikram too.

6. The execution scene near the beginning of the book builds an immediate, intense atmosphere and tension to the narrative that continues as the class divide worsens. How did you come up with the idea for the method of execution, and did it have any unseen effects on the book and the two main characters?

I was brainstorming nasty methods of execution with my long-suffering housemate and as soon as drowning was mentioned I realised there was no contest – it was completely pertinent to the city, and the way that the ocean permeates every aspect of life. I think the execution also added an element of cruelty to the city's leaders that wasn't there before, and the fact that Adelaide has to witness it, and Vikram knows she has witnessed it but can't see her reaction, complicated their relationship down the line.

7. The idea of an underwater prison is both fascinating and terrifying; how important was it to the development of Vikram's character?

I couldn't think of anything much more horrific than imprisoning someone underwater, so that there was literally no way out. Also I liked the reversal of the aquarium motif. Prison was always a crucial aspect of Vikram's character – the experience isolates him even from his closest friends, and the fear of returning to that cell resonates with him throughout the book.

8. There are multiple secrets and agendas in *Osiris*, some we find out about quickly, and others we have to wait for until the end; how easy was it to develop those various strands and use them to build tensions and move the story along?

A lot of that work was done after the first draft – going back through the manuscript and noting every reference, working out when each reveal should be seeded. It's a bit like holding the ends of a hundred different threads and keeping half an eye on where each one of them is going. Not something I find easy.

9. The city of Osiris seems very well thought out; did you have to do much research to build an imaginary city in the middle of the ocean?

Some things I decided on quite quickly, such as the pyramid shape of the towers, which would make them more resistant to extreme weather. Other things were details that I discovered through research – wines made from seaweed, for example. Climate change research suggested that in warmer, more acidic oceans, creatures like squid and jellyfish would be predominant rather than fish or anything with a shell, so that's why they all eat squid and kelp. (A culinary delight I have no desire ever to sample.)

10. The relationship between Adelaide and Vikram goes through various stages, from their initial meeting to their eventual love affair. Will we see more of them together in future books?

I hope so, but now that they have gone their separate ways, who knows what misfortunes may befall them... when I know more, so will you!

11. *Osiris* asks and answers many questions, but also leaves us wondering what comes next. Can you tell us a little bit about what we can expect to see in future books?

You can expect to see what Vikram and Adelaide have spent much of this novel wondering: that is, what really does lie outside of Osiris...